THE SEVENTH GAME

Books by Roger Kahn

NOVELS
The Seventh Game
But Not to Keep

NONFICTION
The Passionate People
The Battle for Morningside Heights
The Boys of Summer
How the Weather Was
A Season in the Sun

JUVENILE
Inside Big League Baseball

EDITED
The World of John Lardner
The Mutual Baseball Almanac

NONBOOK
I.E., My Life (with Mickey Rooney)

THE SEVENTH GAME

BY ROGER KAHN

NAL BOOKS

NEW AMERICAN LIBRARY

TIMES MIRROR

NEW YORK AND SCARBOROUGH, ONTARIO

Copyright © 1982 by Roger Kahn

All rights reserved

For information address The New American Library, Inc. Published simultaneously in Canada by The New American Library of Canada Limited

The lines from "Little Gidding" from *Four Quartets* by T. S. Eliot are reprinted by permission of Harcourt Brace Jovanovich Inc., New York, and Faber and Faber Ltd., London.

 NAL BOOKS TRADEMARK REG. U.S. PAT. OFF. AND FOREIGN COUNTRIES
REGISTERED TRADEMARK—MARCA REGISTRADA
HECHO EN CRAWFORDSVILLE, INDIANA, U.S.A.

SIGNET, SIGNET CLASSICS, MENTOR, PLUME, MERIDIAN and NAL BOOKS are published *in the United States* by The New American Library, Inc., 1633 Broadway, New York, New York 10019, *in Canada* by The New American Library of Canada Limited, 81 Mack Avenue, Scarborough, Ontario M1L 1M8

Library of Congress Cataloging in Publication Data

Kahn, Roger.
   The seventh game.

   I. Title.
PS3561.A39S4   813'.54   82-2214
ISBN 0-453-00420-2   AACR2

Designed by Julian Hamer

First Printing, June 1982

1 2 3 4 5 6 7 8 9

PRINTED IN THE UNITED STATES OF AMERICA

To Ring, for enduring courage.

To Wendy, Gordon, Roger, Alissa,
for the courage to be new.

And for the memories of
Billy Cox and Jackie Robinson.

Oh, how they played the game.

The Teams

The New York Mohawks (National League)

Name/Position	*Birthplace*
Leron "Baskets" Weaver, center field	Philadelphia, Pennsylvania
Kenny Osterhout, shortstop	Santa Ana, California
Harry Truman Abernathy, left field	Gifford, Florida
Anton "Bad Czech" Dubcek, first base	Hammond, Indiana
Dwayne Tucker, right field	McCook, Nebraska
John "Jap" O'Hara, third base	Cody, Wyoming
Ralph "Raunchy" Kauff, catcher	New Braunfels, Texas
Jesus "Saviour" Domingo, second base	Santurce, Puerto Rico
Johnny Lee Longboat, pitcher	Trail o' Tears, Oklahoma
Simonius "Big Cy" Veitch, manager	Poughkeepsie, New York
Dave "Lefty" Levin, pitching coach	Atlanta, Georgia
Bill "Cracker" Tatum, first-base coach	Dothan, Alabama
Daryl Coyle, third-base coach	Quincy, Massachusetts

The Los Angeles Mastodons (American League)

Carl "Spider" Webb, third base	Detroit, Michigan
Lynwood "Duke" Marboro, right field	Pittsburg, Kansas
Verlon "Whitey" Wright, shortstop	Milton, Massachusetts
Rocco Lombardo, left field	San Jose, California
Roosevelt Delano Dale, first base	Mobile, Alabama
Jake Wakefield, second base	Longview, Texas
Fleetwood "Hometown" Brown, center field	Chicago, Illinois
Trevor Jedediah Jackson, catcher	Sewickley, Pennsylvania
Hummin' Herman Calhoun, pitcher	New York City, New York
Frenchy Boucher, manager	Woonsocket, Rhode Island
Nat Natchez, first-base coach	New Orleans, Louisiana
Sorge Sorensen, third-base coach	Oslo, Norway

The Press

Priscilla Drewry Coe	*Scoreboard* Magazine
Rob Brownell	*The New York Standard*
Townsend Wade	*Commentator* Magazine

Others

Augustus "Gus" Vermont III, owner of the New York
Mohawks

Christina Moresby (Mrs. Bradford Moresby),
   formerly mistress to Gus Vermont, presently mistress to
   Johnny Lee Longboat
Rebecca Rae Longboat, presently Mrs. Johnny Longboat
Everett McKinley Taft, attorney to Johnny Longboat
Admiral Amory Haskins Moresby (U.S.N. ret.),
   Commissioner of Baseball
Douglas Bradford Moresby, brother of the Commissioner,
   real estate speculator, sports gambler

The Time

The Seventh Game is played in the approximate present.

Contents

Chapter 1

11:58 A.M., Sunday, October 14

IT WAS Raunchy Kauff who ran for a towel first. Raunchy had been sitting astride a three-legged stool, the kind they give to ballplayers and to milkmaids, and his naked belly jiggled as he chattered.

"Hey, Jawn," Raunchy Kauff said. "What kin a cow do that a woman can't?"

"Piss accurately standing up," Harry Truman Abernathy interrupted.

"This is a white man's joke," Raunchy Kauff said. "Anyways, you got it wrong, Truman. My wife pisses standing in the shower and hits the drain hole damn near every time."

Abernathy, a restless panther of an outfielder, stippled black fingers on a white training table. "That just makes your wife a cow," he said.

"All right," Johnny Longboat said. "All right, goddammit." You had to be careful with the needling. In lighthearted times, banter was central to baseball, the most glorious and the gabbiest of our games.

What can't you give an angry black guy? A fat lip.

I was out with your wife last night and you know what? She's not so hot, either.

These were not jokes to share with Christina Moresby, when Johnny cruised the galleries on Madison Avenue and listened to her chatter about Picasso, Zuniga, and Miró. But in baseball, banter got you through waiting times. Mostly being a ballplayer was that. Waiting. In light-hearted times.

But in an hour now, the New York Mohawks were going on the field at Mohawk Stadium to play what Simonius Veitch said would be the most important ball game of their lives. "More than that," Big Cy Veitch had told them. "Probably for all the rest of your lives you'll never do anything this important." Ballplayers shouldn't cut one another now. You needed to collect yourself, as though you were a soldier.

"Raunchy has a nice wife, a pretty wife," Johnny Longboat said.

"Maudie Sue," Raunchy said. "She was Miss Blue Bell, Jawn. Miss Blue Bell at the New Braunfels Blue Bell Festival."

"And you stop the ethnic jokes, Raunchy."

"I gotta few ethnics myself," Abernathy said. "Like one about fat krauts who can't catch anything but crabs."

"Let's save the jokes. Save 'em all," Longboat said, "until the victory party tonight."

Tired, John Longboat closed his eyes. He was stripped to the waist and he lay prone on the trainer's table. He had a long torso with strong, pliant muscles, but his waist showed thickness. It was not a young man's body. He had been pitching ball games for a very long time, and now he was forty-one years old. "Can't I finish the joke I started to tell you all?" Kauff said. "It ain't an ethnic. It's about women, and there ain't any women here. Besides, women ain't ethnics, are they?"

"I want to hear it," said Claude Youmans, the trainer.

2

Youmans was rubbing hot salve into Johnny Longboat's right shoulder and down into the hard, massive latissimus dorsi muscles that stood like stone ridges on the pitcher's back. Claude Youmans had formulated the salve himself. He wanted Longboat to endorse it. Then, he said, the two of them could market it. He had a trade name ready, the trainer said.

Atomic Balm.

* * *

Upstairs, in the second deck of three-tiered Mohawk Stadium, two hundred reporters composed stories for early editions of newspapers that would be published in New York and Caracas and New Braunfels and Los Angeles and Nagasaki.

Since there was no game to describe as yet, the newspapermen wrote about the sky. They called it "high." That meant the sky was a glare of sunlight, and it would be difficult for the fielders to follow high fly balls. The reporters mentioned three-colored bunting snapping in autumn gusts and the Second Marine Regiment Band playing a march version of the chorale from Beethoven's Ninth Symphony. They retyped names from a celebrity list prepared by Marvin Maas, publicity director of the New York Mohawks. The President of the United States would attend the seventh game of the World Series, provided that he could devise a palliative for the rubber crisis by one P.M. A sudden, inexplicable shortage of rubber had tripled the price of automobile tires in the last four months. The Mayor of New York would sit near first base in Box 11, along with the Governor of California. The politicians supposedly had bet ten crates of California oranges against ten baskets of New York winesap apples on the outcome of the World Series, which had come down to the outcome of a single game. Miss America, a tall, lithe redhead named Alissa Avril, sat in Box 7, near the heavyweight boxing champion, a kind illiterate from New

3

Hebrides, South Carolina. The two regarded each other curiously, then looked away.

Some writers in the second tier were citing the comment that you had to be part small boy really to enjoy a World Series, but you surely had to be a man to play in one like this. Each of the first six games had been decided by one run. Johnny Longboat won the first game with a four-hit shutout. He won the fourth game, struggling, 6–5. Overall, Harry Truman Abernathy had hit three home runs for the New York Mohawks. Rocco Lombardo had hit four for the Mastodons. Three pitchers had won games for the Los Angeles club. The fate of the Mohawks was the forty-one-year-old right arm of Johnny Lee Longboat.

"Right now, while we prepare to shiver in the wind," Townsend Wade of *Commentator* magazine told Rob Brownell of *The New York Standard*, "there's some high strategy being plotted in the clubhouse."

"You read too many war novels," Brownell said.

"They're thinking," Townsend Wade persisted.

"They've thought," said Rob Brownell.

✳ ✳ ✳

"Tell the joke," Johnny Longboat said, lying with his eyes closed, "if you have to tell the joke, Raunchy. What can a cow do that a woman can't?"

Kauff smiled, pleased with attention from Johnny Longboat. "A cow can walk into a river so deep she wets her tits, but keeps her asshole dry."

Where? Longboat wondered. Where do such stories come from? Who makes them up? How do they always find their way into the locker rooms? The same joke appeared at the same time in locker rooms in Pittsburgh and Houston and Seattle. Probably truck drivers made them up, and passed them along on their CBs. Except jokes moved faster than trucks. Maybe airline stewardesses were the couriers.

John relaxed under Claude Youmans' broad hands. It

4

was time to think away the pain and play the head game. It was his own head game, nobody else's, and he had created it to pitch better baseball and to dilute the tension that sometimes threatened his concentration and his dignity. It was a delight to play major-league ball. Years and years of delight, interrupted by moments of inexpressible terror. You would fail. Everyone would know that you had failed. For days the newspapermen and the television announcers would comment on your failure. You would fail. *You* would know that you had failed.

In his head game, Johnny Longboat invented the ball game that he expected to pitch. He reviewed all the batters that he had to get out, and he made up innings, good innings and very bad ones, so that when a very bad inning came, it would not be frightening. He would recognize the very bad inning. Because of the head game, he had pitched through it before. Lefty Levin, who once led a platoon across the Remagen Bridge, said you couldn't play a game like that in war. If you imagined what really could happen during battle, you risked breaking down, screaming and crying, hours before the firefight began. In war, Lefty said, you concentrated on the instant that was now and disciplined yourself not to imagine the future. That would have surprised some sportswriters and even certain managers who liked to talk big ball games in terms of battle.

Leading off for the Los Angeles Mastodons. Carl "Spider" Webb, from Detroit, Michigan. Spindly arms, spindly legs, and jittery as a dog in a lightning storm. Too dumb, really, to panic. Change speeds on jittery Spider Webb. Always change speeds. If you changed speeds with precision, always throwing a little faster or a little slower, The Spider would forever swing one pitch behind.

Lynwood "Duke" Marboro. Good left-handed batsman from Pittsburg, Kansas. Red blond hair and the healthy, toothy look of a rich farmer's son. A smile full of teeth, but the teeth clenched, and if you got the ball inside, the

5

Duke destroyed you. Thinking hitter. Take a chance. Throw the first pitch hard inside. *Last* thing Duke would expect would be the *first* pitch into his power.

Verlon "Whitey" Wright out of Milton, Massachusetts. He had a compact swing and he remembered patterns. The way to pitch to Whitey Wright was out of patterns. Five straight curves. Throw each so that it seemed as if you were setting up the fastball. But throw no fast ones. Five straight curveballs. Good surprise.

Rocco Lombardo. Tall and thick-shouldered and strong. Power and bat control. "Whoosh," Johnny said.

"Hurt you?" Claude Youmans asked. "With your tendinitis, I got to rub in Atomic Balm real good. Know what I mean?"

"Stop chattering," Johnny said. Rocco Lombardo. He's just a *hitter*.

A sharp, skidding clatter made Johnny open his eyes. Raunchy Kauff had kicked over his stool and was running for a towel. Raunchy was naked and sleek Harry Truman Abernathy was naked in the white-tiled training room, and a tall, slim woman stood suddenly in the door. She wore a white blouse and white slacks, and honey-colored hair brushed the woman's white shoulders.

"You got no business here," Youmans shouted. His round face went reddish purple, like a plum.

"I do have business here," the woman said. "I have credentials to cover the seventh game, including the dressing rooms. I'm Prissy Coe from *Scoreboard* magazine." Johnny Longboat gazed at her, without turning his head. Her cheeks were flushed under a California beachside tan. If she were a car, advertising men would have called her color Malibu bronze.

"Your credentials are no good in here," Claude Youmans said. "This is the training room. It's private. I'm the trainer. Jesus Christ."

"His hands have healed the sick," John Longboat said.
"Training," Youmans cried. "Medical. Confidential!"

"Do we go and watch your doctor examine you?" Harry
Truman Abernathy said to Prissy Coe. Raunchy Kauff
had found a towel, but Abernathy slouched on the number-
two training table in cool, indolent nakedness.

* * *

Napoleonic at the top step of the dugout on the first
base side of Mohawk Stadium, Simonius Veitch lectured
twenty-five reporters. "Mental preparedness is a funnel,"
Big Cy said. "You make your thinking narrower and narrower until the only thing on earth that matters or even
exists is the seventh game." The manager of the New
York Mohawks was a hulky, glowering, intimidating man,
who suffered from angina pectoris. Behind the glowers,
Simonius Veitch lived in fright. The chest pains that came
and went would one day swell, like an ocean ripple that
grows and swirls into an angry, deadly sea. Cy Veitch was
afraid the chest pains would finish him. Knowing that, he
put forth fronts that were alternatively philosophic and
intimidating.

"Are the Mohawks mentally prepared?" asked Larry
Pittshoe of the *Middletown* (N.Y.) *Times Herald Record.*

Veitch removed his cap and ran the back of his left
hand against his broad gray eyebrows. He looked about
for a reporter from a larger newspaper. "Say," he said,
dropping his view on Sam Letchworth of *The Washington
Post.* "Do grizzly bears defecate in a grove of aspens?"

"I'm an easterner myself," Sam Letchworth said.

"Our club sure as hell does have mental control," Cy
Veitch said, staring over Letchworth's head. "And yes, sir,
Mister Easterner, bears do defecate in aspen groves. What
do you think they have out there in Yellowstone Park?
Animal Port-o-Johns?"

Several writers laughed. Letchworth's flat face assumed

a look of distaste. "It's a natural thing, Sam," Veitch said. "People do it all the time. Shit."

"What do you mean?" asked Larry Pittshoe of Middletown.

"For a game like this," Veitch said, "you got to keep your asshole tight."

"Oh. I understand." Larry Pittshoe was covering his first World Series.

"Our club has control on both ends," said Simonius Veitch. "They've got tight assholes and they have mental control as well. Gentlemen, I wish I could take you all into our clubhouse, so you could see what kind of total self-control this Mohawk ball club has."

✻ ✻ ✻

"A beaver," Raunchy Kauff called, merrily. "A blue-eyed beaver in the trainer's room."

"I have business here,'" Prissy Coe said.

"But they're bare A, Miss," Claude Youmans said. "I mean they're naked."

"Not all of them. Besides, I'm a professional journalist. Naked bodies mean no more to me than they do to a nurse on duty."

The medical mystique, which requires physicians and nurses to wear white, as though white were innately cleaner than magenta, extended into the Mohawk training room. The two treatment tables were covered with white contour sheets. Beyond you could see white medical cabinets, white heat lamps and in the farthest corner, a white oval tub, four and a half feet high, the whirlpool bath.

"Did she say something chauvinistic?" Johnny Longboat said.

"She was the one," said Harry Truman Abernathy.

"If she were really liberated, she would not be comparing herself to a nurse."

"She would be comparing herself to a doctor," Abernathy said.

"Oh?" Prissy Coe pouted. Her lips were thin and she had an aristocratic, ambitious Ivy League face. "Some of us are so liberated that we admire Florence Nightingale."

"Or Edith Cavell," Longboat said, "but that isn't the point. The point is that liberated people speak in terms of advocacy, don't they, Tru?"

"Liberated women might as well be black," Abernathy said.

"Because without advocacy, there isn't any movement," Longboat said.

"You're Johnny Longboat," Prissy Coe said.

"He's Johnny Lee Longboat," Harry Truman Abernathy said. The table, on which Abernathy slouched, lay between the white-clad woman and Longboat, the pitcher, who still wore his baseball knickers and had not moved. Abernathy arched his long back, posing. His penis fell across a thigh.

"My assignment is to interview Mr. Longboat for *Scoreboard*," Prissy Coe said, staring into Abernathy's left shoulder. "It's pointless to display yourself like that. I'm here to work."

"Maybe you will work and maybe you won't work," Johnny Longboat said. "You don't know whether I'm willing to be interviewed."

"If you aren't, Mr. Longboat"—her eyes had not left Abernathy's glistening shoulder—"then I can write a story about your refusal."

"Uppity," Longboat said.

"Overdressed," Abernathy said.

"A hot damn friggin' blue-eyed beaver," Raunchy Kauff said.

Johnny Longboat spun on the table and sat up. You could see crow's feet radiating from his dark eyes, and carelines weaving from the mouth, though he was smiling. He examined Priscilla Coe, from her honey hair, down the white blouse and the long-waisted white torso. His dark eyes showed nothing; they were the eyes of a poker player or an astronaut.

"I have a sporting proposition," Longboat said, at length. "I never grant interviews before I pitch. Not even to Howard Cosell. There are pressures before a game that I can never turn off. But interviews are one pressure source that I do disconnect. No press interviews before I go to work. But if you were one of us, Miss Coe, if you were a New York Mohawk, I'd discuss baseball. All the Mohawks have to know how I intend to pitch the seventh game."

"I root for you and all the Mohawks," Prissy Coe said.

"I appreciate that," Longboat said, "but so do ten thousand drunks. I didn't say be a rooter for us. I said be *one* of us."

"But how . . ."

"Let me finish. If you were one of us in Claude Youmans' training room, you wouldn't be all bundled up in white slacks and a white blouse. You'd be stripped down."

"Don't be ludicrous," Prissy Coe said. Her poise remained defiant and arrogant, which made it more surprising when she yelped. Harry Truman Abernathy had glided behind her. Suddenly Abernathy pinioned her wrists behind her hips.

"Integration," Johnny Longboat said. "White on black."

"Police!" Prissy Coe cried. "Help me, please. Somebody call the fuzz!"

"There's no need to shout," Johnny Longboat said. "The police nearby are employed to protect the privacy of the Mohawk clubhouse from known gamblers, curiosity seekers, adventurers of every stripe. If the police appeared, Miss Coe, we would have to have you arrested. Otherwise we all would face retribution from Admiral Amory Moresby, the commissioner of baseball."

"Smokey!" Prissy Coe cried. "Where are you, bears? Oh, dear. Oh, balls. Help! Help, someone! Help meeee!"

"You'd better not scream again, Miss," Harry Truman Abernathy said. He clamped his long fingers hard on her wrists.

She winced. "All right; I promise I won't scream. Now please let go of my arms."

"Should I, John?"

"The sporting proposition hasn't been answered."

Raunchy Kauff gripped the towel to his waist. "Pardon, Miss," he said, "but wasn't you in the July *Playboy*?"

Prissy Coe whooped. "I was not. You may have seen my picture in *Esquire*. Coming Media Superstars."

"Was you wearing clothes?"

"Of course I wore clothing. A Calvin Klein knit."

"Then it wasn't you, Miss," Raunchy Kauff said.

Prissy turned her head and clenched her teeth and said to Harry Truman Abernathy, "Will you release me at once!"

The tall, naked baseball player bent toward Prissy's neck. His voice was deep and melodious. "I think I'm falling in fuck with you," Abernathy said.

For the first time, Prissy Coe's face showed alarm. Her blue eyes hurried from one white wall to another.

"You've only been asked to strip," Johnny Longboat said, amiably. "I know a present media star who stripped and did some things beyond that for an interview with Fidel Castro. We're not as demanding as dictators, Miss Coe. We're mere ballplayers."

"All right," Prissy Coe said. "It's a simple matter of displaying bodies. Yours doesn't look so special and, frankly, neither does mine."

"I'll be the judge of that," Abernathy said.

"What about other people?" Prissy Coe said. "You know. Ballplayers. Reporters. The police."

"Raunchy," Johnny Longboat said. "Please guard the door."

The catcher moved quickly and positioned himself with

11

both arms pressed against the clubhouse door. "Nobody gets in," he said. "Nobody gets out." The towel fell from his waist. Prissy Coe giggled.

"You laughin' at my body?" Kauff said.

"How did you get the name of Raunchy?" Prissy Coe said.

Kauff retrieved the towel and held it in front of him. "It was something that happened in New Braunfels, Texas," he said. "We played a series against the Rochester Kodak Bears. John knows the story, or you could ask my wife, Maudie Sue. They gimme the name in Pittsfield, Mass., but it really stuck in New Braunfels."

"Get on with it, Miss Coe," Longboat said.

Abernathy released the reporter's arms. She rubbed her wrists. Then she lowered her head and stared at Johnny Longboat, looking for a response. She turned her gaze to the floor. The three ballplayers and the trainer watched her in the white room. She unbuttoned her white blouse and unhooked a wire brassiere. She made a quick, shrugging motion and was naked to the waist. She wore a gold necklace that spelled the word, "Sweets." She curled her blouse and brassiere into a ball and threw them toward the whirlpool bath. She had wide shoulders and a sturdy rib cage. Her breasts were smooth, just full enough to swing free of her body, and shaped like tears. You would not have noticed her breasts so much, except for the pale contrast they made to the Malibu bronze of her shoulders and arms.

"You were a swimmer," Johnny Longboat said.

"Cal State, Northridge."

"Hiya, Sweets," Raunchy Kauff said.

"I would have thought Bryn Mawr," Johnny Longboat said.

"We were poor people. I grew up in Compton. Integrated neighborhood. May we begin the interview now?"

Priscilla Coe stooped and collected her notebook and her breasts stirred. Straightening, she held the reporting pad high, protecting her breasts.

"She's not all stripped down," Raunchy Kauff cried. "An' she's hiding her juggers with that notebook."

"Juggers?" Prissy said. "What does he mean, juggers?"

"He gets confused with words," Johnny Longboat said. "He's mixed up jugs and knockers. But he's right about one thing, Miss. You haven't stripped down."

"I can make her show pink in ten seconds," Abernathy said. He smiled a skeletal smile.

"I know what that means," Prissy Coe said, "and more force won't be necessary. I don't want that black person to touch me further." She balanced herself carefully and removed her white shoes and her white slacks and turned toward a white tile wall and stepped from white bikini briefs. Her hips were slim but her buttocks were full and sturdy. Protruding, Johnny thought, like twin bumpers. She turned back toward Johnny Longboat. Her pubic triangle was black.

Prissy Coe intercepted Johnny's stare. "As a matter of fact," she said, "I'm Italian. My father's name was Colangelo, but he changed it. He wanted to get ahead at Metro-Goldwyn-Mayer. He didn't get ahead. He shouldn't have changed it to Coe. He should have made it Cohen."

"Ethnic comments are out today," Johnny Longboat said. "They stir up the Mohawks in the wrong ways. Besides our most esteemed coach is named Lefty Levin, out of a fine reform temple in Atlanta, Georgia." He allowed his eyes to flicker from the straight honey hair that framed Prissy "Sweets" Colangelo's face, down to the curly dark triangle.

"Now," Prissy Coe said. "Tell me your thoughts."

Raunchy Kauff barked like a puppy and said, "Hiya, Sweets," again. Suddenly, he had to turn his back on the others in the training room. Harry Truman Abernathy shook his head. "They'll do anything, Longboat. You can get honky broads to do absolutely anything."

"I don't like that word," Prissy Coe said. "I don't like either word. Honky or broad, but I dislike broad the most."

"It's one of John Longboat's favorites," Abernathy said.

"Chauvinism," Prissy said, as much to herself as to anyone.

"Elitism," Longboat said. "There are broads and there are women. There are bums and there are men."

She blinked, surprised at the pitcher's command of words. "I have some questions, Mr. Longboat," Prissy said. "I've lived up to my part of the bargain." The flush was gone from her cheeks. She seemed comfortable in her nakedness. "Are you thinking about the rest of your life?"

"I'm thinking about the game that starts at one o'clock."

"What about the rest of your life?"

"I have all the rest of my life to think about the rest of my life."

"You don't have too many pitching years ahead of you."

"Maybe so. Maybe I have none. Maybe this is the last baseball game I'll ever pitch."

"Does that depress you?"

"It would, if I thought about it, but I'm not thinking in those terms now. I told you that."

Prissy made quick, shorthand notes. "Could I ask you what you dreamed last night."

"I slept sound."

"With your wife?"

"They call that the new journalism," Abernathy said.

"I slept with somebody who's not my husband," Prissy said.

"That's your business," Johnny said.

"If you won't tell me you slept with Mrs. Longboat, I

14

can only assume it *was* with somebody else. Haven't you and Christina Moresby been an item?"

Longboat stared so hard at Prissy Coe's crotch that she pivoted toward the wall. "What are you doing?" she said.

"I was looking for balls, ma'am," Johnny said.

She blushed hard. Just her face and neck. She had a long neck, a pretty neck.

"If you want to be a New York Mohawk," Abernathy said, "all you can assume from Mr. Longboat's remark is that he doesn't fuck and tell. That's a club rule, like no reporters in the training room. It's been a club rule since I got here, four years ago. A Mohawk does not fuck and tell."

"Can I ask this, and then I want to get to pitching. Do you have sex with anybody the night before you pitch? I hear you've been separated and staying with Christina Moresby at Moresby Point. Did you sleep with her last night?"

"We have this problem," Johnny Longboat said.

"What's that?"

"We both come first."

"Holy fucking jumping Jesus fucking Christ." The voice of Simonius Veitch crackled like hail on tin and grated like knives on glass.

Johnny Longboat, in the white-and-blue-trimmed knickers of the Mohawks, sprang from the table. Raunchy Kauff fled toward his locker. Harry Truman Abernathy bound a yellow robe tightly around his body. Only the woman was naked. "Skip," Johnny Longboat said to Cy Veitch. "Say hello to Prissy Coe."

"How do you do, Mr. Veitch," the woman said. "I've been wanting to interview you, too."

The manager thrust a knobby hand in front of his eyes so that he could not see the naked woman. He roared and moved the hand down to his heart. In one sound, Simonius Veitch combined infant terror and storm menace. Priscilla Coe had never heard a cry like that before. She ran across the training room to fetch her blouse and brassiere. Veitch roared again and Prissy forgot her clothing and climbed into the whirlpool bath. She sank as low as she could in the tub, crossing her arms over her breasts.

"Get me Dave Levin," Veitch shouted. "Christ. Moses. God. Longboat. This team is full of cement heads, but you're not a cement head, are you Longboat? You're forty-one years old, and there're a lot of lives and pocketbooks depending on how you pitch today. In one hour you get ready, Mr. Team Captain. And what are you thinking, Mr. Team Captain, Mr. Hall of Fame, Mr. Baseball, Mr. America, Mr. Cement Head?"

"Mostly about Rocco Lombardo," John said, slowly. "I got a feeling that the game will come down to me and him." Longboat gathered Prissy Coe's clothing and handed the bundle to her in the whirlpool. "I hope you got a story, Miss, but if you didn't, come back after the game. You showed some enterprise. If you don't have enough, come back after the game when the other reporters are finished. I'll make some time for you."

Simonius Veitch continued to roar. "Now starting the seventh game of the World Series, on which my job depends, and I have a boy at Cornell and a girl at the Poughkeepsie School of Nursing, now starting a game that will be watched by ninety-seven million Americans, the country's hero, the glorious warrior out of Trail o' Tears, Oklahoma, Mr. John C. M. for Cement Head Longboat."

"Skip, if I got as excited as you did before games, I couldn't pitch. Let's get out of here and let the woman dress."

"Cement Head," Simonius Veitch shouted.

"By the way, Skip," Johnny said, "what do you think of the idea of women reporters in the clubhouse?"

* * *

The Book of Broads. Like most great pitchers, Johnny Longboat kept a mental book of batters, categorizing their strengths and weaknesses, their eagerness, their poise, their terror. *The New York Standard*, through Rob Brownell, had offered John one thousand dollars for his book on the Los Angeles Mastodons. "It would make a great feature for the *Standard* and our syndicate," Brownell said.

"I can't sell that, Rob," Johnny said. "It's twenty years of knowledge out of baseball. It comes from baseball and it stays in baseball."

"I was hoping you'd say that," Rob Brownell said. "We've got a new sports editor, who respects nothing but circulation figures."

"I'm maybe through," Johnny said. "You know it and I know it."

"And your pitching book?"

"The book won't die. I'll pass it on to Lefty Levin. I'll share it with young pitchers. The book comes out of baseball and it stays in baseball. It won't die."

Nobody knew about The Book of Broads. As carefully as he characterized batters, Johnny characterized women, tough or vulnerable, adventurous or lonely, who presented themselves to him in his fame. He did not sleep with many. It was too much, involving yourself with the lives of strangers. He had all he could do, perhaps more than he could do, to balance his wife and his mistress, his baseball and his son.

But once in a while.

Prissy Coe could be once in a while.

He'd goddamn win the seventh game, maybe his last, and then while fans he never knew choired his name, and champagne and whiskey poured throughout New York City, he would hold a private celebration by adding Priscilla Coe-Colangelo as perhaps the final entry in his ultimate baseball secret, The Book of Broads.

Chapter 2
Trail o' Tears, Oklahoma, 1954

THREE MILES northwest of the Sand Springs Cafe, Jerry Lee Longboat rammed his Farrago Port-a-home Trailer, Model 711, the Lucky Lassie, against an embankment of red dirt, silt and scruffy stones. An asphalt hump had bent the front axle of Jerry's Dodge Job-Rated pickup truck as the Longboat family passed the Sand Springs Cafe, which sprawled beside Waynoka Gas and Diesel, on Pearson and Main, at the center of the town called Trail o' Tears. Some days the accident would have agitated Jerry Lee Longboat, but lately he had been avoiding Tupelo Dew, an 86-proof bourbon, and he had held his temper and his last job for seven months. "Ya know something about Lucky Lassie," Jerry Lee said, grinding gears in the front seat of the gray Dodge truck.

"Yeah, I know something about Lucky Lassie," Winnie Longboat said. "It's my home."

"Lucky Lassie is a *dog*," Jerry Lee said.

Jerry Lee laughed and after that Johnny Lee laughed along with Dad. Bent axle and all, they kept heading the Dodge truck and the Farrago Port-a-home northwest, into the wind. On both sides of the two-lane blacktop, they saw small clapboard houses, mostly painted white and clumped together, dirty side to dirty side, although enough raw land stretched in Kingfisher County for fifty new towns or twenty cities. The Oklahoma wind blew with a threatening whine, and it carried red dirt out of the fields and onto the white houses. Some people painted their places red, and these looked better for a time, except other people said, "Your house is a barn." Someone tried dark forest green and, in the Sand Springs Cafe, Ernie Beckham said that it made as much sense painting a house green, as it did to eat a green noodle. So the family who owned the green house, the Elrod Kenricks, were called the Green Noodles. Then Elrod Kenrick repainted his squat, four-room house pale white.

Beyond the dirty houses you saw fields. Alfalfa. Cotton. There was too much of what people called The Bumland. Dusty since the Great Depression. You couldn't farm it, and there was nothing under it, except more dust. No zinc, no oil. Just dust. Still, Jerry Lee Longboat said when he bought the Farrago Port-a-home, nothing out here was permanent, *except* land. Jerry had been a foot soldier and he had lived around. He learned soldiering at Fort Allyn McAlester, just south of the Colorado border, which was where he met Winnie Pike, who had jet eyes and straight black hair and a tight, hard little body the way you found on some Arapaho women. The wars would die. Some women would move on. Only the Oklahoma wind and the flat, naked Bumland seemed permanent.

Jerry Lee was broad and squat and he played catcher for the Fort McAlester baseball team. He was a good receiver, but he wasn't big enough to hit the ball damn far enough. He liked playing ball and he liked fucking Winnie Squaw. The other soldiers told him that there was plenty of prairie animal left in Indian women and when you fucked them, they pumped right along with you. Then, it was said, they clawed your back. She was only part In-

dian, though he called her Winnie Squaw, and the other
soldiers were right to a degree. She did pump with him,
and she made a high whining sound when he fucked her
slow and right, going faster then and faster, riding her
high. It made him feel that he was a real man when tough
little Winnie started whining, like the wind.

The baby, Johnny Lee, was born six months before
Pearl Harbor. Winnie made the high whining sound again
in labor, but she didn't scream, which was amazing, considering how some of them, white, blonde-haired and dignified, collapsed and bellowed while giving birth. Johnny
Lee Longboat came out with a mat of deep black hair. His
eyes turned black in two weeks and he walked early and
he liked to sit up on a frayed green couch and drink in the
room and the people, his black eyes restless as the wind.
Jerry was just learning how to play with his son when the
Japanese bombed America into World War II. The army
flew Jerry's unit to guard the Gatun Locks in Panama.
There was talk the Japs intended to invade the Canal Zone
next. Or send in a big ship or planes and bomb the locks.

Later Jerry Lee laughed about that war. "I was in
Colón when the yellow bastards took the Philippines. Then
the army sent me to Adak Island in the Aleutians. They
said there'd be a woman behind every tree and cold,
fucking damn, if they wasn't right. There are no trees on
Adak Island." He walked wet night patrols on Adak
Island while other soldiers ran into Japanese mortar
shrapnel at Tarawa.

Then all of a sudden, after a cold fucking damn eter-
nity, there was no more war, and the Army sent Jerry Lee
to walk patrols and perform calisthenics in Mannheim,
Germany. Winnie sent him pictures. The boy was growing
sturdy, with high cheekbones and deep, Indian eyes. By
this time Jerry was a sergeant and he had found himself a
German roommate, Traudl Hecker.

That broke up after Traudl drank Riesling wine with a

20

lieutenant. How else could it be, the miserable money they paid a sergeant for soldiering? Jerry Lee transferred home to Oklahoma, where he found Winnie working three nights a week as a checkout cashier in Fort McAlester. By now the baby, John, was six years old.

Six fucking years.

"Well, I'm yer Dad," Jerry Lee said.

"Yup," the boy said. Six years old and already he had developed silent ways. He said "yup," and "nope" and "mebbe," and he didn't volunteer much. Hell, the boy was six years old and he hadn't met his dad.

Well, you couldn't stay in the Army forever, even if you were the thinking-est catcher on any of the post baseball teams. You just put on newer, thicker gut and you drilled newer, thicker squads, more and more of them black, and the drinking got you. Oh, they were very good at drinking in the Army.

They said to choose.
We chose the Ar-meee.
They gave us booze.
We chose the Army.
It's blood and guts for you, they said.
It's clap and pus, for youse not dead.
So drink your booze.
They said to choose.
We chose the Ar-meee.

Jerry Lee resigned from stateside service on October 5, 1953, on the day Billy Martin of the Yankees beat a good Dodger pitcher named Clem Labine with a ground single up the middle in the ninth inning. It was a squirting hit, but good enough to win the World Series. Jerry took his six hundred dollars discharge pay and bought the Farrago Port-a-home, Model 711, the Lucky Lassie, and moved into Nowata County, Oklahoma. There were jobs there, another sergeant told Jerry, driving propane gas trucks for seventy dollars a week, plus a commission on all the gas you sold. But in Nowata, it turned out to be twenty-five dollars a week, and no commission for the first five years —if you could find a driving job at all. Most of the work in Nowata County was pulling cotton in the windy fields. Jerry Lee moved the Port-a-home down to Caddo County, which was flatter, but no better for a man looking for work. Finally, he settled in Kingfisher County, because Jerry Lee said he was tired of lugging Lucky Lassie. He meant to stay in Kingfisher County. "You got to settle somewhere," Jerry Lee said.

"You could find work in the oil fields," Winnie said.

"I don't know how to work no oil fields," Jerry said.

Winnie asked around and got a job cooking in a diner.

* * *

Johnny Lee remembered the afternoon when they had to run. It came in the middle of March, and the sun was cold in a blue-marble sky and the wind whined down from the Panhandle, sweeping through Caddo County toward three hundred miles of Texas flatland called South Plains. The whining wind was part of their corner of southwestern Bumland, like the scruffy dirt and Duckett's Good-Eats Diner where Ma worked. Jerry Lee had tuned in a Cardinal ball game on the radio and Stan Musial hit a home run into the pavilion at Sportsman's Park. Jerry Lee barely listened. He was sucking Tupelo Dew out of a bottle.

"Can't even hear the ball game through this fucking wind," he said.

"Yup," Johnny said.

"Wind whines here like your fucking Indian Ma."

"Yup."

"Don't yup me, ya little mongrel," said Johnny Long-boat's dad.

* * *

It must have been awful in the Army, Ma said, but a man who was American had to fight for his country. That was how things were and she was proud of Dad, but he was a different person, now, she said, not only heavier, but more defeated. He used to like Coors' beer. Years earlier he sat with his beer and he'd laugh and sing. The canned beer made him sing. But whiskey, raw whiskey, like Tupelo Dew, turned Dad mean. He hadn't been a mean man before the Army took him overseas, Ma said.

✱ ✱ ✱

At the Sand Springs Cafe, a low white-washed building designed in imitation Mexican style, a clump of white men talked about a skinny Indian.

"Evuh-where these days people make trouble," Whitey Crowder said. He was a tall, high-shouldered country businessman with an enormous square face and a fine bankroll. Whitey owned the Trail o' Tears trailer park. "I been listening to Senator McCarthy," Whitey said. "They want to give people like us bad trouble."

"Who is they?" asked Jerry Lee Longboat.

"Them fucking Comm-un-ists," Whitey Crowder said.

"I don't know about that 'round here," said Curtis Woodward, who tended bar. "Ain' no Comm-un-ists around the Sand Springs Cafe. Bet there ain't a damn Communist in the whole Kingfisher County."

"That ain't the point," Whitey Crowder said. "The Communists don't have to *be* here to make trouble. Lookit the trouble the Japs done give us, and there ain't a yellow face twixt here and Wichita Falls."

"They was plenty in Hawaii," Jerry Longboat said. "Maybe sixty percent. I saw an Army movie about that. Half the gardners in Hawaii were goddamn spies."

"Did that Army movie," Whitey Crowder said, "happen to mention polluting the races?"

"Naw." Jerry Lee was drinking Tupelo Dew neat.

"Didn't that movie show you Japanese men trying to get with white women?"

23

"Naw. They're little guys, Whitey, and if their peckers ain' bigger than the rest of them, I feel sorry for any white women they do get with."

Curt Woodward, the bartender, started laughing.

"This isn't funny," Crowder said, hunching his high shoulders and swelling with anger. "I seen studies about that, what the Japs want. When two different races mate, you get polluted offspring. You get cretins."

"What's that got to do with Senator McCarthy up in Washington?" Curt Woodward said.

"I got literature back to my house," Crowder said, "that tells how Communists agitate among the races. That's what it's got to do with Washington, and Los Angeles, and everywhere including Jew York City. The Reds will agitate until the Russians are the only unpolluted race around. The rest of us will be a mess of cretins. Senator McCarthy knows that, but he can't say it straight because of politics, the Jews and the lawyers. Pollute the races and you destroy the country."

"There're already a lot of mixed races inside Russia," said Curt the bartender. He had a long, sallow face and he wore plastic-rimmed eyeglasses. "Tartars. Lithooanians. Asiatics. What the Reds *do* want is to get us into another cotton-pickin' depression."

"That too," Crowder said.

"Hey, lemme have another Tupelo Dew, Curt," Jerry Longboat said.

"Ya see, it's the agitating foremost," Crowder said. "The Communists agitate with the other races to get with our women. You seen my wife, Jerry Lee?"

Estelline Crowder was a broad lump of a woman with small, pressed-together features. Winnie Longboat had gone to heaviness in fourteen years, but you could still feel a tight Arapaho body underneath. And you could remember. Estelline Crowder looked as though she had never been tight, any part of her. It must always have been slipping and sliding and skidding. Get to first base, second, third. Then when you get home, you're put out sliding.

"You know that skinny Kiowa Indian down from Kansas," Crowder said.

"Jacob Altus," the bartender said.

"We caught him hanging by the outdoor shower in the back, trying to look at Estelline, when she was washing. I mean this Indian was there and my lady in the shower naturally was bare ass."

Jerry Lee started to wonder how Estelline Crowder looked in a shower stall. He had been drinking for two hours without respite. Estelline had blonde hair like Whitey, like Traudl Hecker, who dropped him for Lieutenant Greenspun back in Mannheim.

"I want to teach that Indian, Jacob Altus," Crowder said. "I want to teach him something."

It was 2:21 P.M. One hour later, Clint Dewey joined Whitey Crowder at the Sand Springs bar.

* * *

According to subsequent investigations by Sheriff Harmon Marlow, defendants Clinton Dewey and James "Whitey" Crowder and possible accessory Jerry Lee Longboat left the Sand Springs Cafe at 4:23 in a red Ford pickup truck. They found Jacob Altus, the skinny Kiowa, driving a John Deere tractor through an alfalfa field in distant sight of Mount Scott, the highest peak of the Wichita Range, south of the tri-town Oklahoma area of Apache, Cyril, and Cement.

Sheriff Marlow typed that Jerry L. Longboat was "staggering inebriated." Crowder and Clint Dewey held their footing well.

"Like white pussy, Kiowa?" Crowder said to the man on the tractor.

("Altus," Sheriff Marlow typed, "might have run the Deere tractor at defendants Crowder, Dewey, Longboat, but apparently failed to recognize danger.")

The skinny Kiowa Indian looked around toward the bald, brown peak of Mount Scott. He looked across the alfalfa fields toward the flat Oklahoma town called Cyril. The land was dry and rolling and you could see a Phillips "66" gas station in a dusty haze. But you could not see people. "I like to work the land, Mr. Crowder," Jacob Altus said.

"You make your living off the land?"

"No, sir."

"How do you make your living?" Whitey Crowder said.

"A little from sharecropping land, Mr. Crowder, but more from doing handiwork for people."

"Like what kind of handiwork, Jacob Altus?"

"Anything, Mr. Crowder. I have good hands. They're small, but strong." The Kiowa showed brown hands with slender fingers. "I can fix a sewing machine or take the transmission out of a Gravely Tractor. I get to do that, if I'm lucky to find somebody who needs my hands. I work at carpentry. I even do some plumbing."

"No reason for the Kiowa to be lying," Clint Dewey said.

"You must make a good living, doing all them things," Whitey Crowder said.

"No, sir. There's not much work of any kind, 'round about here."

"Well, Indian, what was you doing 'round about my house?"

"Your missus said there was trouble with the hot water heater for the shower." Jacob Altus leaned forward on the tractor. "It was a leaking propane line," he said. He climbed down.

"He's lying now," Whitey Crowder said. "You get any report of a leaking line of propane?"

"Propane," Jerry Lee Longboat said. "I only work for the company two days a week. Propane. That's gas. It

26

never leaks unless they screw up a weld. They may not do much 'round here, but they weld good."

"Was you wantin' my missus?" Whitey Crowder said to Jacob Altus.

"Ain' no bad welds this side of Nowata County," Jerry said.

"I fixed it with some solder," Jacob Altus said, "and I'll come look at it again. I had to use the solder because I didn't have my welding gear."

"Was you wantin' my missus, Jacob?" Whitey Crowder said. "In your Indian way, was you wanting a chunk of white meat?"

Jacob looked down from Mount Scott toward the town called Apache, Oklahoma. There was no person he could see; there were no sounds but for the wind. Two hundred yards away, a copse of cottonwood rose near a creek. Jacob Altus started running through alfalfa toward the cottonwoods. Clint Dewey, who had played left halfback at Cordell High School, caught the Indian in thirty strides and brought him down against a slant of rock, where no alfalfa grew.

Jerry Lee wasn't sure what was going on around him, but he felt fright and he shuddered. Big Whitey ordered him to drink another three slugs of Tupelo Dew. "I carry two things with me at all times," Whitey said. "A lot of whiskey, and a little ice pick. The whiskey is warm for courage. The ice pick is cold, for fighting. I know a man held off a brown bear with just an ice pick. Bear ran twelve hundred pounds, but the feller, name of Auker, kept slashing around the nose until the bear ran off, howlin'."

Jacob Altus lay where Clint Dewey had felled him and when Jerry Lee Longboat got close he saw the Indian's shoulders were shaking. He wished Whitey would offer the Indian Tupelo Dew.

27

"Cryin'?" Whitey Crowder said. "Well, sir, that's fair, because my wife, Estelline, cried like a baby she was so embarrassed and scared when you peeked at her in the shower."

"I didn't," Altus said.

"And now you're cryin' like a woman, 'cause you're scared like a woman."

"My knee," Altus said.

"Is he cryin' like a woman, or like a baby?" Clint Dewey said.

After Dewey tackled Jacob Altus into the rock siding, Altus' right knee had bent laterally with such force that both cruciate ligaments tore. That is the injury football players fear more than any other. Years after the assault on Jacob Altus, certain football players who seemed hardest, Dick Butkus and Gale Sayers, squealed like animals when their cruciate ligaments ripped. Jacob Altus had not screamed. He lay still, crying quietly in agony.

"Shee-yit," Clint Dewey said. "A tackle like that calls for a little whiskey. Sheet, I can hit. Coach Bresnahan at Cordell High said I couldn't hit hard enough to bruise a virgin's tit. But I can hit. I got his knee." He drank.

The wind died and sprang up again, rustling the far-off clump of cottonwoods. Jacob Altus rolled onto his back, holding his right knee carefully with one brown slim-fingered hand. He had stopped crying. The wind blowing across the creek threw off a faint sulphuric smell. Jacob drew a sleeve of his plaid shirt across his face. The tears embarrassed him. He shifted and the knee made a popping sound. A long grunt issued from Jacob Altus' throat.

"I had enough of this," Jerry Lee Longboat said.

"What ya mean?" Whitey Crowder said. He bumped Jerry Lee with his chest.

The whiskey was a curtain to Jerry Lee's brain. He could not perceive what was going on, or rather what would happen next, and his tongue felt thick, but he knew that this thing was bad. It was worse than anything that had happened in the Army.

"Hey, who ya bumping, Whitey?" Jerry Lee meant to charge his words with menace, but he was alarmed and the fear made his voice tremble. Fear made his throat shaky and whiskey made his voice sound distant—disembodied, really. His tough words shook with nervousness and sounded distorted and remote through the whiskey that curtained his brain.

"I'm bumping a little fat guy that I could squash," Whitey Crowder said.

The wind increased and Jerry's head felt clearer. "I mean, the Indian if he looked at your wife's quiff, then Clint Dewey here has busted up his knee. That makes you even. The Indian won't be looking at your wife's quiff no more."

"I didn't look at her quiff," Jacob Altus said.

"So everybody's even, and I quit," Jerry Lee said. It was a small statement, but important, Sheriff Harmon Marlow and Judge Walt Burkburnett agreed later. It was unquestionably an important statement.

"Quiff?" Clint Dewey said.

"That's a word English people use for cunt," Jerry said. "I learned it when I was in the Army."

"Didn't I hit the Indian bastard good?" Clint Dewey said.

The wind stopped suddenly. It seemed at once to become ten degrees hotter. Jerry's stomach heaved and he walked toward the red Ford pickup truck to vomit. That was significant, also, according to Sheriff Marlow and Judge Burkburnett. Not that Jerry Lee got sick, but that he actually walked away. First, he said that he wanted to quit, implicitly urging Crowder and Dewey to do the same. Then he walked away. In no sense could he be regarded as an accessory to a crime.

Jerry Lee lay down in the alfalfa, and the ground smelled sweet, which sickened him more, but it made him sicker still to look at Clint and Whitey passing the brown bottle of Tupelo Dew between them. Jerry could remember only two times when liquor had hit him this hard. Once was on a hill, nine miles outside Mannheim, where Traudl Hecker stroked his neck with strong cool hands. The other time, it was so bad, he couldn't remember where he had been or why he had been drinking. Adak, maybe.

Crowder and Dewey dragged the Indian to his feet and Altus cried, "My knee, oh God, my knee." They ran and pulled Altus toward a slim, rough-barked young cottonwood and Clint Dewey held the Indian's hands behind the tree. Big Whitey Crowder ripped down the Indian's jeans and grabbed Jacob Altus's penis with his right hand. "You wanted to stick this into my wife," he said.

"No, Mister. I swear. No."

Crowder squeezed the Indian's penis. "Do you know about the Christian purity of the races?" he said.

The curtain of whiskey at Jerry Lee Longboat's brain thickened, and his stomach heaved, and he thought of jumping Crowder, but Whitey was big and Clint was mean and through the curtain Jerry Lee remembered something about an ice pick.

"Jesus Christ," Jacob Altus said.

"Don't blaspheme," Whitey Crowder said. "Every black cock and every Jew cock and every yellow cock and every Indian cock is a threat to the Christian purity of the white race. Women are weaker. A doctor told me that. They can't sometimes control theirselves. Hell, maybe my Estelline did want to play a little. The women, they can't help theirselves. It's up to the men to guard the Christian purity of the white race. White Christian men. That's what Senator McCarthy is really talking about in Washington, D.C."

With no warning, Crowder thrust his ice pick through the penis of Jacob Altus so that the pick stuck in the rough bark of the cottonwood. Crowder made a growling laugh. "He's coming blood."

Jacob Altus shrieked higher than the wind. Jerry fought the curtain that made it hard to think, but the whiskey was too strong. Jerry Lee remembered how he had gotten a hard-on during an Army physical examination and the nurse, a colored nurse at that, whipped a ruler against the top of his cock. Kee-ripes, that smarted.

But this.

A fucking ice pick.

Jacob screamed in a tone so high that it was a minute before Jerry realized that the Indian was praying.

Hail, Mary.

Hay-eel Maaary!

Full of grace.

"Hey, Whitey," Clint Dewey said. "That's my wife's name. Mary. Mary Grace Dewey. Bet the Indian would like to have a good look at Mary Grace's quiff."

"Maary, Maaary," Jacob Altus screamed. "Maaary. Maaa. Maaah!"

"Ah, shut up, sheep-man," Whitey Crowder said. He found a flat rock and struck Jacob Altus five times on the right side of the head.

The quiet was worse than the screaming. Jerry Lee became sick again in the alfalfa.

✠ ✠ ✠

Judge Walt Burkburnett and Sheriff Harmon Marlow agreed in the judge's office at the Apache City courthouse in Caddo County, Oklahoma. "It was an ugly, drunken, dangerous killing," Judge Burkburnett said, "but you know what could be more dangerous yet? A big, lurid trial, that brings newspaper people here from Oklahoma City and Wichita Falls and Tulsa. If they come here, like vultures, their stories will go out on all the wires and this part of America will get such a black eye, we may not recover."

"I'll handle the prosecution quietly," Sheriff Marlow said.

"You do that, Harmon," said the judge.

Whitey Crowder and Clint Dewey would have to be punished. Sheriff Marlow got a story from them, truth and lies, but when you'd been sheriff for a while, you could tell the two apart. A man talking truth spoke with a certain rhythm. When he started lying, the rhythm changed.

"Seems to me, Jerry Lee Longboat," Sheriff Marlow said in the Apache City courthouse, "all you're guilty of is drinking bad whiskey and running with bad men."

"Yes, sir," Jerry said. "I never been in jail, not even in the Army."

"Which is not to say you're guilty of nothing," the sheriff said. "Judge Burkburnett is an elder in the First Assembly Church and I can tell you he thinks getting drunk and disorderly, which, to say the least, is what you did, is a crime and a sin."

"Yes, sir," Jerry said.

"Myself, I wouldn't put you in jail for that. Probably do more harm than good. Besides you have a boy to support."

"That's right," Jerry said. "I have a good-looking young boy."

"Jacob Altus had five children. He had three girls and two boys."

Jerry sniffed and shook his head and wiped his eyes.

"I'd be in favor of probation," the sheriff said. "You stay sober and you report to me once a month for three months."

"That's the right thing," Jerry said.

"Of course, you'll have to give me your cooperation here. We want to forget that business with the ice pick. Mutilation. Just tell the court the last part of what you saw, Whitey Crowder beating the Indian with a flat rock."

"No, sheriff," Jerry said. Sober now, he thought of Crowder's ice pick. "I can't tell anything about what I saw, less'n they come after me."

"Crowder and Dewey won't come after anybody," the sheriff said. "They'll be locked away in Gracemont Prison."

"They'll get out," Jerry said. "After a while they'll get out. They always get out when all they've done is kill an Indian. And when they get out, sheriff, they'll be after me and mine."

"Maybe," Sheriff Marlow said, "but it will be a good long while, I promise you, and I'll be warning them. You got to work with the law, Longboat. You got to believe in the law." Marlow stroked white grizzle on his chin, around a spoon-shaped scar where no hair grew. "If you don't work with the law, Longboat, we'll ride your ass to Gracemont as an accessory, me and Judge Burkburnett. You think you'll be safe in Gracemont, locked away with killers so mean they'd make Whitey Crowder seem like a warder of the First Assembly Church?"

"I have my boy," Jerry said. "We call him Johnny. He's some damn ballplayer. He pitches."

"You testify," the sheriff said.

* * *

Judge Walt Burkburnett scheduled *People of Oklahoma* v. *Crowder, Dewey* between a drunk driving case and the alleged theft of ten Firestone Champion tires from the back lot of Waynoka Gas and Diesel.

"I'm a little worried, here," Sheriff Marlow said.

" 'Bout what?" said the judge. He was a big, round-headed man who wore string leather ties and collected peach-colored Navajo jewelry.

"Well, this is really first-degree homicide. Murder One."

"Or second degree," the judge said. "We don't know whether there was intent to kill when they headed after the Indian in the alfalfa field."

"It seems we should be taking more time," the sheriff said. "Working with lawyers. Setting up a better jury panel. Building both sides of the case."

"Why do you say that, Harmon?"

"Due process."

Judge Walt Burkburnett laughed and reached into a side drawer of his dark, stained desk and pulled out a bottle of whiskey. It was Jack Daniels, not Tupelo Dew.

The sheriff grinned. "I told the feller Longboat that you didn't drink."

"Horseshit," said the judge. "You deal in horseshit lining up a witness, Harmon. If you knew as much about the law as I do, you'd understand due process is horseshit, too."

"I learned in Cordell High . . ."

"I been to twice as many schools as you, Harmon," Judge Burkburnett said, "and I know lawyers who've been to twice as many schools as me. Drink your drink." He raised his own water glass, four fingers full of bourbon. "To the burial of false belief."

"I believe in due process," Harmon Marlow said. "They taught me that."

"Right now, Harmon, I can tell you that Whitey Crowder will be sentenced to a year and a day at Gracemont. We can't have people putting ice picks into other people's peckers, even if the other is an Indian. Even if the other did some snooping at the first one's wife."

"There's conflicting testimony," Sheriff Marlow said.

"I know Estelline Crowder," Judge Burkburnett said. He sniffed the bourbon and sipped it. "She suffers from what Dr. Hennepin, the psychiatrist from over in Ardmore, would call nymphomania. Or Crowder doesn't sleep with her enough. Or both. Anyways, there's no way she could be around the house with that Indian working, without her showing him some tit, or bumping her crotch against him, or God knows what. Right there is one point we'll never precisely know. But we *assume* at least a little something did happen. We assume further that in Crowder's mind what happened was worse."

The sheriff nodded.

"Clint Dewey gets six months. A field hand with a bad streak. The third one, Longboat, is married to an Indian himself. He gets probation."

"I figured that already," the sheriff said.

"I'm sure this Longboat's found his hell. He has a son, you know, good-looking rangy kid. I wonder what that boy's thinking of his Daddy right this minute." The judge emptied his glass. "Now, Sheriff," Judge Walt Burkburnett said, "you and me and a dozen lawyers could talk about this case for months. But I've spoken to just two lawyers, and reviewed the matter with my clerk, and I've just told you in chambers what's going to happen in open court.

"First, I figure out what's fair and right. *Afterwards* I hear the motions and announce my rulings. I decide. The trial comes after my decision and that's the thing school teachers call due process."

"I never learned what you said in civics class at Cordell High," Harmon Marlow said, touching the spoon on his chin, where no hair grew.

* * *

Johnny Lee Longboat was thirteen years and four months old in October, 1954, when his father had to testify as the principal witness in *People of Oklahoma* v. *Crowder, Dewey.* John had not seen the Apache City Courthouse before. The building rose out of a prairie street in whorls and arches of reddish stone. A squat cupola crowned the courthouse and gold clocks slid their hands on all four sides of the brown-red tower. The courthouse clocks, John had heard his mother say, worked better than anything else in Caddo County.

John knew no details of what happened in the alfalfa field. He only knew that there had been a killing and that his father had not done it. He tried to remember all at once in the courtroom things his father had talked with him about. What happened in the Army. That you hold the fast one across the seams. That when you want to throw a breaking ball you grip the stitches. He looked up and saw a squat man, who should have been taller, waver to the witness stand and talk in the soft, terrified voice of someone who is about to cry. This wavery, watery man was Dad. Johnny felt sorry that he had cut school and sneaked past the deputy into the courtroom. Neither was he able to leave.

The prosecuting attorney, a gaunt man called Mr. Bristow, made Dad describe all that he could remember from the field. Mr. Bristow said he realized that the witness had been drinking and that certain facts might very well be hazy.

"We don't want hazy facts, Mr. Longboat," Bristow said, fiercely. "Just what you remember clear."

"Yessir," Dad said in a little high voice.

Then Johnny's father had to tell the court how they had gone into a field, and there were certain charges, shouting, and while Clint Dewey held the hands of the Indian, Jacob Altus, Whitey Crowder bashed in one side of Altus' head.

"The weapon?" Mr. Bristow said.

"A big flat rock."

"That was the only weapon?"

"An ice pick," Jerry mumbled.

Mr. Bristow turned around and faced the court. His wide mouth leered. "Now you were drinking, Mr. Longboat, and maybe you prefer your poison on the rocks, but why in the world would anybody take an ice pick into the middle of an alfalfa field?"

"I don't know."

"So maybe you just imagined that there was a pick."

"Maybe."

"Maybe or yes?"

36

"Yes. I guess I just imagined it. He killed him with a rock."

"And what did you do, sir, during this atrocious assault?"

"I threw up, Mr. Bristow. Vomited. I drunk too much cheap whiskey. I was real sick."

"Real sick or scared?"

"I was not scared. I been a soldier, Mister. I was sick, not scared."

"But you saw the murder and you did not protest, or cry out, 'Stop this now. Stop this killing in the Holy Name of God!' "

"I didn't do that, no."

"Mostly," Mr. Bristow said, "because the victim was an Indian."

"Now that ain't right," Jerry said.

"Dismiss. No further questions." Mr. Bristow spoke with a wince and a wave of one hand that said Jerry Longboat was distasteful to him.

Judge Burkburnett called for a ten-minute recess and Jerry Lee hurried into the hallway for a smoke. He stopped and cringed when he saw Johnny.

"What are you doing here?"

"Nothing."

"How did you get here?"

"I hitched."

"You ought to be in school, son. How long you been here?"

"Long, Dad."

"You seen me up there on the stand?"

"Yup."

"Don't take that serious, John. It's bullspit and nonsense on that stand. I didn't do no wrong, except I had a drink too many."

Johnny looked down at his sneakers. He didn't want to show that he did not believe his own father.

"John," Jerry Lee said, infusing authority into his voice. "This ain't a good day for any of us Longboats. Wait. I got something for you. Take it and hitch a ride back home." Jerry Lee handed his son a five-dollar bill, straightened his shoulders, and turned back into the Apache City courtroom.

* * *

Johnny caught a hitch on County Road 9, going northwest, and it wasn't much after two o'clock when he reached the Port-a-home trailer in Trail o' Tears. When Dad was feeling funny once, he'd said they lived in Trailer Tears in Trail o' Tears.

Johnny took a new Official Texas League baseball from a drawer under his bed and tossed it up and down to get the feel. In the fluorescent light, the baseball gleamed pearl white. He found his Enos Slaughter model glove and fetched Dad's thin-handled Stan Musial model bat and went outside. Balancing the Musial model bat on the handlebars, he bicycled to Fetterman's Field, a diamond underneath a high wreckage of a windmill, from which the wind had blown loose every spoke. The boys at Fetterman's— Atwood Halligan and Lefty Hammond and some bigger ones, sixteen-year-olds who would work full-time next fall if they found jobs—were throwing an old football. Damn dumb Okie kids, Johnny thought. Can't even get their seasons straight.

"Hey," called Atwood Halligan. "You got a baseball."

"It ain't a pumpkin," Johnny said.

"Could we play?" Lefty said. He dropped the football into the dirt. "Could we play a little ball? Hey, that's a new one."

It wasn't that they were dumb, Johnny realized. They just didn't have a baseball. One thing about Dad was this: No matter what, he *always* made sure Johnny had a ball.

"Okay, you guys can play," Johnny said. "But I wanna try something." Under the spokeless corpse of the old

38

windmill, a shed formed the center of a backstop. Once the shed had been shingled, but winds had blown the building bare and you could see uneven chunks of underboarding. The playing field was more dirt than grass.

As soon as Johnny got infield soil under his sneakers, he felt better. He could not forget what happened in the courthouse but the pain moved from the front of his head where it hurt bad, toward the back, where a curtain dimmed the scene. In the front of Johnny's head now was the brown-green field and the windmill without spokes, and the shiny baseball. "I got a fiver here," Johnny said. "A real five-dollar bill."

"Where'd you get it?" Atwood Halligan said.

"My business. I come by it honest. Now I wanna bet you and the other guys, even the older ones, that I can strike out every one of you." John slammed the ball into the pocket of the Enos Slaughter mitt. "Five dollars."

"What kind of bet is that?" Halligan said. "You know you throw too fast for me to hit. You know that you can strike me out when you go into that special motion."

"My windmill," Johnny said, grinning.

He dropped the thin-handled Musial bat across home plate. Almost everybody Johnny knew in Oklahoma rooted for Stan (The Man) Musial and the St. Louis Cardinals, even though Musial was born in the East in a place called Donora, Pennsylvania.

It must be wonderful to see him hit.

The Donora Greyhound.

Many nights you could pick up broadcasts of the Cardinals playing games against the Phillies, who had good hitters like Del Ennis and Richie Ashburn, or the Giants, who had Whitey Lockman and Don Mueller, and the Dodgers, who had the colored player, Jackie Robinson. Nigger Jack they called him around Waynoka Gas and Diesel, but Johnny Longboat followed Jackie Robinson on the radio and in *The Sporting News* whenever Dad brought one into the trailer. From all that Johnny Long-boat could tell, Jackie Robinson was no shuffling nigger. He seemed like a helluva ball player, stealing second, third and home, and beating you with bunts and homers, and he was Johnny's second favorite baseball player, after only Stan (The Man) Musial from Donora. Dad thought it was a good thing that John rooted for Jackie Robinson. "Root only for the great ones, kid," Dad said. "Rooting for all the others will break your heart."

Johnny threw the shiny Texas League baseball into his glove. He threw it five times and every time the thump was right. A boy learns early the music of ball and glove. Throw the ball too high, into the webbing, and the sound is thin, like a slap. Throw it low, down into the glove's heel, and the sound is thick, a punch against a pillow. But hit the pocket, the dark-oiled center of the glove, which is where a boy learns to catch a baseball, and the sound comes clear and solid and true, as the thump of a good drum.

Magic. The brown-green field, blown flat and bare, made Johnny think of magic. He didn't know why he could always hit the dark-oiled center of his glove; only that he could and some others couldn't. He guessed he must have got the knack from Dad.

He looked toward the hummock. One person sat there. It was Helen Arnett, Randy Lugert's girl. Randy was seventeen and he played flanker back at Cordell High, except he hurt his knee and he couldn't make varsity any more. Helen saw Johnny and gave a little wave.

The older boys, who had been running pass patterns in the outfield, gathered near Johnny when they heard about the five-dollar bill. Cleve Barnstable and Randy Lugert were the biggest. Cleve had a muscled harvester look and Randy was dark, with sloping shoulders and outsized forearms bulging through his long green shirt.

"Have I got this straight?" Randy Lugert said. "You

are gonna pitch to all of us, without a catcher, and strike us out. There's, lemme see, five, seven of us, in all. You're gonna strike us out. All seven in a row."

"If you put up five dollars," Johnny said.

"We got five dollars," Randy Lugert said.

"I want to see it."

The older boy went through his pockets and found the five dollars, but three dollars was change. Randy and John loped toward Helen Arnett, who would hold the money. She had her knees pressed close together, but she had undone her yellow and white blouse one button lower.

"Randy," Helen said. "It isn't right to take money from a kid."

"We're not taking," Randy said. "He's giving."

"I'm not a kid, Miss," Johnny Longboat said.

"My name is Helen."

"I can throw a baseball, Helen. My Ma says that's the one thing I do best in the world."

Helen Arnett leaned forward. Her hair was sandy brown and her eyes were soft blue-gray behind round spectacles. She wore a full print skirt and she balanced a novel in her lap, *Look Homeward, Angel.*

"Where did you get five dollars to lose?" Helen Arnett said.

"From my Dad, and I ain't gonna lose it, and I sure ain't a kid."

Usually Johnny felt nervous bantering with girls who were older than he, but holding the ball and glove, he felt all right. He loped down the slope of green land, sensing he could lope for miles. Then he got Atwood Halligan to take the Enos Slaughter glove, so he could throw Atwood fifteen pitches, to get the feel of the new Texas League baseball, and the feel of the quartering wind that came in gusts, and the feel of his own body this particular day.

"Hey, anybody got an old glove for me?" Johnny said.

Randy Lugert had an old black first baseman's glove,

autographed by someone called Sam Leslie. It was a small glove, made years before, when mitts were almost as small as the gloves that handball players wore.

Johnny bent, straight-backed from the hips, and cupped the baseball in the small Sam Leslie glove. He held the palm toward his face; that way, Dad had told him, his grip was hidden from the batter. He pumped both arms far back and bent forward so that his face paralleled the ground. But his eyes, his dark flat Arapaho eyes, stayed focused on home plate. Then, pivoting on his right leg, John rocked, his left leg rising so that the sneaker pointed toward the sky. With sudden force, the long, young form uncoiled and the baseball sprang from Johnny Longboat's hand. It was a pitching motion Rob Brownell of *The New York Standard* later called The Oklahoma Windmill.

Near first base, the other boys discussed how to split five dollars. "I say the guy that hits a fair ball first gets a simoleon," Randy Lugert said. "Then everybody splits the other four."

"That makes the arithmetic hard," said Charley Capron.

"You been to school," Randy Lugert said.

"Besides," Capron said, "that gives an advantage to the guy we have hitting first."

"Not necessarily," Lugert said. "The kid will be fresh then. He'll be throwing hardest."

"Who calls balls and strikes?" Halligan said.

Lugert pointed toward the windbare shed under the windmill. Someone had painted a black rectangle on the gray boards. "That's the strike zone."

"How about somebody gets hit with a pitch?" Halligan said.

From his windmill windup, Johnny shouted, "I'm hitting nobody."

The other boys made Halligan bat first, and he had seen how hard John could throw. Winding up, John pointed his left toe toward Atwood Halligan's head. Right then Atwood made an awkward stagger, tucking out his backside. John threw hard and low toward the outside corner of the black rectangle. "They hold the bat," Dad said, "at the level of the shoulders. It's easier to hit a high pitch good. Besides, your eyes are high. You see a high pitch better. So when you don't know a hitter, you don't know what to throw, start him low."

"Inside or outside?"

"You feel your way, but start him outside. Feel your way." John threw three fastballs into the low outside corner of the rectangle and Atwood Halligan was out. Randy Lugert shouted, "Ya better wait till the wind is with you, Halligan."

John struck out Lefty Hammond with fastballs that rode toward the center of the plate, then sailed outside. John struck out three more older boys with outside pitches. His arm felt so alive he wanted to lift something. A log. A rock. No, not a rock. The ball was sailing, soaring, and he could throw it to any point he wanted. If they had pinned a playing card inside the black rectangle on the gray shed, he could have hit the card easy, nine for ten.

Before his two-strike pitch to Harry Haskell, Johnny noticed Harry cheating. The first two fastballs had been low, outside. Harry now crowded the plate to get the outside fastballs within bat range. John gripped the ball to make it veer to the inside. He threw a fastball pecker-high that abruptly sailed in toward Haskell's groin. Harry started to swing and swinging cringed and fell down, spinning on his bottom.

John heard Helen Arnett laughing from the green hummock when he made Haskell fall down.

Magic.

But funnier to a girl than to a boy. Watching a pecker-high hard one ride into a batter wouldn't make you laugh, except in nervousness, if you were a *boy* that was watching.

He had to fan Cleve Barnstable and Randy Lugert.

Strike them out. They could be tougher than the others. They could be easier. They had been studying how his fastball moved and that could either help them hit him or leave them scared.

Cleve said, "I wanna use the Musial bat. Is that okay?"

Sure, Johnny thought. You guys lent me the Sam Leslie glove. Besides, its more than okay, if you want to use a bat with a skinny handle, seeing that you can't handle it like Musial.

John rocked and threw a fastball, fist-high on the inside. John threw a little higher, still inside. Cleve Barnstable lunged and foul-tipped the baseball off the skinny handle.

A fat bat, John thought, a Nelson Fox model, and Cleve might have nubbed one past him. A tremulous laugh escaped his throat.

"What you smiling at, you fucking half-breed?" Randy Lugert's voice carried defiant and raw. "Why you smiling that fucking Apache grin?"

John bit his lip and threw Cleve Barnstable another fastball, eyebrow high. Cleve chased the pitch and missed it. He was out.

"Go up the ladder," Dad had told him. That worked in pitching, though there wasn't a soul who could tell why. Start at the fists. That was the hard strike. Then throw one titty-high. That had to be inside. Then throw the last one at the brows or higher. "Damn," Dad had said, "there is no way to explain why certain things work, but damn that works, going up the ladder." Of course you had to push the first two past them. Whoosh.

"What do you mean, half-breed?" Johnny said, when Randy Lugert picked up a brown Adirondack bat.

"Your mother," Lugert said.

"Get in and hit," Johnny said. He was angry, but that made him feel stronger and think better. Everything was magic in baseball, even his anger. Johnny wound up, pointing his left toe at Randy Lugert's face, and loosed a fastball toward the outside corner of the plate. Lugert ducked backward before the ball was halfway to him. Strike one.

"Cocksucker," Randy yelled, and beat the brown bat on the plate. Helen Arnett pretended not to hear. "I'm so dumb," Randy shouted, "I'd give a blow job to a moose." Johnny could tell that Randy was enraged that he had let himself be intimidated, with Helen Arnett watching.

Johnny rocked and Randy Lugert crouched. He was well balanced. You could tell that he would not back off an inch. The ball leaped from Johnny's hand and carried inside, moving up and farther in. Randy squealed and squealing dove for the bare earth. The fastball snarled like hornets, six inches from his cheek. Randy's squeal turned into a grunt when he hit the ground.

He had this batter now, Johnny knew. He could not remember pitching this way before, deliberately throwing a baseball into someone's face. If you want to stick 'em, Dad would say, go for the ribs. They'll feel it. Some could be coughing for a month. But you don't hurt nobody bad, which you are liable to do if you throw a hard ball up around the head.

The wind brushed against his own face and the other boys, lined up around the shed of the windmill without any spokes, stared in surprise. Randy Lugert was a tough one. None of them had heard him squeal before.

Johnny wound up again and threw two outsider sailers, the ball that tailed away from a right-handed hitter. Swinging, Lugert stuck his bottom out. The hitters couldn't help that sometimes. They pulled away just slightly. You could see it in their bottoms, but it was nothing they could help, when they'd been frightened by a baseball, anymore than a horse could help from rearing at a snake.

He threw a third sailer too close to the center of the black rectangle. Not a very good pitch, but Randy did not move his bat. It took all his concentration not to fall away from the magic windmill windup. The ball bounced off the windmill shed and carried back to the flat mound where Johnny grabbed it. Damn backstop had done better than any hitter. Everyone was out.

Johnny laughed. He was ten dollars ahead. Some Oklahoma people, not only Indians but whites, had to work all week to make ten dollars.

When Johnny choked down a laugh, Randy Lugert started to charge him, holding the Adirondack bat above his head. He stopped in five strides. He remembered where the baseball was.

The boy on the flat pitcher's mound shouted in joy. He thought, and more than thought, he knew, that when he stepped out onto a ball field he himself and his life were magic as the sun.

The slim girl in the white and yellow blouse started down the hummock carrying the ten dollars John had won.

✳ ✳ ✳

At Cordell High School, classmates called Helen Arnett "The Bookworm," which was not like being reputed a bookworm at Milton Academy, near Harvard, or at the High School of Music and Art in New York City. Helen read books in clusters, and when Mr. McCurtin, the florid bald teacher of "Mainstreams in American Literature" assigned *Arrowsmith*, Helen went on and read *Main Street, Babbitt,* and *Dodsworth* as well. Then she read *Winesburg, Ohio*. Fascinated by small towns and the people in them, she proceeded to *Spoon River Anthology*. Now, in *Look Homeward, Angel*, she was entering the town of Altamont, and comparing the state of Catawba and the Gant family with persons and places in southwestern Oklahoma. Bookish for Cordell High, pretty Helen Arnett, who was sixteen, had not read a line of Dickens, Balzac, Henry James, or Thomas Hardy.

Some other girls at Cordell said Helen carried books to impress Mr. McCurtin or certain boys, or even her private tennis teacher, Alva Teagarden. But that wasn't why she was bookish, Helen believed. She wanted to explore the world beyond the windy Oklahoma flatness, but Mother disliked travel and her father, Dr. Robin Arnett, a dentist, disliked leaving his practice and never went anywhere, except to Mercedes, Texas, where he shot buck. So to Helen the wonder of Zenith City and Winesburg was that she was transported from the fields of cotton and alfalfa. Later, when the twitting persisted, she did carry books for effect. She felt that she was a step or two higher than the others. Her father did not pump ethyl at Waynoka Gas and Diesel. He was a dentist. If her manner bothered other girls, the children of field hands, very well, let them be bothered. Although her slim body made her a fine gymnast, Helen refused to try out for Cordell's cheerleading squad. Instead she took her private tennis lessons on the cracked cement court at Rush Springs Golf and Country Club. The golf pro, Alva Teagarden, doubled as tennis teacher, and when he worked on Helen's serve Alva positioned her right arm with great care. As he did that, Alva always brushed her right breast. Men had different ways of being pleasing and pleasing themselves. With Mr. McCurtin it was talks about Thomas Wolfe; with Alva it was a broad, caressing hand.

"What do you think is in there?" Helen pointed to the windmill shed blown bare of shingles.

"Animal nests, probably," Johnny Longboat said.

The others had gone. Randy Lugert shouted that Helen had to leave with him, but Helen gazed through her round eyeglasses and said she would just as soon bike home by herself as ride with somebody who fell down trying to hit a fastball thrown by a kid.

"You know I'm not a kid," John Longboat said.

"Let's go see what's inside," Helen said. She fastened a button on her white and yellow blouse.

"Snakes,'" Johnny said. "Could be sidewinders."

Helen yelped softly. "Then maybe we better not go inside," she said.

"I'll go ahead and scout them out," John said. The warped wood door gave slowly to Johnny's forearms. He kicked about. "No snakes," he called. Then he and Helen stood inside the shed. Half-light broke through the doorway and the floor was straw, and there was a little cot on the right side. Johnny kicked the straw and announced, "No squirrels been here lately, either."

Helen placed the Modern Library copy of *Look Homeward, Angel* on the cot and ran her hands along Johnny's right arm. "So strong," she said.

"A good thing, too," Johnny said, "because I'm going to be a big-league pitcher."

"That means you leave Oklahoma," Helen said.

It surprised him that she accepted his hope as certainty. Didn't Helen know how hard it was to be a big-league pitcher? Didn't she know that in forty-eight states and in the Caribbean, there were ten thousand who wanted to pitch in the major leagues?

"There're no big-league teams west of St. Louis," Johnny said. "There're teams in Philadelphia and Chicago and New York."

"I'd like to go there," Helen Arnett said.

"Where?"

"All of them. All those places."

"I'll be going to all those places when I'm a big-league pitcher," Johnny said. "Dad says I just have to grow some and take care of my arm. When the wind gets bad, you can feel it inside the trailer, and I wrap my arm in a sweater 'fore I sleep." Under Helen Arnett's stroking, his arm tingled.

"I'd also like to go to London, England," Helen said, "and Paris, France." She removed her eyeglasses and placed them on *Look Homeward, Angel*. It was light enough to see a soft look in her gray-blue eyes. "That's what I'd like to do most," she said. "Travel."

"I'd like the most to be a big-league pitcher."

Helen unbuttoned John's cuff and rolled his sleeve up and kissed his upper arm. "What would you like to do most right now?" she said.

She's asking me, John thought. I'm not asking her. "For you to take off your pretty blouse and things," he said.

Helen yelped the way she had when Johnny mentioned snakes. "That wouldn't be right," she said.

"Why not?"

"Because it's not as if you were my boyfriend."

"I am for now," Johnny said.

Helen turned her back and unbuttoned her blouse and took it off and unsnapped her brassiere and spun around.

"They're small," John said. Helen cried out and covered her breasts with her hands. "You've looked at too many cows," she said. Then she said, "You shouldn't talk to me like that, if you're my boyfriend."

"They're not *too* small," John said. "Take your hands away. Small and nice and just right, is what they are." It surprised him that a few dark hairs grew about each nipple. He reached and touched a breast and Helen threw her arms around his neck. Her wrists were thin and delicate. He let her pull him onto the cot, where they lay next to Helen's spectacles and *Look Homeward, Angel.*

"Doesn't your thing hurt?" Helen said. "Does it hurt when your thing is hard and pressing against your jeans?"

It was like Dad said about the way you behaved when you pitched. You listened more than you talked. That kept you ahead.

"It doesn't hurt none, Helen," Johnny said.

"But if you took it out, wouldn't you feel more comfortable?"

"Might."

49

She opened his jeans and stroked his penis evenly with both her hands. John made no sound, but shuddered as he ejaculated.

"Oh," Helen cried. "Oh. You're a very strong young man, Johnny."

"My rocket sure went off," he said. His breath came back at once. "Now let me see your bush. You know. Your private hair." He ran his hands up the inside of her thighs, remembering to be gentle and Helen Arnett moaned and shook her head and said, "Wait."

"Why?"

"I can't let you see my parts."

"Why not?" Johnny had risen. He adjusted his jeans and looked down at Helen. Her lips were tight against her teeth.

"Girls get excited, too," Helen Arnett said. "That's why I moaned. If I let you see my parts, we might both get so excited something bad would happen."

"Pregnant," John said. "I'll bike over to Waynoka Gas real fast. In the bathroom, they got this machine. You put a quarter in and out comes a pack of things. They're three for a quarter."

"Contraceptives," Helen said.

"What?"

"Those rubber things are called contraceptives. It's better to use the specific word than to say 'thing.'"

"I'll remember that, Helen. I really will."

Beyond the doorway, twilight threatened. "It's too late, Johnny," Helen said. "And I relieved you, didn't I? You don't hurt."

"Nope."

"Tomorrow, then. You have some money from your pitching. You have time to get the contraceptives early. Buy the best brand."

"'Kay." He was starting to lose his breath.

"Will it be the first time for you?" She was holding him

50

gently by the upper arms. She looked naked although she still wore a yellow half slip and white underpants.

"Yep."

"We'll be together, then," Helen said. "We'll be together for a long time."

"I want to be together with you for a long time," Johnny said.

"Even when you're a famous big-league pitcher?"

"Even when I'm a famous big-leaguer, if I make it. If you'll help me make it. Especially when I'm a famous big-league pitcher."

"We'll see all the great cities then," Helen Arnett said. Her eyes went wet. "London, Paris, Detroit."

"Cleveland and Pittsburgh, too," Johnny Longboat promised.

✳ ✳ ✳

John heard shouting from the Farrago Port-a-home trailer, when he rode his bicycle up the embankment of silt and scruffy stone that was the rear border of the Trail o' Tears Trailer Park. He noticed that the Lucky Lassie had been moved a few yards. It was hitched now to the Dodge Job-Rated truck. From within he heard his father shout, "Why? Because they're a bunch of Indian haters, that's why."

When Johnny walked into the trailer, Mother was packing a long black trunk and tears were on her face, but she wasn't crying. "You promised this was our last move, Jerry Lee."

"How did I know?" Dad paced the trailer living room, between a couch, covered with transparent plastic, and a formica wall that had been treated to look like walnut. "It's a bad thing," Dad said.

Thing. He always said "thing." Dad had never learned to use the specific word.

"It's maybe the worst thing there is," Dad said, "to hate somebody for no reason but color or religion. Or stuff like that. I been to Germany. I seen Dachau, which was a camp where they put living humans on meathooks. The guy I was with, Al Levinthal, he came from Little Rock. Good little outfielder with a pug nose like an Irishman. His grandmother and grandfather got meathooked somewhere else, 'cause they were Jewish people."

"What's going on, Ma?" Johnny said.

"We're moving. Now!"

Helen, John thought. Tomorrow. "We can't move now," he shouted.

"We can," Dad said, "and keep your voice down, son. The thing we can't do is stay here. I got a couple killers coming after me. Whitey Crowder and Clint Dewey."

"I thought they were your friends, Dad," Johnny said.

"Not friends. Just guys I drunk too much with. The jury acquitted them both of murdering Jacob Altus, which they did before my eyes."

"The jury couldn't do that," Johnny said.

"The jury did. They didn't only murder him, they tortured him. They stuck a fucking ice pick through his penis."

John blinked. "I didn't hear you say that up to court."

"The judge. He didn't want me to. I went along with things the way they told me."

"The judge knew they done the killing," Johnny said.

"The judge got sore as bullspit," Jerry Lee said. "He told that jury none of them better come up before him on so much as a traffic charge, else he'd send them all to Gracemont Prison for a year. He said they made a mockery of due process."

"Mockery," Johnny said. "Due process."

"Mockery," Ma said, "is a kind of joke that isn't funny. Due process is how the law is supposed to work."

"The goddamn jury said the Indian had been threatening the purity of Whitey's wife. They said Whitey was really defending the sanctity of his home. And me, Jerry

Lee Longboat, your father, was too crazy drunk to be a witness they believed."

"Now it's all right," Winnie said, but Jerry Lee began to cry.

"Hey. Don't cry, Dad."

Jerry leaned against the Formica-walnut wall of the Port-a-home trailer. He wore a black and red plaid shirt, and jeans. First he leaned and then he crumpled. He was sobbing so hard he could not speak.

Suddenly John thought of running away. He had ten dollars in his left rear pocket and he thought about bicycling to the windmill shed. No. First, he would stop at Waynoka Gas and buy the best contraceptives in the wall machine, even if three cost him fifty cents. Then he would bicycle to the shed and lie on the cot and wait. Helen Arnett would get there tomorrow. She had promised. Must be she wanted to do it, screw, even more than he. Afterwards, he could keep on meeting Helen in the shed and he would support himself, until his arm was ready for pro ball, by doing farm chores. Even now some took him to be seventeen.

But these were his people.

Dad and Ma.

A thought flashed. He could see Helen Arnett's bush, and he was fucking her on the cot and she was moaning and begging him to fuck her harder.

These were his people. How could he leave his people? All you had in life was the people who had made you, unless you were one of the lucky ones who owned land.

Dad wasn't lucky. He didn't own nothing. He listened to a judge and that was bad luck too.

Jerry Lee continued crying, wretched bursts of sobs, so Winnie made her way outside and started the Dodge truck. Johnny sat with her while the engine warmed. Whitey Crowder had told Curt Woodward, who worked at the Sand Springs Cafe, that he was going to kill Jerry Lee "for squealing on what happened with a squealing Indian." He said he would use the ice pick on Jerry Lee worse than he had used it on the late Jacob Altus. Curt Woodward took the message so seriously that he sent his boy running two miles to the trailer. "Dad got scared and shook all day by people like Sheriff Marlow and Judge Burkburnett," Ma said. "You get to a point you can't take scaring any more."

"Dad stands in good against the curveball," Johnny said.

"Some days Dad might have stood in good against that feller Crowder. Just not today."

"I'm wondering, Ma."

"What?"

"Where are all those law people, who looked so strong in court? Sheriff Harmon Marlow. Judge Walter Burkburnett. The lawyer, Mister Bristow. Now that somebody is threatening to kill Dad, I was wondering where they are? They all gone home?"

"Probably, John. You hit the truth."

"They're all lucky ones, I'll bet," Johnny said. "They own some land."

After Winnie raced the engine, to give the battery a charge, Dad climbed in with them and took the wheel. He was calm now. They bumped over the dirt trailer park road and turned east on two-lane asphalt toward Oklahoma City. In a while, Jerry Lee began to sing in a melodious, high, tender baritone. The song was called "The Oklahoma Winddrift Blues." They were coming up on towns called Chickasha and Amber.

Dad sang:

The Oklahoma Winddrift Blues.
You got stardust in your eyes,
But Bumland on your shoes;
That starts the Oklahoma Winddrift Blues.

You got Lana on your mind.
There ain't no Lana round to choose,
Cause in the Winddrift Country
The girls come cheaper than the booze.
Man, that's the Oklahoma Winddrift Blues.

Hear the dirty wind awakin'
Feel your heart and belly achin'.
Come sunlight streaks, or rainstorm,
Okie-man you lose.
Hey, that's the only news.
You heard the Oklahoma Winddrift Blues.

Mother hummed along with Dad, and Johnny had a warm belonging feeling as they sat with their hillbilly music in the front seat of the Dodge Job-Rated truck. Hearing Dad sing, John knew he had done right by not running away from his people. Maybe when they got to the next place, he could write a letter to Helen Arnett, explaining so that she could understand. It would be a hard letter to write. She probably was mooning for him now, getting wet and sticky down inside. But he could write it. He would use specific words.

Dad eased the truck at thirty-five along the blacktop, and every so often someone hooked out and accelerated past them: a flat-hooded Ford sedan, or a Chrysler, shiny with chrome, a Studebaker Starlite Coupe, and once a black Cadillac.

"Times ain't real bad," Dad said into the wake of the Cadillac. "It's just we haven't been real lucky. Ain't that so, Winnie?"

"There's always been enough for the table," Winnie said. "We're luckier than some, but we work hard."

"Where are we going?" Johnny said.

"Northeast," Dad said.

"I know which way is northeast. I mean what town?"

"Don't sass me, son. We're going northeast, on out

towards Arkansas, where there's a town called Pryor, where there's another propane delivery division of my company."

"It's greener there," Winnie said.

Then Jerry Lee said, "It's all the same. Pryor, Oklahoma, or Mannheim, Germany.

> You get stardust in your eyes,
> But Bumland on your shoes,
> Hey, that's the Mannheim, Deutschland Blues.
> Ooom-pah."

They all laughed, and Dad said, "We aren't big people." He stared at the blacktop and the night.

"Johnny's as tall as you already," Winnie said.

"I didn't mean it just like that. Sure if I'd growed bigger, our lives could have been different. I could have played ball on those big-league fields, where the grass is green even in the worst of August. And the crowds and all. The people cheering me. The children asking me to sign my name. I played good ball at 143 pounds. That was my right weight. Not 180 like now."

"An even 143, 'cept that's an odd number, was my exact right weight, but weighing that, I didn't have no power with the bat. That's what they look for first. George Weiss from the Yankees, and Casey Stengel and Branch Rickey look for power in a hitter, because that's one thing that can't be taught. You have to have strength in your hands and Popeye forearms. The power comes from there. The batting coaches like George Sisler can teach a lot of things, but they can't teach a man to hit with power, any more than I could get a prairie dog to kill a cougar."

"Watch the road, Jerry Lee," Winnie said.

Johnny pressed his right hand hard against his left hand. The book, *Secrets of Dynamic Power* by Hal Hercules, explained that tensing one muscle against another

56

muscle was one of the mystic ways in which the Greek Olympians had made themselves strong as gods.

"Baby," Winnie said, hugging Johnny to her. "You must be upset, moving so far from your friends."

"All the boy got to keep in mind," Jerry Lee said, "is that we'll be setting down our trailer a hundred miles from Commerce, Oklahoma. Know what that means?"

"Don't they have lead mines up to Commerce?" Winnie said.

"What it means is Commerce, Oklahoma, is where Mickey Mantle grew up. Mickey Charles Mantle. He hit a baseball at Griffith Stadium, Washington, 565 feet, off the pitcher Chuck Stobbs. Arthur Patterson of the Yankees went and measured it. Don't that mean something to you, John?"

"Yep," Johnny said.

He was going to be a pitcher, not a hitter.

Nobody would ever hit a baseball that far against him.

* * *

At the Resting Knight Trailer Village, just outside of Pryor, a hundred miles southwest of Commerce, Oklahoma, Johnny sat on his foldaway cot and wrote a letter to Helen Arnett.

Helen Dear:

It was a long drive hear to Pryor, specially in a crummy truck with a bent axle, pulling the trailer, but I don't complain to them. They got plenty troubles theirselves.

I can't talk much to Dad, like I can talk to you and Mom, and on the truck it finely hit me why. It isn't that he was away in the Army, over to Mannheim, which is in Germany, like you might think. It's that he doesn't see me. He don't listen. He sees hisself. (Helen, I could go over this and fix the grammer, but then it wouldn't come out as strong as I feel.)

Dad was talking about hisself, I mean himself. That's

what always happens between Dad and me. No matter how we start out, we always finish with Dad talking about hisself and I may mess up, but if I do, it's going to be myself that messes up, not him. Do you find that with your Dad? Does Doctor Arnett like to talk about hisself?

Listen, mostly I'm writing to say that we arrived safe and what we did in the windmill I did respectful. There are guys, all they want with girls is to do something for theirselves, but I see Mom is the one who has held our family together. She even makes sure Dad don't drive right off the road. Ma was a girl once herself, and we arrived safe, and I respect you as a girl, second only to my Mom. I don't want to do bad, selfish things to a person, a woman, an Indian, which I am part myself. Any person.

I acted too prideful the other day. I'm not sure that I can be a big-league pitcher. Striking out field-dirt kids in Oklahoma don't mean much except you know which ones to throw high and throw low. I got that from reading *How to Win the Big Ones*, a book by Dizzy Dean, who used to be GREAT for the Cardinals in St. Louis.

I mean I am going to try hard to be a big-league pitcher, and if I make it, you come too. St. Louis. Chicago. Anywheres. Meanwhile, I got to grow some and to work on my pitching. Little things that would bore you to hear about.

I also intend to read *Look Homeward, Angel* and a book they mentioned in school written by a man with a terrific name for a ballplayer. A better name even then Mickey Mantle. I'll bet you're wondering what that name could be.

The name is Homer. His book is called *The Illiad*. You are too fine a person to marry a Bumland Okie.

Respectfully,
Johnny Lee Longboat
General Delivery
Pryor, Oklahoma

✱ ✱ ✱

Chapter 3
12:02 P.M., October 14

SIMONIUS VEITCH fluttered a blue-bound computer print-out toward Johnny Longboat's face. The men were standing. Big Cy was a square six-footer. The pitcher stood two inches taller. "Would you happen to know what *Fortran* is?" Veitch said. "Or is your head too full of naked women?"

"John has a secret book on women on the road," Raunchy Kauff said. "He calls it the Book of Broads."

"Fortran is one computer language, Skipper," Johnny said. "It's a way you program the machines with information. Putting it roughly."

"That Prissie Coe looked like Chris Evert naked," Raunchy Kauff said. "How you gonna mark her in the Book of Broads, John?"

"We aren't writing today, Ralph," the pitcher said. "Besides, when did you ever see Chris Evert naked?"

"A hundred times. Whenever I see her picture. I take her clothes off in my head to see how she would look serving. You know. With nothing covering her breasts."

"Topless tennis," John said. "But what about the others, with all the muscle, like Martina Navratilova?"

"Do you know what Fortran time costs on a computer?" Simonius Veitch said.

"Neither know, nor care," John said.

"Which is why you had so much trouble in game four for us," Veitch said. "Fortran is very clear on one switching-hitting power dago called Lombardo. He bats 511.6 on letter-high fastballs over the plate. You threw him two that day."

"Skip, they've computerized hotels, which is why we had to wait six hours for rooms in the Happy Day Inn in Chicago. They've computerized hamburgers, which is why they have a leather taste in fifty towns. They've computerized the voting machine in Congress, and they've computerized designs for big-league stadiums. They can computerize the places where we work. But they can't computerize our game."

"First the naked broad," Veitch said. "Now philosophy from a pitcher who made eleven mistakes last time he pitched."

"Fourteen," John said, "but every one was human."

"Maybe they could rig the tennis tournaments," Raunchy Kauff said, "so only the pretty ones played topless."

"Skip," John said, "I've been pitching pretty fair on one field or another for more than twenty years. I pitch my human way. Nobody can translate that into computer language. I pitch my strength against their weakness. My power against their power. My feeling against the hitter's feeling. There're infinite variables. That's how it is for me. I'm getting on. That's how it stays for me. Save the computer for the next generation. All I have to know is whether to pitch a man high or low."

"I caught a no-hitter once where all the guy threw was fastballs," Raunchy Kauff said. "All I had to call was for the pitch to be high or to be low."

"And where might that have been?" said Big Cy Veitch.

60

"Off season, oncit," Kauff said, "in Brownsville, which ain't all that far from New Braunfels, Texas. We whipped the asses off the Rochester Kodak Bears."

"The Rochester team, Mr. Kauff, is called the Red Wings."

"This was a semipro club," Raunchy Kauff said.

"With a Polish manager," Johnny Longboat said.

"Why do you think that?" Kauff said.

"Because bears don't manufacture cameras, Ralph."

"That's right," Kauff said. "Japanese guys, with little fingers, they make the cameras, right? Say, what you said was *funny*, John."

"I saw a black girl dance troupe in Las Vegas last winter," said David "Lefty" Levin, the pitching coach. "All they wore were patches over their pussies. The girls came from the islands. They called themselves 'The Bermuda Triangles.' "

"Fucking baseball," Cy Veitch shouted. "Don't any fucking body talk any fucking baseball any more. When I played, I made a fucking ten thousand dollars per, and all I talked was baseball. Longboat, you're getting near ten thousand bucks a game and considering that this is the World Series, fucking double that."

"Fortran still isn't baseball," Johnny said.

"The Vermont family, which owns the club and which happens to be our employer, Mr. Longboat, has invested eighty-five thousand dollars, almost my pay for a full year, into Fortran reports. You can like it. You can hate it. Up to you. But in this economic system called the U.S. of A., when you take an employer's paycheck, you got to make one compromise."

"Give half you get," John said, "to tax departments of the U.S. of A."

"I don't mean that. I mean you got to do what the employer says."

"Cy, you don't understand. I got a talent. There ain't no one named Vermont who could get a single out, in the first inning at Mohawk Stadium here today."

"But people named Vermont can crush you, John," Simonius Veitch said, kindly. "Kiss ass and live."

* * *

The Vermont family, headed by Augustus Vermont, III, had long ago been surnamed Greenberg. Someone named Guron Greenberg, whose remnants lie in a New Jersey mausoleum, understood iron and steel, or how to sell iron and steel. But the climate of the 1880s precluded Jews from making a success at smelting. The climate suggested simply, "Don't buy Jewish steel." There was even an awkward joke that went, "When you got Jews in the ferrous metal business, the mother irons and the father steals." Steel was closed to Jews, which Guron Greenberg understood. He found a rural corner of the Southeastern Bronx and established a junkyard. In the climate of the late 1880s people would purchase used box springs from Jews, if the price was low enough.

Guron managed the junkyard with such skill that eventually he was able to leave the Bronx for a large apartment on West End Avenue in Manhattan. Then Guron applied in the Supreme Court of New York to have his name changed. The judge was kind. Guron became Augustus. Greenberg translated to Vermont. Still, the old friends, with whom he spent loud evenings playing pinochle, called him Grisslushka. Gus Vermont was a small bear of a man.

Unaccountably (to Grisslushka Vermont), his son, Augustus II, who grew up in a businessman's home and won a Pulitzer scholarship to Columbia College, cared about baseball. The old traditions, business, *chader*, and even pretty women who kept their dark hair bound in kerchiefs, did not stir Augustus II. His passion was baseball and his speech broke into a gibberish of strange names: Matty, Larry Doyle, and Josh Devore.

Death took Grisslushka at the age of seventy-eight, when he was carrying a box spring, afflicted with moderate rust. Augustus Vermont II inherited $1.2 million. For a while he sustained the Vermont Ironworks of the Bronx, New York, but all the time tried to buy a major-league baseball team. The Brooklyn Dodgers, badly run by drunkards, were not for sale. The Yankees were a toy to the iron brewmeister, Jacob Ruppert. That left one team, the poorest buy, the New York Mohawks.

Like steel, organized baseball did not encourage Jews as owners. Or even as infielders. Indeed, one James Hymie Soloman, who played seventy-seven games for the Yankees, in 1930, had to perform under the name of Jimmy Reese. It was 1936, in sour economic times, before Gus Vermont II could use his cash to buy the New York Mohawks.

Gus II knew the game. He loved it with a calculating passion. He sipped whiskey with other owners who were drinkers. Then he made trades. He hired a paranoiac as his manager, because an ordinary team might excel under the pressures imposed by a psychotic. In 1943, the New York Mohawks played in their first World Series since 1908, which was the season when the *Chicago Tribune* hired a young baseball writer away from a paper called the *Inter-Ocean*. Ring Lardner was the baseball writer's name.

Now the third generation had produced Augustus Vermont III, a swarthy, handsome man, profligate only with his mistresses. This Guron Greenberg, Gus Vermont III, neither loved nor disliked baseball. He took two degrees, in business and engineering. He worshipped Fortran.

* * *

"How is the arm?" Lefty Levin said to Johnny in the clubhouse.

"One hundred forty-five years old," said Johnny Long-boat.

They sat alone, beside the Roller-Bang Pinball Machine in the Mohawk Player's Lounge. A uniformed guard, Arnie Fillipo, stood at the clubhouse door. Usually Arnie worked section 14-A, in short left field, but since Prissie Coe's invasion, he had been commandeered for special duty.

The Roller-Bang was a unique machine. Above the rollers and the flippers, plastic ladies posed in flowing dresses. The more points you scored on the machine, the fewer ladies kept their dresses on. It was pinball, John thought, designed by a Raunchy Kauff who had studied engineering.

"Where does your arm feel old?" Dave Levin said.

John indicated a muscle knot, behind the point where his clavicle met his right humerus.

"You know," Lefty said.

"I know," John said. "The elbow gets better. The shoulder never does."

"This could be just as far," Dave said, "as that shoulder lets you go."

"This isn't the seventh game for me," John said. "It's game number 586 I've started in the major leagues."

"And?" Levin was fifty-seven, and spoke with non-committal tenderness. He lifted his blue Mohawk cap and brushed a hand across his crown. Most of the brown hair had fallen out.

"This is beyond the seventh game," John said.

"What's that. For a pitcher what can be beyond the seventh game of the World Series in New York?"

"The last ball game," John said, "that my hundred-forty-five-year-old arm will let me pitch."

"There's doctors, John," Lefty Levin said. He was tight-bodied and five foot nine, too small to have reveled through a long career himself. "Sports medicine is a new

64

field. They have manipulations, under anesthesia. They're supposed to be able to manipulate away adhesions. That worked a little while for Catfish Hunter."

"I tried manipulation. Didn't work for me."

"There's Russia," Lefty said. "There's a whole different sports medicine developing over there. You could go to Moscow. John, this is your career!"

"I went to Moscow last winter, just Christina and me. A professor called Golokin looked at my shoulder and he said something like American medicine was a crime. But for the Soviet sports medicine to work, Golokin said, you have to start doing certain drills at age thirteen. When I was age thirteen, I was getting up my nerve to buy a box of rubbers."

"And here?"

"I've been to Dr. Hylan Bennett at Johns Hopkins so many times, we joke. Like I make house calls on the doctor. Three years ago he gave me a lecture on scar tissue building up and prearthritic conditions and he said all he knew to tell me was to pitch to the point of pain. Warm up and throw harder and harder until the pain became unbearable."

"That spring I clocked you on Gus Vermont's Teen-o-meter Radar at 93.2."

"Did you notice my face?"

"I couldn't look. You were grunting with every pitch, the way I heard Sarah grunt in labor."

"If you had looked, you would have seen tears coming down my cheeks. Lefty, there's Indian in me, and I don't cry. A lot of bad things have happened to me, with my son and Rebecca Rae and all and the day my Dad broke my leg piling up a pick-em-up truck. But I don't cry. That spring you clocked me at 93.2, I didn't cry, but throwing like that made tears run out my eyes.

"How fast was I game four, the other day?"

"84.8 at your quickest," Lefty said.

"Goddamn," John said. "You hate to die and that's what my pitching arm is doing on me. It's dying."

"Would you like to get to the game at hand?" Lefty Levin said.

"Put away the Fortran," Longboat said.

"I don't know if I should do that, John. You can't just oppose Fortran, like it was tobacco smoke in the lungs. It serves a function. Christ, John. Don't fight it. Don't like it. But *use* it."

"You know Christina Moresby?"

"I saw her once at a team party. You were the star, J.L., but she was there in a spangled dress, deep blue. Not purple like a hooker. Just deep blue."

"She wants to get me into this composer called Mahler," Johnny said.

"Can we get to the game at hand?" Lefty said.

"Wait a minute," Johnny said. "I'm not going out to Mohawk Stadium with a dying arm to pick up old score-cards in the outfield. I'm going out to pitch. I got to get my mind set. At Moresby Point we were listening to the radio, FM, seventy-five miles up from New York. This song comes on, like the singer was in the room. Fischer-Dieskau was the singer's name. I asked Chris, in my Okie way, 'How come the goddamn radio sounds so good?' She pulled out a manual. My Dad, who wasn't good for much, could fix electric things. He used to say, when he was working with the Phillips screws, 'When all else fails, read the manual.' I read the tuner manual and it said that the circuits were worked out with eighteen minutes of Fortran time. I'm not opposed to Fortran. I'm just for pitching staying *human*."

"Maybe we can get to game seven quickest, if we go back to game one and game four," Lefty Levin said. "It's 12:15. You'd better stop your musing."

"What is that name *Teen-o-meter*," Johnny said. "I mean the derivation."

"It's just a radar gun," Lefty Levin said. "Harmless. We don't think it causes cancer of the arm. It was developed for cops to shoot a car and get an instant reading of the speed. The Teen-o-meter speed traps kids driving like hell and measures fastballs."

"I never drove like hell. Driving like hell one night, my Dad busted up my body."

"Would it be easier if we started with games one and four?"

"Couple of fuck-ups," Johnny Longboat said. He was tense and even irritable, although generally a gracious, cheerful man. But now John could not drive one thought from his head. This was his last ball game, the last baseball game that he would ever pitch.

"All right, game one," John said. "My first World Series victory. All the years waiting for the team to transit —is there such a word?"

"Change," Lefty Levin said. "Develop."

"I get into the game with this dying arm and what was the fastest I could throw?"

"You got some over eighty miles an hour," Lefty said. "It was 83.8 on the Teen-o-meter."

"Will you stop calling a radarscope by that ridiculous name?" Johnny said.

"Gus Vermont likes labels. Trademarks. He's bought the Teen-o-meter Company as part of the New York Mohawks Baseball Corporation, Inc."

"And *you* have to put up with his conglomerating bullshit," Longboat said. "But in the end, I don't." The broad face hardened and you noticed that John's hairline was receding. "And this is the end," John said. "That's where I am."

"There never was a day in the big leagues, with the old Dodgers—you know I pitched for them—that I could throw 'em eighty miles an hour."

"Then how did you make it to the bigs?" John said.

"They were looking for a Jewish name in the scorecard," Lefty said. "David 'Lefty' Levin. Scouting report: Does not throw very hard and does not throw at all on Yom Kippur."

Johnny laughed.

"Seeing you laugh makes me feel good," Lefty Levin said, "but that ain't the point. I've put away the Fortran. That ain't the point, either. The point is that I won a few big games, and in my prime, I couldn't throw as hard as you can now."

"But how?" John said. He felt restless and walked away from Levin and popped a can of beer, which violated a Mohawk rule. You could drink beer, up to three per man, according to Gus Vermont *after* a game. But none before. (During losing streaks the ration was cut to a single can.)

As John put on his shirt, a blue seven blazing on the back, he felt a twinge in his right shoulder. It was a toothache. Precisely that. A toothache. He was only getting dressed. The toothache would explode when he was pitching.

"I'm not afraid of pain, Lefty," John said, when he was dressed. "I'm just tired of it. You know. It hurts one day and then it hurts another and another and you say to yourself, damn, well, is it worth it?"

"It's worth it," Lefty said, "and don't make an arm pain all that dramatic, Johnny. All that talk of dying. I had an uncle in the clothing business. He sold Palm Beach suits. Tropicals, we used to call them. He had to go to places like Altoona, Pennsylvania, in February, when you couldn't walk for the snow, or breathe for the wind, and push a summer line."

"Tough life," John said.

"Tough guy," Lefty Levin said. "Bone cancer killed him at fifty-two. That, John, was pain. The morphine didn't help much and he couldn't walk away from cancer. There was no relief pitcher." Lefty took off his cap again and brushed back the few hairs. "Abe Levin, a tough clothing salesman—he would have been a stevedore in Israel—died wailing baby wails." Lefty put on his blue and white hat. "So this is only a ball game, and all you have is an aching arm."

"All right," John said. He didn't want to talk about death. Not most days, but particularly not today.

"In game one, which I win, with a bush league fastball, the score is what, 1–0?"

"A classic score, 1–0."

"After you pitch so many you forget. You even forget the classic scores. Anyway, in the ninth, I get three men on base, two out and Rocco Lombardo is the hitter. Big Cy lets me stay in, and I was grateful. Finish what you start.

"Rocco loves high fastballs. The way I handle him is keep the ball down. I get a strike with a good change, around the knees. He didn't think I'd dare do that, start him with a bloody slow ball. Now I'm going for the peak of the cap outside, because Rocco is an impatient hitter."

"Fortran confirms that," Lefty Levin said.

"I confirm that," Johnny Longboat said. "I was in a bar with Rocco once on Rush Street in Chicago and he's so impatient to make out, he comes on to a girl like the U.S. Army. The girl says, 'I don't talk to perfect strangers.' You know what Rocco answers?"

"You never told me."

"Rocco says, 'Honey. I'm not perfect.' "

Lefty yelped laughter.

"In game one I'm trying to pitch Rocco either low or wide. The ball slips. Nothing else. Here comes my lame old fastball at the letters over the middle of the plate."

"Which is his power."

"He hit forty-nine home runs," John said. "I guarantee forty came on fastballs letter high. He is a hitter who can be pitched to. I make a mistake big enough to lose the ball game and he pops the ball to short. I'm a hero. I tell Rob Brownell and Wade and some other writers who understand the game that I am the luckiest semi-Indian in New York City. I won on a mistake. They run the story. I get a confidential memorandum from the office of Admiral Amory Moresby, Commissioner of Baseball, that I should make no such comments in the future. 'They hurt the image of our sport,' the Commissioner said. 'They also disturb the network commentators.' "

"Public relations is his job, John," Lefty said.

"Plus Moresby doesn't like me for reasons I can't tell you."

"You win game four by 6–5," Lefty said.

"But struggling like a virgin with a stallion. Rocco killed me. He hit an outside curve to right that bounced away from Dwayne Tucker. Three bases. Two runs. And in the seventh he hit a beauty of a change, through Jap O'Hara at third. No man in the world could have fielded the ball. Two bases. One more run. That's three runs and I give up five."

"You and Rocco still speaking?"

"Never let business conflict destroy amusing friendships," Johnny said. "Yesterday, Rocco told me he had a new approach for the ladies in the bars on Rush Street. Now he says, 'Honey, I'm going to ask you to do one thing for me. Just one. And if you don't like it, I'll never ever ask you to do it again.' That line has lifted his fucking average to .432."

"Yours has to be .900."

"Never was, Lefty, and maybe something was wrong with me, but I never wanted to sleep with half the world. Sleep with a woman and you touch her emotions so that the woman may not be the same again. This is the wisdom of a man who can hear great age knocking. When I was a kid, hell, I didn't reason things through. But you chase and you get tired and you forget which different stories you told which different girls. Or you get crabs."

"Or the Pearl of the Antilles," Lefty said. "I picked that up one season when the Dodgers took spring training in Havana. The Pearl is the drop at the end of your pecker that tells you you've contracted gonorrhea."

"There's cures for that and crabs, Lefty, but sometimes, I wonder, you know, is it sex that moves the world, or is it money?"

"I haven't had enough of either, John."

"It is 12:32. In twenty-four minutes, I begin my warm-up. What's the temperature?"

"Fifty-nine degrees. Your weather, John."

"Yeah. Only about ten minutes to heat. I don't want to throw a pitch warming up that I may need later. You know there are boxers who have trained so hard, they said they left their fight back in the gym."

"My Uncle Abe Levin fought for three years in the 1930s. There were Jewish fighters then."

"I don't need Fortran, Lefty, but I'll need you. I have too much on my mind, Christina says it's time. Marry her or she moves on. That means leave Rebecca Rae and Jerry Lee, my son. I can't do that, leave the boy and Becky. Or maybe I can."

Levin shrugged.

"You think I'm loaded," Johnny said. "What I've got, besides the house and the Mercedes, is tied up in developmental land in the Bahama Islands. My lawyer told me that he'd found a legal way to beat the I.R.S.

"I asked him hard questions, but Everett McKinley Taft said he was in the same deals himself, and did I think he wanted to go to Leavenworth? Yesterday he mentioned certain problems. That's his phrase. 'Certain problems.' My head was full on pitching. I let it go."

"Is Jerry Lee all right?" Lefty said.

"He's back in boarding school. He's functioning, Dean Miller tells me. But he wouldn't come down today to see me pitch."

"It's 12:36," said Lefty Levin.

"Everybody on the Mastodons can be pitched to," Johnny said. "Spider Webb. Duke Marboro. Rocco. Jake Wakefield. But too much is on my mind, and I have to remember two games back, and stay four batters ahead. You know. The *thinking*. I have to have a thought as well as my back behind each pitch.

"The fans can roar. I'm deaf to crowd noises by now, but with too much in my head, I may—just possibly— have an instant when I lose my concentration."

"Then?" Lefty said.

"I have to know just one thing. Whether to make the next pitch high or low. I'm going to look for you in the dugout. Sit next to Cy Veitch. Tell him when I look in to throw a lot of phony signs. Touch his cap. Rub his hand across the letters. Grab his elbow. Obvious. But not too obvious. We can't give anything away."

"Simonius will go along with that. He wants this game as bad as you. Mr. Vermont is annoyed we didn't win in six."

"When I look at you, I'm asking, should the next pitch be high or low? If your palm is up I go high. If your palm is down, I throw low."

"Semipro stuff, John. Worse than Pittsfield."

"It'll only happen once or twice or three times. No one will know but you and me and Cy. Stay sharp. I'll read you in a glance. If I look hard, that means I'm faking. Shout something. 'Make it a good one.' 'Don't walk him, John.' We'll have Frenchy Boucher thinking you're giving me voice signals. Just do it my way. It'll work."

"I'll do it your way, John. You're the one naked on the mound."

"Everybody on the Los Angeles Mastodons can be pitched to," Johnny said. "It's just a question of executing, and blocking out the pain."

"Think of bone cancer, John," Lefty Levin said.

Chapter 4
Pittsfield, Massachusetts, 1960

THE VILLAGE of Pittsfield is in the Berkshire Hills. It is not of them. The Berkshires are ski runs down Otis Ridge and summer cabins camped around Lake Buel. Pittsfield is commerce and industry: life insurance companies, the transformer division of the General Electric Company, and Sal's Sporting Goods and Power Tools on Division Street, just north of Main. The city sits on a plain one thousand feet above the sea, and in the public green you find a statue of a soldier sculpted by Launt Thompson called "Massachusetts Color Bearer." A reproduction of "Massachusetts Color Bearer" stands on the battlefield at Gettysburg.

Once Pittsfield thrived as a resort, and a village historian points out that Henry Wadsworth Longfellow composed "The Old Clock on the Stairs" when he was living there. Further, Elkanah Watson (1758–1842), who lived at what is now the Country Club, preached passionately for a canal that would connect the Great Lakes and the Atlantic Ocean, by way of Pittsfield. "The Old Clock on the Stairs" is seldom taught, and no canal was built. Pitts-

74

field survives between two forks of the slowly winding Housatonic, which, by surviving, it pollutes.

Even in 1959, the river was bearing poisons. A safer place to swim was Lake Pontoosuc. Except that Harry (The Whistler) Schulte, who managed the Pittsfield Eagles, would not permit his ballplayers to swim. "Swimming weakens the muscles," Harry Schulte said, "especially for pitchers, even more than having sex before a game. Swimming is an automatic $50 fine. A pitcher having sex is an automatic $100, and if he does it twice, $500. Do all you bushers understand that? Five hundred dollars."

Johnny Longboat did not like being called a busher. Sly Donoghue, the old Pittsfield left fielder, had watched him pop fastballs into Ralph Kauff's fat glove and called him "Magic."

"Magic?" Johnny said.

"Yeah, kid," Sly Donoghue said. "Throwing that easy and popping a mitt that hard is magic, kid. You're gonna make the bigs—the big leagues—very large, kid, if you get a little more control, and if'n you don't get hurt."

"I already been hurt," Johnny said. "In an auto wreck."

"Which is why," Sly said, "the Mohawks was able to steal you out of high school."

John limped for a while after his father drove the Dodge Job-Rated pickup into a row of concrete guard posts 5.7 miles outside of Pryor, Oklahoma. Dad banged his head against the windshield, his chest skidding across the top of the steering wheel, and after that he got bad aches above the neck. Then the pain would make his temper blow. His head would hurt and he'd drink Tupelo Dew— he said just to make pain move out away from him—and the damnedest littlest things would set him off.

"Shit, why you limping, son?"

"I broke my leg."

"Be tough, goddammit, son. If you're gonna pitch don't limp. If you're gonna limp, don't pitch." The puffy face reddened. The voice became a shout. "What are you gonna be, a fuckin' fairy?"

Well, that was quick to say, except Dad hadn't broke his leg, or felt the pain, a thousand nails shooting up and down below the knee. And John saw his own slivery, naked bone that afternoon, but through the pain he could see something worse. His father, still as a rock, blood running down the forehead. John knew his leg was broken, but he made himself get up and drag Dad out of the pick-em-up truck, 'fore it blew up. Gas tank was almost full. Payday in Pryor, Oklahoma. Fill up the tank and me. I just might go round the back and take a sip of Tupelo Dew.

"Dad. I couldn't live without my pitching."

"Then pitch without limping, goddammit. Are you trying to ruin your arm?"

"Go easier on John," Winnie Longboat said. "He's a good boy."

Dad took the next swig from the bottle, forgetting the glass of Tupelo Dew on ice that Winnie had poured him.

"You're a goddamn half-breed, Winnie," Jerry Lee Longboat said.

"What kind of name is Longboat?" Winnie said, snapping with weariness. "That's not an English name or Scotch. Don't go telling me there's no Indian blood on your side."

"God damn limping kid," Jerry screamed. "God damn kid. God damn you, John. Why does my head hurt so God damn much."

* * *

After the snapped left leg was healed, it didn't bother John, except when he threw baseballs. His natural motion was overhand, and the ball veered in or out, or sailed or even sank, depending on how he gripped it. "Beautiful,

beautiful," said Rusty Coombs, the coach at Pryor High School. But John's left leg smarted every time he landed on it and he began to let his pitching arm drop. That way he could slide the left leg after he threw.

"Come over," Rusty Coombs pleaded. "Come up top the way you did."

"Couldn't get through a whole game like that, coach," Johnny said. "I've got to go three-quarter."

"Any way John, long as you keep throwing smoke. But be careful. It's different throwing three-quarter overhand. Different muscles. Different ligaments. If your shoulder starts to hurt you, John, ease up."

Either way, overhand or three-quarter, Johnny could pop the catcher's mitt. He was barely seventeen years old. Popping a catcher's mitt made him feel better than anything else.

"Helen, Dear," he began a letter.

I know I have not been such a good correspondent, but I am a better pitcher than I ever was. I wrote you about the wreck and Dad's headaches and all and it was wonderful that time you came all the way out here to see me play.

But here's a bad thing. I can tell this to nobody in the world but you. My shoulder hurts. I'm throwing different now. Maybe your Dad would know about this, but I sure don't.

I mean I never had bad pain, 'cepting when I broke my leg, and now I've got a kind of toothache in my shoulder. Which means sometimes I ease up on the fastball. Or ease off. Which is the correct word? You would know.

So what happens? We're ahead, 8–0 against Muskogee High. It was mostly me. I was pitching the shutout and I knocked in five of the eight runs and it's only the fifth inning, so I can maybe ease up, and quiet that toothache starting in my shoulder.

You shouldn't do that as a pitcher. Don't ever ease

up. Because then, when you want to go out full again, you can't. It's like shifting into neutral, and all of a sudden you can't find second gear.

I couldn't find no gear. Muskogee got five runs and then Rusty Coombs took me out.

That day, darn, April 11, is when the Yankee scout, Lynn McGraw was watching. He came over after the game and said the Yankees had very high standards and were always careful before they invested. I shouldn't be discouraged, he said, but the Yankees wanted to see if my pitching endurance improved.

Endurance. I mean, what could I tell him? You know back in Trail o' Tears, I could pitch all day and all night, too, before I broke my leg. And I'll be able to again soon as my shoulder and my leg are mended, which could be next year. But what could I say to Lynn McGraw? That I was in a bad auto wreck? I figured that would be worse than saying nothing. So I said nothing, except Thank you, sir, which is the same thing. Thank you, sir, can be nothing.

Anyway, it don't matter at all whether I'm a Yankee or not. I mean, there are other teams. I'll let you know which big-league club wants me most. If I get a bonus, I'll be able to get a car and drive over to see you.

That would be nice, for me and you, because I miss you.

With deep respect
John

✳ ✳ ✳

Harry (The Whistler) Schulte, the manager of the Pittsfield Eagles, was a short, thick-necked man from Decatur, Illinois, who had a theory for every situation in baseball and a theory for every situation in life. He even had theories, one sour old newspaperman suggested, for situations that didn't exist.

Medicine? Harry knew what caused pitchers' sore arms. It was self-abuse. "That hurts two ways," Harry said. "You're working your arm, when you should be resting it, and then you lose your strength. I can always tell those guys from the healthy ones. The self-abusers, they can't go nine innings."

Politics? "The fairies have ruined it, them and the Communists." Harry (The Whistler) Schulte pronounced the word "common-ists." "When I was in Decatur we had a fairy and we beat him up every day. It was in the sixth grade. I never got no further in school. By the end of the term, he wasn't a fairy no more. We had a atheist, which is all right, although I'm a Catholic myself, but we didn't have no Common-ists. What we ought to do with that fucking state department is beat up the fairies and the Reds. In a couple of months, they'll all come around and then we can get tough with Russia. But that Mister Eisenhower he don't have the guts. I'm not saying Mister Eisenhower is a fairy. I know all about the bimbo he had in England. But he may be Commonistic. I hear he is."

Horse racing? "Two years I was out of baseball, I made good money handicapping at the California tracks. Horses is like ballplayers, except they don't practice self-abuse. I can tell being around a ballplayer if he's a good one. Ask me about the first time I seed Ted Williams. And I can tell being around horses. But I'm not gonna let you know *how* I can tell about the horses because if something happens in baseball I might have to go back to handicapping again."

Race relations? "It don't matter none to me what their color is. The only white ones that the black guys bother are humpty-dumpties. Everything bothers humpty-dumpty ballplayers because they're no damn good."

Baseball. "Ballplayers is dumb. That's the trouble with the game. The ones that play it, I tell 'em how to hit and field, and when I was with the Yankees I showed some famous guys how to throw the spitter. But they don't listen. They don't wanna learn. I managed Fort Smith Arkansas oncit and we won three pennants cause they listened.

They had to listen. It was the Depression. Don't listen to the manager, then, and it was Whoops. Hot damn. Goodbye, Dolly Gray. But now there's too much money around and if they don't listen to me, they can make good money working in an airplane factory. It's ruining the game, the good times. Except for the black ones. That's why I like the black ones. They play baseball like it was still the Depression."

Harry was an infielder with the Washington Senators in 1925 when, he said, Big Walter Johnson threw too many fastballs. "I tole him that. Everybody knew about his fastball. He'd throw'd it for fifteen, twenny years. But now he'd lost a little, so I went up to him and said, 'Walter, they're all looking for the fastball. Go to the curveball more.' I tole him what to do and the old man did what I said and won his twenty games."

"About my fastball," Johnny Longboat said.

"You was born throwing it," Harry Schulte said. His features were clumped about narrow, blue eyes. "But with your curve, you come a little to the side. You don't come straight over. So I can tell when you're gonna throw the curve."

"The hitters," Johnny said.

"Is dumb," Schulte said. "That's why they're in the minor leagues. You make it come straight overhand with the curve and then I'll show you a change and when you have the three pitches you'll be outa the minors so quick, they'll think you got a rocket up your ass."

"How come you're still in the minors, Skip?" John said.

"The Yankees give it to me," Harry said. "DiMag."

"DiMag? But he was great."

"It got screwed up. There's this one day in 1949, eleven years ago, when I seen a pitcher doing what you do. Changing his motion when he starts to throw his curve. I'm coaching third base at Yankee Stadium. I call time-out. I say to the big Dago, 'Hey! He's tipping his pitches.

I'll whistle when he's gonna throw his curve.' The Dago don't say much, except to blondes. He looks at me and then he nods his head.

"The next damn pitch, the guy changes his motion. I figure curveball, so I whistle. DiMaggio hangs in. Trouble was, I didn't reckon just how dumb this pitcher was. Now he changed his motion to throw the *fastball*! He was that dumb. DiMag hangs in, and the dumb pitcher's fastball damn near hits him in the head.

"Next thing, DiMaggio's the one who's calling time. 'If you whistle again,' he says, 'I'm shoving this bat right through your teeth.' The story got around. The Yankees started calling me The Whistler. You get a name like that, you can't beat it. That's why I'm here. I know as much as Stengel, more than Durocher."

Nothing in Johnny's life had prepared him for Harry Schulte. Some of the Pittsfield Eagles mocked the manager because of his obsessive use of the word "I." But how, Johnny wondered, could you make fun of somebody who knew as much baseball as Harry Schulte and who had played ball on the same team as Walter Johnson and been a coach in uniform with Joe DiMaggio?

"I never heard a guy talk about hisself so much as Schulte," Ralph Kauff, the catcher, said.

"If Schulte wrote a book," Sly Donoghue said, "he'd only need one letter on his typewriter. The ninth letter. You dummies go figure it out."

"We're supposed to be here to learn," Johnny said, "and the Skipper can teach us."

"What?" Sly Donoghue said. "How to make a speech about himself? I went to a father-son breakfast at the Country Club last year, and Schulte was embarrassing. When I was at Fort Smith. When I tole Walter Johnson. When I was coaching the Yankees. I-I-I-I." Sly glowered. "Fans may be dumb, but not that dumb."

"Schulte says the ballplayers are dumb."

"If *he's* smart, how come he's working in the bushes," Sly said, "eating cold hot dogs, and drinking warm beer at his age? He's sixty-two."

Sly was a good fellow, blandly handsome, somewhat stiff-bodied and going nowhere. He'd been up with the Mohawks for two Florida springs, but each time they threw him back like a sick fish. You only had to watch him bat to know that he couldn't hit good stuff, as long as you kept it low. At twenty-six, he was old for a busher, and this was probably the last season in which he could make a living playing ball. The Mohawks didn't want competent career minor-leaguers. You had to pay them a higher salary each year. It was cheaper constantly to use new kids, although if the minor leagues truly were developmental, you'd always want to keep mixing some veterans with the apprentices. That would create a better learning situation. Anyway, Sly Donoghue, a good fellow, six feet two, who could hit a high fastball five hundred feet, had become bitter.

"Schulte is in the bushes," Johnny said, "because he couldn't get along with Joe DiMaggio."

The three Pittsfield Eagles were drinking beer at the Idle Hour, a roadhouse on Route 7, six miles south of Launt Thompson's "Color Bearer."

"That's not smart," Ralph Kauff said. "If you're managing, you have to get along with everybody, particularly a great one like Joe D."

"He was *coaching*," Johnny said. "He made a mistake."

"I get along with everybody," Sly Donoghue said, "even the coons."

"What's hard about getting along with black guys?" Johnny said. "I'm damn glad to have Billy Dunn running down the long ones in center field."

" 'Magic,' " Sly said, "when you come over with your curveball, you don't have to worry about your center fielder. They ain't gonna hit the ball that far. Another head!" Sly shouted at the barmaid, a blue-eyed black-haired girl called Becky Rae Carpenter. "It's one thing playing ball with coons, but you wouldn't want them in here ogling at Miss Becky Rae."

"John," Becky Rae said. "When you pitching next?"

"The night after tomorrow, Saturday. We go against the Waterbury Yankees."

"The best team in the league."

Sly Donoghue said, "Becky, I don't fancy talking baseball with a pretty woman. There's other things to say. But don't you worry about John going against the Waterbury Yankees. My friend, Johnny Magician here, is the best pitcher in the Eastern League."

"His fastball turns my hand near purple," Ralph Kauff said.

"John," Becky Rae said. "You're gonna be something."

"Yup," John said. He stood and moved his pitching arm in the motion of a fastball.

"He's magic," Donoghue said.

"John," Becky Rae said. "You got a girl?"

"Back in Oklahoma," Johnny said.

"And he'll have more," Sly said.

"Nope," Johnny said.

"It must be pretty back in Oklahoma," Becky said, " 'stead of like this in Pittsfield. The hills on all sides closing you in, and all of the good people gone."

"There's good people here," Johnny said.

"But the best moved out. They went into the cities or the West," Becky Rae said. "My father told me that."

"It ain't real pretty back in Oklahoma, Becky. You got dust and wind and people scratching to get by."

"I'm coming out to see you pitch Saturday night against the Waterbury Yankees. Sure it's pretty, John, in Oklahoma. I saw a movie they made there. The land looked good and all the people were real friendly."

Someone down the bar clamored for a Seven Crown and Seven-Up.

"I'll be rooting real hard," Becky said to Johnny.

* * *

"Rebecca."

Only her mother called her Rebecca; she was Becky Rae to Daddy and her friends.

"Yes, Mom."

"What were you doing out so late last night?"

Becky sighed and pouted and said, sarcastically, "Yes, Mom."

"You were out with that short boy who wears eyeglasses again, weren't you?"

"Yes, Mom." Becky heard shrillness in her own voice.

"Don't sass me, Rebecca. I'm trying to raise you right." Her mother, Charlotte, had a round-faced prettiness, but her body was bloated and her hips looked enormous, even in loose-fitting slacks. Mother said glands made her overweight, and Becky accepted that, although Mother certainly loved to nibble fudge and chocolate candies.

"You didn't sit in his lap, did you, Rebecca?"

"I don't like to be quizzed. Yes, I did sit on his lap."

They were in the kitchen of the Carpenters' small yellow house near the northern edge of Pittsfield. Mother was eating brownies out of a paper bag.

"When you sit on a boy's lap, you get him excited. They can't help themselves." Her mother nibbled. "Did you get the boy excited, Rebecca?"

"Either that, or else he had a pipe in his pocket."

Charlotte took a large bite of the brownie, chewed noisily, and shook her head. "What's going to become of you, Rebecca? What are you going to become?"

They had been having such jousts for five years, since Becky turned fourteen and Mother joined a fundamentalist church called The Assembly of The Lord. Becky's father, Carl Carpenter, tended bar at the Country Club, and freelanced behind the bar of the Veterans of Foreign Wars. Working nights, he slept much of the day and Charlotte Carpenter told friends that before she found The Assembly of The Lord, her life was so lonely that she actually had thought of suicide. Now Charlotte talked about the Lord and how we would all stand before him naked on Judgment Day, when only the pure and merciful would be saved. She talked about the Lord and nibbled brownies.

Becky wanted to run. She loved her father, a diffident man, defeated by long struggles to earn a living. She supposed she loved Mother, too, but the new religion had turned Charlotte into a chronic kitchen evangelist. "Only the pure and merciful will be saved, Rebecca. Are you merciful, Rebecca? Are you pure?" The fat woman waved both hands, the way she had seen the preacher gesture from the pulpit.

"Have another brownie, Mom."

"Rebecca!"

Becky wanted to leave this frame house and go somewhere far-off, to Oregon or California, but her beaus never took her anywhere, except the drive-in, or the Lucky Strike Bowling Alley (twenty-two lanes). She did well at high school English and thought of writing stories for the magazines. She was a cheerleader and made the girls' gymnastic team. She learned typing, but her shorthand was poor and besides, when she graduated, there were no jobs for secretaries. She dressed in short skirts and carried her body very straight and read novels and wondered, in low moments, if she would ever find a magic beau, who would enfold her in his arms and lift her beyond the Berkshire Hills. At length, she took a job serving cocktails at the Idle Hour.

Intelligent, but trained for no career, Becky was not equipped to make her own salvation. But she could cook and sew and offer sprightly conversation. She was equipped, indeed conditioned, to be a wife. In her better moments she thought it was only a matter of time before the magic beau appeared and a new life, a real life, could begin.

She liked working at the Idle Hour because she met baseball players, even some from Oregon and California. They were good-looking and they liked her conversation. She rejoiced with them when they won and comforted or gently teased them when they lost. It was, Becky Rae concluded, when she was feeling neither high nor low, a matter of both time and luck for someone to find her and save her from the salvation sermons that droned interminably, amid bites of brownies, in the oppressive holiness of her mother's kitchen.

* * *

Wahconah Stadium sat so close to the Housatonic that when the river rose, center field turned into swampland. But Johnny thought the little ballpark was a pretty place to work, with all the green around it and the trees standing way back of center field on the hill that rose beyond the river. It was Friday night. The Eagles were to play the Binghamton White Sox, but Harry Schulte made time to work with Johnny.

"All right, the change-up," Harry Schulte said. "Gimme the ball."

They stood in the bull pen sixty feet from Ralph Kauff. "Now," Schulte said, "you reach and go with your usual fastball motion, until you're about to release the ball. Then you pull down. You pull down hard, like you were pulling down a windowshade. That's the motion, pulling down the shade. Forget about Venetian blinds."

Harry Schulte grinned and whistled shrilly. "Now what happens when you pull the shade, is that the ball spins like a sonuvabuck, but it don't go fast. The batter sees your motion and he sees the ball spinning like hell, and he thinks *a fastball* and he swings. Whoops. The ball ain't there yet. But you got a strike. I'll show ya, kid."

The Whistler went into an awkward windup—he had been a second baseman, not a pitcher—and threw as hard as he could, pulling down the shade. The ball bounced short of home plate and glanced into Ralph Kauff's collarbone.

"Aaafh," Schulte said. "Slipped."

"I better get my chest protector, Skip," Kauff shouted.

"Stay where you are. Gimme the ball." The Whistler's second throw sailed off at an odd angle into a corner of the left-field grandstand. "I got this arthritis," Schulte said. "I ain't been taking enough blackstrap molasses. You get older, you gotta take blackstrap molasses. This guy sends it to me from a special place in Alabama. He seed me play oncit, when I got three hits and I stole home. You try the pitch now, kid," he said to Johnny.

John rubbed a new Eastern League baseball, and lobbed a half dozen throws to Kauff. Then he threw a fastball that hissed and buzzed and crashed into Kauff's glove. "All right," John said.

He went into his loose windup, kicking his left leg high. Holding the ball along the seams, he pulled down as he released it. He pulled down as hard as he could. There was no strain. The ball spun furiously and floated up to Kauff at the level of a batter's uniform letters.

"Keep it down," Schulte said. "Most of the time you want to keep your change down."

"Good pitch," Kauff shouted. "Good damn pitching. I knew what was coming and it *fooled* me."

"Fooling you don't get a Yank to Oxford," Schulte said.

"What do you mean?"

"Nothing," Harry Schulte said. He laughed a hacking laugh and whistled again. "Keep the change down," he said.

It was a curious thing, throwing a change of pace. With a fastball or a hard curve, you threw. Then in the blinking of a thought the ball was in the catcher's glove. But with the change of pace—a slow ball they called it on the field at Trail o' Tears—you got a sense of being disembodied. It was your pitch. You'd throw it. But when it was out of your hand, it wasn't yours any more. It went floating, spinning toward home plate and there was so much time to think. The ball sat in the air, and it seemed ridiculous, throwing a slow pitch to a professional batter. A girl could hit it, Helen Arnett or Becky Rae Carpenter. The closer the slow ball moved to the plate, even to the plate in the bull pen, the bigger it seemed to get, until it was a basketball, not a baseball. How could any batter miss it?

"When I was at Fort Smith," Schulte said, "we had a pitcher, broke his arm. Left-hander called Les Merrill. He was driving with a woman, and his left elbow was outside the car and someone bashed him. Well, sir, with that bashed left elbow barely healed, he won twenty-two games for me at old Fort Smith, and you know what his best pitch was? I taught it to him."

"The slow ball," Johnny said.

"Say change-up," Schulte said. "Slow ball sounds bush."

Johnny threw five more change-ups, all at the knees.

"Yeah," Schulte said. "You got it quick." He didn't whistle. Johnny began to realize that Schulte's whistle was derisive.

"Now switch," Schulte said. "Throw fastball, change-up, fastball, change. Like that."

Ralph Kauff began chattering to an imaginary batter. "Ur-up. Look sharp. You ain't gonna hit this guy. Ur-up. Cain't hit him batter. Watch your head."

Schulte whistled. "It's a change," Harry shouted. "It wouldn't dent you if it hit you in the temple. Besides, there ain't no batter. Ballplayers is dumb."

Schulte turned to John. "Work on that change tonight. Throw some in the bull pen in the last three innings. That way the Binghamton White Sox might think I'm gonna use you in relief. I'll throw 'em off. Whoops. Good-bye, Dolly Gray."

"They'll see the new pitch," John said. "They'll tell the Waterbury Yankees."

"Not with these Pittsfield lights," Schulte said, "and them sitting way in the dugout. They won't see nothing. It'll look like you're loosening up."

"You mean you want me to use the new pitch *tomorrow* against the Yankees?"

"What you got a new pitch for? Your girl?"

"Helen's back in Oklahoma."

"You got to use it, Johnny," Schulte said. "You got to have confidence in it. Your first pitch tomorrow night. I want a change."

"Okay, okay," Johnny said, "except I don't really need it."

"I wouldn't be teaching you what you don't really need."

"I beat the Yankees twice so far with fastballs."

"You want to be on home relief?"

"No," John said. "I've seen people on the home relief. One old lady, Molly Squires, in Pryor, Oklahoma. I caught her eating cat food."

"Then learn the change. Learn to believe in it. Look, before you get to be old like that lady eating cat food, you're gonna need it. I know some things. I hear them call you Magic. You got as good a natural fastball as Bobby Feller, 'cept you got to keep coming over for your curve. When you come over, the curve gets to the plate and, whoops, it falls off a table. Then the hitter is swinging at nothing 'cept the air."

"Good-bye, Dolly Gray," John said.

"That was a song. I knew that song and I read McGuffy's reader, but I got no education. I never read a book. But listen to me and you'll learn to be a pitcher. Not a thrower. A pitcher. What are you kid? Nineteen?"

"Right. My birthday was in June."

"Most people who is nineteen usually is going on twenty," Schulte said. "Think of the blocks the babies play with. You want to build something. I never had a baby. You want to build with blocks till you become a pitcher, not a thrower. But you got to start with the right blocks. That's what I'm giving you here. Start throwing change-ups now and when you're thirty, which is an old man for some pitchers, and you do need a change, you got it. I'm giving you the blocks, and don't forget it and you'll be a pitcher not a thrower right away and you can go on till you're forty. I'll be dead."

"You won't, Skip. You're in some shape, hitting infield practice every day."

"Nah," Schulte said. "I keep forgetting to take my blackstrap molasses and, since my wife died, there ain't no one to remind me."

"What was her name?"

"Dolly," Schulte said, "like in the song. I'd sing the old song for you, but I got a foul tip in the throat one day in Fort Smith, Arkansas, and I can't sing good no more."

"How'd you get hit there?"

"Catching, kid. I could play anywhere, catch, pitch, infield, outfield. 'Cepting for this. I could do all them things pretty good, but none great. I didn't have the size. But you, you got the size and like I say, I hear them call you Magic. I seen the great ones, Mathewson, near the end and Grover Cleveland Alexander, and I played with Walter Johnson. They called Mathewson 'Big Six,' because having him was like having six pitchers. Johnson was the Big Train. He could bring it. And 'Mose' Grove and Dizzy Dean and Feller and that kid in Cleveland that got it in the eye, Herb Score. Shame, but if he'd been playing for me, I'da showed him how you follow through so your glove is near your face. So you're protected. Glove at the face. Cup on your nuts."

90

"How's my follow-through?" Johnny said.

"I'll work on that after you pitch next time. You just remember finish with both hands up in front of your face, like Floyd Patterson when he's boxing. I'll show you all you got to know. I seen these great ones, the drinkers and the sober ones, and the ones that broads ruined, which is a lot, and I got a lot of things to tell you. Stay with the beer. Maybe a Scotch once in a while. Martinis kill you. Them and stingers. And the bimbos. Look for one like my Dolly. She was three years older than me, so's she had sense. Kids, they look great, but after you marry them they grow up and what happens? How you gonna know what they'll be after they're all growed? Hey, kid, you listening? I know a lotta things for a guy never got past grade six. Like I know you, and with that arm you got, I'd call you Magic, too, 'cepting it wouldn't be right."

"Why not?"

"There ain't no magic here. This is the bushes. Only place there's magic is the major leagues."

*   *   *

The Binghamton White Sox defeated the Pittsfield Eagles, 11–5. The crowd at Wahconah Stadium numbered 106 people. "More peanut sellers than customers," said Sly Donoghue, who was assigned to manage the bull pen for The Whistler. Ralph Kauff hit a home run so high up in left center field that it hit an electric cable that ran between wood poles thirty feet above the fence.

"He's some hitter for a fire hydrant," Sly told Johnny.

"I think if you jam him he's in trouble," Johnny said.

"Who can tell down here in Double A?" Sly said. "How many pitchers got that much control?"

"Jam him," Johnny said.

"How can you tell?"

"I don't know how I can tell, but I look at the way a hitter stands, and I watch him swing batting practice, and I know."

"You don't have to know with that fastball. You can throw it by them. Eight straight wins. Ninety-seven strike-outs. What do you have to know to throw it by them?"

"I don't want to be a thrower," John said. "Some day I'm going to be thirty and I'll have to be a pitcher. So I want to start becoming a pitcher now."

The small crowd specked the wooden grandstand and from the bull pen John could see three different types. There were the children, pursuing foul balls and frankfurters, restless as feeding chickens.

Old men sat stiff-necked and still, sometimes with hands against their faces as though remembering. *You know Lou Gehrig played first base in Wahconah Stadium once, but he had to use another name. He was still going to Columbia College and . . . well you remember Larrupin' Lou, the Iron Horse. We had real crowds in those days, crowds in the thousands, and they all stood up the day Larrupin' Lou hit one clear into the river. Can you believe it? The crowds are gone for good. And Gehrig died and Babe Ruth died. Those weren't men, but giants. On their death beds, I read it in the paper, both Gehrig and Ruth weighed less than a hundred pounds.*

Then there were girls, like Becky Rae Carpenter, and every single girl had a favorite player, and each girl studied her favorite and throbbed with secret hope. The ballplayer would fall in love with her and marry her, and he would go on to the major leagues and the girls, not baseball girls any longer, but baseball *wives*, would travel with the ballplayers to distant cities like Milwaukee and Chicago, where the last two World Series had been played. The girls would fly high over the mountains that clamped Pittsfield, the town which Longfellow and Nathaniel Hawthorne knew, and where a ballplayer, even a ballplayer from as obscure a town as Trail o' Tears, exuded magic promise.

Becky Rae waved to John as he threw to Sly Donoghue in the bull pen. Black hair, in a pageboy bob, outlined her oval face. Becky Rae had a pretty snub nose and she was compact. Not slim but compact.

"I can't talk now, Becky Rae, I'm working." Violation of Eastern League rule 807.3. A player may not fraternize with (or be sororized by) fans, during the course of a regularly scheduled game, or during the postseason championship playoffs.

The change-up wasn't hard to throw. Once in every twelve pitches it slipped and went high, but that happened with the fastball too. Wild high. Except with the fastball you could miss and throw it into the hitter's power. And the hitter would swing too late to hurt you. With the change, you wouldn't want to make a mistake.

Fatty Pfister started for the Pittsfield Eagles. Fatty Pfister threw all kinds of junk: a palmball that sank, and a screwball that broke backwards, and three different kinds of curves, all slow. Pfister was never going to pitch in a better league. He knew it. He was a sorrowful, open man, five-foot-ten and two hundred pounds, who tried with intense passion, but simply did not have the arm a pitcher needed to advance.

The Binghamton White Sox hit Pfister hard after the fifth inning. It was a matter of timing. Once the Sox adjusted to the variety of slow pitches, they pulled long drives. The White Sox scored nine runs. They led by 11–4.

From the seventh inning, Hawk Heron warmed up on the other bull-pen mound, alongside Johnny, who was working on his new pitch. Hawk threw a hard fastball that sank. That was all he threw. It was good for an inning or two, particularly after Pfister's slow stuff. Hawk would have to pitch that last inning. "Goddamn housemaid," he said to John. "The Whistler's gonna want me to mop up."

John was concentrating on his change of pace and did

not answer. It surprised him in the top of the ninth when Harry Schulte whistled from the mound and held his hands together and drew back, spreading them apart, like a magician who materializes an explosion out of the air. It was his sign for Johnny, who jogged in. That was one of Harry Schulte's rules. A relief pitcher jogged. "You got to work your legs every chance you get. It ain't just the arm, remember. Every time you throw, you got to lift one leg and push off the other. Can't pitch without strong legs. I had a guy at Fort Smith, arms like a goddamn soldier. An old-fashioned soldier, the kind that swung a sword all day. But he wouldn't listen to me. He didn't work his legs. I tole him. He didn't listen. He never could go nine. He plain ran down and you can find him now in a filling station, pumping Esso, in Alma, Arkansas. He couldn't stay at Fort Smith, even though I tole him."

At the mound, Ralph Kauff said, "I'll use one waggle for the fastball, and two for a breaking ball, and three for the change, if you want to throw it. You want to throw a change?"

"He wants to throw it," Schulte said, " 'cepting to the bad hitters, Leonard and Minton. Those two guys don't get their bats around. Never throw the change-up to weak hitters. You overpower them suckers."

"Why me and not the Hawk?" John said. "I thought I was supposed to pitch tomorrow."

"You're pitching tomorrow," Schulte said. "I was in Japan oncit with the Yankees, and them little Japs are so small they can barely grip the ball but they made guys pitch every day. You lose a little speed, maybe, but you get great control. I tole Tommy Byrne on the Yankees what to do, but he don't listen. Could have had some big year. I tole him how. He didn't listen. Whoops. Good-bye, Dolly Gray. He's back in Carolina."

"Come on," said Dink Slatterer, the umpire. "Get started. You ain't coming back with any seven runs."

"Fuck it," Schulte said. "Don't go telling me what we're gonna do."

"What do you say?"

"I said fuck it."

"Well, it's a good thing you didn't say fuck you, cause if you said that, I'd run your ass right outa here, Schulte."

"You in a hurry?" Schulte said. "You got a date with some bimbo?"

"One more word, you're gone," the umpire said.

"Pitch good, John," Schulte said. Then, walking toward the dugout, over his shoulder, "That's three words, Slatterer."

The umpire shook his head in anger.

John started Rick Rosenthal, the White Sox's best hitter, with a change. Goddamn. The thing went high. It sailed up slowly, spinning hard, right into Rosenthal's power. John shuddered while the pitch was in the air. It surprised him when Rosenthal never moved his bat. John had a strike.

"You long-nosed son of a buck," The Whistler shouted at Rick Rosenthal. "You couldn't hit that one with your nose." Then John struck out Rosenthal with fastballs. Kevin Ryan nubbed a roller to the mound. Two out. John started Russell Rentzel with a hard curve. Strike one. He blew a fastball by the fists. A second strike.

Ralph Kauff waggled his fingers twice. He wanted another curve, down and away. It could even be a little wide. Rentzel would be tense enough with two strikes on him to swing at a pitch beyond the strike zone.

John shook his head. Kauff waggled once. A fastball on the thumbs could get the strikeout, too. John shook his head again. He was trying to be a pitcher.

Kauff waggled three times. Johnny threw the change. It went low, a fine, surprising pitch, and Rentzel hit it on a rising line into left center. Billy Dunn fled and leaped and reached across his chest and grabbed the ball.

John jogged into the dugout and said to Schulte, "What the hell?"

"He was guessing," Schulte said. "I shoulda tole you. Rentzel is a guess hitter. I shoulda warned you with the guess hitters."

"What?" John said.

"That when they guesses witcha, they hits ya hard."

"But how can I anticipate their guessing?" John said.

"You can't, but you can do something else. While you're pitching, *think* what the hitter is thinking. Be the hitter and the pitcher both. You got to teach yourself to do that. Then the guess hitters won't bother you none, because they'll always be one guess behind."

* * *

John had rented a room in a tall, white Greek Revival home, set behind drooping spruce trees off Spadina Parkway. Mildred Vancil, an accountant's widow, who owned the big house, rented two rooms to Pittsfield baseball players each season. She was a large, red-faced, hearty woman, who liked golf and bridge and the idea of young men in her home, but she imposed two conditions in her leases. The ballplayers could not have women guests, even in the living room. "They may mean well, but they have a drink," she said, "and get boisterous and they could break my Waterford glass decanter." The second condition was that the ballplayers had to be white.

Most of the Eagles lived in old houses near Spadina Parkway, but Billy Dunn, who was black, had to live in the northeast corner of town, in a squat old yellow house, that belonged to a black janitor who worked for General Electric. Once in a while, when Johnny took Billy Dunn to the Idle Hour, Pittsfield beer drinkers shuffled their feet and mumbled. That bothered John and bothered Billy and even bothered Becky Rae Carpenter, the barmaid. She always asked Billy Dunn what he wanted to drink before she asked any of the other ballplayers.

"It doesn't make sense," John said to Kauff in the sitting room of Mrs. Vancil's home.

"What don't make sense?"

"They put a statue in the square to commemorate the soldiers who fought the Civil War. You know what that war was about, Ralph?"

"Lincoln freed the slaves. But that don't mean we got to live in the same house with Nigras."

"Don't say Nigras, Ralph. It's a bad word, like the time Wilkie Willis called you a lumpheaded Texas kraut. You ever take history?"

"They didn't teach history, if you was studying to be a diesel mechanic at Bowie Vocational High."

"The war was about the Union, the United States. Whether one state, South Carolina, could quit the Union. Afterwards it was about slavery and, Ralph, if Billy Dunn was good enough to catch that ball today, he's good enough to room here with you and me. That's what that Civil War statue, *Color Bearer*, is supposed to mean."

Kauff squinted in thought. Then he said slowly, "They didn't explain things the way you do, John, at Bowie Vocational. The coach I had said baseball was all legs. You got to have speed. I got no speed. The coach said the Nigras was gonna run us all right outa the game. We played this one black school. They bombed us. Our pitcher wasn't like you. He took forever to release the ball. They ran on his big windup, and the Nigras stole eight bases. Eight goddamn bases. I was catching. That's why I had to study to be a diesel mechanic. I thought I'd never play baseball beyond Bowie High."

"You're a good receiver, Ralph, and I'd guess you'll hit enough. I can tell looking at a hitter."

"I'm trying to hit one five hundred feet," Kauff said. "Then maybe the Mohawks will know they need me. I hate them diesel tractors and them trucks. The engines smell and the greasy diesel fuel foams like beer. You get it on your pants and you start to smell from oil. My girl don't like that. Maudie Sue."

"They all have two names. Maudie Sue. Becky Rae. I'm glad you have a girl back home, Ralph. That's important."

"But I want other girls. I want every girl I see. They look at me and they see this stumpy look. One day The Whistler called me 'Fire Pump.' The girls turn to someone who's smooth, like Sly, or someone big and good-looking like you."

"One girl's enough," John said. "Schulte told me that, but I knew it anyway. You can talk to other girls. It makes you feel good. The big thing is that the one girl should be the right one."

"You got the right one?"

"Helen Arnett. I'm gonna win twenty games this season and then they'll move me up to Knoxville, or even the big club. Either way, I'll make almost eight hundred dollars a month. Then I go back to Oklahoma and tell Helen Arnett and we'll be married. I haven't told her yet. It's a surprise."

"But don't you want to *be* with the others?" Kauff said. "I mean fuck them. Don't you want to fuck Becky Rae Carpenter?"

"A little bit, Ralph. Sometimes a lot. But you can't fuck all of them, Ralph. That can't be done."

"I was thinking about fucking Becky Rae, 'cept she won't look at me. Schulte, like he could read my brain, he says, 'Hey, Kauff, you're raunchy. From now on that's what I call you. Raunchy Kauff.' "

"That's not a good name, Ralph. I'll speak to him. After the ball game tonight. You wouldn't want that name to get around."

* * *

The next day's mail brought Johnny a five-page letter, written in longhand, from Norman, Oklahoma.

Dear John,

I have grown a lot since the delightful days we had together in those dusty fields as children. But we're not children any more.

I follow your work in *The Sporting News* and so does my Dad, and we are pleased to see you are winning so many games in Pittsfield and Waterbury and Elmira and those other old Eastern towns. It must be fascinating to travel from one to the other.

I am still a great sports fan; in fact, I'm on the Sooners' cheerleading squad (for next autumn), but I have other interests now. I am majoring in art history, studying Western painters such as Remington and Bierstadt, who has a wonderful work called "Sunset at Wind River Canyon." Beyond that I study the great Europeans, as well, not only Rembrandt but Monet, Picasso. And many others!!

John, dear, this is the hardest letter I have written. There is a man here in Norman, that you would like very much, Norris Oakwater. He is an obstetrician. The wonderful thing about his being *that kind* of doctor is that his patients are healthy. He deals with health and life, not sickness and death.

His wife was killed in a fire and he's so lonely. His house burned, killing his wife, and he has not been able to bring himself to live in a house since. Norris lives in an apartment building, here in Norman, with several people from the university, including the assistant dean, who's my advisor. Norris owns two original Remington paintings!

This is the hard thing. Norris has fallen terribly—wonderfully!—in love with me. He says I am his youth and his resurrection. He loves the sketches that I do—I have to make myself draw more from life and less from my imagination!—and he says that after we are married, he will support me very well and I can continue art studies as long as I like. He doesn't mind. He delivers 150 healthy babies a year. There. I have said it.

The hardest thing I have ever said in a letter. Norris Oakwater wants to marry me!

When he asked, I was surprised and confused and I said let me think. Norris is fourteen years older than I am. When I'm confused, I talk to Daddy and I told Daddy that I had loved you and that I wasn't sure with Norris, and Daddy said, 'You will be sure. Johnny is far away and that makes him romantic. Norris is here. But honey,' Daddy said, 'you know love is something you learn to do, and how can you compare a doctor of medicine with a mere ballplayer?'

This is not coming out the way I meant it. Nothing will replace the loving times we had, you and I alone. I write *loving* very carefully. That is really a special word to a young woman! And *I* did not say 'mere ballplayer.' Daddy did.

We have had six family meetings. Norris and I will marry July 11. This letter is so hard for me to write. Such a hard thing!

John stopped reading Helen Arnett's letter. He lay on a maple bed in the large hall bedroom of Mrs. Vancil's home. Not moving anything but his right hand, John crumpled the letter. Then, still lying down, he threw it toward a brown imitation-leather waste basket, pulling down as he released the balled paper. Spinning hard, it dropped into the basket.

Ralph Kauff knocked at the door.

"Come in, Raunchy," Johnny said.

"I thought you told me 'Raunchy' was a bad name," Kauff said. "Why you using it?"

"You got to put up with the way things are. Schulte's name is gonna stick."

"But I don't like it."

"Life is a bitch," Johnny said, "and the worst thing about it is that cunts are pricks."

✳ ✳ ✳

The Waterbury Yankees, leading the Eastern League by six games, swaggered as though they owned the City of New York. Although the Connecticut town in which they played was nothing like New York, they had their reasons. The Yankee management paid each Waterbury player one hundred dollars a month more than comparable Eastern Leaguers earned and required everyone to wear a jacket and tie on travel days. A Yankee rule, the players said. A big-league rule. We'll all be Yankees some day, winning the World Series and walking out of the big ballpark carrying winners' checks, wearing hand-tailored suits and Sulka ties.

Wilkie Willis, who managed Waterbury, cackled with the most arrogant needling John had heard. You could like individuals on the Waterbury club, but it was hard to like the team. You wanted to beat the Waterbury Yankees every time you played them, but winning was chancy. Pumped full of Yankee dollars and Yankee pride, they played like hell.

"We'll all be wearing pinstripes in the big town," Wilkie Willis yelled at Johnny on May 16, "but the only way you'll ever wear stripes is if you go to jail."

John knew people who should have been in jail back home. Wilkie Willis wasn't funny, simply nasty. He had been a New York Yankee across two seasons and played in only eleven games. That must have been embittering, being with the best, Rizzuto, Tommy Henrich, and Di-Mag, but not being good enough to *play* with the best. Only to shout at people from the dugout. You could understand what frustration did to a man, but you didn't have to approve. Life, Johnny reminded himself, was a bitch.

"I'll get that loudmouthed fuckhead," Whistler Schulte promised his players. "Don't you listen to what Wilkie Willis says. In Fort Smith there was this loudmouth who come from up Wyoming and one year he got a disease.

Gonorrhea. He's batting and I holler, 'Hey, how's the sheep?' The guy wasn't no loudmouth after that."

The Pittsfield Eagles waited, but so far Whistler had never nailed the fuckhead, Wilkie Willis, who was just as quick as he was nasty.

John decided he would pitch mean baseball against the Yankees. He had pitched mean only once before, on that day under the Oklahoma windmill when Randy Lugert said he was a half-breed. Damn Helen Arnett.

Dad told him about Walter Johnson, who could throw faster than anybody and was always frightened that his hard one might kill a batter. The cruel hitters, like Ty Cobb, knew Johnson's fear and stood up close to the plate, making Walter Johnson throw his fastball wide. Or so Dad said.

Johnny's fastball made a snarling noise. There was a whoosh of air, and then a hard buzz that seemed to spin right off the stitches. Whoosh-buzz. The fastball always made a threatening noise.

John stood six feet two inches tall now, and he had thick forearms, but a lot of thick-armed six-foot-two-inch men couldn't throw much. There was no way John could explain where the fastball came from. It was part of himself, and something beyond him: his own pitch as he gripped it, and a thing apart from him when he released the ball.

He did not throw the fast pitch into batters. They were alert to it and sometimes frightened. The disembodied pitch made its own point.

Whoosh-buzz.

Tornadoes. Beehives.

The hitters would back off.

Warming up on Saturday evening, July 12, John decided to throw half a dozen fastballs at the Waterbury Yankees. He didn't know whom he'd knock down. He wanted to throw at Wilkie Willis, but the manager never hit. He stayed in the dugout and shouted, safe from spikes and safe from fastballs.

John pitched three shutout innings, using his hard curve and fastball. "Where's the change, kid?" Schulte said. "You don't use a new pitch, it rusts on you, like lousy plumbing."

"There's something else I want to try, Skip," Johnny said. Next inning, he got two strikes on Harry Templehoff, a big, moon-faced third baseman. He wound up and loosed his fastball at Harry Templehoff's head.

The hitter froze.

"Duck," John bellowed.

Templehoff threw himself backward. His bat sailed toward first base and his baseball cap hung in the air. The ball hurtled between Templehoff's head and cap.

Whoosh-buzz.

"Busher," Willis shouted. He stood in the dugout holding a bat. "You throw at my guys again, you'll be picking splinters out of your bush-league teeth. Not just hairs, you goddamn muff-diver. Splinters. Ya hear that, ya bush muff-diving bastard?"

Johnny turned his back on Willis and Templehoff and rubbed a new baseball. He had heard Willis and now he heard Becky Rae Carpenter call from behind the plate, "That's scaring them, John."

An inning later, he knocked down Bump Igoe, and Dink Slatterer, the umpire, walked over from first base. "What's going on?"

"Wild," John said.

"Only with two strikes? You don't have to pitch that way, Johnny, and I'm not gonna let you. Nobody gets killed in a game I umpire."

"There's lights." Schulte had sprinted to the mound. "Them hitters ain't goddamn blind. He ain't pitchin' to Helen Keller, Dink."

"We got a rule on intentionally hitting someone," Slatterer said. "It's a hundred-dollar fine and expulsion."

"How can you determine intent, Dink?" Johnny said. "You study mind-reading?"

"I can tell intent," said the home-plate umpire, Frank Lovecione. "I can tell by the count."

"Then why did I yell duck at Harry Templehoff?"

"To make it look good," Slatterer said.

"Bush bastard." Willis stood near the mound, holding a bat.

"Get outa here, Willis, before I run you," Slatterer said. Dink was the senior umpire.

"I'm protecting my boys," Willis said. "Valuable Yankee property. Nice kids. This is baseball, not the damn Korean War."

"You got a point," Slatterer said. "Throw one more too high and too tight, Longboat, and the Eastern League office hears about it."

"I got a kink," Johnny told The Whistler. "It's in my shoulder."

"Eight pitches," Schulte said. "The rules give him eight pitches to test his arm."

John threw the first of eight into the screen behind home plate. He bounced two outside curves. He threw two fast strikes and another wild one.

What happened next was just what Johnny planned. The Yankee hitters, standing under minor-league lights, thought that the fastest pitcher in the league had lost control. He didn't know where his next pitch was going. That meant their head and ribs and knees, and who knows what, could be crunched by Johnny's plummeting fastball.

Jack Rickerby cringed as John wound up. He was still cringing as the change of pace floated across the plate.

A *Yankee* cringing from a slow ball. John snapped a curve and threw a fastball into Rickerby's thumbs. The hitter swung with a wild eagerness and missed. He was wildly eager to get back to the dugout. John had the Yankees cringing at his change-up and suddenly he was aware that he had four pitches. A fast ball, a curve, a change of pace, and a knockdown.

Schulte sat next to him in the dugout but said nothing.

"Four," John said. "I got four now, Skip."

Schulte squinted a smile. "An' last week, you had only two. An' I showed you one and you learned the other by yourself. Kid, win this game and I'm calling the Mohawks, if I got to pay the long-distance bill myself. They don't always listen to what I say, but you belong up there now, kid. You ain't a thrower no more, but a pitcher, 'cept in a few years it wouldn't hurt for you to learn a slider, which I will be glad to show you when it's time."

John put an arm around The Whistler's shoulders and said, "Thanks."

"I'm prouda ya," Schulte said. "Never had no kids myself. I never had a kid of my own that I could teach to be a ballplayer."

Billy Dunn hit another home run and in the seventh John was leading 2–0, when Templehoff came up again. The third baseman glowered. He was no coward.

"Get in and hit," said Frank Lovecione, the umpire.

Goddamn, Johnny was thinking, I'm a pitcher, which is what I always wanted to be. I'm nineteen and I'm a pitcher, which is a glorious thing, and my girl has run and she's gonna marry a doctor. John felt rage and Templehoff still glowered and John thought, if you're going to give me a hard look, stupid, you shouldn't do it while I have the ball.

"Hey, Okie," Willis yelled. "We're gonna get you now, Okie, and send you back to where your family is. On home relief."

John let his fastball go so that it would sail slightly

behind Templehoff, kidney high. The hitter took a small stride, ducked backwards and then—everything happened in half a second—he realized he had moved into the path of Johnny's fastball. Templehoff uttered a high, girlish cry of fright. The ball crashed against his ribs, drawing the grunt of a bull. Johnny had never heard a sound like that before, "Aieee—urghh." Templehoff lay outside the batter's box, spinning and kicking.

John saw players from the Yankee bench come charging. Raunchy Kauff thought quickly enough to throw back the ball. Three of the Waterbury Yankees ran toward him but when they realized John held a baseball, they stopped short.

"You better hold it, damn ya," Schulte yelled, running to the mound. "This man is armed."

Near home plate Harry Templehoff retched.

"All right, Longboat," Dink Slatterer said, "I'm running you and it's a hundred dollars. Now get outa here."

"We're playing this game under protest," Schulte said.

"We protest *your* protest," Wilkie Willis said. "Your Okie is trying to kill my Yankee hitters."

"If I was trying," John said, "there's two or three that would be dead, already."

John walked toward the plate. Templehoff was on his feet, shaking his head. The fight was gone from him. "I think you broke my fucking rib," he said to John.

"Listen, Templehoff, nobody's mad at you, but if your manager keeps mouthing at us, you guys pay. Checks and balances. Willis mouths *us*, you guys get hit."

"I didn't say nothing," Templehoff said.

"Well, you better say something," Johnny said. "Tell your manager to zip his fucking lips together. There's needling and needling. I don't want to hear another word about my family. Not now. Not ever."

"I can't tell him, John. I can't fight with my manager. I want to make the bigs."

John indicated the mess beside home plate. "Think of the bigs," he said, "but think of your insides first."

Templehoff nodded. "Look," he said, pointing.

John fastened a hand on Templehoff's shoulder and wheeled. Schulte and Willis were wrestling on the grass alongside the mound. It wasn't fair. Willis was twenty pounds heavier and fifteen years younger. Before Johnny could reach the managers, other players and Dink Slatterer had pried them apart. Willis stood up. Schulte lay on the grass, wincing.

"Skip, are you all right?" John cried. "Skip, did he hurt you?"

Schulte's complexion had gone gray. "Okay," he said through grinding teeth. "Willis couldn't hurt me. Chest," Harry Schulte said. "Heart."

"Stretcher," Slatterer hollered. "We got to get this man to a hospital. Get an ambulance."

"No ambulance," Schulte said. "Take my car. Blue Ford. Mohawks pay me eight cents a mile."

*　*　*

The Waterbury Yankees, wearing neckties with suits or sports jackets, tramped on to an air-conditioned silver bus. They were silent, except for Wilkie Willis. "Goddamn," Willis bawled at Johnny, "if you hadn't started throwing those knockdown pitches, Schulte would be alive."

"Hey," Harry Templehoff said. "Lay off him, Wilkie. There's been enough trouble tonight."

Willis chewed gum, considering.

"Get on the bus, Wilkie," Templehoff said.

"Listen," Willis said, "who in the fuck is managing this club, Templehoff?"

"You are, Wilkie, but there's been enough trouble tonight."

"Thanks," Johnny said to Harry Templehoff.

John walked with Billy Dunn toward his own pale green 1952 Chevrolet convertible. He remembered the salesman at O.K. Used Cars on Route 44, who said the Chevy wasn't green, but honeydew. "Dinah Shore drives the same color car," the salesman said. He suddenly sang inanely,

See the U.S.A.
In Your Chevrolet
America is asking you to call

"That was a bad death," John said to Billy Dunn.

"He died on the field," Billy said. "That's where he liked to be. And it was quick."

"But it was stupid. Getting into a fight at his age. It was absurd. I'm reading a book about that. Absurd deaths."

"Does it help?" Billy said. "Do you feel you can deal with Harry dying better because of a book?"

"I don't know," Johnny said. "Not yet, I don't."

"Where you going?" Becky Rae Carpenter said. "Can I come?"

"To the Idle Hour," Johnny said. "I've got to do a little drinking."

"You can just drop me," Billy Dunn said. They wedged into the front seat of the honeydew Chevrolet, Dunn positioning himself carefully so that his left hip would not touch the right hip of Becky Rae Carpenter.

"You come along, Will," Johnny said.

"You don't need me," Dunn said. "You've got a girl. You'll have a drink. What you need an old black center fielder for, John?"

"How old are you, Billy?" Becky Rae said.

"Well, the Mohawks think I'm twenty-three, but my mother knows I'm thirty-three. That's C.P.A."

"C.P.A.?" Becky said.

"Colored people's age."

"I'm nineteen," Becky Rae said. "That's H.G.A. Honest Girl's Age. Gee, it feels funny coming to the Idle Hour on my night off."

108

"Nothing is funny tonight," John said. "Nothing at all. Our manager just died before our eyes."

* * *

John wished that he could order Tupelo Dew. If he was going to drink hard, he might as well drink the way Dad did.

"Drink my stuff," Billy Dunn said. "White Turkey. Hundred proof. You got no troubles when the Turkey flies."

"I'd like a Tom Collins, Kathy," Becky told the waitress.

"When the Turkey flies, Harry Schulte's still alive," Billy Dunn said.

Three drinks, and the shock of the ball-field death shook Billy Dunn from his customary manner: whiter than white. "Thirty-three," he said, "and every year a war. I grew up in Long Island, a town called Lawrence, and there were mostly nice houses, except for one block. The people in nice houses called my block Nigger Street. All the cleaning women lived there. That's what my mother was. A cleaning woman."

"Nothing wrong with that," said Johnny Longboat.

"Oh, thank you, Oklahoma liberal."

John gazed. Dunn was a high-shouldered man with a wide, large-eyed, open face.

"I'm a gentle lover," Billy said to Becky Rae. "The ladies 'round New York call me 'Honey Horn.' Do you know why?"

"I haven't the faintest notion, Billy Dunn."

"Because when they go down on me, my horn tastes like honey.'"

Becky Rae blushed. "I wouldn't have the faintest notion about that, either."

"What's in your drink, Bill?" Johnny Longboat said.

"White Turkey, man. You know what they say about a colored guy. He ain't a real man until he's finished a fifth of 100-proof bourbon, and got a white fox to go down on him."

"I certainly wouldn't have the faintest about that," Becky Rae said.

"You don't have to comment on what this hostile bastard says. It isn't him talking, anyway. It's White Turkey bourbon whiskey."

"A long bar filled one wall of the Idle Hour. Below, in a smoky mirror, drinkers saw dark images of themselves. At the rear of the Idle Hour, you found two pinball machines, Bat 'em Out (nineteen runs wins a free game) and Rocket Ball (Score A Million and Win Five Free Games of Rocketing).

It was supposed to be a natural thing for ballplayers to drink, and more than natural, it was expected. The baseball people talked of the great singles hitter, Paul Waner, called Big Poison. It was said Paul Waner kept a flask in the dugout and nipped whiskey between innings.

"How do you hit with a load on, Paul?"

"When I see three baseballs coming up there, I swing at the middle one."

There were stories about Cletus "Boots" Poffenberger, the prince of curfew-breakers, and Flint Rhem, who claimed he could not pitch for St. Louis during an important series in Brooklyn because he was kidnapped by gamblers and forced, at the nose of a gun, to consume great quantities of liquor. Branch Rickey, the professional baseball man who was Rhem's boss, accepted the story, pleading, "You couldn't disprove it by the way Rhem's breath smelled." There was the Babe. Say, didn't he drink New York dry of ale and hit four home runs on the very next day?

All the stories were genial, Johnny thought, and all were wrong. It was no joke-scene living your time half-bombed.

"I got a proposition for you," Billy Dunn said to Becky Rae.

"The Turkey's taken over, Will," John said.

"You fucking, white-man clown. You ought to be a house-cleaning man out on Long Island and learn what life is about, you cocky Oakie."

John seized Billy Dunn's right arm and said, "Go home."

"Yeah. Maybe I better."

John released him. "Hey, Becky Rae," Dunn said, wavering as he stood. "You know where I'm going, Becky Rae?"

"Home."

"Yeah, home. Except that Pittsfield and Lawrence, Long Island, is the same. In this town they also make me live on Nigger Street."

* * *

The whiskey invaded Johnny invidiously. His head began to hurt, above the right side of his neck, the way Dad's head would hurt, and Becky Rae Carpenter became, quite slowly, Helen Arnett.

"Don't sleep with ballplayers," Johnny said.

"I don't. There've only been four guys. They didn't play."

"No ballplayer would respect you if you slept with any," Johnny said.

"But I respect you, Johnny Longboat, for the way you behave and the way you throw a baseball."

"Like I'm as good as a doctor," Johnny said.

"Better," Becky said. "My doctor was examining me, in a private way, and then he tried to date me."

"With his thumb?"

"No, he was proper. He tried to date me in the consulting room afterwards."

With each drink of bourbon that John took, Becky Rae looked more like Helen Arnett.

"Would you sleep with a mere ballplayer?" Johnny said.

"No, John, but I'll sleep with you. Please, John, don't get too drunk!"

"Helen, I wish . . ."

"Who's Helen?" Becky Rae said.

Helen was there and Becky Rae was here and bourbon whiskey made both appear the same.

"I will not sleep with you unless you marry me," John said.

"I want to marry you, Johnny Longboat," said Becky Rae Carpenter.

Chapter 5
1:05 P.M., October 14

THE SECOND REGIMENT Marine Corps Band, fourteen musicians trying to look bellicose, behind horns, drums, flutes and a xylophone, broke into a portentous clattering overture to "The Star-Spangled Banner." Above Mohawk Stadium, an October wind stirred two dozen flags. The breeze, Johnny noted, blew from the north in toward home plate. It was clear and fifty-eight degrees. A good day to pitch; and the wind was a pitcher's wind.

"Ooooh."

As she sounded her opening note a quarter-tone flat, a blind soul singer named Mary Lou Loomis mispronounced the first word of the National Anthem. Oooh, as in pain, instead of Oh, as in exultation, at Fort McHenry long ago. Where have you gone, Robert Merrill? Johnny thought.

Mary Lou Loomis, he knew, represented one price the Mohawks chose to pay for playing baseball in New York City. The stadium, a stout-walled, concrete fortress of a ballpark, rose amid deserts of decay. The neighborhood around it had disintegrated until it was barely a neighborhood at all. Most of the old red-brick tenements had been abandoned. Welfare families and squatters occupied others. Some of these people were Haitian. Some were Hispanic. Some were American blacks. All were bent by poverty in a city of towers, wealth, and ballparks with stout fortress walls.

They bred grim, desperate children, who in turn bred fear. "We've got to be damn careful our fans are not scared off," growling Gus Vermont announced to his staff six years earlier. "Talk up the neighborhood to the writers. Use urban renewal, phrases like that. I want the city to install brighter street lights. I want more cops."

"Maybe we can work a little with the neighborhood people," said a young publicity assistant named Douglas Hamilton.

"How's that?"

"Let in some kids free on quiet afternoons," Hamilton said. "Then hire musicians. The local people like to sing the National Anthem before big games. Give them rhythm guys like Josalito Caguas and soul singers like Mary Lou Loomis. Make the neighborhood part of the Mohawk family."

"No—to the kids in for free," Vermont said. "Those fucking spooks would steal the goddamn bases. Okay—to any musicians you want. The National Anthem bores everybody anyway."

Patriotism mingled with soul and marimbas played well in the newspapers and on the networks, but it made no difference to the people in the rubble beyond the fortress walls. That point was underscored after the All-Star game in 1978, when a crowd of Latins surrounded Josalito Caguas' dove-gray Rolls. They might have overturned the car, except for resolute work by a battalion of elite policemen. Cocaine, as much as race, was the issue; cocaine and the cash to buy it and the lack of cash to buy it. But by the time everybody realized, that, soul, and Latin Anthem singers were a Mohawk tradition (and the publicity assistant named Douglas Hamilton had enrolled in Fordham Law School).

Mary Lou slid her note downward. Flat, flatter. She held a warbling contralto moan. Briefly, Johnny felt annoyed. They ought to sing the Anthem straight before the seventh game. Then he shrugged and said, "I guess the lady is coming."

"Wrong, man," said Quincy John Coleman, the Mohawks' bull-pen catcher. "When black ladies come, you don't hear no moans. You hear sirens."

"Right now an NBC camera has you in close-up," Johnny said, "and eighty million people are reading lips."

"Hi, mutha," Q.J. said. He laughed in a chesty baritone. "I end up giving them half a word."

The warm-up, roughly ten minutes of throwing to Q.J., was proceeding tolerably well. At forty-one, you never knew how your pitching arm would feel until you used it. The variables became more significant each year. Alcohol. Mood. The rotator cuff. The position of your arm as you slept the night before. How soundly you slept the night before.

Christina.

Age made you uncertain. You felt less sure about your arm, the course of your life, or even where you really stood with the black ballplayers. Mary Lou's version of the Anthem rumbled slowly. She was making an operetta of the line, "by the dawn's early light."

The blacks ripped you and you ripped them, and both sides pretended it was fun.

Why is a nigger on a five-year contract like a busted Winchester rifle? Won't work and can't be fired.

They came back and Harry Truman Abernathy could be slick. How many WASPs does it take to change a light bulb? Two. One to mix martinis and one to call the superintendent.

Yeah? Well how do you stop five blacks from raping a blonde? Throw them a basketball.

Did this go at work in the worlds beyond baseball? John didn't know. He had read Townsend Wade's essay in *Commentator* Magazine which Wade titled "Ethnicity as Love." The point was that bantering, back-and-forth humor most profoundly meant affection. "However harsh, barbed, tasteless the ethnic humor may appear," Wade wrote, "just telling a so-called black joke to a black, a so-called Polish joke to a Pole, and having them come back at your own roots, signifies affection and trust on both sides. It is great progress from the days when such ball-players as Hank Greenberg and Jackie Robinson were assaulted with vile epithets."

"Quite simply the best essay yet on American sports humor," George Plimpton decreed grandly from his WASP heights. But from the south of France, James Baldwin cabled, "Merde."

John's mind was wandering, like Mary Lou's version of the Anthem. The difference was that he had to go out and pitch the seventh game.

* * *

At the first-warm-up throw, Johnny grinned. His arm felt loose. Not like an iron whip. That was what Rob Brownell once called it in *The New York Standard*. Not Magic. That was back home, under the wreck of the windmill in Oklahoma. But the arm, weathered and worn by a quarter-century of baseball, began loose and stayed loose. Then John threw a spinner to Quincy John Coleman.

"Aagh."

"You grunting with the strain, or are you hurting?"

"Both," Johnny said, "but mostly disgust." An old pitcher was an ambulatory orthopedic report. Pain here. Pressure there. Signs and symptoms. More than the worn and weathered arm, that was what spawned disgust. Here he was, young by most standards, well-conditioned, strong and at the same time he was a creaking baseball dinosaur. He saw suddenly the truly old people who lived at Golden Billow Shores, a trailer park west of the Mohawks' training base near Melbourne, Florida. Plump and stately, the lady wore khaki Bermuda shorts and rode a giant tricycle to the medical center where she would have tests performed on her circulation and blood pressure. He was frail, since his last coronary. No tricycle riding for him, the doctors said. He sat outside the laundromat with nothing to do on earth but wait for the dryer to stop whirling. "Aagh," Johnny said aloud to himself.

He threw more spinners, limbering muscles in his arm and shoulder, along the strain-line of his overhand curve. Come over. Come up top. Reach for the sky. When you follow through, grab a blade of grass. Like under the windmill. The arm itself becomes a windmill.

His shoulder stung at the first spinner, and radiated geriatric pitching pain. He threw another spinner and another. The pain held, neither more nor less. They had stretched the arm, to snap adhesions, and pumped cortisone into the shoulder and fed him Butazolidin Alka three times a day. If technicians found Butazolidin in the urine of a horse that won at Belmont, the horse was disqualified and placed last. The stewards ruled that the animal had been drugged. But it was accepted medical practice to drug pitchers with Butazolidin for two-week periods, before, the specialists said, "changes commence in blood chemistry." And after that? Tylenol and codeine. But no one, not even the specialists, knew just when the drugs would exhaust their usefulness, and the pitching arm would die.

He stepped up the speed on the spinners and the ball made a louder baroom as it hit Q.J. Coleman's glove.

"Good, John. You're throwing good."

"Compared to what?"

"Hey, John, pitch to me, man. Pop the mitt, man. Just hum that pea."

Why the hell was he warming up alone? Suppose the pain got worse? Oh, he was through long-term. There would be no more summery years with twenty-seven victories. He understood that. But suppose a stab of pain finished him right now, a little before one o'clock on October 14? Then how was he going to pitch the seventh game? John didn't know, and if he didn't know, how on earth could Simonius Veitch have any idea? He threw mechanically to Q.J. Coleman, loosening the worn and weathered muscles.

Casey Stengel or Harry (The Whistler) Schulte would have warmed up two pitchers for a game like this. And let the other side wonder which man would start.

Few managers possessed the courage to be sly. Unlike ballplayers who could be judged coldly on performance— in the agate type that told their hits, home runs, earned-run averages, and errors—managers were measured subjectively. Veitch had poise, presence and an accomplished, sometimes witty manner with the New York press. He *seemed* to know what he was doing. Frenchy Boucher of the Mastodons moved with exuberant vulgarity, spouting obscenities and lusty platitudes. "If my mother was a catcher blocking home plate," Boucher would say, "and I'm the runner coming home, I slide spikes high. I spike my own fuckin' mother, but I score the winning run." That played dramatically for the press, even though it was only an exercise in fantasy, headline-grabbing, or both.

Veitch and Boucher projected images for the press. Stern Cy Veitch. Suave Cy Veitch. Boucher the Battler. The Fearsome Frenchman. A few younger sports writers even referred to Boucher as Ol' Mother-Spiker. Stories about the men fed one another until now their images had become grand enough to win them entry into an invisible company union called the major-league managers' association.

Once you entered that club, once your image made you a card-carrying major-league manager, you'd be employed for most of your useful life. You'd work a few years for the Mohawks or the Mastodons, or at Cleveland or Atlanta, and after a while you'd be released. Teams win and lose in cycles, and you'd draw your release when your team touched the bottom of its curve. Smile wanly. Check your bond portfolio. Criticize nobody. Say, "I gave it my best shot." Then, in a week, a month, a year, you'd be hired to take over another team close to the bottom. Now say, "I don't come to lose." Say, "To win, I'd spike my fucking mom." Thus you were reemployed, to general applause.

Major-league baseball is a successful business with a history running back more than a century. The men who own ball clubs respect and romance baseball tradition with its rosters of great names and its decades of profits. "Innovate?" said Commissioner Amory Moresby. "Well, we do innovate in baseball, but only where necessary. We certainly don't want to innovate our great game into a state of innovative bankruptcy."

Safety was the password. Why hire a manager whose experience somewhere else ended with failure? Well, he was an experienced hand. The men in front offices felt safe hiring a manager with major-league experience, rather than a newly forceful man, like John Felske in the minor leagues, or a creative instructor, like Wally Moon, who somehow taught English majors to hit at a tiny university in Siloam Springs, Arkansas. Experiments frighten baseball men. Tradition comforts them. "If the people who run baseball ran the United States," Bill Veeck said, "Nebraska would still be trying to get into the Union."

Safety dominated, drowning invention. When a club went sour under a veteran manager, team executives safely told the press: "We thought we'd do better than this. Our manager, after all, has been around." If Johnny's game today went badly, he knew what Cy Veitch would say by way of eulogy on network television. "I went with my most experienced man. Maybe that was wrong, gentlemen, but I hope you can respect my thinking. After all, I'm an experienced man myself." Safety. Cy Veitch was a double-rubber guy. He managed partly to win and partly to look good in the papers the next day. Managers embraced safety and general managers embraced safety and the Commissioner embraced safety; only the ballplayers truly risked. They risked their bodies and their psyches, winning and losing. And then a young writer would appear, cowlicked, and shiny faced, and ask, "Do you think ballplayers today are overpaid?"

John flicked his glove forward, indicating fastball. He rocked far back, the way he liked to wind up with bases empty, the way he wound up in the Oklahoma winddrift days. As he whipped fastballs straight and hard, the pain in his shoulder receded.

Rock back. Rock back so far that your left toeplate points toward the sky. Stare at the dark pocket in the center of the catcher's glove. Windmill (and don't forget to grab for grass).

After throwing for nine minutes, Johnny turned his back on Quincy John Coleman and rubbed a new baseball. The feel of the cowhide and the intricate red stitches pleased him. The new baseball, sewn by black seamstresses in Haiti, felt like a friend. He wanted to absorb and remember every good feeling that touched him this October day, and he walked to the outfield fence, bounding the left-field bull pen, and climbed a bench and looked toward the pitcher's mound at Mohawk Stadium, 315 feet away.

"Watcha doin'?" Coleman shouted. "You got to throw more."

John would climb that mound at 1:15 and 65,777 people would look on, chattering and breathless, and he would hold a new baseball, an old friend, in his right hand and all things, even time, would be suspended. They would all be watching, the young advertising man proud to have tickets, and Gus Vermont, growling and rooting, and Commissioner Amory Moresby and Christina and Becky Rae, and the cab drivers, risking a day off, and the doctors, temporarily liberated from the sick, and the super-lawyers, like Everett Taft now briefly fans, and head-waiters from the finest restaurants and the children. The children would watch and dream that they might climb the same mound Johnny climbed.

He flushed with pride. Then he stepped lightly from the bullpen bench. "I've warmed up enough," Johnny said.

Q.J. Coleman was thirty-seven, big as a football player, and he could still hit a high fastball five hundred feet. Six weeks after Coleman broke in with the old Milwaukee Braves, every pitcher in the National League knew how hard Q.J. hit the high ones. Everybody had to pitch him low. That finished Coleman as a serious batter. His promise flamed and died in fifty days. He could hit the high ones hard, but he could only hit the high ones. Word of a hitter's weakness flashes from pitching staff to pitching staff with the speed of gossip. "Pitch the big guy, Coleman, below the boilers, and you got him."

After that Q.J. played irregularly across fifteen seasons. He retained a bit of value as a backup catcher. Once in a while, when a pitcher made a mistake and sailed a fastball high, Coleman hit a five-hundred-foot home run. At such times baseball men lusted to teach Q.J. how to hit the low ball. He went from team to team, eight clubs in all, and tried a dozen batting stances. None helped. Fifteen years of listening to chirping coaches and watching better hitters when he caught batting practice and playing once a month and making out and waiting always for the headsman who would hand him an unconditional release. This would be John's last major-league game and it would be Coleman's last major-league game. A career of glory was ending alongside a career of obscurity; yet each man was giving up the same thing.

"We've both throwed enough," Coleman said. "Every time some sucking pitcher throws the ball, I got to throw it back."

"We'll just play catch," Johnny said. "I'll just throw hard enough to stay warm, like the way you keep a diesel running in the cold."

"I ain' got a diesel. Can't afford no Mercedes, man."

"I know that," John said, "but Volkswagen makes a diesel, too."

"Anyways, I buy American only. Detroit is the place where I growed up."

The ball flying easily between them punctuated casual talk.

"Then buy a Caddy diesel," Johnny said, "or an Olds."

"No bread."

"The wife?"

"She's outta the wheel chair. She's on a cane."

"Cerebral accident."

"You talking doctor-English, man. She had a stroke." Coleman fired the ball at Johnny. "Hey, sorry, man. I got upset. Sorry, John. Thirty-four and she has a stroke. You figure it. I can't figure it myself."

"I can't figure it, either, but maybe I can do something about it."

"What's that?"

"Win this ball game. Get you a winner's share. Pay some expenses."

"Yeah, John." Coleman spoke plaintively in his low baritone. "That would be good, John." He walked toward the pitcher. "Johnny, win this mother."

122

It was at this moment that Mary Loomis hit her first uncertain note.

*　*　*

"Ooooh

"Say-huh

"Kin

"You see?"

Mary Lou Loomis used arpeggios for single syllables and single notes for phrases. She pushed her voice from contralto to naked squeals.

"Whut

"So prou-ow-owd-ly . . ."

Honor America is what Joey Frankfurter, the public address announcer had demanded when he asked the crowd to join Mary Lou in singing. Honor America? Mary Lou was honoring Zimbabwe. Where else could these swooping sounds have come from?

The fourteen Marine musicians blared and thumped under the steady white baton of a bantam-rooster master sergeant. Honor America? This was the U.S. military vs. C.O.R.E.

"An-uh-rockets-sa-red-glare. The-huh bombs burstin' in-uh-air . . ."

She reached "gleaming." After "perlis fight," the lady reached "gleaming." Two syllables. She overwhelmed the word with six notes and a swoop. Above the bleachers in left center field, words flashed on an electronic score-board. Then, for "gleaming," the scoreboard showed a beige picture of an American flag, surrounded by elec-tronic simulations of bursting bombs.

They used to sing the song straight. There used to be scoreboards with white numbers on a dark background and every scoreboard was a little different from every other. That helped a traveling ballplayer remember where he was. Now the electronic scoreboards were a plague of sameness, with the same cartoons of bombs and the same disembodied hands clapping to the same electronic rhythm, after home runs in New York, Pittsburgh, and Kansas City. The new ballparks looked the same and the new scoreboards looked the same, so where the hell were you? Ask the traveling secretary.

Singing against the Second Regiment Marine band, Mary Lou was getting to the clutch, the high note that carried the word "free." It might have been an uneven contest, one blind soul singer against a uniformed contingent of Marines. But Mary Lou Loomis had the microphone.

"O'er the lay-yund of thuh-uh free-ee-ee—

"Fur-ee if we'ee

"Kin

"Ovuh

"Come."

Nobody had rehearsed. As Mary Lou oversang of overcoming, the Marines played the accompaniment to "home of the brave." The service band finished and the echo died. Mary Lou still held the microphone. She waited and sang *a cappella*.

An endless bray. "Bray-ay-ay-ay-vuh." At last the trial by cacophony was done. Mary Lou and the Marines strutted off in different directions.

John looked annoyed and Q.J. Coleman must have noticed. "Rhythm is what we got," he said, "not perfect pitch."

John nodded and grinned.

"Oh, fuck," Coleman said. "Just win this one, buddy. Huh?"

"I'm heated fine, Quincy. You've done your job. Thanks for the catch."

Johnny opened the bull-pen gate and jogged slowly across the outfield, toward the other Mohawks, who stood along the first-base line, in the old Mohawk colors of blue and white. The Mastodons stood on the other foul line in uniforms of white and black and gold. They were a relatively new team, a so-called expansion franchise, and they were also a California team. Both considerations worked against restraint. So the Mastodons had to perform in colors that suggested honey bees.

Why dress a ball club in the colors of a bug? The owner of the Mastodons, an Orange County real estate hustler named Jeremiah Maloney, remembered that his high school football team wore yellow and black. Why call the bugs the Mastodons? Maloney had visited the LaBrea tar pits as a child and he believed that Mastodon was a name that symbolized tradition in the Los Angeles basin.

As Johnny jogged, carrying himself very straight, people stood in the grandstands and applauded. They rose and clapped their hands in respect and enthusiasm and farewell. He wanted to stop, but that was wanting time to stop. Actors and politicians drained moments dry of clapping. He was something purer than an actor or a politician. He was a ballplayer. Neither Mary Lou Loomis, with her squeals, nor Jeremiah Maloney, with his bee-colored Mastodons, could detract from that essence. He was a ballplayer. That was an essence that could not be mocked or stained.

He halted at the first base line next to Harry Truman Abernathy. The fans were cheering so loudly, you could barely hear Joe Frankfurter's announcements over the loudspeakers.

John waited. The crowd would not stop. He stepped from the line of blue-and-white Mohawks and lifted his cap. The cheering rose, a wave of adoration.

Johnny turned back to the line of Mohawks. Tears welled in Abernathy's eyes.

"You're crying," Johnny said. "They're cheering me and *you're* crying."

"Goddammit," Abernathy said, "I want to play ball with you for another ten years."

They stood at attention as the announcer commanded in carefully solemn tones:

"Play ball."

✻ ✻ ✻

At forty-one, you cannot afford to waste energy on the pitcher's mound. As the announcers were prattling on television, an old pitcher needs both head and heart. But he also needs physical strength—and muscles have no memory. A tiring muscle in the ninth inning does not remember whether the earlier, wearying exertion came in the game or during warm-up pitches. At forty-one, a pitcher must conserve himself, as surely as he must exert himself. It is not even a good idea to let the mind drift into agitating thoughts. Think of the hitters. Think of hitters striking out. Think of a cold drink of water. Think of the hitters. Don't tax your arm warming up.

John had eight pitches in which to get a sense of the mound at Mohawk Stadium. It was a mound he knew better than his living room in Ridgefield, Connecticut, and he knew what he wanted to do. Throw four curveballs, gradually increasing the sharpness with which they broke. Then throw four fastballs to secure his pitching rhythm.

Without asking, Raunchy Kauff knew what Johnny wanted. Catching the same pitcher across many seasons, a man comes to know the patterns of the pitcher's attack. This is part memory, part repetition, part intuition. No one had ever called Raunchy Kauff's thought processes quick. His collection of mental tricks consisted of one. When playing Hollywood gin rummy, Kauff could keep the score without taking notes. That was the sum of his cerebral achievement. But somehow this stolid, rather simple man had learned to anticipate the subtleties of Johnny Longboat's pitching.

Kauff made a twisting motion with his bare hand, suggesting curve. John nodded. He threw successively a spinner, two easy curveballs, and a hard one. Spider Webb, who would lead off for the Mastodons, shook his brown bat as though it were a rug-beater. Nervous energy. Diffuse discharge. The sight of the fourth warm-up curve may have bothered him.

Then John threw hard. Rock back. The sky. The toe-plate. Windmill down. He wanted Spider Webb to see his fastball. The brown rug-beater bat slowed into measured swings. The Spider, a good fastball hitter, was roused by Johnny's fastballs, which were swift, but not so swift as they had been.

John wanted to bother Webb with curves. He wanted to excite him with the fastballs. Let Webb step in to hit with faint apprehension and a reckless eagerness.

John breathed deeply, filling his lungs with delicious autumn air. He wanted to be conscious of his body. He breathed again and he was ready.

Webb batted left-handed. Kauff squatted in his catcher's crouch and showed three fingers. John wound up and fired, pulling down Harry Schulte's window shade. The ball hung in flight, rotating furiously. Webb whipped his bat and swung through the plane of home plate while the slow-moving baseball still spun ten feet away. Strike one. John had started the seventh game with a slow ball. A change of pace. A change from the warm-up fastballs he had thrown to excite Spider Webb.

Webb stepped back from the batter's box and leaned the brown bat against a hip. He shook his head and rubbed his palms on elbows and knees, wiggling his torso in a spidery dance.

John looked. Kauff showed three fingers again. John threw another change of pace, in toward Webb's knuckles. Webb lunged, but kept his bat cocked. Off balance, he tried to slap the pitch into left field. Instead he rolled a foul ball at the Mastodon dugout.

"That's his hard one," bellowed Frenchy Boucher. "That's the only hard one he has left. Hey, John-boy. How's the wife?"

The words were ambient filth, the faint pollution of a pellucid autumn day. John threw a fast curve, down and outside. Spider Webb blinked. After the two change-ups, he had expected John to waste a pitch.

"Steey-up thruh," called Danny Merullo, the home plate umpire, jerking his right hand high, in vaudeville overstatement. John had begun the seventh game with a three-pitch strikeout.

Duke Marboro liked fastballs over the plate. He rode them in whistling arcs toward distant corners of the ballpark. But he could not hit good fastballs thrown near his fists. Thus, the margin between Marboro's greatest batting strength and greatest weakness was less than a foot. The scouts said, "You get him on the inside hummer, when you smoke it, but don't ever let that hummer get away." John rocked and threw a fastball toward the inside corner and Marboro, swinging furiously, popped a high foul to Bad Czech Dubcek alongside first base. Johnny's forty-one-year-old fastball was precise as a rapier thrust. Everything depended on timing and accuracy. Years before it had been overpowering, the stroke of a broadsword. Which was the better pitch—the rapier or the broadsword? "Hell," Harry Schulte had told him, "it don't matter how you throw. The best pitch in baseball is always the same."

"What's that?" Johnny said.

"A strike."

Whitey Wright, the Mastodon's number-three hitter, had no distinct weakness. He hit high pitches with power. He hit low balls with greater frequency. You could pitch either to his power or to his average. The scouts and Fortran said, "Move the ball on Wright. Don't throw two pitches to the same spot. Vary your pitches and vary your speeds." John breathed deeply. Then he threw three hard curveballs low and outside. Whitey Wright swung a foot over the last one.

John turned and briefly caught the eye of Frenchy Boucher, who was walking in front of the Los Angeles bench. He fixed the manager with a glare. He felt so good, Johnny meant the glare to say that he could defy the book and Fortran, actually pitch into the Mastodons' strengths, and still snap the bats off in their hands. He also meant the glare to say, "Shut up about my wife."

"Good drill," Kenny Osterhout said, trotting past Johnny.

"Keep jerkin' them around like that," Abernathy said, "and you'll give me the day off in the outfield."

"You don't look like an ancient pitcher in pain," Lefty Levin said, his creased, flat-nosed face showing a smile.

"I'm not in pain." John put on his blue-and-white warm-up jacket. "I'm not young, Lefty, but I'm not in pain."

"Who's young?" Lefty said. "The rookies and the night clerks and the ballpark cops are young. Everybody else has gotten old."

"Everybody's gotten old," Sy Veitch announced, "but only a very few have gotten smart."

"Ralph," Johnny said, "is my fastball moving enough to let the big boys swing at it?"

"It's got a nice sinking tail when you throw it low," Kauff said.

"I got it at 85.8 miles an hour on the Teen-o-meter," Levin said.

"That's damn near the precise average for a major-league fastball," Cy Veitch said.

"But there ain't no radar gun can tell you how a ball moves," Kauff said, "or whether it's throwed to the right spot, like John here did to Duke Marboro."

"They'll have that next," Veitch said, "a machine that tells you everything about a pitcher. They'll have that as soon as they get the right transistors invented."

129

"And when they get them," Johnny said, "you'll be obsolete. By 1990 this ball club will be managed by a computer."

John glanced at the Teen-o-meter, a rectangular box, with a digital read-out panel on the top. Warming up, Hummin' Herman Calhoun threw a fastball 96.7 miles an hour.

"We'll just spot *our* fast one," Johnny said.

"Fucking aw-right with me," Kauff said.

"Even Sandy Koufax spotted his fast one," Levin said.

Johnny scowled. "I don't need sympathy, Lefty. Koufax spotted the fast one, sure, but sometimes, he just flang it. I saw him clean the Mets one time, just firing, just gunning the fast one past them. Same way with me ten years ago. I could just fling. Hell. Forget old times. Let's watch the game."

"Hey, John," Raunchy Kauff said. "If they get a computer for a manager, how they gonna know if you break curfew?"

✳ ✳ ✳

Calhoun's pitches crashed into Jedediah Jackson's glove with the sound of old artillery pieces firing. The kid, six-foot-four, sullen, skinny, and strong—the longest whippet John had ever seen—threw explosive fastballs. Baskets Weaver popped one to shortstop and Kenny Osterhout took another for a third strike. When Osterhout, a stylish, graceful rookie, watched a third strike, you knew he had been overpowered. He preferred being called out to offering an awkward, defensive swing.

But Harry Truman Abernathy, small whippet against a larger one, lined a ninety-four-mile-an-hour fastball between outfielders in right center. The ball bounced 275 feet from home plate and skidded toward the wall. Abernathy fled toward first base and Hometown Brown in center field raced toward a spot ten feet from the outfield wall. He had gauged the drive, imagined the carom, and when the baseball ricocheted, he gloved it, spun, and threw so fluidly that all these things were a single, complex motion.

Racing past second base, Abernathy looked to Daryl Coyle, the third-base coach. Coyle spun his right arm in a large circle, shouting, "Come on. Come on."

The shortstop, Whitey Wright, caught Brown's throw, chest high, and turned and relayed the ball toward third. Abernathy slid, throwing his body toward the outfield and hooking the base with his left foot. He was safe, but only because of his deceptive slide.

Tactical mistake, Johnny thought. Two men were out. Daryl Coyle should have stopped Abernathy at second base. It would probably take a base hit to score a run and a single would score Abernathy from second, as surely as from third. Why take a pointless chance? The coach's mistake created an exciting play and Mohawk Stadium resounded to good-hearted, ignorant cheering.

"Come on, Anton," Johnny shouted to Bad Czech Dubcek. The Mohawk first baseman was a powerful man, out of a family of sturdy millhands and big-boned middle-European women. He was quiet and genial; it filled him with joy, he once told Johnny, to think of himself, "Prushka Dubcek, a big dumb nobody from Hammond, Indiana, playing in the major leagues alongside great stars."

"We're all big, dumb nobodies from somewhere," Johnny said, and Dubcek's large, dark eyes burned with sudden pride.

Now Anton looked grim. Harry Truman Abernathy glided about third base. It was Dubcek's job to crack a buzzing, hopping fastball sharply enough to drive him home.

Herman Calhoun's second pitch was high, and Dubcek hit under the ball. But his stout blacksmith forearms powered the pitch far into right field where it carried and carried toward the fence. The wind worked against Dubcek's high drive, but it had a chance to drop into the right-field box seats. Then Duke Marboro sprang so high that his glove was almost ten feet in the air, and stole the ball from the spectators.

"Three fuckin' inches," Lefty Levin said. "The goddamn wind. Shit, we don't score and their kid pitcher gets faster as he goes."

"Why do you Jewish people worry so much?" Johnny said.

"Because of all you Christians," said Lefty Levin.

John grinned and strode cheerfully toward the mound. His arm was alive. His pitches were moving. It was a lovely day to play a ball game.

Rocco Lombardo, the best of all the Los Angeles batters, would lead off the second inning. Rocco was tall, olive-skinned and strong, with a prominent jaw that showed a haze of stubble, even after he shaved with the swiveling, twin-bladed razor he personally endorsed for twenty-five thousand dollars a year.

"Hiya, folks," began the television commercial. "I'm Rocky Lombardo. Some say I'm the toughest power hitter in baseball. I don't know about *that*, but I do know this. In the shaving league, I've got the toughest beard."

[Camera shows Rocky shaving.

[Cut for makeup. Powder Rocky's face for next shot, so that no stubble shows.

[He pulls on fitted shirt in front of clubhouse mirror. We see other ballplayers in background. He strokes chin again, but lightly so as not to dislodge powder and reveal stubble.]

"Ah, that's smooth. The Clatterbuck has tamed my Hall of Fame beard. [Smiles. You can tell Rocky has a date.] "Now, gentlemen and *ladies*, I'm ready to play."

Lombardo's power and swarthy Mediterranean look led sportswriters to beg their muses for nicknames. Rob

Brownell referred to Lombardo as The Muscular Medici from San Jose. With a practical sense of public relations, Lombardo began calling his black thirty-four-ounce bat "The Godfather." Venice and Sicily were different places on different seas, with distinct tradition, history and climate. The Medici were not simply northern Mafia. But what did that matter in a media world where, after shaving with the Clatterbuck twin-bladed, swiveling razor, you had to powder your face to hide your beard?

Leading off the second inning, Lombardo pumped The Godfather up and down behind his shoulders, loosening Sicilian-Venetian-Californian muscles. Stepping in to hit, he winked at Johnny.

"You need a shave," Johnny called. "Again."

Lombardo grinned. John could see Danny Merullo laughing behind his umpire's mask. Was there a more affable man on earth than Rocco Lombardo? John disposed of him with a splendid curveball that Lombardo bounced to Jap O'Hara at third. This was a *helluva* lovely day to play a ball game.

Roosevelt Delano Dale looped a change of pace to right field, where Dwayne Tucker caught the ball in stride, charging toward the foul line. Then Jake Wakefield hit a fastball off the end of his bat, pulling the pitch softly to the left. Abernathy raced in and dove and lay in a tight knot, squirming as though in agony.

Had he made the catch? No one could tell, but by the time Larry Wellington, the third-base umpire, reached Abernathy, the baseball was secure in the webbing of Abernathy's enormous Wilson glove.

Had he made the catch, or worked the ball into his glove while squirming?

"Out," Wellington bellowed.

He had made the catch.

In the dugout, other Mohawks chattered at Abernathy. "Good play. Way to scoop 'em. 'Attaway, Tru."

133

"You caught it?" Johnny said.

"I must have caught it. When I dove my elbow hit my gut and I blacked out for a couple seconds. When I came to, the ball was in the glove."

"A shame," Johnny said.

"Huh?"

"If you were acting, Tru, you were acting so damn well. Maybe I could have my lawyer book you for a Clatterbuck razor commercial."

"I can't act," Abernathy said, "and haven't you noticed? The Clatterbuck Company doesn't hire blacks."

"Well, I'm glad the Mohawks do. Hell of a play, Truman. Thanks."

"But the Mastodons hire blacks also and that kid pitcher they got out there is one very rapid dude." Calhoun overpowered Dwayne Tucker, Jap O'Hara, and Raunchy Kauff and it was time for Johnny to go back to work.

Lovely day or not, he had to maintain concentration. Brown, Jackson, Calhoun. The top of the third inning brought him the bottom of the Mastodons' batting order.

Hometown Brown tapped a curveball back to the mound. Jedediah Jackson struck out, missing a high change of pace. John worked with delight on Hummin' Herman Calhoun. His rival was not only sullen but arrogant. John threw a fastball that rode in toward Calhoun's knuckles, catching the inside corner of the plate. Then he threw a slider at the knees on the outside corner.

"The tall guys," Johnny's father said, "will always have trouble with pitches at the knees. If you don't know the hitter, and he's a tall guy, pitch him low."

It was sometimes true—of course, the other times could kill you—but what could Dad have known except a blur of failed athletes, living poor and playing baseball, intense and maladroit, in the winddrift Oklahoma country.

John threw a low curve and Herman Calhoun struck out awkwardly. Kauff flipped the ball to Calhoun, who promptly dropped it. For an instant Calhoun's arrogance had won its due. Behind John the electronic scoreboard hands clapped. About him fans cheered. To his right Frenchy Boucher stood shouting, "Next inning your fucking arm comes up with the baseball. After that you ain't even gonna be able to choke your chicken."

It would be nice, John thought, to shove a fist into Boucher's prominent teeth, on another day, perhaps Christmas. But, hell, Boucher was working. If he could break John's concentration, then he was working effectively.

"Hey, Frenchy," shouted Jap O'Hara, "you come a long way for a sewer rat."

"You better watch it, ya bush-league bastard," Boucher said, "or else when the Mohawks get rid of you, I ain't gonna take you, and then you're gonna have to work for a living, busher."

"I wouldn't ever play for him, John," O'Hara said in the dugout. "I'd go to work in my father's gas station first."

"Now don't go crazy," Johnny said. "Gas station attendants have to get up at seven o'clock."

O'Hara's complexion always seemed jaundiced. Now he looked both jaundiced and hurt. "Forget him," Johnny said. "You're a big-league third baseman, Jap, and what's Boucher? Just a garbage mouth. High voltage, but just a garbage mouth."

"Damn right," O'Hara said. "I'd like to fucking punch that garbage fucking mouth."

There was no score. John had pitched three innings. Nine outs. One third of twenty-seven. No hits. No pain. Johnny didn't want to pitch just six more innings. He wanted to pitch on and on, for as long as he could imagine.

He had better seal himself against his own romanticism,

the way he sealed himself from Boucher's taunts. Garbage mouth. That was a decent phrase. Garbage fucking mouth, Jap O'Hara said. That was a baseball phrase. Double garbage. Johnny grinned. It was a lovely day, despite the fucking garbage it was a lovely fucking day.

Next inning would be Webb, Marboro and Wright.

Chapter 6
Moresby Point, New York, 1966

SHE WORE a sleeveless dress of cornflower blue, open at
the collar, like a shirt. A pearl necklace stirred below her
throat. She was driving a white, gullwing Mercedes—a
curiously beautiful and remorselessly impractical automobile—driving too swiftly on the narrow blacktop
carved into the western slope of Tuscarawra Mountain.
Even as she drove, the cornflower blue skirt covered her
knees. (She would express disdain for miniskirts as "obvious, sleazily obvious.") Johnny studied, of all things,
her naked arms. They were slim and tanned and downed
with white-blonde hair.

They passed a sign that shouted: "Radar Patrolled;
Speed 35." She pressed the squat, exotic car toward 60
miles an hour.

"Hey, pardon me," said Johnny Longboat.

"Ummm." She was watching the road, but had an inward look.

"I can't pitch for the Mohawks tonight if I get killed
this afternoon."

"Ummm." Christina Moresby allowed herself to smile.
The car rose and fell in its severe suspension, and from

time to time, you could feel the Mercedes bottom. It was, Johnny thought, one of those machines that handled as if it would not skid, much less spin out, until it did. After that, despite the gullwing doors and the heavy, sculptured grill, you might as well be spinning in a Corvair.

"Hey, pardon me again," he said, "but I'm riding wing this trip, and the Hudson River is six hundred feet straight down."

Christina Moresby continued smiling. Her face was too thin for perfection, but not for elegance. She was high-cheekboned, with Scandinavian blue eyes, a straight, thin nose, and cheeks that made soft hollows within the cheekbones. Her mouth was wide and sensuous and that was all the more suggestive within an ascetic face. Christina whipped the Mercedes into a turn that arced behind five bluestone boulders, guardians that could themselves be as lethal as a catapulting fall into the river. John heard Michelin radials squeal. "The idea," Christina said, "is to come all the way down Tuscarawra Mountain without once touching the brake. I have never actually been able to do that."

"My idea," Johnny said, "is to live to beat Philadelphia tonight. Listen, I was in a bad car crash once."

Christina shook her head, as though impatient, as though she didn't care to hear about auto accidents that had happened to somebody else. Blonde hair rustled near her neck. The speedometer read sixty-five. John looked down the Hudson Valley, toward Bear Mountain Bridge and yellow city haze beyond. "All right," he said. "Slow up. You're not going to make it without touching the brake pedal this time, either."

"Are you frightened?" Christina said. "Are you feeling chicken?"

"I'm not frightened," Johnny said, "but I'm not suicidal, either."

"You are a little chicken. Oh, there's a new nickname I

can give Rob Brownell to use in the *Standard.* Chicky Longboat. The great young pitcher Chicky Longboat."

John heard a hot wind rasp by the windows of the gullwing. They were approaching a forty-five-degree right turn.

"Slow fucking up," he said.

Christina laughed.

More boulders stood sentry at the roadside. These were triangular. The white car with the implausible vertical doors might flatten against the triangular rocks and then break through; John imagined a long, end-over-end fall into the river, then gullwing doors bent permanently shut. He remembered his father's slurred assurance before Dad wrecked the Dodge Job-Rated pickup. "One thing I can do kid, any time of day or night, drunk, kid, or dry, is handle a moving vehicle. I mean a car."

John placed his left hand in a fold of the cornflower blue dress, directly above Christina Moresby's right knee.

"Aagh," she cried in eagerness or pleasure or alarm. She gave a rapid, blue-eyed glance.

His large hand surrounded the pretty woman's leg, and he squeezed hard. Her cry died in surprise. Johnny lifted her right leg, so that she could not reach the accelerator, and placed his own bulky left foot on the brake pedal. The sports car shuddered. He eased the pressure. Still holding her right leg as tightly as you hold a lifeline, he pumped the brake until the gullwing—"the vehicle" his father would have said—slowed smoothly. Johnny threw his right hand to the steering wheel and guided the Mercedes onto a narrow shoulder, next to the triangular boulders that screened the mighty Hudson River gorge. When the car stopped, Johnny released the wheel and Christina Moresby's right leg.

"You've driven gullwings before," she said.

He shrugged.

"Perhaps at Lime Rock."

"Perhaps I've driven on a fucking Okie farm. Perhaps a Dodge, fucking pick-em-up truck, with the left front door held closed by fucking rope."

Her inward smile returned, although a flush simmered through her tan. "You speak two languages." Christina said. "You're a bilingual ballplayer. You speak English and then you speak another language."

"What's that?"

"Baseball."

"Fucking baseball?"

"If you wish."

"You say it," Johnny demanded.

"Fucking baseball," Christina said.

Childlike, Johnny thought, I've gotten this elegant lady to say fuck. He felt a rising electric buzz of alarm. There was a delay in his nervous circuits that helped him pitch but could make living perilous. He did not always react with immediate emotion to every emotional circumstance. Sometimes he found himself in situations that should prompt fear or joy, but his reaction at first was like an electronic printout. *You should feel fear. You should feel joy.* He recognized the emotion that he should experience, but he did not actually feel it for minutes, hours, even days. Then, when the emotion did strike, sometimes it struck most fiercely.

Seated in the parked Mercedes, above the Hudson gorge, he began perspiring. She could have killed him; she could have killed them both. He'd known an outfielder from Provo, Utah, Eddie Paulson, who died playing no-braking-on-the-hill, shattering his car and himself at the foot of the Wasatch Mountains. John scowled in anxiety, and this first delayed alarm—his slow-fused fear—set off another. What was he doing on a mountain road at three o'clock in the afternoon, when Becky Rae was back in Riverdale Towers with the baby?

A ballplayer traveled too much. You missed birthdays

and anniversaries and the Fourth of July picnic because you had to pitch a ball game two thousand miles from home. Now, when the Mohawks were not traveling for two weeks, he ought to be home constantly, making up for the long absences. Oh, the cool, blonde Mercedes-driving lady in the pale-blue dress had talked of certain paintings he should see. "There's more to art than baseball cards and Norman Rockwell." She had asked him with only a suggestion of eagerness to visit her family's art collection, and he had accepted in a calculating way. He would consider the paintings, but not so intensely as he considered Christina Moresby. Johnny continued to scowl. He knew what he was doing—what they were doing—and so did she. This could hardly have been the first time she said fuck.

"That was deft," Christina said. "Your hand is a vise."

"Sportswriter talk."

"What do you mean?"

"The sportswriters who can't write very well, which is a lot of them, say my hands are like vises or like hams, which are clichés."

She smiled and tossed her head and smoothed her hair with a tanned, slender hand. "It's remarkable," she said, "maybe even odd, how you switch from speaking baseball . . ."

"Fucking baseball."

"Fucking baseball, then. How you switch from speaking that to speaking decent English."

"It isn't odd at all," Johnny said. "I work in rough company. The team is pressured and competitive and scared and all male, maybe like an Army platoon in Vietnam. Oh, we have Christ-ers who play that they're at Sunday school six days a week. They thank Jesus whenever they get a big hit. But mostly it's a good rough scene, so in the clubhouse I talk rough like everyone else."

"Why?"

141

"Because it's easier. It's easier not to seem off horse or aloof. I use rough fucking language, protective coloring, in rough company and when I get into company that's not so rough, there's a spillover."

"How do you know I'm not so rough?" Christina said.

"I don't. That makes you interesting." They paused. She looked toward the river. "You wouldn't know," Johnny said, "from the way I am in the Mohawk clubhouse, that I'd ever read a book."

"And you have read a book? Not a sports book?"

If she was mocking him, he declined to notice. "Since I was sixteen years old, I've been reading." He remembered sitting in a house trailer turning pages, escaping from the house trailer through the pages he turned. "I've read old-fashioned poetry, the kind that rhymes, and farm equipment manuals and novels and particularly histories. *The Conquest of Mexico and Peru. Jefferson the Virginian.* The only good education you can get in the Oklahoma winddrift country is the education that you give yourself. Out there, even the doctors say 'seed' for 'saw.'"

If she was mocking him, he thought, she had no right. "Yes, I've read a fucking-not-sports book, and whenever I hit a new word, I write it in the back and when I finish a day's reading, I look it up. Sang froid, or culch, or caco-demonomania, which is the fear of being possessed by evil spirits."

He had meant to impress her. She looked amused. The lean face with the suggestive mouth glowed gloriously. "My, and to think I'd expected to be showing the paintings to a rather simple man of the earth."

"I want to learn about paintings the way I've learned about books," Johnny said. He shook his head. "Man of the earth? I've pulled some cotton, if that's what you mean. If my arm goes, I might have to pull cotton again."

"You never would. You're famous now. No matter what, you can always use that fame. Unless, of course,

142

you'd want to farm cotton." She surveyed him from head to waist. "Would you want to farm cotton again?"

John looked past her toward a wind-beaten white pine springing from a fragile rooting out of sight. "You know enough about me," he said. "You talk."

"I don't know anything, really, about what it was like to grow up in western Oklahoma."

"We made love in the back of pick-em-up trucks, except the ones who found oil in their backyards. They made love in the backs of Bentleys." He opened a gullwing door. "You talk now," he said. "I'll drive."

* * *

She was born Christina Knox-Albright to a tall, sedately beautiful English Catholic mother, and an affluent Episcopal father, who traced his lineage to General Henry Knox, a passenger in the boat that carried George Washington across the Delaware River on December 24, 1777. "Probably General Knox was drinking that Christmas Eve," Christina said, "and telling Washington he had to drink to keep warm."

"It's a leveler," John said, swinging the Mercedes onto the highway.

"What is?"

"Drink. There's no good families and there's no bad families; there's no rich families and there's no poor families when there's hard drink. All families with a drunk are just the same."

When Christina was seven, her mother left Sanford Knox-Albright (and the One True Church) after Sanford fractured, but did not displace, her left cheekbone. They had been discussing the décolletage of her most recent Lily Pulitzer gown, which Sanford regarded as extreme, and his next martini, which Helen Knox-Albright thought had best be postponed until tomorrow's lunch. Sanford stirred his drink and sipped and spoke about Helen Knox-Albright's bosom. It was firmer, he said, and worthy of deep cleavage before she breast-fed Christina. No longer. "You're just showing your sag."

"You are a bastard," Helen said, in a composed, hateful tone. The tone was what upset Sanford, he said later. Finishing the martini in the company of policemen summoned by the cook, he explained that after his wife cursed him calmly he struck her because he wanted to watch her cry. He hammered his wish to truth. First, Helen screamed in pain and shock; then she wept in humiliation. On page four of the *Daily News* two days later, Christina read a story about herself. The headline announced: Moppet Sees Society Mom Slugged.

After the divorce, Helen Knox-Albright married a lean, aloof tax lawyer called Henry Wales, who disliked androgynous names like Leslie or Chris. So as her mother became Helen Wales, Christina Knox-Albright became Tina. "We're doing *everything* together," Mother said, before the wedding. Tina, formerly Chrissie, made a radiant flower girl, until she began to weep.

John was holding the white Mercedes at fifty, when they passed a blue-and-yellow state police car, which had caught a plum-colored Citröen station wagon. "I'm glad you made me stop," Christina said. "Otherwise it would have been worse. I would have been stopped by Trooper Renfroe."

"Which name do you like better," Johnny said. "Chrissie or Tina?"

"I've outgrown Chrissie."

"Chris, then?"

"If it pleases you, I'll be Chris for this afternoon."

Her mother's second marriage was successful, Chris said, and they moved from nine rooms on Park Avenue to fourteen rooms on Fifth. "But Henry had children from another marriage and my mother wanted so obsessively to succeed the second time, that there wasn't any place for me. You drag debris into second marriages. The Romans had a word. Impedimenta. I was part of the impedimenta Mother carried."

Christina remembered servants called Helga and Colleen, and boarding schools at which she learned English riding and American literature, and studied ballet, flute, and landscape painting. "Enough of everything to be a fine companion, and not enough of anything for a career."

"Did you want a career?" John said. The highway curved away from the Hudson, through clumps of juniper and canoe birch.

"It was a matter of caste," Chris said. "In our caste, a woman's career was marrying well, which I've done, after the fashion, and serving as a brood mare which doesn't interest me."

"I mean, didn't you *want* to go to work?"

"Work, in our caste, is what one does on a volunteer basis for New York Hospital. Or else one works by selling tickets to the Antiques Show in the Seventh Regiment Armory."

"Work is play."

"Exactly. You grasped that quickly. Of course, being paid to pitch must help you understand."

The coupe felt sure and heavy on the twisting road. He was beginning to enjoy her car and he was beginning to enjoy her manner. She spoke with undertones of condescension, as though he were an interesting hired hand, a gardener, who knew better than she where to place a forsythia bush, but who still would have to strain his back digging in soil she owned. All right. Her manner introduced competition into their reckless game.

"You think that pitching big-league ball is play?" John set his jaw.

"Isn't it?" Christina tossed her head and touched blonde hair near cornflower blue at her neck.

"Once pitching was play," Johnny said, "and once they called you Chrissie. But in the big leagues everybody is grown up. You have grown men playing against each other for money and almost everyone is pretty good. Fun was playing in the fields with other children. What I do now isn't the same."

"But you enjoy it."

"Sometimes. I'm *proud* to be a major-league ballplayer, but it's damn hard. When the reporters press me, or the manager gets on me, or the travel grinds me down, or when I plain and simple don't pitch well, being a major-league ballplayer is hard as hell. I'd get down, except then I think: What else in the world would I like to be?"

The road sloped back toward the Hudson and Johnny downshifted. The back of his right hand, a clumsy instrument for passion, rubbed Christina's left thigh. "You've got me talking about myself, again," he said. "You talk."

"I've told you everything there is to tell you."

"You left something out."

"What could that be?"

"Your husband?"

Christina giggled and said, "Caught."

"We're both caught," Johnny said.

She nodded, smiling. "Brad is what one calls a sportsman." She leaned back and the long, tan arms made graceful bows.

"What does that mean?" John said. "That he plays squash, or scored some hockey goals for Yale?"

"Princeton," she said. "He won three hockey letters at Baker Rink. But, no, that isn't what I mean. Brad is a gambler. His hobby, and his love, is making bets."

"Making bets, or winning bets?" Johnny said.

"Making bets. He doesn't win that often."

"I read that can be a disease," Johnny said, "as bad as boozing."

"My therapist says that each is an aspect of compulsive, neurotic behavior. The difference is that gambling doesn't corrode the liver."

146

Johnny was trying to catch up with her world all at once. "Now why would you need a therapist?"

"I won't discuss that," Christina said.

"We didn't have therapists in Oklahoma, and we were probably less crazy than people in New York. Or anyway, no more crazy."

"Oh, look," she said impatiently, "people think therapy is where women talk about their sexual secrets, but this isn't that way at all. I'm just getting support in adjusting to my marriage encounter."

"Encounter?" Johnny said. "That's a word I'd use for a date, not for a marriage." When she did not respond, he said, "Where did you meet this guy you married?"

"I met this guy—my husband—through your employer, Gus Vermont." Johnny knew Vermont as a chunky, black-haired, angry-looking man of forty, with an irritating laugh and the manner of a spoiled and willful child. The ballplayers said, "Never cross Mr. Vermont. He blows higher than a geyser."

"I dated Gus three times," she said, "and the third night he took me to Mohawk Stadium, where we sat in his box, glassed in against spring breezes. Gus is an indoor person. His playground would be an office with six telephones and three stock market tickers. Anyway, that night, he was entertaining another guest. My husband."

She had found Vermont driving, restless, and so bright in matters of debentures and tax shelters that he made her feel both frightened and sad. Frightened at the ferocious nature of his intelligence. Sad that it was directed entirely at getting and spending. She had considered Vermont as a marriage partner; she was conditioned to consider all affluent single men as marriage partners. But she felt that the next woman Gus Vermont married would be treated alternately as a virgin goddess, tall on an alabaster pedestal, and as a particularly expensive whore. There would be alimony later, in the scenario she fashioned, but no alimony could be worth all those battering rides from goddess to hooker—and from goddess to victim—and back. She remembered her mother's fractured cheekbone.

Bradford Moresby possessed the look and manner of the men she had been raised to charm. She and Brad, she said, felt a shock of recognition when they met in Vermont's box at Mohawk Stadium. ("Brad's date that night was a beauty, with just a suggestion of tackiness.") Moresby called Chris intermittently in the ensuing months, but never pressed. Then when summer and autumn were gone (along with the somewhat tacky beauty), Brad suddenly conducted an intense courtship that ran through Eleuthera, Moresby Point, and St. Jovite, Quebec. He proposed at a fireside in St. Jovite after a cold, white day of skiing the Laurentians. She was exhilarated by the crackling air, and by Brad's long-legged form on a downhill trail called Timberlake. "I thought I was getting a dignified, decent man," Christina said. "I was as careless about Brad as I was careful about Gus Vermont. Odd, isn't it?"

"No," Johnny said. "It's tough to be careful twice in a row."

She blinked in surprise. "I didn't know about the gambling. There were signals, I suppose, but I missed them all."

"I don't understand serious sports gambling myself," Johnny said. "I don't understand why a stranger would risk important money on the condition of my arm on a particular Friday night."

"Oh, there are books about it. The theories run from a man's relationship with his father to his discomfort with sex."

The road swerved to the left, toward a valley. A green and white sign read: "Moresby: 2 Miles."

"You may not understand gambling, Johnny, but you understand drinking. When Brad loses a big bet, two thousand dollars on the Green Bay Packers, five thousand dollars on the Los Angeles Mastodons, he drinks himself into a stupor."

"Does he get violent?"

"I'm perfectly safe. He gets maudlin and then infantile on the way to his stupor."

"You might have done better with Gus Vermont."

She whispered in a rousing, earthy voice, "I might have done better with you."

John slowed the car at a sign marking the entrance to Holy Redeemer R.C. Church. "Now," he said, "you're being careless *twice* in a row."

"Perhaps."

"Anyway, I'm taken."

"You haven't always been taken."

"Oh, yes, I have," Johnny said. "I've always been taken. There was a girl in Oklahoma once and after that came Becky Rae, who's my wife."

"Nobody's taken for life," Chris Moresby said.

"Except I asked Becky to marry me, and she did. And she's had my son, Jerry Lee. So yes I am. I am taken for life."

Christina tossed her hair and made a loose fist with her left hand and drew her thumb inward across the forefingers. A lovely, tanned hand. A slim, seducing hand. Being taken, John thought, was different from being owned. He remembered Sly Donoghue's definition of cheating. "It's getting laid in the same town where your wife is."

He wanted very much to tell Sly's joke to Chris Moresby. Instead he said, "Say, what kind of a little village is this place Moresby?"

It was a crossroads with a yellow blinker light. On one side, Johnny saw Marino's County Place—Groceries & Gas, and a white salt box with a scrolled sign that read Van Deeren Realty. Across the highway stood Cobb's

Tavern and Paul's Wines & Liquors, which shared a mustard-colored building with the U.S. Postal Service.

"That's all?" Johnny said.

"That's all, except for a few houses and trailers in the woods."

"It's smaller than an Oklahoma town," Johnny said.

"This is a private corner of the world. Go slowly, now. You make a sharp left turn in seven tenths of a mile."

Past Moresby the main highway twisted south, but a narrow blacktop curled upward to the northwest. "There," Christina said. "At that buff sign that says private road." John eased the Mercedes onto the blacktop and three hundred yards farther slowed for a high cyclone fence, topped by a v-shaped frame that supported parallel strands of barbed wire. Christina touched a black button on the dashboard, and a panel of fence slid open. "Go through," she said. "It closes automatically."

John drove slowly past a stone gatehouse, a Williamsburg-blue gardener's cottage, and proceeded under a long corridor of ancient maples. The branches arched and leaf touched leaf, creating a shadowed glade. He drove through leaf-strewn sunlight, cleared a rise, and had to suppress a gasp. Before them rolled a lawn that was larger (and greener) than the playing surface at Mohawk Stadium. Beyond that rose a white stone manor house. John stopped the Mercedes and counted eleven chimneys.

"So," he said, at length, "this is yours."

"No," Chris said. "This is what I married."

John let his right hand fall to her knee. She did not stir. "Then why do you worry if he loses a few hundred dollars betting the ponies?"

She laughed a rueful laugh and shook her head. "I don't suppose my worries are as significant as the worries of the trustees." The estate, with its gatehouse and manor, was called Moresby Point after a granite outcropping that jutted above the Hudson. It was not owned by herself or

150

by her husband, Christina said; rather, it was one portion of the assets of an organization called The Moresby Foundation. She folded her hands in her lap, managing to look prim, and said she would explain certain facts of American economics, if Johnny cared, and if that was not too dismal an activity for such a splendid summer afternoon.

"Economics is dismal," Johnny said, "when it's about people who don't have money."

The river towns, Christina said, spaced far below, towns called Beacon and Peekskill and Poughkeepsie, were populated by people who didn't have money. The towns had prospered once, with heavy industry and railroading, but industry went south for cheaper labor and the railroads, if not yet dead, were stricken. It was hard to make a living in the river towns today, but blacks had moved up from the south with fantasies of better living. Then in the river towns fantasy turned to irony, for the poor whites railed against the new blacks who were poorer still. These beats of a harsh life sounded in the great gorge that the Hudson carved. But the estate called Moresby Point, eight hundred feet above the river, remained as distant from the river towns as Heaven. Depression, inflation, even taxation could not assault inheritors of great New York State fortunes, the Harrimans, the Rockefellers, the Moresbys. They hired extraordinary tax lawyers to shelter all their holdings and, of course, paid the lawyers generous (tax-deductible) fees.

"They're not afraid of ups and downs in the economy," Christina said, "but what frightens these families, or at least frightens the Moresbys, is what they see as an enemy within. A spendthrift son."

"Christ," Johnny said, "one man all by himself can't spend a family fortune like this."

"You're probably right," Christina said, "but the one man I'm married to has certainly tried."

The Moresby fortune had been built through five generations. First came shipping and furs. Then timber and real estate. After that the Moresbys diversified into investment patterns that became, she said, too complicated for laymen to understand. Her father-in-law, Amory Moresby, Sr., trusted his lawyers more than he trusted his children and placed most of his wealth into the Moresby Foundation, which was organized officially "for the betterment of natural science, medicine, other sciences and the useful arts," and which unofficially protected Moresby wealth from what the old man called "America's socialistic inheritance tax." But after the first son, Amory, Jr., followed a specific Moresby tradition and went to Annapolis and then to sea, his father rewarded him with three hundred acres, fronting on Peachblossom Creek, near Easton, Maryland, and a tax-free trust that provided $400,000 a year.

"Admiral Moresby," Johnny said.

"The nuclear admiral," Christina said. "The nuclear admiral is my brother-in-law and if the Republicans find a way to defeat Lyndon Johnson in '68, if Nelson can get nominated and win, Amory says he'll become Secretary of Defense. After that he doesn't say. But everyone knows he wants to run for president."

John was trying to comprehend what Christina called the Moresby wealth. It seemed to be more than one man could earn; from the look of the manor house it had to be more than ten men could earn. It was more than everyone on the Mohawks earned combined. All the salaries of all the big-leaguers put together, a year's pay for Koufax and Mays, Killibrew and Gibson and Yastrzemski, that might come close. Or it might not. And the people back in Trail o' Tears, and even Pittsfield, dreamed that you could get rich playing baseball. Rich? As a ballplayer you could end up well-to-do, like Ty Cobb with his Coca-Cola stock.

And you could end up just as easily begging strangers in cheap bars to buy you drinks, like the old Philadelphia sluggers, Al Simmons and Jimmy Foxx.

"Brad calls the main house our castle," Christina said.

The gorgeous lawn, rolled, watered, limed, and nourished for generations, plucked free of knotwood and plantain, made a glistening carpetway in front of the huge house. The building was a rectangle, three stories high, very long, but so carefully proportioned that it appeared less massive than it was. A center pediment suggested Greece; the house at large suggested an English manor. Two wings extended from the portico and on the topmost corners, the architect had designed notched battlements, as medieval battlements were notched for archers.

"It is a castle," Johnny said.

"I call it a sand castle," Christina said. "We don't own it. We merely live in it, more or less like squatters. The Moresby Foundation owns this place." An undertow of anger stirred her voice. "At any time, at the whim of a dour lawyer, the Foundation can evict us. What looks limestone to you, is merely sand to me."

The father, Amory, Sr., did not trust his second son Brad, who liked to gamble. Alive, he sustained Brad on a generous dole. Then, when the old man died in 1962, he left a ninety-seven-page will, making reasonably certain Brad would be looked after and making absolutely certain that Brad could not touch Moresby capital. The dole, $100,000 from municipal bonds each year, would continue, and Brad, his wife, and any issue could reside at Moresby Point so long as Brad conducted himself "in accordance with accepted familial, clerical, and public standards of responsible behavior." At semiannual intervals Brad was required to review his finances with a senior partner of a law firm called Klinch and Wales.

"We're children on an allowance," Christina said. "All

that's different, really, is the scale. And the cash-review meetings with Edgar Klinch, are demeaning." She lifted thin blonde eyebrows. "Amory Moresby, Sr., was a cold-faced old man, with chalky lips. I met him at one of my stepfather's parties when I was seventeen. He spent ten minutes with an arm around my waist and everyone thought, how charming. How avuncular. We were standing with our backs to a Moroccan marble fireplace and I was the only one who felt Amory Moresby's ancient hand probing toward my bottom." She blew a puff of air. "The hand felt like a scalpel, but what could I do? Shout, 'Mommy, Stepfather! The third richest man in the state of New York is goosing me?' "

John grinned. "Do I get to see the inside of your sand castle?"

She led him through the Grecian portico into a white marble rotunda and opened darkwood doors that rose beneath an ivory-colored archway. Nothing in John's life had prepared him for the parlor of Christina Moresby's sand castle. The room was a long rectangle under a vaulting ceiling of black oak. The walls had been painted soft violet, and Persian carpets of reds and blues picked up violet traces. Gilt-framed paintings marched across the two long walls. John saw an English woman of high breeding; a beckoning valley under a twilight glow; a Paris street of small, exquisite houses; and a red-coated horseman, reining a white stallion, which frothed with foam. Light fell from globes set in the black oak ceiling and light filtered through mullioned windows at a far end of the parlor. The windows were set within an arch that picked up the arch of the ceiling, and every pane but one was Tiffany glass. The clear pane, precisely centered, framed mountains rolling far beyond the Hudson.

John let the room, the paintings, the window, and the woman called Christina Moresby fill his senses. She was smiling and considering him and he felt her look. "Why are you staring at me?" Johnny said.

"To see if you're intimidated," she said. "Besides, I like to look."

"I'm more curious than intimidated," he said.

"Look all you want."

For a moment he thought giddily that the house and room were his and he heard himself telling Dr. Norris Oakwater and Helen Arnett, "Welcome to my home."

"The paintings," Christina said, "are also the property of the Moresby Foundation. We retain viewing rights."

He noticed her graceful, long-legged, cornflower-blue walk as she spoke to him of Gainsborough and Reynolds. "I don't know what's prettier," he said, "the etchings that you have here, Chris, or you."

"Oh, that's an easy thing to say, Johnny, and not very good."

She was being condescending again. Well, he was *not* a gardener, working land she owned. "That wasn't easy for me to say; I suspect it's not easy for *you* to take a compliment." He stood beneath a red-coated English horseman, and wished that he had dressed more elegantly. He wore fitted blue-gray slacks and a rust-colored knit shirt with a yellow pelican flying above his heart. "Just take it in," Johnny said, "when I try to tell you that you're beautiful."

Christina stopped beneath the high-bred English woman, creamy-skinned and dead two hundred years. "Not beautiful," Christina said. "My eyes are set a bit too far apart."

Beautiful women always knew their flaws: a curve of jaw, a flair of nostril that deviated from someone's paradigm of beauty. Beautiful women studied their faces and their bodies until they knew them better than the most discerning lover. That must make them self-absorbed, Johnny thought. Like athletes.

155

"Oh, I'm pretty, I suppose," Christina said, "but not quite as elegant as Lady Anna Southwyck, who's above me. I'll get us drinks."

"I can't drink," Johnny said. "I have to pitch later."

"Then let's just sit." She indicated a sculpted couch, covered in pale yellow linen, which looked too delicate for Johnny's weight. He sat, half expecting the legs to buckle. "Does this room intimidate *you*?" John said suddenly. (The sofa legs held firm.)

"Not the room, but everything the room suggests. The Moresby Foundation. The control strangers can exert now over my life."

"When something scares you," Johnny said, "charge it."

She shook her head, impatient, disappointed. "That's even easier than calling me pretty, and it's as silly as baseball talk, if you think about it."

He would not respond.

"In baseball," Christina said, "you charge at the team that's hard to beat. All of the ballplayers say that. But none of the ballplayers, not even you, charges at the real enemies. The Mohawk organization. The antiquated contract laws. Gus Vermont's Mussolini manner. The baseball bylaws that insist you aren't allowed to have an agent negotiate your salary."

"I'll charge that stuff later on," Johnny said, "when I've built up the right arsenal."

"Will you? I don't mean to sound cynical, but you're a star now. I've read in the *Standard* that you've won twelve straight baseball games."

"I'm a young star," Johnny said. "You know more baseball than you've been letting on, isn't that right?"

Now it was she who would not respond.

"To make a system better for myself," Johnny said, "and everybody else, I have to be first what they call a superstar."

156

"But when you're a superstar," Chris said, "you'll have so much invested in the system that made you super, that you won't be able to charge it. You won't even want to."

"You may not mean to sound cynical, but you do sound cynical."

She moved to his side on the yellow couch and placed both hands on his shoulders. "When you win so many baseball games, you get used to winning. You look ahead with confidence and optimism. When my husband loses bets, the opposite happens."

"Meaning?"

"I mean he literally shrivels."

She looked vulnerable. The husband was far away. John leaned to kiss her.

"The paintings first," Christina said, "and damn you and your pitching schedule. I want a martini."

"Sober," Johnny said, "we'll get each other's names right."

* * *

They had met three nights before at a party Gus Vermont organized in the Wahoo Room at Mohawk Stadium. It was a major-league tradition that management and ballplayers did not mix socially, except for unusual occasions such as the celebration of a pennant. The risks of cross-socializing were apparent. Substitutes wanted to play regularly. Regulars wanted to be paid as much as stars. At a party, after several drinks, a ballplayer might shout at management people, or even throw a punch at the chairman of the board. The stars themselves could burst with suppressed anger, or simply drink themselves sloppy. As one traditionalist who owned a ball club put it: "The players have their pubs and I have mine. There's safety in that territoriality. It's best for all of us, until they bring back prohibition."

Gus Vermont developed a different view. He was running a team in New York City, a celebrity town, a media town, a money town. Why not, he reasoned, throw careful parties and display celebrity ballplayers to the other celebrities of New York? The celebrities could gape at one another, chatter, mingle, and move on. That way the Mohawks would be talked about beyond the sports pages and Toots Shor's. The basic Mohawk audience might be enlarged. Although traditionalists denied it, baseball was becoming more and more a subdivision of show business. Bring out the stars, Vermont reasoned. Don't keep them curtained. (But make sure the bartenders in the Wahoo Room poured for the athletes with a temperate hand.)

The Mohawks announced this party with one hundred engraved invitations:

The New York Mohawks
and
Augustus Vermont III
Request the pleasure of your company
at the Wahoo Room
To Meet the Mohawks' Newest Luminary
(and his luminous lady)
Mr. and Mrs. Johnny Longboat

"Should I wear a long dress?" Becky Rae asked, in the uptown apartment they had rented.

"Do you want to sit through a ball game in a long dress?" Johnny said.

"I'll wear my sensible wheat-colored suit," Becky said. "Can I take the baby? I'd like to show him off."

"It's not that kind of party," Johnny said.

"Who's going to be there?"

"All I know for sure is you and me."

Nelson Rockefeller declined, but Senator Jacob Javits would attend. So would Sammy Davis, Jr., who was starring in a musical version of Clifford Odets' *Golden Boy,* and Patricia Lawford, fresh from what the newspapers called "the first Kennedy divorce" and Arthur Goldberg, weary after a day of defending the Vietnam War, at Lyndon Johnson's command, to batteries of visiting delegates at the United Nations. Limousines, hired by Gus Vermont, bore the celebrities to Mohawk Stadium and a good ball game. New York defeated Chicago, 5–4.

The Wahoo Room was a brightly lighted windowless rectangle, served by a private elevator. You stepped off the elevator and walked through a canvas opening that was supposed to suggest a wigwam. Inside, the Indian motif disappeared. There were two darkwood bars, a collection of tables, covered with red and white checked cloths, and walls busy with portraits of the eleven former Mohawks who had been elected to the Hall of Fame.

Marvin Maas, the publicity man, led Johnny and Becky toward the imitation wigwam and Gus Vermont, who was standing inside, smiling and nodding. "Well," the owner said, "I want to introduce you both. Everyone's here to meet the two of you."

Becky gaped, although she didn't mean to gape. "Isn't that the Mayor?" she said in the voice of a small girl.

"That's John," Vermont said. "Mary couldn't make it."

John Lindsay smiled a golden smile and Becky blinked.

"So this is the new star pitcher," the Mayor said. "I hear you're doing very well."

"How are you doing with the city?" Johnny said.

"Our worst problem could be solved with one invention."

"What's that?"

"A shitless dog," said Mayor Lindsay. He moved on, behind his golden smile.

Still gaping, Becky blushed.

"Don't be embarrassed," Vermont said. "That's his standard line when he doesn't want to talk politics. Get a drink, Johnny. I want to chat with Mrs. Longboat."

Vermont had noticed Becky's awe. This seemed a good time to read her the commandments. Vermont led Becky to a corner table, where a waiter brought her Canadian whiskey and ginger ale. "I want you to take in this party for a minute. See who has come. Recognize your family's new fame. That's one of the pleasures of being a baseball wife."

"Thank you for asking me."

"But there's a downside," Vermont said. "There are days and days alone, when your man is traveling."

"I know."

"That's baseball," Vermont said. "It's the nature of the business. Now the Mohawks are going to be fair to Johnny and generous, but you have an obligation also. Be cheerful. Keep yourself happy, even when he's away. A winning pitcher needs a happy wife to come home to. I can take care of the paychecks. You have to take care of the home. I've got a feeling, Mrs. Longboat, that you'll be terrific."

Johnny moved about with Marvin Maas. The actors and politicians seemed impressed to meet him, or at least as impressed as he was to meet them. Johnny kept his footing. The guests had not come to meet him as a man, but as a pitcher. Lose his fastball and assemblages like this would vanish.

At the corner table Vermont complimented Becky Rae on her stability. She did not know what to say. She repeated, "Thank you." She thought of her mother in the kitchen at Pittsfield. She herself would grow into parties like this, but she needed time.

At that moment Christina Moresby, a cool, blonde party guest, asked Johnny if this all seemed as strange to him as it did to her.

* * *

Her invitation had been a smiling suggestion that Johnny examine the Moresby Collection. Not quite certain of himself with a lady who was beautiful, stately, smiling, seductive, and married, Johnny said that where he grew up the only paintings anyone saw were magazine covers. Candor was a sensible approach when you were not confident in new country. Candor on your part often disarmed the other side. At least it had in this case.

"Here," Christina said, leading Johnny into a long, ivory dining room, "is where the best impressionists are hung."

Johnny stared at a Monet cathedral, a blend of purples and whites. Although no cathedral in the world showed the colors Monet had used, the painting was astonishingly true. Johnny continued to gaze. The painting was true because the canvas was, in a sense, a world all by itself. The artist had created his own world. "Where do you find these things?" he said.

"The Foundation retains an art consultant," Christina said. "A driving, black-haired witch of an art historian who calls herself Tami Goldsmith. These *things*, as you call them, are worth millions of dollars. Tami and the lawyer Edgar Klinch and a Wall Street broker, whose name I forget, decide what to buy and when to buy and when and if to sell."

"At least you get to hang them," Johnny said.

"Tami Goldsmith suggests where to hang them."

"Why listen?"

"Because Tami Goldsmith speaks with the voice of the Moresby Foundation."

Christina made a little angry shrug, and directed John toward the Rose Room, reserved for Vermeer, and then to the Music Room, where he saw a delicate white spinet and pale blue walls aflame with the colors of Gauguin.

Even the hallways glowed with art. As Christina led him about, John felt a sense of museum vastness. The proportions of every room and every hallway were correct. The colors made radiant patterns. But the whole effect was too large, and too demanding for a home. "It could be hard feeling comfortable here," he said.

161

"Could be?" Christina said. "It *is* hard." She guided him from the Juan Gris hallway into a tidy darkwood den, unadorned except for arrays of hunting horns and steins. "I am going to have a martini," she said.

"All right," John said. "It's pretty early. I'll take a beer."

He moved behind the bar and found a gin called Lamp-lighter and a sleek silver pitcher and a machine that made chunks of ice in the shape of the letter *M*, for Moresby.

"That is something," he said. "Monogrammed ice."

"I call that something gauche," she said. "Why don't you have a martini, too?"

"Damnedest thing," Johnny said. "When I met my wife, she was serving drinks to me and here I am serving drinks to you."

Christina sat on a leather couch, slim, graceful, a pastel portrait. Long tanned arms. Cornflower blue. Blonde hair. "I'll take a martini, but only one."

She smiled. "Have you ever taken one of anything in your life?"

Within half an hour, they were upstairs. The bed was a small fourposter, under a flowered white canopy. He sat lightly on the mattress and said, "Why?"

"I'm so damn curious," Christina said.

"Would you mind," Johnny said, "just getting undressed and walking around?"

"It's my turn now to ask why," Christina said.

"I guess we have something in common," Johnny said. "We *both* like to look."

When she was naked, she tossed her head and walked before him.

"You're so relaxed about this," he said, "because you know your body is beautiful."

"But it isn't," she said. "My breasts are a bit narrow for my rib cage." She was standing sideways to him. John noticed the white of her breasts and felt the old boyhood excitement at seeing beyond where a woman's suntan ends.

"And my thighs are a bit too sturdy. There must be Swedish or Scottish peasant stock buried in the genes." Her thighs were firm and the light brown pubic tuft worked like a magnet on his gaze. He undressed quickly.

Their rhythms were alike. He kissed her deeply and just before he was about to break for air, she drew back. "At our first kiss," she said, with a slow and knowing smile, "we're nude."

"Someone should paint you nude."

"Sssh." They kissed again and she guided him back to the fourposter.

* * *

Their rhythms were alike and they had been alike. She lay against his shoulder. "Ah," Chris said, "that fateful, fatal Lamplighter martini."

"Are you laughing at me?"

"No. Oh, no, dear. I'm feeling happy for us both."

"I'm not," Johnny said.

"Why not?"

"I have a wife and a baby. You have a husband. That's why not."

"You still have a wife and a baby," Christina said. "And I still have a husband, dammit."

Naked beside him on the fourposter, she seemed extravagantly poised. "You seem to take this easily," he said, "in stride."

"You mean have I been sleeping with many men?"

"Close enough."

"Lately I've been restless, but I won't talk about that any more. Right here, right now. There's only here. There's only now."

"No," Johnny said. "You can't escape from before and afterward."

"You mean emotions?"

"Yes, I mean emotions."

"You're feeling fond?"

"You're easy to be fond of."

"Is fondness new to you?"

"No. Once before. In Oklahoma. Her name was Helen, and I lost her."

"But what about your wife?"

"I don't want to talk about my wife. That really would be cheating, talking about my wife, with the two of us here in your bed."

"I'll talk about my husband," Christina said. "When Brad loses bets and drinks, he can't perform. I'm twenty-four years old. I have normal drives, and a semi-impotent husband."

"I still don't want to talk about my wife."

She sat up and turned. The white breasts, under the suntan line, moved before him. "You're taking everything so seriously," Christina said, "but, Johnny, it's only fucking."

"It isn't only fucking. There's no such thing as *only* fucking."

"You mean," Chris said, smiling again, "that you're not any easy lay."

"I'm not one of those damn road-bum ballplayers," Johnny said. "We've got guys on the Mohawks who would turn your gut. The kids come 'round, little girls of seventeen, and the road bums fuck them. Older ones, women with hairy arms and dumpy and maybe forty-five, the road bums fuck them, too. Sometimes there's two or three road bums get in a room and they pass a girl around. One is on top of the girl. The other two are watching and clapping their hands in time to the pumping."

"The women ask for that by coming around to the hotels where the ballplayers stay."

164

"Sometimes the road-bum ballplayers rough up the girls. They rough up seventeen-year-old kids who don't know what they really want."

"But the ballplayers are little kids themselves," Christina said. "Kids in a playpen."

Johnny sat up. "And you," he said, "in this house, Chris. What are you?"

"I'm not a little kid, Johnny. Don't make that mistake. And this house is hardly a playpen."

"What is it then?"

"Try another word," Christina said. "Try prison."

But she was free and beautiful and chose to stay here, Johnny thought. No one made the prison but herself. And he, abruptly fond of the smiling, stately, seductive married woman, wasn't he walking into a prison of his own?

There was more to being a ballplayer than winning ball games, and there was more to being a man than being a ballplayer.

* * *

She dropped him six blocks away from Mohawk Stadium, on Bolivar Boulevard and 165th Street. A few indigent men stared at the gullwing.

"Why here?" Johnny said.

"The better part of valor," Christina said.

"Oh, yeah. Discretion." Johnny stepped out of the Mercedes into a bright, hazy summer evening and looked about quickly, like a thief.

Chris laughed. "We've been discreet, Johnny. And indiscreet, Johnny. Go, Johnny. It's all right, Johnny. Win the game."

Ordinarily, he reached the ball park by five o'clock on nights when he was to pitch. He liked to lie on Doc Youmans' training table and close his eyes and feel the hot salves on his arm and think through the innings that were ahead.

"Where you been?" Youmans said. It was 6:08.

"You wouldn't believe me, Doc."

Youmans, short, muscled, and florid, looked like a worn-out football guard. "I've got to believe what winning pitchers tell me," he said. "Supportive therapy, they call that. It's part of my job."

"How'd you train for the job, Doc?" Ralph Kauff asked. "I mean, how do you learn to be a trainer?"

"Two years at Valley View Osteopathic College, outside Pittsburgh," Youmans said, "before I went broke and had to quit. I was going to specialize in spinal arthritis. If I knew I was going to end up treating ballplayers like you, Kauff, I would have majored in crabs."

"I was looking at paintings," Johnny said to the trainer.

"Broads?" Raunchy Kauff said. "Was you looking at broads without clothes?"

"Git off my table, you raunchy rookie bastard," Youmans said. "Let a major-leaguer in here, so I can do some work."

"John?" Rob Brownell of *The New York Standard* was calling timidly from the doorway.

"That's me. I'm John."

"Can I ask you some questions?" Brownell said. He was slight and spare, and wore a mustache.

"The league rule is clear," Johnny said. "No reporters in the trainer's room. Sure, Rob. Come on in."

"But keep it brief," Youmans said, guarding his territory, "and don't ask him upsetting questions. He's got to pitch."

"I know he has to pitch," Brownell said. "Uh, Johnny. You've won twelve straight. Do you have any feeling about thirteen being unlucky?"

"What was your question?" Johnny said.

"Thirteen."

"I'll know if it's unlucky after the game."

Writing in a blue, looseleaf pad, Brownell said, "Can't you try to do better than that? Thirteen is supposed to be unlucky because of 'The Last Supper.' The twelve apostles and Jesus."

"I don't intend to be crucified," Johnny said.

"Neither did Jesus," Youmans said.

"That's good, Johnny," Brownell said. "That's a nice first edition quote. Seeking his thirteenth consecutive victory, young Johnny Longboat, the Mohawks' rookie right-handed ace, announced . . ."

John felt careless. "If you look up Norse legend, Rob, you'll find references to thirteen in there, too."

"What?" Brownell said. "Norse legend in the locker room? I am amazed."

"We've got a very high-toned ball club," Youmans said. "They can all read and some of them can spell."

"Where did you pick that up, Johnny?" Brownell said. "Norse legend. Do you know Wagner's operas?"

"I don't know anybody's operas, but I do have a secret, Rob. Can I trust you with a secret?"

"Sure."

"I've read a book."

"In Oklahoma?" Brownell said.

"Yep, and another one in Pittsfield. I'm thinking of reading a third book now that I'm in New York."

"Can I do a Sunday feature on you?" Brownell said. "Or maybe a piece for *Sports Illustrated* or *The New Yorker*. Wouldn't you like a story with a little depth? I'm sure it would sell."

John waited.

"It is a surprising kind of image for a lot of people," Brownell said. "A rookie who reads."

"Except," Johnny said, "if you make me out to be an intellectual, I'll have problems. The other benches here get on a fellow pretty good." He made his voice guttural.

"Motherfuckin' intellec-shul." He lifted his voice into falsetto. "Oh, dearie. Shall we look at the Monet paintings over tea."

"An extremely high-toned ball club," Youmans said. "If it wasn't for Kauff here, we'd give our voice signals in Latin."

"I'll see you after the game," Johnny said, dismissing the reporter.

"With a win," Brownell said. "You can handle Philadelphia."

* * *

Johnny felt curiously listless on the mound. His fastball sailed high and his curve broke onto the plate and he walked the first two Philadelphia batters. What had his father told him? "They call a walk a pass, but it's really more of a gift. Never, dammit *never*, give a damn gift to the enemy."

He eased up, seeking control and threw a lazy curve. Home run. He walked two more and aimed a fastball hand-high at the inside corner. The pitch drifted to the center of the plate. Triple. He was out of the game at twelve minutes after eight.

"You got nothing tonight," the manager, Mush Kramer, said. "Not a fucking thing."

"Sorry," Johnny said. The crowd was making subdued sounds of sorrow and shock. Ralph Kauff scratched the back of his short, thick neck. "I never seed you throw like this before."

"You haven't got a fucking thing," Mush Kramer said.

"Is that right?" Johnny said. "Is that maybe why they got those five runs off me?"

"Don't be a bad-ass," Kramer said.

Johnny looked toward the murmuring crowd in the triple tiers of Mohawk Stadium. He blinked and saw the violet room; he saw the high-born English lady, Anna Southwyck; he saw Christina's long, tanned, downy arms.

He put the baseball into the hairy hand of Clyde Killifer, the relief pitcher. Mush Kramer patted his rump and Johnny walked dully from the mound, touching his cap and wincing in response to consoling clapping from the crowd.

Harry (The Whistler) Schulte had been right, Johnny thought. Despite Schulte's advice, he'd had "sex with a woman" before a game and now Philadelphia bombed him. Score one for Philadelphia. Score one for Harry Schulte's intuition. Score nothing for Harry Schulte's reasoning. Johnny moved through the dugout into the long, cream-colored corridor that led to the locker room. His spikes clacked on the wooden floorboards.

It was not, as Schulte believed, that good sex weakened you. It wasn't that at all. Rather, good sex touched your mind. It made you dream. And nobody, except maybe a few poets and songwriters, ever prospered by dreaming about a blonde.

In the clubhouse, he continued to think of Chris. Had she seen the Phillies knock him out? To business, he thought. To business. He would wait in uniform for the newspapermen who would arrive for interviews after the game. If you gave interviews when you won, you'd better give them on the bad days, too. Christy Mathewson, who, Dad said, was the best of all the pitchers, lost 186 games in the major leagues, not counting five lost in several World Series. Matty, best of all, was a 191-game loser. Johnny had now lost only one.

Philadelphia defeated the Mohawks, 11–4, and when Rob Brownell saw Johnny sitting on a three-legged stool in front of a locker, the reporter assumed a pallbearer's look. "The number was unlucky," he said. "Thirteen turned out to be unlucky."

"It wasn't bad luck," Johnny said. "I just pitched horseshit."

"You looked out of rhythm."

"Out of rhythm. Out of focus. I was horseshit."

"Look, Johnny, about that story I wanted to do, the magazine piece about the reading rookie."

"The reading horseshit rookie? Sure. Go ahead."

* * *

Robert Ervin Brownell majored in English literature at Williams College, amid the pines and maples of the Berkshire hills, where he wrote his senior thesis on the heroines of Thomas Hardy's novels. Praised more for content than style, the thesis earned a B. By his senior year in college, Brownell knew he would not go into the family business—a busline that ran from New York City into the Adirondack Mountains. He thought briefly of becoming a teacher. But sport tugged him. Sport tugged Brownell as surely as it would tug at Johnny Longboat. It was clean, exciting, attracted crowds. As he sometimes now explained to other newspaperman, sport was for him the green light Gatsby saw but never reached.

The management of the *Standard* liked quiet, thoughtful men from proper Eastern colleges. Management people were offended by the idea that newspapermen drank hard, wore fedoras, and wrote with more passion than literacy. Rob Brownell of Williams College was what management regarded as the *Standard* type. At twenty-two, he was hired as an editorial assistant in sports.

His career advanced more quickly than his writing skills, which was hard for Brownell to understand. He read constantly. Hardy. Dickens. More Hardy. Lardner. Flaubert. His tragedy—he was inclined to call it pathos—was that he could read so much better than he wrote. He envied Red Smith's grace and Jimmy Cannon's power. Was the difference that they thought more gracefully or more powerfully than he? He could not be sure, but when Brownell sat before a typewriter, his fingers tensed and his heartbeat accelerated. Then he wrote wooden, workmanlike columns. His noblest concepts became bland as they reached paper. He knew this without understanding why, but at forty-seven, he remained a hopeful man. He would yet capture fire, this time with a story on Johnny Longboat.

The New Yorker rejected "The Reading Rookie," with a courteous, impersonal note that mentioned a full inventory of sports pieces and did not comment on the submitted article. *Sports Illustrated* responded with a letter that said Brownell's premise was not sufficiently remarkable. "We believe we're a long way from the days of Ring Lardner's illiterates, who stirred their coffee, or highballs, with their index fingers," an editor wrote. "Increasing numbers of ballplayers are college graduates. A rookie who reads does not strike us as unique." An editor at *Esquire* telephoned to say the story had great promise, but needed revising, in ways the editor intended to outline by mail. When no letter arrived in a month, Brownell called the magazine and learned that the editor had been dismissed.

Brownell then decided to transform the story into a column for the *Standard*. It ran on September 18, when Johnny Longboat's record was 19–5.

THE SPORTING LIFE
By Rob Brownell

You wonder about a lot of things in my job. Kids are dying every day in Southeast Asia and you get to write, "Ralph Kauff is beginning to look like a hitter." But in truth people like Ralph Kauff—and like Johnny Longboat—may be as important to our national consciousness as our soldiers. Professor Sheckard at Williams used to teach, "You can know a nation by the nature of its wars and by its games." So ballplayers, who play our games, cannot be said to be unimportant.

Friends wonder about a sportswriter's job, too. Some say, "You get paid to go to ball games." But, ah, my friends, no sportswriter ever earned a nickel *going* to a ball game. You're paid to *write* about the games, which is a different thing.

You see, ballplayers arrive in droves each spring, from farms or maybe out of service stations where they pumped gas. They appear, suddenly noticed, and they try to act nonchalant. They have a chance for fame, and seventy thousand dollars a year, and they work hard to convince everybody that they're relaxed. According to the new California phrase, they are laid back.

As you can imagine, most of them blow it. They blow the experience—coming to New York from Ottumwa, Iowa—and they blow the money. They move into a suburban split-level, commute to a ballpark and never get to a Manhattan theater, an art gallery or a library. The money? Not all financial advisers are equally reputable. One third baseman, some years back, was advised to invest thirty thousand dollars in a "sure-fire Cuban sugar deal." The thirty thousand was guaranteed to grow to ninety thousand in three months. When it turned out there was no ninety, no thirty, no sugar, no deal, the ballplayer was too humiliated to sue.

Pensions and Penchants

That is hard stuff. It's not the bland brew TV people (except for Cosell) stir up, which, incidentally, is one reason we need our newspapers. And adventures like the third baseman's are a reason modern, laid-back ballplayers become excited by such relatively dull matters as pension plans.

Well, this is a story about one man who, I'd bet, will never have to haunt the mail box for his pension check. Johnny Longboat, the Mohawks' extraordinary right-handed rookie, is not merely a pitching man but a man who reads and thinks. Here, with the help of a brand new tape recorder is how conversation goes with this unusual rookie. He is not just interesting as a ballplayer. He is interesting as a man.

Q—What was it like growing up in Oklahoma?

A—Flat was what it was like. It could be hard for New York people to understand the flatness. You have skyscrapers here, and the Palisades. Go into Westchester County and you see hills and that wonderful Hudson River gorge. Where I grew up, it was flat in a lot of ways. Not as much dimension as New York.

Q—Where does a ballplayer come off using words like gorge and dimension so easily?

A—Where does a newspaperman come off asking a question like that? From what I've seen so far, the average IQ of ballplayers and sportswriters could be about the same.

Q—Meaning?

A—Somewhat lower than Einstein's.

Q—Are you suggesting that you have to be intelligent to play baseball?

A—It doesn't hurt. But first you want to define the type of intelligence. Is it imagination? Now that can hurt a ballplayer, if he imagines bad things, like a Russian novelist. Harry Schulte, who was a great minor-league ballplayer and manager, never read a book. But he knew how to win. A specific intelligence—game intelligence—absolutely helps a ball player. Christy Mathewson was a checkers champion.

Q—Where did you hear about Russian novelists?

A—I said it was flat in Oklahoma, not dead. There are schools there, books, even courses in world lit.

Q—Back home you must have been the best ballplayer around.

A—For my age. There are always older guys who are better.

Q—I heard a well-known author say that he was thinking of writing a novel with this theme: Baseball is what gives the ballplayer's life depth and height. That is, when you're a kid and life is tough, you can always go out and play well and rise above it.

A—Rise above life? He must believe in resurrection.

Q—He meant rise above your troubles.

A—Not that much. I was a good ballplayer as a kid, but suppose I'd been a great biology student. Instead of excelling for three hours on a field, I could have excelled for three hours in the biology lab. In important ways, that's pretty much the same thing.

Q—Except ballplayers are more famous than biologists.

A—And that can make things not easier, but more difficult. As a kid, I didn't consciously want to be famous. I just wanted to be a good ballplayer.

Q—Is money important to you?

A—No, except I like to go places and buy things.

Q—Do you want to be rich?

A—Yes, but possibly not out of greed. If I had plenty of money, there would just be one less damn thing to worry about.

Q—What worries you now? Maintaining your pitching standard?

A—(Pause) No, that really doesn't worry me. I'm not conceited but I know I can pitch. I do that better than I do anything else in the world. It's the rest that gets hard and worrisome, the life beyond the ball field. Adjusting to change. Change is always painful for me. That's an honest admission.

Q—How do you think you'll handle all the changes, all the fame?

A—Read a little more. Think a lot. Enjoy the sunlight. Try to limit myself to two drinks a day.

Q—What do you have in mind for the days after baseball?

A—Come see me in 1982, if the politicians let the world survive.

We know the world will survive the politicians, if only because it always has survived them. We know, too, what Johnny Longboat's place in the world will be, when his pitching days are done.

At the top. Or pretty close.

Rob Brownell tried to read the column, which he had liked when he was composing it, as though it had been written by someone else. He was less pleased as he reviewed it. He recognized for the thousandth time that he could not write a sports column with Red Smith or Jimmy Cannon. The thought depressed him until he decided that the column gave the reader a sense of what it was to sit and chat with Johnny Longboat. That was something. Not everyone could do that.

The thin, wispish newspaperman thought briefly of sport as Gatsby's beckoning green light.

But *writing* about sport was once removed from sport and besides, Smith and Cannon had already reached the dock where Gatsby's light shone across a phosphorescent bay.

Maybe, Rob Brownell thought, he should go to Vietnam and write his stuff about the dying soldiers.

And maybe not. He resolved to have a catch with his boy this weekend. Disappointed in the column, which was one of his best, one of the finest pieces of his own, the newspaperman took down a book and began to read a Dickens short story in which a mother engages a physician to restore life to her son, who has been newly hanged.

Chapter 7
1:51 P.M., October 14

In the fourth inning, spindly Spider Webb bunted Johnny's second pitch, a tailing outside fastball, and the bunt rolled between third base and the mound. The Spider had wanted to bunt along the foul line, but the tail on the fastball surprised him and cost his bunt direction.

Johnny moved as quickly as he could. At forty-one, you can move rapidly once you are under way, but there is a blink, a stay in time, that does not delay a man of twenty-five. John saw the bunt and knew he had to react. Younger, he simply reacted.

As Johnny rushed to his right, the spin on the baseball bit into the grass, and the ball twisted from him. Straining to make the play, he perceived elements in motion. Jap O'Hara was hurrying in from third. Kauff had torn off his mask and ran forward from home plate. The three, O'Hara, Kauff, and himself, formed a frantic triangle contracting toward a spinning, dribbling baseball. John would reach the baseball first. He shouted, "Mine."

He plucked the ball from the grass with his bare hand and leaning now and spinning himself, snapped a hard throw across his chest toward first base. His spikes skidded and Johnny sprawled forward, barely feeling the impact of the ground. But a bulb of pain exploded in his right shoulder.

The crowd cheered and applauded; he had made an excellent play. Johnny sat up. He had nursed his arm carefully while pitching. Now, a simple, snap throw across the infield . . . His black-eyed, high-cheekboned face burned with inexpressible anger. "Damn," he said.

He saw Bad Czech Dubcek throw the baseball to Kauff, who threw to Saviour Domingo, who threw to Kenny Osterhout in a casual, graceful ritual of success. Johnny stood and bent to brush dirt from the knees of his blue and white uniform. The hot bulb in his shoulder cooled. He breathed deeply, taking measure of himself. His shoulder ached. The muscles around it felt fatigued.

✳ ✳ ✳

He remembered the bespectacled Ivy League doctor at New York Hospital, who examined his right shoulder last August. The man wore a checked shirt, kept him waiting for fifty minutes, and put questions in a patronizing way.

"If you can't show me a dot of pain, can you at least show me a rectangle? That's like a square."

"The pain is fan-shaped," Johnny said. "It radiates from a point near the joining of the clavicle and the humerus. You know the humerus? It's the big bone in the upper arm."

"A joker," said the doctor in the checked shirt, "but is a sore arm really funny for a pitcher?"

In the white, windowless room, the orthopedist spoke to two colleagues. Humerus socket. Rotator cuff. Caracoid process. Trapezius insertion. A stranger's fingers stabbed John's shoulder. Pain. "What the hell you trying to do?"

"Sorry. We're just checking into your shoulder."

"Looking for what?"

"Your father was a truck driver, wasn't he?"

"That's right."

177

"In terms you can understand," said the smug New York Hospital man, "we're trying to determine if the gears are gone."

* * *

Now he had thrown out Spider Webb, but—in understandable terms—had the snap throw shattered the final cog? Johnny stood on the grass at Mohawk Stadium, in shadow thrown by the triple tiers. He bent and gripped his knees.

"You all right?" Cy Veitch stood over him.

"I'm all right, but I better throw a few."

"For how long?"

"I don't know for how long I better throw."

"We ought to warm up Cardwell and Torchyzer."

"They should stay loose," Johnny said. "They should have been throwing from the beginning. I'm forty-one years old and this is the seventh game." The pain was making him irritable.

"I know what game this is," Veitch said. "You don't have to tell me what game this is." Tension grated against the manager. Neither pain nor tension customarily is ennobling.

Johnny puffed and inhaled.

"If you don't want to go any further," Veitch said, "now is the time to tell me. You say you're hurt and we get time to warm up the next man. Is that what you want? Do you want out?"

"Throw a few, Johnny," said Kenny Osterhout, the shortstop, his voice sounding a supplication. Kenny was twenty-two. John had been nineteen and jabbering with Harry (The Whistler) Schulte the summer Osterhout was born in Orange County, New York. "You're our big man, Johnny," the shortstop said.

"No, I don't want to come out," Johnny said to Veitch.

His passion to win was a spotless white plume, and to win he had to make himself ascend. Above years. Beyond pain. He wanted to win the game for Quincy Coleman, the old guy who never succeeded, and he wanted to win for Kenny Osterhout, the kid who was his fan. He wanted victory to defy certain people. Cold Gus Vermont, with his business-school approach to baseball. He'd show the bastard something you couldn't program into a Fortran computer. He'd show him guts. The white-haired, sharp-featured commissioner of baseball, Admiral Amory Moresby, prattled to writers about the integrity of the game. Beneath his glacial manner, Moresby would be rooting for Johnny to lose. Their lives had crossed once, in a shattering collision of personality, background, and ethics. Afterward John found himself one of the few who knew the Commissioner was a fraud. Win to help people. Win to defy people. Win to show people. Mostly win it for yourself. If this was to be his last ball game, it simply had to be a victory. For the rest of his life he would remember October 14.

"Gentlemen," said Danny Merullo, the plate umpire. "We don't have time to hold a convention here."

"Goddammit," Veitch said. "Don't start up with me now. My pitcher may be hurt."

Goddammit, Cy, Johnny thought, don't start up with *him*. Talk softly. Give him respect. Call him mister. Start up with him and he may take the corners away from me.

"Are you hurt?" Merullo said to Johnny.

"I just want to throw a few, if it's okay with you, Dan."

"No more than eight pitches," Merullo said. "That's the rules and that's enough to see how your arm is. Then you either gotta go, or gotta stay."

"I'll just need maybe five, Dan. That okay?"

"Sure. Hell, why don't you take your eight."

Johnny threw two fastballs and a curve. The ache and the weariness around the ache were constant. Not unendurable, but constant. The ball moved nicely. It would be mental then, and here at last was an advantage that came with years. The young athletes had winged swiftness, but pain confused and frightened them. It was an early reminder of mortality. The old pitcher no longer confused himself with a god. The years had schooled him in mortality; in his own mortality, and in how to live with pain. He had learned simply to think of another part of his body. If your pitching shoulder hurt, concentrate on a great toe. Pain, the old pitcher thought, played a game of terror. If you did not let it terrify you, pain could be resisted, even dismissed. He was certain of this as he nodded at Danny Merullo, indicating that he was ready to resume.

Duke Marboro of Pittsburg, Kansas, was the next batter. Marboro must sense that the pitcher was wounded, Johnny thought. He would be excited by that, and eager as a predator.

Kauff wagged his fingers for a fastball. Johnny shook his head. They went around until Kauff signaled for a change of pace. Meanwhile, Duke Marboro pumped his bat. John threw the change, a few inches higher than he wanted, but Marboro, the lusting predator, took his stride early. With his weight already committed, he had only enough power to drive a soft fly down the right-field line. Dwayne Tucker caught the ball at his knees after a hard run.

"The change is all he's got," Frenchy Boucher bellowed from the Mastodon dugout. Boucher must have liked this theme. "He's got no hard one left. Ya better feel sorry for his wife."

"Hey, Frenchy," yelled Kenny Osterhout from shortstop, "how come your mouth looks like an open sewer?"

"Hey, sewer-mouth," called Jap O'Hara. Boucher sat down.

A man could enjoy this, Johnny thought. You could laugh at the coarse dialogue, this secret, dissonant music of big-league baseball, except you had to work. You had to pitch.

180

Boucher was a gutter guy, but a game-smart gutter guy. Otherwise, he'd still be prowling gutters. As with Johnny Carson's talk, Boucher's working conversation was charged with purpose.

You got no hard one. Your hard one's dead.

Set aside the noise, Johnny thought; ask what the noise means. He knew at once. Boucher was challenging Johnny to show that his hard one was alive. In short, to throw a fastball. Whitey Wright, at bat, punished pitchers who threw him fastballs. The bellowing, game-smart, gutter guy was prodding the pitcher toward an angry mistake. Johnny grinned, but not at the dugout dialogue. He grinned because he had figured out Boucher's clever, sewer-mouthed game.

He threw another change of pace. Wright blinked. Strike one.

A third straight change. As the spinning slow ball crossed the plate, Wright spat. Strike two.

Now Johnny threw a fastball, a good foot inside the plate. Wright swung—hitters swing wildly when they really want a certain kind of pitch. Wright had wanted a fastball—*any* fastball. Johnny had his strikeout. Another inning. No hits across four.

Johnny sat by himself on the right-field side of the dugout, near the wood-floored runway to the clubhouse, and toweled his neck. A red-eyed television camera peered at him. John winked at the camera and seventy million people, and waved his right arm, as if to show that it felt fine.

Kauff approached. The peeping camera turned toward the field. "That was a real nice strikeout, Johnny," he said.

"Was there much on the fastball, Ralph?"

"It didn't matter, seeing as where you put it. He like to hit it with his thumbs."

"But was there much on the fastball?"

"You can keep using it, if you spot it good," Kauff said.

"You got much pain?" asked Lefty Levin.

"No more than I can handle," Johnny said.

"It's Boucher who's hurtin' now," Kauff said. "Right, Johnny?"

"Needling you about hard ones," Levin said, in sour disdain. "That broken-down bastard had a physical last year and you know what the doctors found when they checked his cock?"

"What?" Kauff said.

"Cobwebs," Levin said.

"Let's stay in the ball game," Johnny said.

✷ ✷ ✷

"Does it look to you as though your man pushed the last fast ball, when he should have flang it?" Townsend Wade of *Commentator* magazine asked Rob Brownell of the *Standard*.

"It looked to me the way it looked to Whitey Wright. He used the same motion he'd been using on his change of pace."

"Two dollars to a dollar your man does not go nine," Wade said.

"I'll give you three to one," said Prissy Coe of *Scoreboard* magazine.

"I'll take both bets," Brownell said.

Prissy shook her honey hair and looked pleased. Acceptance of anything, even a bet, came uncertainly to a woman in a press box.

"It's been a nice ball game," Wade said. "No runs. A pitcher against a thrower. But your man, the pitcher, has to beat more than the Mastodons. He has to beat the years."

"You're talking in leads, Townsend," Brownell said. "Besides you're repeating what you've already stated with your money."

"Do you happen to wonder how come I'm covering the seventh game?" Prissy Coe asked.

Brownell felt annoyed. Why was she talking about herself, instead of what she had been assigned to cover? The new journalism was nothing more than the old egomania.

"You slept with your editorial director," Wade said.

"Not right away," said Prissy Coe. "He wanted me to move up within *Newsmakers* magazine, and handle the section called Women. If you're a woman they think you can only cover women, the menstruation beat. I said no without thanks, and the editor said what was my dream and I said, 'Do you mean after my girlhood dream of playing center field for the New York Mohawks?' So he said would you write baseball for *Scoreboard* and I said yes."

"Which is how you came to sleep with him," Wade said.

"Maybe."

"But, Priscilla," Brownell said, "how did the idea of promoting you to a major writing job occur in the first place?"

"The editors at *Newsmakers* are sexist," Prissy said. "They kept a file on the women researchers and the secretaries. They called it 'Scouting Reports.' The women staffers were rated not on talent but on compatibility, tits, and ass. All on a scale of ten."

"Was this stuff in writing?" Wade said.

"In ink. I'm a strong reporter and I got hold of the file and I put it to them. Either promote women to real jobs, or we start a class-action suit against *Newsmakers* and introduce the file. By the way, I rated high in tits and ass."

"This offends me," Brownell said.

"Sitting next to a woman in the press box offends you?" Prissy Coe said, setting her strong, triangular jaw. "That is the sort of shit we simply do not intend to take any more."

"What offends me," Brownell said, "is sitting among people who insist on chattering about matters other than the marvelous ball game unfolding in front of us."

That was, however, not all that offended him. Brownell was a sensitive and conventionally proper man; women talking about menstruation or saying "shit" discomfited him. Priscilla Coe was hardly a lyric heroine, the peony-mouthed girl that he (and Hardy) so admired. Yet her story about *Newsmakers'* sex file was true. Indeed, it was just the sort of material that *Newsmakers* would have printed, in an article weighted with outrage, had the sex file been discovered somewhere else. By all accounts, Priscilla Coe was a fine reporter. She would go anywhere—some said to any bed—to get a story.

Sadness touched Rob Brownell. She was less sensitive to the beauties of baseball than he, more willing to ask rude, prosecuting questions. But the brashness helped make her a strong reporter. Strong reporters probed the wounds of subjects, as callous to the pain they caused as young, ambitious doctors. They said (like doctors) that causing pain was part of the job.

As for himself, Brownell practiced good manners in drawing rooms and dugouts. But could he argue that journalism was at length a mannerly game? No. It was as unmannerly as baseball.

Prissy Coe, first-generation woman sportswriter, accepted that without sentimentality. Brownell believed he would be more comfortable with the second generation of women sportswriters, whether they were peony-mouthed or not.

He shouldn't muse. Later there would be a long story to write quickly. Like Johnny Longboat, Rob Brownell told himself to stay in the game.

* * *

Leading off the bottom of the fourth inning, Kenny Osterhout let a fastball nick the shirtsleeve of his upper left arm. Frenchy Boucher charged at Danny Merullo roaring, "He just stood there."

"That's right," Merullo said, "and now he's just gonna be standing on first base."

"The fucking rules say, Mr. Umpire, that he's gotta fucking try to get out of the way." Boucher gestured with one hand and two pitchers stood up in the bull pen of the Los Angeles Mastodons.

"You can say what you want for one minute," Merullo said, "as long as you're not abusive."

"You're fucking-ay right I can say what I want." Boucher's face was red and his short, bulbous nose was turning red. He ran toward first base and pulled off his hat. The bald top of his head was reddening also.

"Looking good on the color TV," shouted Lefty Levin.

Boucher kicked at his hat in the base path.

"Why don't we send the kid?" Levin said to Cy Veitch. "Get something started." Veitch touched his belt buckle so that Daryl Coyle, the third-base coach, could see that he wanted Osterhout to steal. The manager tapped his chin twice. Steal on the second pitch.

Boucher continued to stalk in rage. He was reminding the umpire that narrow calls against the Mastodons would create loud, offensive scenes. He was reminding his players that this wasn't college baseball. He was giving his bull-pen pitchers extra moments to warm up. "You think," Boucher shouted at Merullo, "that if you don't call anything the hard way, it'll look like you're doing a good job."

Merullo looked at his watch. "Thirty-eight seconds. I know you need your network time."

"Yeah," Boucher said, making a sweeping gesture, so that both hands circled to his chest. "Be nasty to me, but do it quiet. You got the power and the blue suit, Mr. Umpire."

185

"Thirty-three seconds more," Merullo said. "That's all I give you."

"You give me nothing, Merullo. You think you can stand back there and act real composed and the Commissioner will think you're doing a good job. Well, I'm telling you, Merullo, you blow any more calls, and I won't let you stay composed. My players are working, and I'm working and goddammit, I want you to work. This is the seventh game."

"I know this is the seventh game," the umpire said. "Twenty seconds."

"You ain't scaring me," Boucher shouted, "because you ain't throwing a manager out of the seventh game."

"Fourteen seconds."

Boucher kicked dirt to the right of the umpire.

"That's it," Merullo said. "Time's up."

"Hey, Danny," Lefty Levin shouted from the Mohawk dugout. "Give the son of a bitch his Academy Award and let's play baseball."

Boucher was walking toward his own dugout. He turned and said, "Merullo! You gonna let a kike tell you what to do?"

Johnny Longboat stood in the Mohawk dugout, and lifted his right arm in a Nazi salute. "Sieg Heil," he shouted. Other Mohawks picked up the words. They chanted along with Johnny. "Sieg Heil. Sieg Heil."

Boucher's face contorted. He was truly angry now. He roared at the plate umpire, "Now you're taking orders from a kike and a half-breed?"

"Sieg Heil," the Mohawks chanted. "Sieg Heil."

Merullo bent himself into a twisting stoop. He was preparing to throw Boucher out of the game; he wound up for a regal sweep of an arm. Boucher turned quickly and trotted toward the Mastodons' dugout. The stooping umpire abruptly scratched his own right thigh. You could not

banish a manager when he scampered in full tactical re-
treat.

"Kike?" said Harry Truman Abernathy. "Half-breed?
How come the sucker left out nigger."

"He's not destructive," Johnny said. "He's a bastard,
but he's not destructive. There are no Jews or Indians on
his ball club, but he's got blacks playing for him. He
doesn't call anybody 'nigger' because he doesn't want to
lose his own guys."

"There's rules," Lefty Levin said, looking pale. "You
take some things if you're a Jewish ballplayer and some
things are all right to take. Like they'd shout, 'Levin, if
you had a nose fulla nickels you'd be a millionaire.' But
that Boucher, when I played in the same league with him
in Carolina, he was always yelling 'Christ-killer,' or things
like 'How the hell did Hitler miss your mother?' That's
beyond the rules."

Johnny wanted to get his head back into the game. "He
got to you in Carolina, Lefty, but we sure got to him just
now."

"He's so tight," Abernathy said, "he's ready for a heart
attack."

"Impossible," Lefty Levin said. "Frenchy Boucher
couldn't have a heart attack. The worst thing that could
happen to him is a hernia."

* * *

On Hummin' Herman Calhoun's second pitch to Tru
Abernathy, Ken Osterhout broke for second base. He
started smartly, stealing fractions of a second on Calhoun's high-kicking motion. Two-thirds of the way along
the base path, Osterhout's legs went out from under him
and he fell. Jake Wakefield, the Los Angeles second baseman, caught Jed Jackson's shoulder-high throw and
trotted toward Osterhout. He was grinning.

Lying prone, the young shortstop crawled toward first

187

base. His arms flailed and his spikes beat against the ground. He was a powerful, lithe swimmer, using his best sea stroke on the beach. Wakefield laughed as he tagged Kenny Osterhout on the butt.

"What did he trip on?" Cy Veitch growled. "A goddamn shadow."

"He's a kid," Lefty Levin said, "and he's nervous as hell."

"We're all nervous as hell," Johnny said.

Osterhout slunk into the dugout, staring at his spikes. He threw his batting helmet to the floor. "I had it stole," he said, shaking his head. "I had it stole, clean as my mother's rosebush in the rain."

"Yeah," Jap O'Hara said, "and the throw was high."

Osterhout sat next to Johnny and folded his arms and hugged himself. "I never done that before," he said, "even in high school where the field was full of ruts."

Abernathy lined his second hit, a double over third base, and Cy Veitch cried, "Christ. There was our run if the kid don't trip."

Osterhout continued to hug himself. He looked as though he were about to weep.

"Come on," Johnny said. "We've got a man on second base, and a good hitter up there."

"Belt one," Osterhout shouted to Anton Dubcek.

Dubcek hit a hard ground ball directly at Whitey Wright, the Los Angeles shortstop. Abernathy was frozen at second. Dubcek was out at first.

Tears welled in Osterhout's eyes. "The New York papers will kill me," he said, "and my mother up in Newburgh likes to read the New York papers."

"We still got a hitter up there," said Lefty Levin. "Hey, Dwayne. Pop one, Dwayne, baby."

Dwayne Tucker hit an outside fastball into deep left center field and the entire Mohawk bench rose, rooting the baseball toward the fence. The ballplayers were still standing when "Hometown" Brown ran down the drive near a sign that read 417 feet.

"No," said Osterhout. "Oh, good God, no."

"Kenny," John said, "forget it. Forget the New York papers. Forget this inning. If I'm gonna win it, I need your great glove to back me in the innings we still have to play."

* * *

Coaches and managers worship concentration. Johnny was trying to relax as he warmed up. The coaches in every sport. Chris Evert wins because she *concentrates*. Reggie Jackson *concentrates*, especially in the October wind. Jabbar sometimes loses *concentration*. Vince Lombardi's football teams *concentrated*. According to the managers and coaches, loss of concentration was a sin. But the real sin, Johnny believed, was blind belief in any single pattern or doctrine.

Relaxing, as he warmed up, Johnny thought Ken Osterhout probably had been *overconcentrating*. He was thinking of Calhoun's release time—the span from the start of Calhoun's windup to the instant when he released the pitch. He was thinking how you balanced your weight, as you took your lead, and how you kept your fists clenched so that no finger could be spiked, and how you broke into full stride from your left foot. He was thinking, too, that this was the seventh game and that the New York newspapers, which his mother read, were covering the game with a legion of reporters and a blur of photographers. Concentrating on the game, on his role in one particular moment, he had caught a spike in smooth earth. Relaxed, careless, Osterhout could have run from first to second ten thousand times without the suggestion of a stumble.

Johnny threw easily to Kauff, aware that Rocco Lombardo was *concentrating* on his motion. Lombardo kept pumping his staunch black bat, The Godfather, behind his neck, loosening shoulder muscles, although it was not so much stallion strength as game intelligence that made him a home-run champion.

"We got the long boat now," Frenchy Boucher shouted. "The long boat is sinking down to the bottom. He goes to the old-age home tonight. That old-age home for half-breeds."

As Lombardo set his feet to hit, he looked toward he mound. His lips formed one word: "Sorry." Guinea and nigger; kike and half-breed. Foul punctuation amid golden dialogues in the American game. John didn't like it. Lombardo didn't like it. But it was there. He nodded acknowledgment toward the big-shouldered black-browed hitter.

Johnny started Lombardo with a slow curve. The book, and the computer, warned that Lombardo hit off-speed pitches except when he was swinging with two strikes. Rocco, in his concentration, knew that. Surprised, he watched the suddenly arcing baseball break past his knees.

"Steey-yup," bawled Danny Merullo.

Lombardo blinked and glowered. Without looking at the umpire he said, "The pitch was low."

"It's a strike, Rocco, because I said it was a strike."

"Okay. I'm not arguing, Danny. I'm only trying to make a living. There's a lot of hungry Italians in San Jose and they're all named Lombardo."

Johnny threw his tailing fastball, high and wide. Lombardo all but leaped—he actually stood on his toe spikes —trying to reach the pitch, and fouled it into Danny Merullo's mask. Merullo shook his head. "If you keep swinging at those sucker pitches," the umpire said, "all those Italians are going to be even hungrier."

With two strikes, pitcher and batter embarked on a lofty game of chance. Lombardo had to set himself for a fastball. He could not let himself be overpowered. He would *set* for the fastball, but what would he be *looking* for? Remembering his first pitch, Johnny guessed that Lombardo would look for another, defiant slow curve.

Kauff signaled for a straight change of pace. Johnny would throw a great change-of-pace hitter a great change of pace. He was not matching Lombardo muscle for muscle. Rather he was matching game-sense against game-sense.

Johnny curled and threw, jerking down the baseball, closing Harry Schulte's window shade. He felt something pop deep within his shoulder.

Lombardo strode too early, but the big black bat, The Godfather, still was cocked.

The change hung in the air, like an enormous wafer. Lombardo whipped The Godfather across the plate. The change still hung. Lombardo had swung too soon. "Hell of a strikeout," shouted Kenny Osterhout.

John inhaled three times. He would not wince, or let his arm dangle. But the pain was clear now and defined. It burned at the point on the back of his upper arm where humerus and clavicle join, within thick bulbs of muscle. Because the pain was clear, Johnny no longer felt certain that he could finish the seventh game. The gears, the smug Cornell doctor's gears were slipping. From now on every pitch had to be an "out" pitch, a pitch that could retire the batter. He could no longer afford to waste one pitch to set up another, simply because he didn't know how many pitches he had left.

Rosey Dale bounced up the middle where Jesus Domingo made a back-handed stop and threw him out. Jake Wakefield pulled a buzzing, hooking line drive which Jap O'Hara caught, springing high and to his left.

Slipping gears or not, Johnny had pitched five innings of the seventh game and nobody had reached first base.

* * *

"All the signs and symptoms," Rob Brownell said in the press box.

"Seldom fails," Townsend Wade said.

"What?" Prissy Coe said.

"Tradition," Wade said.

"Which tradition is that?"

"You must know it," Wade said, "if you wanted to be a ballplayer."

"Let her up," Brownell said.

"He doesn't have me down," Prissy said.

"Taste, madam," Wade said.

"The tradition here," Brownell said, "suggests that when a pitcher is working on a no-hitter, like Johnny Longboat, and line drives start getting caught, he's going to make it. The pitcher's going to get his no-hitter."

"Wouldn't a no-hitter in the seventh game be unusual?" Prissy said.

"Go cover the Joffrey Ballet," Wade said.

"Silence," Brownell said. "No bickering in the press box."

"I'd like to add no chauvinism," Prissy said, "and Townsend, how come your dialogue is so crackling and the stuff you write in the magazine is so flat?"

* * *

According to the Teen-o-meter in Lefty Levin's leathery hands, Herman Calhoun began the bottom of the fifth with a fastball that moved at 98.4 miles an hour.

"Sometimes," Levin said, "a pitcher peaks like that, then loses it. They peak and then come falling off the mountain."

Calhoun struck out Jap O'Hara and Raunchy Kauff. An inside fastball snapped Saviour Domingo's bat. The baseball trickled to the mound and Domingo, as though in shock, stood at home plate, staring at the severed bat handle.

192

"You got to run 'em out," Cy Veitch shouted. "You got to run everything out, Domingo." Then he muttered, "Domingo's playing lazy, like this was Santurce against San Juan."

"He knows this isn't Santurce," Levin said. "He never saw no fastball like that in Puerto Rico."

"He didn't see it here," said Johnny Longboat.

Chapter 8
Moresby Point, New York, 1972

ACROSS SIX YEARS, the semisecret romance had spun dark, magic, threatening threads. They were getting along, Christina said, but where were they going? Would they ever possibly marry? They were long-since married, Johnny said, although not to each other.

They knew complacencies before a fire and heaving lust. Furtive luncheons in Connecticut inns, where wide-pine floorboards listed, and careless dinners at two-star steak houses in New York, where the bus boys were trained not to ask for autographs. Dreamy talk and easy word play that broke into laughter. Shopping trips to Henri Bendel's and to a pompous British tailor, where she whispered, "I like to dress you almost as much as I like to undress you." Concern and joy and fondness and rumbling guilt. Oh, they were well-acquainted and knew each other's ways. Perhaps, they may even have been in love.

"You've gotten comfortable in this violet room," Christina said. She smiled approvingly, and looked both maternal and provocative.

"It's been six years."

"Now you can distinguish a Munch from a Vermeer."

"That's freshman art appreciation. Now you can tell a fastball from a slider."

"That qualifies me to coach Little League in Peekskill."

They had developed teasing games, but each was smart enough to stop before the teasing wounded. She sat on a George IV couch, graceful and elegant, and her downy arms were covered by the long sleeves of a black velvet blouse.

"You can coach if you love the game," Johnny said.

" 'You got to love the game.' I'm quoting Willie Mays. 'Nobody can teach you nothing and you can't teach nobody nothing, unless you loves the game.' "

Christina's blue eyes filmed. She was wary of what she called jock-talk. "Love a game?" she said. "You love people, Johnny. You like a game."

"*You* love the game of love," Johnny said, and looked away.

She was the leader in the semisecret romance. Even when she clung to him in passion, she was the leader. (He wondered sometimes, did any leader have a more willing follower?) Now she had asked him to meet her about something "important, even urgent." He cherished the casual times they spent together and the idea of something urgent touched him with alarm. Would she want to talk about the future? They had the rest of their lives to live the future. Why talk about it now?

He had learned to sit on ocher Queen Anne chairs, without worrying lest one collapse, and he had overcome his wonder at violet walls and mullioned windows, but he was not comfortable in the violet room. Johnny felt uncomfortable in rented cars, in rented tuxedos, and in other peoples' places. The things we own feel safer than the things we rent. Borrowed coin stings the honest hand. He sat familiarly, but not comfortably, in Moresby Country, with another man's wife.

"The *Standard*," Chris said, "reports that you pitch against Chicago tonight."

"What does the *Examiner* say?"

"That you're favored to win, thirteen to five."

"The damn *Examiner* ought to run its printouts of the odds next to its editorials on the evils of gambling."

"Come on, honey. You can't be a morality policeman for the world."

"I am pitching tonight," he said, "but thirteen to five? How do the gamblers know if I feel like working?"

"They know your record. They know what happens when you pitch. I know what *doesn't* happen before."

"We can't go to bed," Johnny said.

"That's nonsense," Chris said. "That's in your head."

He remembered his rookie game against Philadelphia, after he had lain with Chris, and how dreamily he threw away the game. "You're part right," he said. "It's in my head, but it isn't nonsense."

"The idea that intercourse weakens a man belongs with witchcraft and the plays of Strindberg."

"Look," Johnny said, "it doesn't weaken me. But it's distracting. If we make it at three, I think about you at nine. Two men on base. A hungry hitter up there. And I'm thinking about your muff."

"That's inelegant," Chris said, "and flattering."

"It's simply the truth, at least the truth for me."

"The truth for me is that I'd rather be making love." She made a tinkling, beckoning laugh.

The kids, they said in baseball, could fuck all night, drink a glass of milk, then fuck (or pitch) all day. But he was thirty-one, middle-aged for a ballplayer. Indeed, already he felt a symptom of middle years: touches of boredom with his profession. He was not bored when he pitched, but he only pitched one day in five. He was bored with riding in jets and hearing chummy, unknown captains say: "Ah jes want you all to know it's a real thrill for us to be flying a great ball club like the Mohawks, and, uh, there's jes a few li'l thunderheads ahead, so if you'd fasten your belts, gentlemen, you'll be more comfortable, when we hit the li'l chop." He was bored with hotel living; the plastic coffee shops; the muted print of a Dufy, nailed to the wall as though it were worth stealing; and the feel of overlaundered, overstarched bed sheets. He was bored by sitting on a bench and watching other people play ball, four days out of every five. Sometimes now, he experienced a vague weariness that ten hours of sleep failed to relieve. These first tendrils of middle age confused him.

"We can make love after the game," Johnny said.

"You'll want to be with Becky and look at your son."

"Then there's tomorrow."

"You used to be impetuous," Christina said.

He followed her out of the violet room and down the Juan Gris hallway into the darkwood den. He made her a martini, six parts Lamplighter gin to one part vermouth, and stirred and wanted to make another for himself. He had to pitch. He opened a bottle of Harp's Irish Lager.

She sat on the rosewood arm of an easy chair and sipped. He wished to hell he didn't have to pitch.

"I'm going to divorce court," Christina said. "I'm leaving Brad."

Johnny put down his beer. "On account of me?"

"No. On account of Brad." She averted her eyes and began speaking quickly as people do when they believe they have made a final decision. "Next week Brad's going to a tennis camp in Tucson. The day he goes, Delray Movers are coming to take my things, all my things, but none of his. The things go to storage, and I'm moving to Mother's until I get settled. I feel inertia. Dr. Groisser says that if I don't make my break now the inertia will become so strong that I could spend the rest of my life with Douglas Bradford Moresby. I'd rather spend it with you, Johnny, but you aren't the reason I'm getting a divorce."

So many thoughts erupted that Johnny said nothing.

"A blank face," Christina said. "Is that all you can give me, a handsome blank, Arapaho, no-comment face?"

"If it was me," he said, "I'd fire the psychiatrist."

"Oh, that's wonderful. That's simply smashing. I finally set a sensible course and you tell me to fire the navigator."

"You know what I'm thinking?"

"What are you thinking?"

"Two things at once. First, you may be right in getting a divorce. There are no kids. Second, Brad is not a bad guy."

"I was hoping for support. You're just straddling."

"I know I'm straddling," Johnny said, "but I'm a man and I see things from that side. I see Brad coming home with a new carbon fiber tennis racket, and a new improved backhand, wanting to tell you that he's gotten rid of his slice. And he finds the bed gone and the silver gone, and nobody here to talk to. What happens to him then?"

"Don't," she said.

"You're right," he said. "I'll close my Arapaho mouth. I'm probably just ducking my own guilt."

She finished the martini. "But, you see, the whole point of Dr. Groisser was that I make my own decision. I even had to promise him that before I married anyone else, I'd let him interview the man." Her eyes welled. "So there isn't any reason for you to have guilt."

"Damn," Johnny said. "Goddamn."

She moved to him and kneeled and put both hands to his face and fixed her eyes on his. She tried to speak but could not.

He made a cry of pain, not for himself but for Chris. "I have these old values," Johnny said. His voice trembled in this small storm of life. "Once you have a child, and Becky Rae and I have a child, divorce is unthinkable. I don't know if that's right or wrong, but, Chris, it's what I feel and I can't make myself feel any other way."

"You know I want you. Whatever Dr. Groisser says about not going from man to man, I want you."

Soon he would pitch a ball game he didn't want to pitch and go home on a night when he wanted to stay with Chris. He thought, how much time did people spend doing things they didn't want to do? And at the end, when there was no more time . . .

Christina recovered first and rose and shook her shoulders. "I'm being demanding," she said. "I can't stand people who demand."

"You can't help being you," Johnny said, "any more than I can help being me, and there's nothing wrong with that. I'd say we're both good people."

"Baseball players," Christina said, speaking through a lovely wounded smile. "The modest idols of children and television announcers. Awed by old men. American heroes. Johnny, do you know any ballplayers who have good relationships with women?"

"We have an honest relationship right now."

"Without tomorrows."

"It's hard to grow up when you're a professional ball-player," Johnny said. "Hard as hell. When you work, you play and when you play, you work. You move around a circuit that's a merry-go-round. It's hard to grow up in a children's world."

"And the groupies hurling themselves at you all the time," Christina said. "Pathetic, sorrowful, unfulfilled young nymphomaniacs."

"They're not all sad, and some groupies are forty-five."

"Where are we going, Johnny? Where the *fuck* are we going?"

"You are the furthest thing on earth from sorrowful or pathetic," Johnny said, "and I hope you give the tennis player one more chance. Support him a little more. Think of ways you can help each other. Don't go rushing to moving companies and divorce court."

"Oh, hell," Christina said. Her voice was bravado. "The hell with you and Brad and Dr. Groisser. Dammit, I'll wait."

"Look," Johnny said, "I wouldn't have passed Groisser's interview anyway."

* * *

The rutting swarm of ballplayers, Johnny observed, alternated in their ways with women. Sometimes they were obsequious. Sometimes they were cruel.

Spinning on the major-league merry-go-round, where it was so hard to grow up, the athletes saw the world in vivid, childlike ways, with no gray areas. You won a ball game or you lost it. There were good guys—agents who brought contracts for commercials—and bad guys, mostly in the press. Women, those fragile, spikey, haunting, breeding flowers of the field, were too complex for ballplayers to understand, without grappling also with maturity. So they reduced womankind to a pair of classes. There were the wives and there were the broads.

The basic baseball wife had been a cheerleader. Good face, without much character. Nice legs. Accomplished at cooking, childbearing, and meeting late-night charter flights. Patient with sex; grateful for favors there, and generally undemanding. Discreetly silent about infidelity by husband-ballplayers on trips. The baseball road was not a wife's domain. A cheerleader once and a cheerleader still, rooting for a team of which she was no part. (Only a few baseball wives become morning drinkers by thirty.)

The ballplayers rewarded baseball wives with fine houses, functional second cars, and extravagant respect. They respected wives as they respected mothers, who after all, were only wives grown older. Basic ballplayers behaved like choirboys with basic wives. One of the foulest mouths in the game once said, "sure as shit," in front of Becky Rae Longboat. He blushed and winced and stammered, "Uh, pardon me, will you, uh, ma'm?" "I sure as shit will," Becky Rae said, merrily, prolonging the offender's blush.

Broads, ballplayers believed, were hair and meat. Ballplayers used broads, ridiculed them, passed them about, and fucked them passionlessly in turn. Such casual affection they showed broads was condescending, like affection offered to a pet.

John tried to elevate himself from ballplayer attitudes with inconsistent success. The society in which he worked affected him, and besides, as Christina said, he could not be a morality policeman for the world. He found himself adopting mocking humor, to wall himself from the ways of basic ballplayers with basic broads. He would not sink into moral anarchy, but neither did he want to be Johnny Bluenose.

At the Hotel Pennsgrove, where he had shared Room 1056 with Ralph Kauff three weeks earlier, a hard-faced Philadelphia blonde appeared at the door. "Mr. Kauff," she said. "I'm Cleo. Jeannie's busy, but she gave me your note."

John was lounging with a novel by John Fowles, *The Magus*, which illuminates a Greek island with blinding whiteness. He looked at Cleo. Round button face. Button nose. Button mouth. The button blonde waited tables in a ballplayer's drinking spot called Temperance House.

"I was wondering, Ralph, if your pecker is as sturdy as the rest of you, because if it is, you'd make one hell of a lay."

Kauff made a joyous, yelping noise.

"Just like that?" Johnny said. "Are you that easy?"

"I need two tickets for tomorrow's game," Cleo said.

"I'll get you four tickets," Kauff said.

"I'd like to try you second, Mr. Longboat." Cleo, the button blonde, walked into Room 1056, unbuttoning her blouse.

"Wait till I close the door," Kauff said, in a shrill tone. "You know we got a manager on this club."

"Sure I know," Cleo said. "He's drinking stingers downstairs. You don't have to worry about *him*." She closed the door. "I'll take you both on, and any other ballplayers. Somebody got a joint?" She tossed her blouse onto Kauff's bed.

John closed *The Magus*, marking his place with a fly-leaf. "We don't use joints during the baseball season," he said.

"I can maybe get you some from Daryl Coyle," Kauff said.

Cleo snapped off her skirt and her bra. She stood in front of the door wearing only flesh-colored panty hose. The button blonde had little round breasts and you could see that her pubic triangle was dark.

"Your hair doesn't match," Johnny said.

"I wouldn't dare use peroxide down there," Cleo said. "Peroxide can burn."

"Who cares about hair?" Kauff said.

"Now you do, Ralph," Johnny said. "You told me that after Maudie Sue won the Miss Bluebell contest in New Braunfels, and you finally got her to bed, you liked how the hair on her head matched the hair around her pussy."

"You crazy, John? You trying to kill something live. Don't you mention Maudie Sue."

"Who's Maudie Sue?" Cleo asked.

"His wife," Johnny said.

Cleo drew off her panty hose without pause. "Why should I care about her? She isn't here."

"I'll call Daryl about the joint," Kauff said.

Soon Coyle, and three other Mohawks were convening in Room 1056. Cleo asked them all to sit on the beds while she performed a "secret Oriental belly dance. And please," she said, "don't nobody touch me until my Oriental dance is over."

"Okay, but then make way," said Coyle. He was a thin-nosed man from Quincy, Massachusetts, who looked like an undernourished priest.

Undernourished, Johnny thought, and excommunicated. "Make way for what?" he said to Coyle.

"Make way for the last of the great straight up-and-down fuckers."

John moved for the door. "I've got an appointment," he said.

"You're carrying your fucking book," Coyle said.

"It's an appointment to give a reading," Johnny said. "Say, I hope you guys make out." John read *The Magus* in the lobby for two hours.

The next evening in Room 1056 at the Pennsgrove, John told Kauff a traveling man's joke.

"Hello, baby," says the traveling man. "Let's fuck."

"Okay, you sweet-talking son-of-a-bitch. Your room or mine?"

"Well, if you want to argue, let's forget about it."

Kauff laughed. "For sure, a good one, John," he said.

"I don't know why you press so," Johnny said. "If you have to bang your brains out, go ahead and do it, but relax. There'll always be more talent."

"I ain't smooth like you, John."

"Christ, Ralph, go down to the lobby and look around. Then throw the room key in the air. Somebody will catch it before it hits the rug."

Kauff nodded and left. He returned twelve minutes later with a girl of seventeen, who smiled on and off, a nervous, flickering light of some parents' life. "Ralph," John said, "there are standards. You don't romance children."

The girl, long-faced with straight, dark hair, stopped smiling. "I'm no kid."

"Right," John said, "and Mr. Kauff and I are going to take you downstairs to the Imperial Room where we can have a sophisticated tea."

"She's live," Kauff protested.

"Raunchy," John said, shaking his head.

"I don't much like that word," said the dark-haired girl.

In the Imperial Room, a red-jacketed waiter served tea and scones to Johnny and the girl, whose name was Nancy. Kauff ordered whiskey and ginger ale. Nancy looked pleased to be taking tea, instead of trying a stranger in a hotel bed. "I come from a fine family up in Yardley," she said. "I'm studying art in Philadelphia. I just happen to be crazy about baseball, like my Dad."

"What would your father say," Johnny asked, "if he found out that you were trailing ballplayers to their hotel rooms?"

Nancy bit her lower lip and looked into a blue tea cup. "I never did before. Besides, Daddy couldn't say. He died last week. My Dad is dead."

"Why did you come here?" Johnny said.

"I don't know why I came. I just know I felt like doing something really nutsy, really wild."

"Life is a bitch," Johnny said, "or maybe a bastard." Nancy smiled wet-eyed and Johnny moved the conversation to painting. They parted warmly and a little sadly. "Luck with the brushes," Johnny said. "Stay close to Monet and keep away from deplorable characters like Kauff and me."

"I'm going to root for you every time you pitch," Nancy said, just before she walked out of the Hotel Pennsgrove, with her clothing in place and her dignity intact.

"A real neat one," Kauff said. "It's a damn shame we let her get away."

"Ralph, you know how some ballplayers hire a sportswriter to tell their life story when their careers are finished."

"Sure, Mantle and Musial did that. What are you getting at?"

"Well, because their careers are over, not that many people care. I have another kind of book in mind for you."

"What's that? How you call pitches on the tough hitters?"

"Something more deplorable and more commercial, Ralph. Write about your adventures off the field. Your hits. Your misses. Your after-hours moves."

"You kidding me? I wouldn't even know what to call a book like that."

"I have your title," Johnny said. "I renounce all rights to any similar work. You call it Raunchy Kauff's Book of Baseball Broads."

The trouble with mocking humor is that at length it mocks no one so much as the humorist. Johnny was trying not to be upset by the seventeen-year-old art student named Nancy and by memories of his stumpy, horny friend.

What was he then?

Kauff and Coyle each had a basic baseball wife and moist, interminable histories with basic baseball broads. Johnny forced laughter at their ways, and all the while loved variously both a wife and a mistress. Was he better off, happier, wiser, more grown-up than the swarm of his road-bum colleagues? He went back to Room 1056 and an escape into John Fowles' harsh, white novel.

* * *

Within the sheltering, darkwood den at Moresby Point, Johnny asked Christina if she had spoken to a lawyer about the divorce she had just agreed to cancel.

"Not one but three," she said. "The first two wouldn't help me, because they did business with the Moresbys. Talk about rejections. I've just been turned down twice by men I was offering money."

"So you've spoken to three lawyers."

"Three. You look worried."

205

"Lawyers, doctors, anybody, when they drink, they talk. And if these lawyers talk, gossip reporters can hear them."

"I know that," Chris said. "I don't see why divorce stories are so titillating. What about all of the people who stay married and miserable?"

"Some would argue that's the American way," Johnny said. When Chris didn't smile, he spoke to her intensely. "Where I grew up, people stayed with marriages better than they stayed with churches. My Dad gave my mother a thousand bad times but she stayed with him and after a while, the bad times came less often. It took years and pain, but they got to love each other. In time, they became very kind people. Maybe that will happen with you and Brad. I'm trusting that's what will happen with Becky and me."

Johnny stood and paced the red and dark blue carpet. "Then there's my son, Jerry Lee, named for my father. He's almost seven and, damn, he won't pick up a ball. He plays with blocks and little racing cars and he moves quickly. He's in and out of a room like a chubby cat. But he doesn't like to catch a ball or throw a ball, and I'm waiting for him to come around, so I can teach him a little pitching. Oh, he'll come 'round. I know he will. Soon he'll be old enough to understand the game, so he can come down to Mohawk Stadium and be proud right through his toes, that his father won a big one in the major leagues. The father he lives with and plays with. Not a father living with somebody else. Not a father who's gone and broken up a home."

Intensity was spinning John when Brad Moresby walked into the den. Moresby wore a dark, pin-striped suit, over a blue-checked shirt. His narrow tie was loose; he looked distracted.

Johnny clutched his beer stein. Christina blinked. "I thought you were in Lucaya," she said.

"Nassau," Moresby said. "Whoosh, did I ever have a darn bad time. Every darn wheel in the island was rigged against me. How's that for paranoia? Hello, Johnny."

Did Moresby perceive that the moment was awkward? Did he care?

"Hey, big right-hander," Moresby said. "Why are you sucking a darn brew. How's for a real drink?"

"I'm pitching later," Johnny said.

"A snort in the afternoon clears the head."

Johnny looked at his mistress' husband. "It's just been cleared."

"I'm delighted to have you home," Christina said, "but what brings you back early? Me, I hope." She rose and kissed Moresby drably on a cheek. That is how, John thought, a woman kisses her second favorite brother.

"Primarily you, of course," Moresby said. "Secondarily an empty purse. I tapped out on that wicked sand spit." He laughed and shook his head and winced. He had a pleasant, even-featured face, on which the bulb of the nose was just beginning to swell. His gray eyes lacked intensity. Moresby resembled nothing so much as a road company leading man, whose impressive appearance withers by Act III, even when the theater is underheated.

"Can I have a lollipop, honey?" he said. It was their code word for Jack Daniels over ice. Envy touched Johnny. Even in a wilting marriage, small private talk endures; hearing it can make the most confident lover feel like an intruder.

"Chris," Moresby said, "I've got to talk to John alone."

Her lips pressed tight. "Oh?"

"It's essential, Christina."

"Very well." Her thin-lipped voice cut like a shard of glass. "I'll retire to the laundry room and do your shirts." As she walked out, she touched Johnny's right arm. "Throw strikes tonight."

"There's no better pitch in baseball," Johnny said. The three of them laughed three strained, separate laughs.

But what did Moresby want of him alone? What could the vague, darn Ivy League hockey player have in mind? Johnny thought he knew. He was afraid he knew. And how could he respond?

Look, old fellow. I'm darn sorry I'm fucking your darn wife.

I'm darn sorry, but your wife and I appear to be somewhat in love. My own wife and I also appear to be somewhat in love. All in sport, old fellow. I am darn sorry I'm fucking your wife. But please don't ask me to refrain.

Moresby moved behind the bar and motioned for Johnny to sit on the black leather sofa.

"I feel like standing," Johnny said.

"I'm in real trouble," Moresby said. "I'm in a darn mess of trouble that in a way relates to you."

I'm sorry I'm fucking your wife.

"You can bail me out," Brad said, "if you'll just stop doing what you've been doing and be a darn good guy."

"I am a darn good guy," Johnny said, "most of the time." The word "darn" stuck in his throat like an obscenity. He was more comfortable with ballplayers who used the word "motherfucking" as casually as Bradford Moresby said darn. He preferred vulgarity to what he took as affectation.

Johnny looked at the man behind the bar. Possibly, if Johnny were not careful, there could be a fistfight, a lusty old-fashioned fistfight about Christina. About lean, sparkling, sexual, laughing Christina. Put simply, he could have to fight Brad Moresby for fucking rights to Chris.

Moresby stood six feet one, and trim, with remarkably wide shoulders. The old Princeton hockey player slouched as he stood and the vague eyes suggested a man who had known some fights and felt some beatings. He might not be a hard man to fight, but Johnny didn't want to fight at all. He had to pitch. "I try to be a darn good guy," he said.

"Just groove a couple of pitches once in a while," Moresby said. "That way, both of us can make a fortune."

"I hear you," Johnny said. He was surprised at how loudly he spoke.

Moresby giggled again. "Say, how much do you make from the Mohawks?"

"Seventy-one thousand dollars this year."

"That's nothing," Moresby said. "Nothing for the best young pitcher in baseball. Do you know what Gus Vermont takes out of the game? About $750,000 every season. That's ten times what you do."

"The Mohawk Corporation, or Vermont Industries, makes that much, I guess."

"No. The corporation makes $4 million. Gus likes to live well, and he has nifty tax write-offs, so he personally receives $750,000. Have you seen his place at Hobe Sound? He has his own nine-hole golf course. He takes out three-quarters of a million, you make $71,000, and Gus hasn't gotten a batter out to this day."

"There's always someone richer," Johnny said. "Anyway I don't like golf and besides, no matter how much you make, there's always someone richer."

"Sure, and his name is Nelson Rockefeller. But you're not getting your darn share out of your own work. That's something that could be straightened out by my group."

"Group?"

"A darn nice bunch of guys, from all walks."

"The word you mean," Johnny said, "is syndicate."

Moresby laughed as he poured his third bourbon. "You see too many movies on the road. You think of Sicilians who need a shave. I'm in a group with darn good guys. They like sports and they like to bet sports and win. That doesn't exactly violate the Ten Commandments."

"No. It only violates the law."

"But the law itself is crazy. Inside the cyclone fence at Belmont Park, a bettor is a sportsman. Go outside, go outside by one yard, and the same bet makes you a criminal. Hey, John? Do we have to be crazy because the laws are crazy?"

Johnny's face darkened. He did watch televised movies when he traveled and he thought, corruption, if it came at him, would sound through the voice of a heavy-jowled man, who chewed a cigar and wore a hand-painted necktie, showing a strip-teaser whose breasts went incandescent in the dark. But the bribe was being offered by a narrow-tied Ivy Leaguer, five steps beyond the famous Juan Gris hallway.

Moresby read John's face and said, "Don't answer yet." Then he began to tell a story.

Almost a dozen men had met once in the old Toots Shor's restaurant on Fifty-second Street in New York. They included a dour, mustached man who had made millions in Manhattan real estate. He took government money to build so-called middle-income housing, but by the time each development was completed, the rents had somehow tripled. He then sold the buildings. Subsequently, he (and certain legislators) shared the profits of the sale, which were five times the original investment. A second party was a lupine, white-eyebrowed Florida broker who specialized in corporate mergers. He had spent nine months in a Federal prison for violating "Full Disclosure" regulations of the Securities and Exchange Commission but all the men gathered under Shor's cavernous stucco ceiling agreed that the broker had done nothing any other broker wouldn't do, given the chance. It was his singular misfortune to stumble into one of Bobby Kennedy's vendettas. "Your liquor sideline put you on old Joe Kennedy's kill list," the Manhattan real estate man told the corporate broker, "and you know how much chance that gave you."

210

"How much?"

"About the same as a drunken, blind man, steering a sports car through a mine field."

There was an executive of a Union Pension Fund, who liked to boast that he'd done well enough so that he would never need a pension himself. A Washington lawyer lobbied for the Arab bloc and, as a sideline, resolved paternity suits filed against Congressmen. There was an "interface" between his activities, the lawyer said. The gathering, nine men in all, surged—a Supreme Court of American power. But to casual customers they looked only like nine middle-aged men, drinking without the sparkle of dates.

The men regarded themselves as sportsmen and as winners. Being a winner was the essence of their camaraderie. "Show me a good loser," the union man said, "and I'll show you a guy whose American Express card has been revoked."

They liked to bet college football—at least two had interests in professional teams—but here they were defeated, often as not, by an anonymous Las Vegas character, called The Wizard of Odds. The Wizard was variously described as "a computer genius," "the best mathematical brain since Einstein," and "a guy who, if he'd gone into coaching football himself, would have made Vince Lombardi seem like a nun."

The Wizard set a betting line for college football games each week, then relayed it on private teletypes to wholesalers, so to speak, who in turn telephoned The Wizard's odds to individual bookmakers. Along the route, everyone paid for The Wizard's service. The Wizard of Odds was reported to be as wealthy as Bob Hope.

Nebraska would defeat Oklahoma by seven points. Yale was six points better than Cornell. Texas over L.S.U. by fourteen. This information flashed through integrated circuits to Houston, Seattle, New Orleans, Palm Springs,

New York—anywhere bookmakers flourished, which was everywhere, except, perhaps, Bountiful, Utah.

After three years of uneven results against The Wizard, the lupine, brush-browed Florida broker made a proposal.

"Premise," said the man, who talked in memorandums. "The Wizard may not be the second coming of Einstein. He may simply garner information that we lack.

"Probability: He has informants working on college campuses, possibly team managers or student sports-writers."

"You sure as shit can't trust the kids after Vietnam," the union man said. Others frowned at the interruption.

"Solution," said the memo-talking broker. "Engage our own informants on the campuses. Pay them a fixed retainer, with variable bonuses for winning results."

"That would even things," said the union man, whose jowls did not disguise a light-heavyweight boxer's face. "Betting's a little like collective bargaining and for bargaining to work, both sides have got to have input. The fucking thing here . . ."

"Who'll bell the cat?" the Washington lawyer said.

"Final point, preceding suggestion," said the Florida broker. "Assistant college football coaches are poorly paid. Example: When George Steinbrenner, the Great Lakes shipping guy, coached at Purdue, he was trying to borrow money from his father."

"The next step is obvious," said the union man.

"Not at all," the lawyer said. "Whom can we get to recruit our informant coaches?"

"I've done preliminary work," the Florida investor said. He ordered a white telephone from a swarthy captain and placed two calls. He first reached a legendary baseball manager who lived in Rancho Mirage, outside Palm Springs, and who, since his last and apparently final firing, was spending nine hundred dollars a month more than he drew from pension and lecture fees. "Father-and-son banquets," said the manager, "pay cowshit." He next found, at a country club near Elkhart, Indiana, a storied Midwestern football coach, who had been dismissed for what he regarded as a minor malfeasance. He had seduced the nineteen-year-old daughter of the university chancellor and, suddenly impotent, spanked her vigorously. He was affluent, thanks to investment advice from the brush-browed Florida broker, but unemployed, unemployable, and bitter. He believed the girl's father, the chancellor, had spread gossip among the directors of universities, alleging that he was "a moral leper."

Both the legendary manager and the storied coach agreed to start work for The Group at a retainer of nine hundred dollars a month. They would travel, first-class fare paid, and meet informally with assistant college coaches who admired them. They would elicit information on the health and attitude of important college players. Then, proceeding slowly, very slowly, over many visits and many weeks, they would draw out information on the general strategy, the so-called game plan, that the college team would follow. Through the legendary manager and the storied coach The Group would give assistant college football coaches cash rewards.

"Now hold it," said the union man. "Suppose the Feds find out? You know what they been doing to Jimmy Hoffa."

"Item One," said the man from Florida. "We deal, like in the movies, with small, unmarked bills. Item Two: The President, Mr. Nixon, is a sports nut. Item Three: He's scared to death that he's going to be voted out next year. Conclusion: He wouldn't dare run for Pennsylvania Avenue on a platform that includes indictments of two great sports heroes."

"If you weren't an ex-con," the Washington lawyer said, "you could have been one hell of a president. You'd have made Harding and Grant look like minor-leaguers."

213

"Which they were."

"Double-brandy all around," said the large-jowled union man.

Bradford Moresby told Johnny that all he himself remembered saying was "darn."

* * *

According to Moresby, The Group was prospering. Not every bet worked. Sometimes a sore-armed college quarterback recovered with the bubbling blood of youth and surprised everyone with three touchdown passes. Sometimes a head coach changed his game plan Saturday morning. Some games turned on luck.

"Gambling is a darn risky business," Moresby said in the darkwood den, "but we're way ahead in football. The important thing is that we're making The Wizard of Odds a loser. The most important thing is that I'm a winner now."

"Why talk to me?" Johnny Longboat said.

"Because roulette wheels on the sand spits and baseball betting chew me up."

"I can't believe the story," Johnny said. "I don't want to believe the story. If you know about it, a lot of people do. What about the writers?"

Moresby had a scorn for journalism common to wealthy men. Journalists were people who had never fixed on a career. Journalism was nobody's ambition. It was the loser's walk away from utter rout. "We've got guys in our group who *own* newspapers," he said, "and own newspapermen."

"The attorney general," Johnny said.

Moresby's right hand quivered as he drank his tepid lollipop of bourbon. But he was growing stronger. "Bobby Kennedy," he said, "got himself a reputation as an incorruptible man, am I right? I mean forgetting the darn Marilyn Monroe stuff. Bobby was supposed to be beyond corruption."

214

Johnny wanted to sprint for his car, but he wanted more to hear about Bobby Kennedy.

"I've been betting a darn long time," Moresby said, "and bettors hear about other bettors, the way pitchers find out about other pitchers."

"No," Johnny said. "We hear about batters. What do I care what Tommy Seaver's throwing? He could send his fastball through the postal service and I still couldn't hit it."

"All right," Moresby said. "That's a darn point The Group is glad to know. Anyway, after old rapacious Joe Kennedy made his fortune and his sons, he only cared about three things. One was the Catholic Church; he figured he had more to confess than anybody. The other was Gloria Swanson; that stuff will come out in some journalist's smut book. Winning bets. That was the third big thing for old man Kennedy.

"Now Joe wasn't crazy about the Jews, but he had a buddy named Carroll Rosenbloom, who owned the football team in Baltimore. Darn wonderful team; you couldn't beat them. But they could win by twenty-seven points or seven. The two, Joe and Rosenbloom, bet a fortune and they won a fortune, betting different ways, different weeks, for and against the Colts. They used parties, maybe fifth parties, to handle the cash, but they sure knew about the betting wires themselves. They darn well knew about The Wizard of Odds.

"You couldn't bribe Joe's boy Bobby Kennedy with cash and Bobby wanted to do nice things for the Negroes. A good man and I wish the Arab's bullet had missed. But Bobby was quick and tough and informed and he darn well knew about The Wizard's wire. I hear he even knew The Wizard's name. Then he closed his eyes. Why? He sure as darn hell wasn't going to run an investigation that would lead up to Daddy's electric gate in Hyannisport."

"I guess," John said, "it makes sense. It makes sense at

least the way you tell it." He frantically thought of Marilyn Monroe. The itinerant wiseacre manager, Frenchy Boucher, claimed he had been with her and that blonde as she looked, the pubic hair was dark. Johnny grabbed a drink, three fingers of Scotch neat.

A long sip calmed him. He extended his neck to let the Scotch spill more gradually down his throat. "We better forget this," Johnny said.

"You can't forget what's happened."

"Nothing's happened yet, except talk. My contract with the Mohawks specifies that I have to report any approaches from gamblers. So does baseball Rule 21A. I don't have the words verbatim, but I know the sense. Look, I'm willing to bend a little. You're not a guy I'd want to hurt and besides, you've been talking football and all you've given me is hearsay. That's why I'm willing to bend."

Conscience struck behind his eyes and Johnny saw the den as a dark blur. Hearsay? Football? *He was thinking like a cheating tax accountant.* He thought the name, Christina, and his mind cleared and he could see.

"What do you want from me?" Johnny said.

"You start almost forty games a year," Moresby said. "Not all are equally darn important. Now take tonight. The Mohawks are in first place by a mile. According to The Wizard, you against Chicago is a two-and-a-half-to-one bet. Well, groove a few. Throw fastballs down the middle. Promise me that and you can have fifteen thousand dollars in small bills now."

Moresby killed his lollipop of bourbon. "In a month you'll double your income, tax-free. In a few years you'll have your own golf course, like Gus Vermont."

"Good hitters can pop up fastballs down the middle."

"That's the darn beauty part for you," Moresby said. "The Group isn't asking for guarantees. And they aren't asking you to groove pitches every game. Just like now, when the Mohawks have a darn fat lead and the darn betting price is good. What are we talking about, five or six games, fifty or sixty pitches out of three thousand? We'll have spotters behind the plate at Mohawk Stadium. If grooved fastballs get popped up, that's our problem not yours. In fact, I'm supposed to be one of three spotters tonight."

"*Not* grooving pitches is what I do," Johnny said, "for seventy-one thousand dollars a year. All right. After taxes that's no fortune, but my wife and I don't lack material things. We have a nice house in Ridgefield, Connecticut, with a mortgage I can handle. We have a pool. We aren't suffering."

Moresby face had been changing. He had straightened his tie and his gray eyes were flat and hard.

"What kind of car do you drive?"

"An Olds wagon."

"That's a shoe salesman's car. Wouldn't you rather drive an XKE?"

"Subject to oil leaks," Johnny said, "but, sure, I'd want a Porche Turbo Carerra."

"Your down payment is in my pocket," Moresby said.

"But I can live without the Porsche and the damn last thing that I could live with is knowing that I'd let crooks into baseball."

"Crooks," Moresby said. He put a strong hand gently on Johnny's shoulder. "You're sure a darn, nice, naive Okie kid. The crooks have been there for years, only they're called magnates in the papers. They skim on admissions and cheat the tax people with double-entry bookkeeping. They buy some Congressmen and get a tax-depreciation law that's thievery."

"I'm a ballplayer," Johnny said. "I do my work and feed my family and give some people joy. They think I'm a hero. But I've got heroes myself. Babe Ruth, the first man to hit sixty homers. Joe DiMaggio, who hit in fifty-six straight games. Jackie Robinson, the first black in the Hall of Fame. Now you want me to be the first modern pitcher to dump a dozen games."

"I've said all I intend to say, but you might not be the first. There might be others."

Johnny slammed his crystal old-fashioned glass against a coaster on the bar. Christina appeared in a pale blue dress and asked Brad to take her to the game.

"You bet," Moresby said. "This is one I really want to watch.

"You bet," Johnny said. "I don't."

* * *

That night Johnny pitched a three-hit shutout against Chicago. He also doubled home two runs. The Mohawks won, 4–0. Johnny was out the down payment on the Porsche Turbo Carrera and Brad Moresby and The Group had Johnny's answer. It spoke thunder.

* * *

The clubhouse telephone rang nine minutes after the game and Doc Youmans, the trainer, said it was "a broad for Mister Longboat."

"Hey-up," Daryl Coyle shouted, "do to her what you did to Chicago."

"I get that," Raunchy Kauff said. "You mean he'll fuck two in one night."

"When you die, Kauff," Daryl Coyle said, "I'm going to have your brain sent to the Smithsonian Institution. There's a spot waiting for you in a section called Advanced Monkeys."

The carpeted clubhouse resounded with ballplayers who whooped in victory.

"I heard," Christina said on the clubhouse phone.

"You'll have to speak up," Johnny said. "The boys are noisy." He covered his left ear with a finger.

"I heard about the gambling," Chris said.

218

"Don't say any more about that on this phone. Where's Brad?"

"He's in the Wahoo Room. He's drinking hard with buddies. I'm calling from a booth in an empty corridor that's full of dirty hot dog wrappers. I admire what you did tonight. I love what you did tonight. I'm feeling sad."

"Look," Johnny said. "I mean listen. Listen as hard as you ever have."

"Okay." Christina was beginning to cry.

"Except for the pitching, I've messed up my life in a lot of crazy ways. I can't go on messing your life, too."

"Hey-up, Johnny," roared Doc Youmans. "What a ball game you just pitched."

Christina made a restrained wail.

"I'm a country kid in a big city," Johnny said into the telephone, "who's messed up some and sure as hell will mess up more."

"No." Her voice was tight. "You're so much more than you realize."

"I can't go to Moresby Point ever again."

Now *she* was stronger. "I realize that."

"Please now." His own voice was choking. "Don't interrupt me. Let me finish."

" 'Atta fucking ball game," yelled Dwayne Tucker.

"I've tried to give you the best of me, Chrissie. And I've learned so much from you. So much. I've grown up enough to realize that I can't contend with my life. Listen, now, Chrissie. Hear me. I have to give you up."

"Just because you can't come to Moresby Point?"

"I'm trying to say good-bye. You go ahead with your life. Forget me. Do great things. You—" he choked and sobbed—"you are my life."

Christina said, "We can still meet in quiet hotels. We can meet in little country hideouts."

"I can't meet with you in one-night cheap places."

"No motel room I ever shared with you Johnny, if you'll still have me, could be one-night cheap."

So they agreed on two telephones in a ballpark, that they would stay together as best they could.

Johnny was crying as he hung up. He did not sob, but tears of silence ran on his cheeks.

"Big Chief?" Doc Youmans said. "Your arm hurting you real bad?"

Johnny shook his head and thought the word "Christina," and noticed through tears that Daryl Coyle was snapping a blue-and-white Mohawk towel toward the glans of Ralph Kauff's short, stubby penis.

* * *

John now had to answer the sportswriters' questions, while sitting on his three-legged stool. "I'm lousy copy tonight," he began. "Everything went smooth. You guys would say routine. The slider worked. The change was good. I was watching the corners. Kauff called an excellent game. So did the umpire."

"What about your two-base hit?" Rob Brownell said.

"I've been swinging for that since I was seven years old. After Koufax, I'm the next worst hitter in modern baseball. I always seem to swing in the same plane. The poor bastard pitching for Chicago just happened to throw one into my blind-swinging plane. A thousand-to-one-shot. Okay guys. Let me dress, huh?"

The reporters milled toward the manager's blue-and-white office. "Rob," Johnny said, sharply to Brownell. "I have something for you. Complicated."

"I have to write," Brownell said.

"Say two hours from now in P. J. Clarke's. I'll take a table in the back room."

Wally, the short, scraping maitre d' at Clarke's, asked Johnny why he'd been such a stranger. "Sometime," he said, "you ought to bring me an autographed ball."

"Will you settle tonight for an autographed cocktail napkin?"

"I will," Wally said, "and that's one free drink. There's a good group. Hedy Lamarr. You're too young to remember *Ecstasy*. Richard Boone. Dave Brinkley. We're just missing Jackie O., the Queen."

"I need a two," Johnny said. "When Rob Brownell from the *Standard* comes, send him back."

"Okay, Johnny, but keep him close to you. We don't want him interviewing the clients here. You know the show 'Meet the Press.' Here we have to say, 'Fuck the Press.' "

Brownell and Johnny sat at a rickety table in the back room, which was lighted so cleverly that it would have depressed a plastic surgeon. You could see the sculpted features of people whom gossip columnists dog, but you could not see the crow lines at their eyes or the rooster wattles at their necks. "I don't come here much," Brownell said, "but the way some genius has this lighted makes me think of the opening to *Cabaret*. The men are beautiful. The women are beautiful. Even the bartenders are beautiful."

They ordered Watney ale, on draught. "And even the *brew* is beautiful," Brownell said. "I wish I could afford to drink here more often."

Johnny recounted Moresby's story and the bribe offer.

"I've heard," Brownell said. He drank hard, a small, decent, kindly, sometimes sorrowful man. "Not in all that detail, of course. But conspirators who conspire at Toots Shor's ain't exactly Caesar's wife."

"Meaning?" John said.

"They're not above suspicion. Some word gets out."

"I want you to write this whole fucking thing," Johnny said.

"There's a helluva risk involved," Brownell said. "It's known as libel."

"What do they call the thing that you guys like to win? The Pulitzer Prize."

"I can't write it. Not even a line. I've discussed these gambling rumors with Max Taylor, our managing editor. He's a good Groton guy, as much as any managing editor can be a good guy. He balances power and peril and his own sense of righteousness. What's good for the paper? What's good for circulation? What's good for the country? What's good for the onrushing career of Max Ballard Taylor III? How's that for an anticlimax?"

"It's like another newspaperman's anticlimax. For God, for Country, and for Yale. I think they told me the writer's name was Brown."

"Broun," Brownell said. "Heywood Broun. A Mathewson of columnists. A Big Six."

At the next table, the actor Richard Boone shouted at a waiter that he wanted acquavit in his martini, not, goddamn Polski vodka.

"Sorry, Mr. Boone. We fix that up right now. But *please* lower your voice."

"That waiter," Brownell said, "is showing us how to use the words of a lance corporal with the manner of a brigadier." He drained his Watney's and asked politely for another stein. "Max Taylor has that manner," Brownell said. "He is courteous and nicely bred and indisputably the boss. He works with a balance scale of many platforms. I've heard him say that certain stories were worth the ultimate risk: turning over the keys to the executive suite at the *Standard* and losing his own five-story brownstone to a fleecing libel lawyer. He means some pieces are so important that you risk a ruinous libel suit. He says that rule went for something like turning around the war in Vietnam. He says no baseball gambling story could ever be worth that risk."

"I can't believe this," Johnny said. "I can't believe the

First Amendment is a bunch of curveballs, like the standard baseball contract."

"Max likes his house," said Rob Brownell.

"Can't you go over Taylor's head, to the chief lawyer at the *Standard*?"

"I like my house, too," Brownell said, "and my forest of native spruce trees in Katonah. The chief corporation counsel for the *Standard* is an old Princeton tackle, called Eddie Klinch, who represents not only the *Standard* but certain Moresby interests. Turning in a Moresby to Big Ed Klinch would be giving up my baseball writing job. They'd have me typing lists of ship arrivals and departures by five o'clock that day."

The maitre d' named Wally interrupted, bearing a National League baseball as though it were the philosophers' stone. "I'm the only guy allowed to interrupt our guests," he said. "Sign this to Elizabeth Searing."

John wrote, as ballplayers learned to write autographs, holding the pen vertically against the baseball. He finished with "always my best, whoever you are."

"Two more Watneys for the gentlemen," Frankie cried.

"It really could be some story," Johnny told Brownell.

"Agreed."

"Maybe you and I could work with the district attorney."

"He's a tired old man named Hogan, with forty variously venal assistants."

"So?"

"The world isn't turned by a bunch of lanky cotton-pullers like you, John. Half these D.A.'s want Frank Hogan's job. They work for a good press. They all have favorite newspaper guys. You know what a leak is?"

"It's what we'll need after finishing Frankie's free Watneys."

"Don't be joking, now, John. Don't use humor to put

223

off serious thought. The woman. It's inevitable that something will come out about you and the woman."

Johnny looked through Clarke's artful half-light. A white hand stroked a coffee-tan arm. A man sat back, languid, confident—and the woman facing him spoke quickly in Italian. She was holding her torso erect. Damn, Johnny thought, he wasn't the only man with a mistress and he sure wasn't a road-bum ballplayer. He wasn't the only one who played beyond the field, but that didn't make it right. How could he ever justify hurting Becky Rae?

"Rob, you know about Christina?" John's words hurt as he spoke and he felt pain, as a boxer feels pain, when he is punched below the heart.

"I know. Other sportswriters know. Max Taylor loves gossip. I'll bet he knows."

"Then why the hell hasn't it been in print?"

"Does it ever strike you that journalists are capable of being decent?"

"Some, but I've seen awfully sloppy stuff."

"We don't have mighty company unions like doctors or lawyers," Brownell said. "Making the mortgage payment scares a lot of us. The doctors' union and the lawyers' union call themselves professional associations and they make up complex codes of ethics. But get in trouble with a doctor and a lawyer and you'll find out who the ethical codes protect. The professional men. Not the customer.

"Now journalists aren't really professionals. Professionals have licenses and usually run their own businesses. Journalists, including sportwriters, are at most craftsmen, which is an honorable estate."

"If you behave honorably," Johnny said.

"Let me finish," Brownell said. The ale was making him aggressive. He pointed a curling index finger at John.

"We have to make up our own ethics, while we worry about the mortgage, which is harder than wrapping yourself in a set of self-protective rules that other guys figured out. Now my rule, and it's the rule of most good journalists I know, is turn it around. Ask how would I like what I'm writing, if it were written about me?

"Am I drunk, or for whatever reason, close to deadline, so that I report a double as a triple? Inept, but harmless.

"Am I so drunk I throw in items short of libel about a black rookie making it with a white pop singer? So drunk, I threaten two marriages when my assignment is to write who won the game? That would be unconscionable and I should have my license to write pulled, except under the First Amendment journalists can't be licensed."

The ale was also making Brownell prolix. "You're talking mostly about drinking," Johnny said. "I was talking about Christina."

"You think," Brownell said, with thick lyricism, "Christina is unique?"

"Yes."

"Ah," Brownell said, and quaffed. " 'Chris' as in the fabled Son of God. 'Tin,' not as in base metal but in long, *teen* thighs, as yet undimpled. 'A,' as in the cry of sexual release. Christina. Damn, Nabokov would have done it better."

"You're drunk," Johnny said.

"Prefer tipsy," Brownell said. "That happens to be the word that I prefer. But not so tipsy as you might imagine, old cotton-puller. Christina is not unique."

"She is to me," John said. "Hey, waiter. Bring us coffee and a check."

"Shakespeare has had his Christina. Max Ballard Taylor III has his Christina. Brad Moresby may have a private Christina, too."

"And you?" Johnny said. Where was the damn coffee? Where was the fucking check?

"Not like yours," Brownell said. "She was a book saleswoman at Famous-Barr in St. Louis. Her thighs were badly dimpled and I was not the first. Far from the first. But we had moments. Her moments. My moments. The best were reading passages from Shakespeare, when we were naked in Room 802 of the Park Plaza Hotel. The best was not the obvious. 'My naked weapon is out.' *Romeo and Juliet*, Act I, Scene 1. Nor even Act I, Scene 4, 'This is the hag, when maids lie on their backs, that presses them and learns them first to bear, Making them women of good carriage.' "

"What was the best?" Johnny said.

"As I told you, we were naked and my Christina, whose name was Jewell, read, 'The bawdy hand of the dial is at the prick of noon.' 'Your hand,' she added. 'My dial.' "

"Life turns on moments like that," Johnny said, "although I'm not real good at Shakespeare."

"Turns?" Brownell said. "It fairly sprouts and germinates and flowers. There is a child in a modest house, near Lindbergh Road now, who bears my seed but not my name. That's why I'm broke."

"You want another beer, or something harder?" Johnny said.

"All I want is a quiet bed now, Johnny, and you not blaming yourself. There is a time that grips you, Johnny— you, me, everybody with decent normal sex drive—when something bellows, 'Reproduce the race.' It's like a powder charge that anything can blow. A tone of voice. A crack showing between a lovely woman's thighs. A cry for help. Even, forgive me if I sound like Studs Terkel, the fuzz that grows around a woman's anus."

"I'm gonna take you home," said Johnny.

"Wait," Brownell said. "Hear me for my cause—our cause—then take me home. Don't fight the Christina thing. Love her and Becky and make them both as happy as fuzzy birds."

"I got to deal with the gambling thing," Johnny said.

226

"The Commissioner has brightened the lives of fuzzy birds," Brownell said.

"Amory Moresby? The Nuclear Admiral? He sleeps around?"

"When he was at the Pentagon," Brownell said, "his nickname was The Nookie Admiral."

"Well, goddamn," Johnny said.

"Well, goddamn," Brownell said. "But you get older and the bawdy hand of the dial turns down toward 6:30, and stays there round the clock."

"I got to read more Shakespeare," Johnny said.

Brownell made a muttering sound into his beer stein.

"And I got to settle this gambling thing."

Looking worn as a sea-scraped Triton, Brownell said, "Go see the Commissioner. I'm going home and I'll get sober."

"Would you type up a memorandum of this conversation?"

"Why?"

"To protect me. Sort of guarantee my security down there."

"A guarantee," Brownell said, "is what comes with Pinto cars." He drained his Watney. "As I see it, this is you against the Commissioner, corruption against integrity, and it's also Christina against Becky Rae. A damn memo from me would be just worthless."

"Why?" Johnny said again.

"Remember this. Remember this thing. Blood is thicker than baseball." Brownell rose, leaning on the table. "Shit," he said. "Blood is liquid and a baseball is solid. As usual, my image doesn't work."

Chapter 9
Easton, Maryland, 1972

SOME OF THE sports columnists described the Commissioner of Baseball as "The Great Stone Face," but the nickname never really took hold, possibly because the young people who followed their columns no longer were required to read Nathaniel Hawthorne's short stories. The grand tale of that granite visage set godlike on a godlike mountain now was as obscure to many as the codes of Zoroaster.

"Hawthorne and Melville," Rob Brownell complained to Townsend Wade. "There should be a law that says no one can get a high school diploma unless he reads five hundred pages of each."

"Do you believe President Nixon has read five hundred pages of either?" Wade said in his dry way.

"I'm not even sure that son of a bitch has a high school diploma," Brownell said.

The features of Amory Moresby's face were rather like those of his brother, regular and clearly aristocratic. But where the younger man, who gambled, had a look of eroding elegance, Amory Moresby's face did indeed suggest New England granite. The jaw was strong and square. A strong, slightly bent nose parted the Commissioner's face. His mouth, as one sportswriter put it, "customarily looked as severe as the mouth of a banker who is turning down a request for a loan from an alcoholic." His hair was iron-gray and he stood a lean five foot eleven. Amory Moresby, Czar of Baseball, formerly admiral and chief of staff of the United States Navy, was physically one imposing executive.

"I've looked forward to this meeting," Commissioner Moresby began. "I regard you as an ornament to our game, Johnny."

Silence.

Then Johnny said, "I'm glad you agreed to see us, Commissioner."

Moresby looked pleased. He liked the way the roles were defined. The articulate, possibly overly intelligent, probably overlusty national hero was simply a first name, "Johnny." He alone bore a title. "Commissioner." A title against a first name was an advantage. Doctors learn this early in their art of subduing patients.

"I'm particularly glad you brought your young family, Johnny. I've wanted to meet them, too." Moresby's voice was soft, with a suggestion of the refined South, an accent you might hear in the libraries of Vanderbilt, or at the Naval Academy in Annapolis. "It's because I wanted to meet both you and your family in a relaxed, and, if I do say so, refined, setting, that I've asked you here to Easton, instead of to my office in New York. I think you and your family will find the driving time well spent, even though it's a long trip from New York to the Eastern Shore."

"Also no reporters know I'm here."

The Commissioner had been smiling within his commanding gaze. The smile flew from his face and Johnny thought of a country buzzard taking off at the sound of a shotgun. "Of course," Commissioner Moresby said. "Everyone in public life, from President Nixon on down, has had unpleasant experiences with the press. Now why don't you and your family explore this little place that we call Boxwood? Then we can meet in the main house for lunch. Say one o'clock?"

"When do you and I meet alone?" Johnny said.

"Why, after the soft-shell crab and some cool, pale vintage wine, son. We'll talk more easily then. A full stomach maketh a man mellow."

The estate called Boxwood occupied four hundred yards along a broad, slow-running estuary called Peachblossom Creek. The swimming was good there in June, until the jelly fish moved in. Summer stillness idled on the trees. You could see cottonwoods and dogwoods, and deep red florabunda roses and a bent grass lawn inclining toward Peachblossom Creek. The foliage was tended like a Devonshire garden.

John had put the luggage—the Commissioner recommended at least one change of clothes—in the guest house, a simple, two-story, cream-colored stucco box, with large windows welcoming the sun. Now he and Becky Rae walked along the shining bent grass lawn, the two gazing at Peachblossom Creek, and hearing, perhaps, its songs of summer ease.

"It's a damn hard thing I've got to do," Johnny said. "Turn a man in to his brother."

"Whatever you have to do, you just do, John," Becky Rae said. "You know I'll stand behind you."

"But I'll be in there alone."

"Not really," Becky handed Johnny a note she had printed carefully on pale blue stationery headed, "Mrs. John Lee Longboat."

"You don't want to lose your temper with the Commissioner," Becky said. "In the bar where I had to work, I've seen the crazy things men do when they get mad."

John read the note.

I love you!
Do not lose your temper!!
I love you!!!
Becky Rae.

"If you feel you're getting mad," she said, "just pull out the note and read it. Maybe that will help."

He squeezed her hand. "But suppose I don't get mad and the meeting still goes badly?"

"I've been thinking about that," Becky Rae said. "I think if it starts to go badly, you just excuse yourself."

"Then what?"

"You can always schedule another meeting."

As he walked hand in hand with his wife, whom he believed he loved, whom he believed was a good, loyal, if unexotic woman, he thought about Christina for no reason that he understood. He doubted if Christina, with all the magic of her tanned, downed arms, offered Brad Moresby the support Becky Rae gave so naturally. Or ever had.

"I wish we could live in a place like this," Becky Rae said.

"You know the Longboat family motto," Johnny said.

"Only in Latin," Becky Rae said, and she giggled. "How does it go in English."

"There'll always be somebody richer," Johnny said.

"I thought the motto was 'Life is a bitch,' " she said, "or now that you're getting liberated, 'Life is a bastard.' "

"Uh-uh," Johnny said. "That isn't ours. That's the motto for the whole world."

They paused under an old, surviving elm. He knew he had a better life than Bradford Moresby. A better life and probably a better wife. Why couldn't he content himself with what he had, with a single, loyal, and adoring woman?

231

Brownell had talked of the body, in its strength and sinew, crying out to reproduce the race. Johnny was strong and he knew that he was strong and sometimes his own strength frightened him. He was afraid that a fastball would slip, and a batter would freeze, and the ball would make its hundred-mile-an-hour impact just below the helmet on the batter's brow. The hitter would die. Ray Chapman had died, after Carl Mays fractured his skull with an underhand fastball. When Johnny pitched, he buried this fear so deeply that it actually ceased to exist. The batter was the enemy. You couldn't worry about him while you were pitching, any more than you worried about Japanese beetles when you sprayed pesticide.

But, God, Becky was right about the temper. He could not let his temper loose and with it his great physical strength against the Commissioner of Baseball.

Why did he stray? He didn't know. Why, holding Becky Rae's hand under the elm tree did Christina's lean arms stir his thoughts and, ever so slightly, his loins? The irony suspended in the summer air, as mysterious as the stillness.

He put her note in a back pocket and squeezed Becky Rae's hand again.

"Sometimes I feel I'm losing you," she said.

"You'll never lose me, you or Jerry Lee. I just get restless."

Except for certain stretch marks on her belly, she had not altered much across the seasons. The oval face, framed by a pageboy bob of dark hair, still looked free of care lines. She wore a wraparound denim skirt below a starchy white blouse. She looked like an Akron school teacher, a Tulsa law secretary, or even a waitress in Pittsfield, which she had been. Pretty without being breathtaking. She reminded Johnny of one of those girls in the old Andy Hardy movies, which he sometimes watched very late on the nights before he had to pitch and he felt too tense to read. Crazy, he thought. Your own wife reminding you of somebody you never met with a made-up movie name like Donna Reed.

"Sometimes," Becky Rae said, "I feel I never had you. I was just somebody along the way, you know, like on the road, when you were down because you lost that woman back in Oklahoma."

"Helen," Johnny said. "Her name was Helen Arnett, Becky. But, believe me, that was very long ago."

"Pittsfield and that wonderful crazy manager Harry Schulte were very long ago," Becky Rae said. "But wasn't it easier then? You pitched and you loved to pitch, but you weren't real famous. Now there're reporters and interviews and your name in the New York papers all the time, and if you lose, someone can write you made a stupid pitch and we can't even sue."

"We have a nicer house," Johnny said. "I bought us a really nice colonial in Ridgefield."

"And the Little League people there want you to make seven speeches a week."

"I like helping kids, and if I'm tired, what the hell, we both know how to say 'no.' "

She looked up at him, her face alive with mischief. "Oh?"

"You have your sick headache."

"The doctor calls it a migraine."

"And I have my aching back."

"You're right," Becky Rae said. "We both do know how to say 'no.' " She spun and leaned against the elm and arched her back. "I'd like a kiss," she said.

"Yes," Johnny said, hugging her. "Yes."

When they paused to breathe, she smiled, still leaning lightly against the elm bark. "You know," she said, not harshly, "I've heard about you and Christina Moresby."

He stood straight. His first response was confused anger. The note in his pocket said, "Do not lose your temper," but he was angry at the woman who'd written the note.

"The bloody New York newspapers," he said. He felt relieved. He had directed the anger away from Becky Rae.

"Oh, not the gossip columns," Becky Rae said. "The gossiping wives. The gossiping baseball wives."

"Who?" Johnny said.

"Several."

"Shit."

"But I'm not going to give you any names."

"And I'm not going to lie," Johnny said. "I'm not going to tell you nothing's happened."

"You know I respect that," Becky said. "You know I think that being honest like that is brave."

"It, uh, she"—he did not seem able to articulate Christina's name—"is something I just can't seem to get away from. And I'm sorry because I guess it hurts you."

"If I did it with somebody else," Becky Rae said, "would that hurt you?"

"Have you?" Johnny said, fiercely. "Have you slept with anybody else since we've been married?"

"Once."

"Who?"

"A boy from Pittsfield. He said he was only visiting around New York. You were away."

"A fucking road-bum bush-league ballplayer?"

"No. Please. This is hard, but it's important to me. A junior high school teacher. You never met him. He's five foot four inches tall and he wore eyeglasses."

"Why," Johnny said. "Why dammit? I know my cock is big. Don't I foreplay you enough?"

"No, it isn't that at all. It isn't foreplay. You must read too many sex manuals when you're traveling."

He could not speak.

"It's not mechanical. Women aren't machines. Press the

starter. Touch the throttle. Go! Mr. Vermont told me once to create a stable home. I try."

It was a stable home, Johnny thought. His life was exciting. Winning games was exciting. Even contending with the Commissioner was exciting. But his home and his wife were merely stable. At least for now—he hoped not forever, he could not be sure—he needed more.

Becky Rae turned and walked away from the elm. "I get lonely and when you're lonely it's hard to say no, even though you and I both can say no sometimes, to somebody who makes you feel he really likes you and that you are an important person."

"Oh, Christ," Johnny said. "*I* really like you. You *are* an important person to me."

"But not all of the time."

Anger seized him again and he looked at Becky Rae's soft, wounded face. "Oh, hell," he said. "It's not all right, but it is all right. Do you know what I mean?"

"No."

"I mean I love you and you're important to me and I also mean that I don't own you." He grinned. "I mean this women's independence thing makes a little sense. They tell me women can even vote in elections these days."

"I need things like any other woman," Becky Rae said. "To be kissed and made love to and touched and held. A lot. You can't help the way you are, but you're so much into yourself."

"What a pair we are," Johnny said. "Mr. and Mrs. Adulterer. The priest and the nun."

"I know you have to be into yourself," Becky Rae said, "because the pitching comes so much out of yourself. And all the reporters always asking questions about you. How do *you* feel? How is *your* arm. What did *you* throw. And the children. Can I have *your* autograph. And the groupies. Can I have *you*?"

235

"I've never touched a groupie," Johnny said.

"I love you, Johnny. I love the way you pitch and I love you for taking me out of Pittsfield and I love you for giving me Jerry Lee."

"You've said everything, Beck, except that you love me for myself."

"But I was trying," Becky Rae said. "Maybe if I had a better education, like the other one. She has a better education, doesn't she, Johnny?"

* * *

Wandering quietly, they came to a weathered wooden footbridge over a narrow stream. Beyond they saw Commissioner Moresby's main house, white clapboard with shutters of dark wine. A small, abandoned playground aged to one side. Becky had dressed Jerry Lee in blue and white, the colors of the Mohawks, and the boy was pumping on a rusty swing.

Odd, Johnny thought, when the children grow up, the garden is better tended and the playground rusts. Fifteen feet past the swinging child, a trampoline still looked serviceable.

Seeing his parents, Jerry Lee cautiously slowed the swing. When it had stopped, he waved. Then he climbed awkwardly, blue bottom bulging, onto the trampoline.

"Jump, Jerry," Johnny said. "That's what the thing is for. Jump up and down."

The boy hopped tentatively. As he landed on the resilient canvas, he looked alarmed.

"Jump higher," Johnny said.

"I don't want to jump high," Jerry said. He was small for his age and had his mother's oval face.

"Look, silly," Becky said to her son. She mounted the trampoline and pressing her skirt close to her thighs, leapt gracefully.

"I want to go swimming," Jerry Lee said.

"Jumping is fun," Becky said. She leaped three times, landing on her buttocks, feet extended and bounced to an upright position.

"That's more than all right," Johnny said. "Where did you learn to do that?"

"On the gymnastics team at Nessacus Middle School. We had a marvelous coach, a marvelous fat man named Paul Patrick McKernan."

"Can you flip?"

"Oh, sure. Pat McKernan couldn't bounce, but he could teach."

Still holding her denim skirt to her thighs, Becky leaped into gliding somersaults.

"Mommy," Jerry Lee cried. "Don't hurt yourself, Mommy."

"Mommy's an acrobat," Johnny said. He lay a hand on Jerry's shoulder, as lightly as the landing of a moth.

The Commissioner and his wife appeared silently, studied the family scene—the trampolining mother and the father lightly touching his son—and when Becky Rae finished tumbling, broke into courteous applause.

"What a fine, athletic family, Catherine," Commissioner Moresby said to his wife.

Catherine Moresby was a tall, gaunt woman, whose long face spoke of beauty in her young years, but now bore the look of being hunted. "The toys haven't been used much, since Laurie left our hearth," she said. "There's been nobody to bounce on the trampoline." Mrs. Moresby's dark eyes, which showed flecks of sunlit ocher, reminded Johnny of the eyes he had once seen on the mounted head of a sable antelope.

"Laurie?" Becky Rae said.

"Our daughter," Catherine Moresby said. "She's gone out to a farm near Medford, Oregon. She's a modern young woman, who likes jeans, electric musical instruments, berry picking and—well, we're afraid to think of what else."

"I don't know why she'd prefer such things to Box-wood," Becky said.

"Young people," said Commissioner Moresby, "always look for a place far from where they started. Young people, and I could perhaps include you in that reckless category, Johnny, are not mature enough to understand what the poet wrote."

"Which poet?" Johnny said.

"Thomas Stearns Eliot," the Commissioner said. And he recited:

We shall not cease from exploration
And the end of all our exploring
Will be to arrive where we started
And know the place for the first time.

"The Commissioner loves the modern poets," Catherine Moresby said, "and he has an eidetic memory. Remembers everything."

"I understand you're a closet intellectual yourself, Johnny," the Commissioner said.

"Oh, I can do the crossword puzzle in the *Standard*," Johnny said. "I'm not an intellectual, but I'm good at word games, especially when they ask for a three-letter description for somebody who's overweight that ends with an 'A' and a 'T.' "

"Fat," Jerry Lee said, proudly, and was ignored.

"Baseball," said the Commissioner, "is the most intellectual of our games, particularly when you consider the art of pitching. Yet within the game—among owners as well as you players—one is forever discouraged from showing evidence of intellectual interests."

"On the field, it's the needling, Commissioner," Johnny said. "You don't want the guys in the other dugouts to

238

know anything about you that's different from the way the other guys are. If you're different, like you knowing T. S. Eliot, they call you 'off-horse.' "

"Curious," the Commissoner said. "Say, Johnny, would you and your son like to play catch? We have balls inside and gloves, including some new experimental Japanese models."

"No baseball," Jerry Lee said. "I want to go swimming."

"There are jellyfish in the water, dear," Becky Rae said. "Pretty purple things, but they sting you worse than bees."

"Worse than hornets?"

"Anyway," Johnny said, "the admiral is Commissioner of Baseball, not a swimming coach."

"I don't want to play baseball," Jerry Lee said. "The baseball stings my hand bad as a hornet."

"A will of his own," Catherine Moresby said. "You'd better watch out for that one, Mrs. Longboat. He could end up picking berries in Oregon."

"The soft-shelled crabs are succulent and steaming," Commissioner Moresby said.

"You people have the loveliest house," said Becky Rae.

✳ ✳ ✳

At 3:18, the Commissioner led Johnny into a leaf-shaded sun room, furnished with a small desk, simple hardwood chairs, a flowered settee, and walnut book-shelves. Three electronic data transmitters stood in a corner, and one, clearly a hot line, was colored red. Johnny walked about, hoping to feel less tense, and considered the Commissioner's books. Sailing volumes mingled with poetry and baseball classics. *Pitching in a Pinch*, the Every Boy's Boy Scout Edition of 1912, sat beside Ring Lardner's *Lose With a Smile*, Zane Grey's *The Shortstop*, and *Bang the Drum Slowly*, an abiding work that the author, Mark Harris, completed in 67 days.

239

"Each is autographed, Johnny," the Commissioner said, "and which autograph do you think I prize the most?"

"Well, Harris is alive and replaceable," Johnny said, "and Zane Grey wrote mostly kid stuff, as I understand it."

"Hollywood stuff or kid stuff, indeed," the Commissioner said. "I sometimes think they're the same thing."

"I guess the Ring Lardner autograph," Johnny said.

"Curiously no," said the Commissioner. "It's *Pitching in a Pinch*, ghost-written though it was, signed by the great Mathewson himself. Besides, Lardner had a nasty habit of depicting ballplayers as dolts."

"Hey," Johnny said, "I read a story of his called 'My Roomie' after a ball game I lost in St. Louis in May, and there wasn't a single dolt in it."

"Difference of opinion," the Commissioner said, "makes horse racing, literary criticism, and the baseball player draft."

"What's the red teletype for?" Johnny said.

"A private, absolutely off-the-record hot line, wired into the office of the most important and responsible executive at every ball club office in the major leagues."

"Have you used it?"

"On one or two occasions."

"Like when?"

"There was a transvestite pitcher for Pittsburgh, whom we learned from private sources wanted to go public with a book."

"We all knew about that," Johnny said. "How Patty Wilson liked to put on dresses in the Pittsburgh clubhouse, after the last reporter left."

"And we knew you all knew," the Commissioner said, "but Clause 21F in the baseball *Blue Book* forbids any ballplayer from acting—in this case gossiping—in a manner detrimental to the game. Not that *you* would, but if some dunderhead like your catcher Kauff talked about his sex life to a reporter from a scandal sheet, we'd have an action."

"Kauff is a good catcher," Johnny said. "He calls an intelligent game."

"But the Patty Wilson book was so potentially foul that I wanted a consensus from lawyers for different clubs on preventive action. I got that. The specifics are confidential. Certain ballplayers, not by the way including Kauff, were warned, by certified mail, and their wives were warned as well, not to speak of Patty Wilson, under penalty of suspension without pay. The notes to the wives included even harsher sentences, which I say, regretfully and truthfully, I have forgotten."

"Who thought of that?" Johnny said.

"As it happens, an attorney whom I do *not* reach by the red telex. He represents certain private interests of mine. He's not as famous as Louis Nizer or Ed Williams, but he does well for certain family interests of mine. For me. For my brother, Brad. For Mrs. Moresby. And for my sister-in-law, Christina. His name is Ed Klinch and he is, I assure you, one cold computer mind."

The Commissioner produced two ponies of Remy Martin. It was 3:26.

"Even allowing for Mr. Klinch," Johnny said, "I guess you better make sure the red teletype is plugged in before I start talking."

"It is, son. It's tied to a lock-plug, with an auxiliary generator in the basement."

"Well, let's start," Johnny said, "because I've got to be at Mohawk Stadium for wind sprints tomorrow by eleven in the morning, else I could get fined. That's in the *Blue Book* or the standard contract somewhere."

The face of Commissioner Moresby turned from stone to flesh. He smiled and looked like an avuncular old man. "You can skip a day of wind sprints, Johnny, and you won't be fined, or even reprimanded. I happen to know it's three days before you're supposed to start another game. I'll look after you, son. My rank hath not only privilege but power."

"Here is what I've come to tell you," Johnny said.

"And influence beyond what you imagine. Your arm will go, Johnny. Early Wynn's arm went, and Bobby Feller's arm and Sal Maglie's arm and even the mighty arm of Mathewson. I know certain people at the major networks. I see you, when you can no longer pitch, earning a hundred thousand dollars or so a year for ten years as a color man at a major network. I'm a sailing man but in this job I've had to learn how to make contracts. I'm prepared now to make out that long-term guarantee in writing. Think of it, son. An aggregate million. At least. Ed Klinch will help you with tax shelters. Figuring, roughly, your arm wears out at forty, here's what's ahead. You talk baseball on the networks for ten years. That's in essence a one-day-a-week job, with a small expense account you can cheat on. Ed Klinch assures me you will not have to cheat. Play the game, Johnny, and I mean both baseball and the harder game. Life. Pitch the ball games as only you can pitch them. You can conclude this meeting with my personal guarantee that you'll have a largely tax-free income of a hundred thousand dollars a year, even aside from your baseball pension. You'll have a gorgeous place, like Boxwood, Johnny. Does Santa Barbara appeal to you? Think of it. A home with a pool and a year-round swimming. Play tennis. You'll be club champion in a week and tennis is a pleasing easy game. The ball is soft. You can read and relax . . . I don't mind telling you," the Commissioner said, "I envy you this offer that I'm making."

"I'm here to report, sir," Johnny said, "that your brother has asked me to go into the tank."

The flesh of the Commissioner's face returned to stone.

"Tank? Swimming. I'm not personally sure that swimming during the season would be good for your pitching motion, but in ten minutes I can get a consensus of ortho-pedists."

"He wants me to throw games, Mr. Commissioner. He wants me to dump. He wants me to pitch to lose."

Johnny tried to soften the Commissioner's granite mien. "That's worse, sir, than wearing a dress in the clubhouse."

"Oh, indeed," Commissioner Moresby said.

"And I feel, uh, remedial action should be taken."

The Commissioner held his body so rigidly that he seemed, while sitting behind his desk, to stand at atten-tion. "Your father died of alcoholism," the Commissioner said.

"Yeah. Some guys in Oklahoma used to joke that his liver should be sent to the Hall of Fame for livers."

"But it wasn't funny for you or him or your mother."

"No, sir, it wasn't any funnier than a scream of pain. Daddy was a rugged guy, but he died crying and scream-ing."

"Which is why you limit yourself to two Scotches a day."

"How did you know that, sir?" Johnny said.

The Commissioner rose and walked to a tan box with a green screen. Despite the heat, the Commissioner wore a gray suit, set off against a narrow crimson tie. He punched several keys and the computer began to perform.

Longboat, J. Lee. Pitcher. Born Okla. trailer camp, 1941. Fastball clocked 101.2 mph, July 2, 1962. Mohawks prop. Habits moderate; road deportment good. Married waitress Becky Rae Carpenter, August 4, 1960. Gam-bling connections: none. Closest friend, catcher R. Kauff, cf file #7890-B. Kauff poor road habits, possibly subject paternity suits and/or statutory rape. Recommendation: Discourage J. Longboat discussing Kauff with press. Longboat in long-term affair Christina Moresby, cf file #101529. Moresby woman has met known gamblers. Sexual habits unknown. Recommendation: Encourage

Longboat to sever ties with Moresby woman. Casual encounters safer. Sum: This man, barring injury or scandal, will be in the Hall of Fame.

Johnny wanted to gasp. "Who did this?" he said, "the computer or private cops?"

"Both," Commissioner Moresby said. "We have files on all persons, matter, and data relevant to the game. Would you like to see something more of how it works?"

"I am reporting a bribe offer," Johnny said.

"Yes," the Commissioner said, "and the computer has just reported, on the basis of witness reports, that you are involved in continuous acts of adultery."

"Look," John said, "I'm not perfect. God, who maybe doesn't exist, knows I'm not perfect. But people are trying to turn the game crooked. They'll kill the game." John started to tell the story of the meeting in Shor's. But Commissioner Moresby cut him short. "That's in a computer also. I'll punch that up for you, if you require."

"But they're still trying to bribe guys, Mr. Commissioner. Suppose it wasn't me, but some twenty-thousand-dollar-a-year kid, or a good man, which Ralph Kauff is, who's scared to death of a paternity suit?"

"Son," Commissioner said, standing at last in his admiral's posture. "You had a bad sheep in your family, a drunken dad."

"I resent that," Johnny said.

"And I apologize," said the Commissioner. "I meant only to analogize. Brad is our bad sheep."

"Mr. Commissioner, I'm sorry for your family trouble, but I want a written acknowledgment from you that I've reported the bribe offer from your brother. It says in *Blue Book* Rule 21A, under misconduct, "Any person who shall fail to report solicitation—and it means gambling, not hookers—to the Commissioner, shall be declared permanently ineligible.""

"Trust me, son," the Commissioner said. "I am the Commissioner, not you."

"I want to trust you, sir, but I want the written acknowledgment more."

"No," Commissioner Moresby said.

"No, what?" Johnny said.

"The game is important," the Commissioner said. "The game is magnificent. But I will not turn in one of my own family to a computer, or to the private cops, or to some venal publicity-mad district attorney."

"Then I will," Johnny said. "I'll turn him in somewhere."

"Think of Santa Barbara," the Commissioner said. "Have you ever watched junior champion girls play tennis? Their bodies sleek. Their underarms shaved naked. But once in a while the tailored panties slip and you can see the crack in the buttocks. Sometimes when they serve you see a pubic region that I can only imagine as delicious, in clear outline against the tailored underpants."

The Nuclear Admiral, Rob Brownell said, was also famous as the Nookie Admiral. "You could have them," the Commissioner said, "maybe for as long as you want. We have a subfile on certain junior champions, as sports-related persons. It suggests that they have normal lusts."

"Just write the damn acknowledgment," Johnny said. "Sign it and date it, and we can watch my wife bounce on the trampoline."

"Give up the other woman, Longboat. Thou shalt not have my brother's wife."

"Or else?"

"The computerized reports on your love affair will become public," the Commissioner said. "Exposure of your affair with Christina would not be pleasant for anyone, but I prefer it to prison for my own brother. We have certain writers and columnists who covet information leaks from our machines. Ask Pete Rose. Ask Johnny Bench."

"Meaning?"

The gray-suited, granite-faced Commissioner said, "Your adulterous situation will become public knowledge. You came down here with a cocktail-waitress wife, for whom you have a certain affection, perhaps love."

"Meaning?"

"If you exact a statement from me, I promise that you'll be in every American gossip column by July. By September, divorce court. I rather suspect Eddie Klinch would find someone to represent the cocktail waitress—"

"Her name is Becky Rae," Johnny said.

"For a minimal fee. Or a maximal fee that you'd be stuck with."

"Meaning?"

"You will be a lonely, weeping single man on Christmas Eve," the Commissioner said.

"Anything else I should know about your meaning?"

"Yes. Five words more, in our prolix talk. Leave my brother's wife alone!"

Johnny sprang across the desk and with his left hand lifted the Commissioner of Baseball, a hundred ninety well-conditioned pounds. Grabbing shirt collar and lapels, Johnny slammed the Commissioner against a wall of the sun room at Boxwood. A daguerreotype of Ty Cobb fell to the floor.

Johnny made guttural noises and cocked into a fist the right hand which could throw a baseball 101.2 miles an hour.

He was coherent enough to say one word—"cocksucker"—and to hear the Commissioner shout "Adulterer!" Then Johnny heard an ugly splatting noise. Three breaths later, he realized that Commissioner Moresby had defecated in his pants.

Johnny let his right fist go loose. The meeting was adjourned for a change of linen.

✻ ✻ ✻

"Look, son," the Commissioner said at 4:06. He had seemingly recovered his poise and presence.

"Don't call me 'son,' Amory," Johnny told the Commissioner. "From here on the name is 'Mr. Longboat.' "

"Very well, Mr. Longboat, if that pleases you."

"I want that written acknowledgment of the bribe report."

"We are not enemies, Mr. Longboat, but at this moment, neither are we friends."

"I wouldn't threaten me any more, if I was you." He heard himself make the grammatical error. In a time of tension he had collapsed into rural Oklahoma speech. If this bastard Commissioner ran a divorce suit, Johnny might not make the most eloquent witness for himself. Besides, hell, they had him. How many times can you fuck a beautiful woman without the wrong people finding out? Two times at most, Johnny guessed. Worst of all, he didn't want to lose Jerry Lee and Becky Rae.

"Where are we, Amory?" Johnny said.

"Well, *Mister* Longboat . . ."

"Save your sarcasm for Charley Finley. I know he hates you."

"We are at the point where the broadcasting offer has been withdrawn." Moresby had changed not only his underpants, but his suit. He now wore a solid charcoal brown. "Other athletes are as well-spoken as you. We are at the point where you'd better forget Santa Barbara."

"I can accept that," Johnny said. "There's other places."

"And I am now formally withdrawing my warning to destroy your marriage."

"Can I have the written statement on the bribe offer?"

"And I am imploring you not to ask me for that. You could lose it, misplace it. The press."

"I'll put it in my vault at the Irving Trust Company,

245 Park Avenue. I won't even tell my banker, Tom Heckman. I will tell nobody."

"Will you give up the woman, my brother's wife?"

"No, sir."

"Then we're back to square one, or perhaps two. I have your report. I have heard it. You go forth and win twenty-five games. I will handle the gambling problem, which is, after all, an aspect of the Commissioner's job."

"You know what will happen without your written note," Johnny said mildly.

"Nothing. That's what I'm trying to tell you, son. Nothing will happen."

"Wrong," Johnny said. "I'm going to beat the shit out of you. Painfully. And while you're lying on the floor and ruining another set of underpants, I'm going to punch everything that's happened into that computer machinery. By then, you'll be coming to. I'll cuff you some more. Then I'm going to call Ben Bradlee at *The Washington Post* or Abe Rosenthal at *The New York Times*. Whichever I get first. You know the press, Commissioner. I kind of like the press, Mr. Commissioner. When you win as many as I win, you don't just meet the sportswriters. You get to some stylish luncheons in newspaper executive dining rooms. Your brother bets, Amory. You want to make a bet with me?"

"On what issue?" Moresby said. "At what odds?"

"That by the time I'm through cuffing you, punching the computers, and using your phone—and I ain't gonna call Rosenthal or Bradley collect—this story will have a place on the front pages of tomorrow's *New York Times* and *Washington Post*. And after that you'll get to read a couple of columns neither you nor that Ed Klinch guy will forget."

"You'll be arrested for criminal assault."

"I can accept that, too," Johnny said, "and here's a second bet for you. That if you hit me with the mud about

Christina—" his throat caught. Christina and mud. They didn't match any more than roses matched excrement. "That if you hit me with mud, my wife, Becky Rae, will still stay with me."

"A good woman doesn't like to go through shit," Moresby said.

"That may be." Suddenly Becky Rae, not Christina, was the flower. "But if they have to they can. Roses grow beautifully through manure."

"You're a reckless man, Mr. Longboat."

"I'm a ballplayer and I have to risk every day I pitch. Do you know what a line drive back at the mound can do to your face or your nuts? Destruction. That's what it can do. But consider your own risk. No more Nuclear Admiral. No more Mr. Commissioner. Just time, nothing but time, to ride your Gravely tractor around Boxwood."

The Commissioner began to write, beginning with the date.

"Use carbon," Johnny said.

"If you were more observant you'd have noted the Xerox among the computers."

The Commissioner wrote with calligraphic beauty.

> *July 7, 1972*
> *Bribe from Bradford Moresby reported to this*
> *office on this day by pitcher J. Longboat of*
> *New York Mohawks.*
> *Amory Moresby, Commissioner*

"Two Xerox copies," Johnny ordered, "one for you."
"Why the third?"

"That goes to Becky Rae's vault in a bank in Connecticut, just in case the Irving Trust burns down."

＊　＊　＊

"You realize you are losing the broadcasting job."
"We've discussed that."

"You realize also that your arm will go. Koufax's arm

went overnight. And if, in your declining years, certain of my close professional friends, such as Walter O'Malley of the Dodgers, ask about employing you for spot pitching, I am going to inform them in full candor that I don't recommend their employing you at all. I know what you are, Longboat. A troublemaker. A Bolshevik. A baseball Bolshevik."

It was only when Johnny placed into his left hip pocket two copies of the Commissioner's written statement that he remembered the other note concealed there. Becky's loving warning against losing his temper.

"I'm tired of this, Amory," Johnny said.

"Not nearly so tired as I."

"So I'll be saying good-bye to your wife, but I want to ask a question first."

"So long as it's brief."

"We're on the same side. We don't want fixed games. So what the hell was all the fuss about?"

"My brother, whose keeper I am not. My brother's wife." The Commissioner stood naval-erect in his clean brown suit. "I am going to make a little metaphor here that may sound fused or indistinct."

"What's that?"

"Blood is thicker than baseball."

"I've heard that before," Johnny said.

* * *

As he drove the station wagon north, past the ultra-green of Maryland fields, Becky Rae said, "Did you remember my note? Did you control your temper?"

"Sort of, but I did lose my temper. I went after him."

"And?"

"Terror. Nobody will ever call Amory Moresby a tight-assed Commissioner again."

After a time Becky Rae said, "Gross." But she smiled.

Chapter 10
2:17 P.M., October 14

JOHN'S FIRST warm-up pitch in the sixth inning surprised him. He rocked and threw a medium-speed fastball, and the pitch fled from his fingers, a crossbowman's arrow. He hadn't pushed or overthrown the baseball. Near the plate it sailed upward and crashed into Raunchy Kauff's glove. Kauff blinked. "Nice drill," he shouted.

John threw again, letting the power flow from his right ankle, through his calf and thigh, and up his back. Another popping fastball.

He felt dull pain in his shoulder, but the pain and these fastballs were unrelated. He noticed the next hitter, Fleetwood "Hometown" Brown, a free spirit from the projects on the South Side of Chicago. Brown's eyes widened.

At the fifth warm-up, John threw a curve. The ball broke sharply. He threw another, then a fastball, and concluded by throwing a fine change.

Elation made him giddy. "You've seen 'em, Hometown. Now all you got to do is guess and swing."

Go forth, Johnny thought, as Commissioner Moresby would say, and figure out a pitcher's arm. Go figure it, doctors reigning at Johns Hopkins. Go figure it, pitching coaches, spitting Red Man tobacco juice in the bull pen. Go figure what you're facing, big-league hitters. A pitcher's arm was vibrant and alive. A natural glory, sure as Maryland grass is green. If medical experts had developed a technical nomenclature—rotator cuff, caracoid process, and the rest—that did not mean they understood a pitcher's arm. They developed words for diseases they didn't understand either, like cancer.

Nor indeed did Johnny understand the magic. But beyond pain, for reasons no one could explain, his arm again was young.

Now the enemy was emotion. He had not surrendered to despair in the fifth inning, when his arm felt as gnarled as a cottonwood shaped by its survival battle against the prairie winds. An inning later he could not let this mysterious new power make him careless. This was the major leagues, the World Series, the seventh game. He could not simply throw. He had to pitch. Hometown Brown did not hit hard stuff below the boilers. That's what the scouts said. Fortran concurred.

Boilers? He could hear a dry, electric computer voice say, "The power plant. Humans call them balls."

Johnny gripped the baseball on the seams and as he threw, released the pitch so that it spun off the outer edge of his middle finger. The ball carried toward the inside corner, sank and swerved. Strike one. John threw another sinker. Brown beat the ball against his left instep, yelped, and fell. He squatted on the dirt, wincing and clutching his foot.

The Mohawk dugout shouted dog-pack sounds. "Arrf. Bow-wow, a-woooo!"

"Hey, Brownie,'" someone bellowed. "We got mustard." Mild dugout humor. An aching foot was a hot dog.

A fast pitch fouled against an instep hurt outrageously for a few seconds. As the pain passed, the hitter was embarrassed for having cried out and writhed under the gaze of thousands of spectators. An embarrassed hitter was likely to swing more in anger than in guile.

Kauff asked for a third sinker, moving his glove to the outside. John shook his head twice and Kauff trotted to the mound. "You don't want to give him nothing good," the catcher said.

"High, hard, and outside," Johnny said.

"He kills the high ones."

"We're gonna give him one that he can't reach."

John gripped the ball along the stitches, as he had held the sinkers, but this time released it straight, across the tips of his middle and index fingers.

The ball sailed toward the outside corner, shoulder high. Brown all but jumped to swing. As he did, the fastball veered wide and upward. He missed the sailing pitch by five inches.

"Aarf, aarf," someone called cheerfully from the Mohawk bench.

Jedediah Jackson was next. Four pitches did the job. Then Johnny struck out Hummin' Herman Calhoun with three curveballs.

It was easy when you had your good stuff. It was like having money. When you had money, you didn't worry about bills. You simply paid them. When you had your good stuff, you simply pitched.

Anyway, he was through six perfect innings.

* * *

Sometimes at World Series games, even at those as fine and fiercely battled as this one between the Mohawks and the Mastodons, people leave the ballpark early. This phenomenon occurs mostly among those who go not to see but to be seen. Deputy Mayors for Sanitation, actresses in failing musicals, executives engaged to rescue American automobile companies, along with mortals of lesser eminence, who recognize that buying a Series ticket can pay dividends in publicity. Newspapers run lists of distinguished people in attendance and television cameras probe about for what television announcers call notables. (Somehow, executives of the network that paid to telecast the Series always qualify as both notable and distinguished.)

But the newspaper stories are written early, often from lists prepared by publicity people, and the television executives and their distinguished wives and notable children, have all been shown on home screens during the first few innings.

"Can you believe it," Prissy Coe said in the press box.

"Believe what?" Rob Brownell said.

"People are leaving a scoreless tie in the sixth inning."

"It happens every fall," said Townsend Wade.

"But why?" Prissy said. "Why would anyone walk out on a magnificent game like this?"

"Numerous reasons," Wade said. "Their toes may be starting to feel chilled. They may be hungrier for something tastier than a hot dog. Or perhaps, in an elegant apartment on East Seventy-ninth Street, a lady may be waiting in passion."

Dammit, Prissy Coe thought. I'm not only the junior member of this trio, I'm only the woman, and I went and asked a dumb schoolgirl question.

Rob Brownell suddenly remembered a long-ago ball game. The pitchers he thought were Dizzy Dean and Van Lingle Mungo. Both looked unbeatable. In the seventh inning he remembered his father announcing that they had to leave.

"Why, Dad?"

"Important contract I've got to sign for the Pine Hill Route. We don't want Greyhound beating out our little bus company. In fact, we can't afford to be beaten by Greyhound to Pine Hill. You understand."

Brownell remembered understanding that he wanted to cry, but he would not let his father see his tears. Were

254

boys brought up like that today? he wondered. His last memory of the game—he had even forgotten who won—was Van Lingle Mungo kicking high to throw a fastball, and his own father's firm hand forcing him into an exit tunnel, where he walked in dry-eyed grief.

The girl—he really could not train himself so quickly to say "the person"—was all right. She might not yet know the intricacies Casey Stengel had known, but she was enthralled by this game. Thrall was a beginning. Brownell knew baseball had enthralled all its finest reporters from Heywood Broun to Ring Lardner to today.

Maybe he had underestimated this first-generation woman-in-the-press-box. After all, the first generation of black baseball players included such fine and balanced people as Monte Irvin. And the first generation of Elizabethan poets . . . Stay in the ball game.

"Townsend," Brownell said to Wade, "would you pass me a piece of copy paper?"

He took the paper and elaborately wiped the palms of both hands. "I'm actually perspiring," Brownell said. "This is one magnificent brute of a ball game. I don't see how anyone can leave myself."

"Thanks," Prissy Coe said, with murmuring intensity.

* * *

The Mohawk dugout was suddenly a small southwestern town, among farmed-out alfalfa fields, where oil gushed from exploratory wells. It was alive with hope. The ballplayers had picked up the change in Johnny's pitching. They were cheering for him, and more happy for themselves with sweet awareness that each winning player's World Series share would exceed thirty-two thousand dollars.

"Hey-up," Anton Dubcek said to Johnny, "you got them swinging like the bats was magazines. It's like they was trying to hit your stuff with copies of *Sports Illustrated*."

Johnny would lead off the bottom of the sixth inning; he was wondering what he could do against Herman Calhoun's fastball. Black hand. White lightning.

" 'Attaway to fire," Kenny Osterhout said.

"We're gonna win this mother," cried Baskets Weaver.

"Let's get some runs," said Harry Truman Abernathy.

"Hey, John, you're throwing great," said Raunchy Kauff.

"I am gonna win this mother," Johnny said, "for all you guys and for your wives and for your tax lawyers."

"How can you think about money at a time like this?" Kenny Osterhout said.

"What should he be thinking about?" Lefty Levin said. "Pussy?"

John blinked and saw Christina. He grabbed a light bat, thirty-one ounces, and stepped forward to encounter Herman Calhoun. He could bunt. Indeed, he would surely have bunted ten years earlier. But he was forty-one and he knew that he was forty-one and that the beats of time had stolen his quickness. It would take him perhaps half a second longer to reach full running speed. The kinetics of his body, like the geometry of baseball, were remorseless. The batter had to run ninety feet to first base, whether he was forty-one or twenty. A good infielder's throw to first moved at seventy-five miles an hour. If you ran the ninety feet in 3.2 seconds, as Mickey Mantle had, or even 3.5, you had a good chance to hit the base before the speeding, snarling baseball died in the first baseman's glove. If you took a half-second longer, the throw, like body kinetics and the geometry of baseball, would nail you against an umpire growling, "Out!"

"Take a minute," Danny Merullo, the home plate umpire said.

"I'm ready," Johnny said.

"But they aren't."

"Who's they?"

"The people. The people who have paid to see you pitch."

John stepped out of the batter's box and heard for the first time jubilation from the crowd. He was pitching a no-hit game in Mohawk Stadium and the fans were making Praetorian cries of tribute.

He looked sidelong toward the grandstands. Everyone was on his feet. The noise was not a shouting, but rather a mixed, primitive, mindless cry of love.

"Stay out of the box," Merullo ordered. "If they got a minute, we do."

"I ain't a farmer's kid," Johnny said. "I don't want to milk this."

"If I coulda throwed like you, and they cheered like this for me, I'da milked this," Merullo said.

"Ain' no way," Jed Jackson, the Los Angeles catcher said, "they'd ever cheer for an umpire like this, lessen he dies."

Johnny laughed and tipped his blue-and-white Mohawk cap and the jubilation turned into a wailing sound of adoration.

"You tellin' me, you didn't hear this noise when you come up?" Jed Jackson said. "You tellin' me an umpire had to remind you?"

"I was concentrating," Johnny said, "and when I concentrate too hard, I get a little deaf." He looked quickly into his own dugout. Dubcek and Abernathy, Dwayne Tucker, Jap O'Hara, Lefty Levin, and even Cy Veitch, were standing and applauding, too.

"I guess they love you in October," Danny Merullo said.

"Herman and I loves you all the time," Jedediah Jackson said, "but before this game is over, we'll whip you ass."

Johnny bunted a low inside fastball toward third base. He could feel, he actually felt, two beats of time, as he

257

drove his body through the bunter's ritual. Drop the bat. Flee toward first. He ran hard but he knew the beats had cost him running strides and he remembered that baseball's geometry was remorseless.

When John was three strides from first, Rosey Dale of the Mastodons abruptly let his gloved hand droop. As John crossed the bag, he heard Dale say, "Shee-yit."' Then John knew he was safe with a lead-off bunt single.

"What happened?" he asked Cracker Tatum, the first-base coach.

"Their third baseman, Webb, he fell down."

"Good bunt?"

"Rolled up along the line a little hard. If he'da kept his feet, he'da got you by two, three steps."

"But he didn't keep his feet," Johnny said.

"Stay in the game now, John-boy," Tatum said. "Take your lead real careful. You're the winning run. Take a slow look toward third and read them signs. You can read them signs great, Johnny-boy."

John watched Daryl Coyle at third begin to dance. A slight knee-bend. Finger to nose. Hands across the uniform letters. Hand to wrist. Arms folded. Arms unfolded. Hands clasped. A whistle. A shout. "Go get a good one, Basket-man." The arms stirred constantly. Johnny thought, A noisy country scarecrow in a gale. But all the gesticulations were only decoys. Coyle stood with his right foot on a chalk line of the coaching box. The scarecrow arms were camouflage. The position of Daryl Coyle's right foot, after the finger-to-nose indicator, was the order. Baskets Weaver was to bunt.

Calhoun, rangy and high-cheekboned, glowered at John and fired a pickoff throw to Rosey Dale. John stepped back and studied Calhoun. The two were staring at each other, but only Calhoun appeared to be glowering. Slants of October light broke against the severe planes of his face and made him look as ugly as an Aztec killer-priest.

Now Baskets Weaver bunted, calmly, professionally toward first. Johnny slid safely into second base on the sacrifice. He thought, a sacrifice against an Aztec priest. He thought, do not drift. Stay in the game. A single can score you.

Calhoun went with his rising fastball against young Kenny Osterhout. As a rule, young ballplayers hit speed. They have worked up through the minor leagues against strong, young pitchers. Youth against youth. Power against reflex. Their survival, specifically the survival of young Kenny Osterhout, was testimony that he could hit a good fastball. He had hit them in Sioux Falls, Keokuk, and Ogden, Utah, and in night games where the minor-league floodlights offered batters only a pale glare.

Osterhout fouled Calhoun's first fastball back to the screen. He bent angrily and called for the pine-tar rag and rubbed it vigorously against the handle of his bat. He cracked Calhoun's second fastball over shortstop into left field.

John paused to make sure the drive carried higher than the leap of Verlon Wright. Then he began to run, fighting yet once more against the beats of time. As he turned third base, hitting it with his inside foot to make a tighter turn, Daryl Coyle wildly waved him home. Coyle's right arm was an Oklahoma windmill.

But the years, enemy of every athlete, every dancer, the years. The years extended Johnny's turn into a lazy arc. He fought the years and fought the lazy arc and stumbled. He hit the grass with his left arm, bouncing up like a child learning to ice-skate, and kept his footing. But fighting time, he had lost time.

"Home," Mastodon ballplayers bellowed toward Rocco Lombardo in left field.

John heard their shouts. "Home," he roared within himself. "God. Fuckit. Home!"

Lombardo's throw reached the catcher, Jed Jackson, when Johnny was eight running strides away.

One final chance. John covered up and drove into the catcher, hoping the impact would dislodge the ball. The two rolled over and over in grotesque, brawling intimacy. The ball stayed in Jed Jackson's right fist.

"Ya-rout," bawled Danny Merullo.

Jed Jackson rose first. John was stunned for six seconds, not sure where he was. The veil cleared. He was out, but Ken Osterhout, making the right play, had kept running and stood on second base.

"What a fucking shot," Jed Jackson said, without anger.

"We aren't playing softball," Johnny said.

"That's right," Jackson said, "and just because you bumped me and I tagged you, don't mean we got nothing against each other personal."

"You play the game," Johnny said.

There was still a base runner in scoring position, a young, leggy base runner who could make that sharp turn at third and score on a two-out single.

But Harry Truman Abernathy popped up. With three innings remaining, neither team had scored.

* * *

In the dugout, Lefty Levin told Johnny, "Take a blow. Breathe hard."

"I'll stall Merullo," Cy Veitch said.

"I'm all right," Johnny said. "I got my left shoulder into his ribs. I'm not dumb enough to hit him with my right shoulder. The guy made a damn good play to hold the ball."

"You made the damn good play," Levin said. "You're giving everybody a lesson in how you play a seventh game."

"Or baseball," Veitch said. "I'll stall Merullo."

While Johnny breathed, the manager walked toward the umpire. "Come on," Merullo shouted. "Get him out here."

"What about the mirror in center field?" Veitch said.

"What mirror?"

"My hitters say somebody's flashing a mirror in their eyes. Must be an actress visiting from Los Angeles."

"Okay," Merullo said. "I'll give your guy a minute until Boucher comes running out here screaming. Wave your arms. Act like you're mad." Veitch beat his arms and said, "Thanks. My pitcher deserves a minute to catch his breath."

Merullo stuck a finger furiously toward Veitch's nose. "And if it was up to me, and not the rules, he could have five minutes."

Veitch tore off his cap in a gesture of rage. "Okay," he said. "Good going. Thanks. When we win this thing, you're coming to the party."

"Hey," Merullo said, shaking the forefinger. "I go to no victory parties, theirs or yours. I'm just giving Mr. Longboat his due."

Frenchy Boucher was screaming as he ran from the Los Angeles dugout. "Make him pitch. They're fucking stalling. Make the old bastard pitch."

The crowd had begun shouting during the mock argument that mixed raging gestures with soft words. Now the shout rose and mock argument ended.

"He's telling me there's a mirror in center field bothering the hitters," Merullo said, "and I'm telling him I don't see none."

"Damn right there's no mirror," Boucher bellowed. "The man is fucking stalling for fucking time."

"I have to check it out," Merullo said.

"You have to make the son of a bitch pitch," Boucher shouted.

"Don't tell me what I have to do," Merullo said.

Before Boucher retreated, two minutes passed. Johnny warmed up easily, his wind and composure restored.

"Worked," Veitch said to Levin in the dugout. A small, satisfied smile creased his long face.

"Umpires are neutral toward the loudmouths," Levin said, "the way I was neutral when England was fighting Hitler."

"Never bait the bastards," Cy Veitch said, "or they give the other side the breaks."

"Unless the ump is chicken," Levin said. "There's some that Boucher can intimidate."

"Not Merullo," Veitch said, still smiling. "He sure as shit ain't chicken, which isn't saying he doesn't have moments of blindness."

* * *

"That dive into Jackson was worthy of a fullback," Townsend Wade said in the press box.

"It was more than that," Prissy Coe said.

"Oh?" Wade did not like being corrected by a woman.

"A fullback plays in armor," Prissy said. "Johnny might as well have been naked when he took on the catcher with the catcher's chest protector, shin guards and all. And more than that. I can't just put it into words."

"Perhaps," Rob Brownell said, "you mean that this game is a kind of art form that's complete in itself, and why drag in extraneous images from some no-face game like football."

Prissy leaned toward Brownell with a cool, approving little kiss.

"No kissing in the press box," said Townsend Wade.

* * *

John had not scored the run that could win the seventh game. His dive for home had bruised his left shoulder but had failed to make Jed Jackson drop the baseball. Still, he felt triumphant.

He threw a sailing fastball to Spider Webb, a fastball hitter. Surprised, Webb popped to Jap O'Hara at third. He jammed Duke Marboro with a fastball tailing in and got a foul ball for a strike. Then Marboro tapped a low inside slider to Saviour Santo Domingo at second base. Whitey Wright must have anticipated a fastball because he stroked John's first pitch on a high line to right center. Baskets Weaver sprinted and caught the ball over his left shoulder, hit the wall, and sat down and held the ball. Another three.

Calhoun cut his fastball through the Mohawks. Dubcek struck out. Dwayne Tucker popped to shortstop. Jap O'Hara hit a foul pop fly that Spider Webb caught halfway in to home plate.

Seven innings were done. More than two-thirds of a game. No Los Angeles runner had reached first base. The Mohawks had made five hits, but neither team had scored.

Chapter 11
Mohawk Stadium, January 11, 1976

A club, by placing the name of a player on a list, can reserve exclusive rights to his services from year to year for an unstated and indefinite period in the future.

I find this unpersuasive. It is like the claims of some nations that persons once its citizens, wherever they live and regardless of the passage of time and the wearing of other allegiances, are still its own nationals. This "status" theory is incompatible with the doctrine of policy of freedom of contract in the economic and political society in which we live and of which the professional sport of baseball ("The national game") is a part.

Arbitrator Peter Seitz,
December 23, 1975.
Labor Arbitration Reports
Dispute Settlements
Volume 66, page 116

The long bondage was over and stumpy, black-haired Augustus Vermont III glowered at the blond, round-faced lawyer called Everett McKinley Taft. "I don't like shysters tramping in on contract negotiations," said the president of the New York Mohawks.

"Welcome to the Twentieth Century," the lawyer said in a soft, Midwestern voice. As some children, particularly in medieval paintings, appear to have the face of an adult, Everett Taft's face was that of a child who had never grown up, or perhaps the face of an enormously overgrown baby.

"John here and I could work out this contract in fifteen minutes," Vermont said. "Isn't that right, Johnny?"

"If I thought that was right," Johnny said, "I don't suppose Mr. Taft would be in here with me."

"What the hell, John," Vermont said. "We've been doing contracts for years. Why bring in a shyster to muck things up?"

"You can ask that question of Peter Seitz," Johnny said.

"Another shyster," Vermont said, "and we fired him. He's not baseball's impartial arbitrator any more."

Vermont's office was huge and formless. A thirty-foot color mural of a sold-out Mohawk Stadium covered one wall and when you drew back gray drapes, revealing glass walls, the real stadium appeared outside. The effect could be described as repetitious, overstated, or tasteless.

"I want you to know, Mr. Vermont," the round-faced lawyer called Taft said, quietly, "that I don't intend to muck up anything. John is my client, true, and I'll represent him as well as I can, but you're a man I honestly wish I *could* have for a client. The job you've done, sir, with the Mohawk franchise. In a baseball sense, winning all those pennants. In a business sense, drawing all those fans. The way you handle the wolves of the New York press. Really extraordinary."

"Don't try to stroke me, Taft," Gus Vermont said.

"I'm just telling you my feelings."

"You're promoting, Taft. You're probably on commission and you're promoting. I know something about promotions. That's one reason why I'm successful. Let me give you a tip. Never promote a promoter."

"I'll try to remember that, sir," Taft said.

"You better remember it," Vermont said.

If he had not been the centerpiece, John might have laughed. Gus Vermont was blustering and Everett Mc-Kinley Taft was fawning. But the blusterer was unarmed and the fawning lawyer had the cannon, thanks to the decision lately announced by arbitrator Peter Seitz. A ballplayer was free now to go from team to team, matching offer against offer. A ballplayer at last could truly bargain.

"Now, John," said Gus Vermont, his growl softening toward civility, "I have a proposition. Get the shyster out of here. Then I'll make two proposals, one upside, one downside, for the good of you and for me. For the Mohawk franchise and for baseball."

"Make the proposals within earshot of my attorney," Johnny said.

"Sure," Gus Vermont said. "*You're* not promoting me, John. You're getting older and maybe you're feeling a little scared. Okay. I'm going to take care of you. You and I hack out a contract. The numbers will be fair. I'm aware of what you've meant to the Mohawks. Banish the shyster and the upside is this. When your arm goes, you get a front-office job. You help to direct player personnel. Check out the farms. In a few years you could be general manager here. You could be set for life five years after you throw your last pitch."

"That's a fine offer," said Everett Taft.

"The downside," Vermont said, "is this: Keep the shyster in here and after you throw that last pitch, there will be no place for you *anywhere* in the Mohawk organization." Vermont stood before the color mural of the ballpark. "Shysters," he said, "can ruin the game of baseball."

"I hear an upside offer and a downside offer," Johnny said. "Isn't there any offer in between?"

"Let me speak, Johnny," Ev Taft said. He gazed at Vermont. "Sir, can you give us five minutes to weigh the offers?"

"In the fucking hall," Vermont said. "None of my players talks to their shysters in my office in front of my mural. You got your five minutes out in the hall."

Outside, in a fluorescent corridor carpeted with Mohawk blue, Johnny said, "I've always thought he was an unpleasant bastard."

"Bluster," the lawyer said mildly as though unoffended, "is just one way of doing business. The business he's trying to do goes something like this. If he blusters you out of using a lawyer or an agent, the deal personally could well be better for you. But then he tells a dozen other Mohawks, I bargain head to head with Longboat and he's a damn sight more valuable than you are. I'll be damned if I'll bargain with agents for mediocre bums like you when I bargain head to head with Longboat." The enormous baby face looked forlorn. "The deals could be much, much worse for each of your teammates."

"You stay," Johnny said.

The lawyer nodded.

"One other thing," Johnny said. "You bargain just as hard as you can, but we aren't going to bargain with any other ball club."

"Why not?"

"I've become a kind of New York guy. I don't want to end up in Kansas City."

"Understood," Taft said. "Now I want you to understand something."

"What?"

"We keep that between ourselves. In Vermont's office I need every pound of leverage I can get."

✷ ✷ ✷

Everett McKinley Taft, related neither to the presidential McKinley nor the presidential Taft, was the son of an Ohio doctor, Hayes Alan Taft, who raised his children in the Tudor comfort of Shaker Heights. It was a time when physicians still practiced in their homes, and the Tafts lived in a half-timbered corner house three blocks from Cleveland's rapid transit line.

Dr. Taft was not a spendthrift, but he had certain elegant tastes that he felt were appropriate to an internist who had graduated with honors from Western Reserve Medical School. He drove a black Buick Roadmaster on his house calls, a sturdy and dependable car that enabled him to reach sick patients promptly in the cold Ohio nights. For no reason that he knew, Dr. Taft also stabled a Bugatti in his garage. Something was always going wrong with the sports car, and the one mechanic who could service a Bugatti charged more for his time than did a physician. Dr. Taft dressed his wife in splendid furs, but he also provided extravagantly for an English nurse who worked for a colleague, and with whom Dr. Taft had the misfortune to fall in love.

His practice, someone noticed, began to include an increasing number of women patients. Young women patients who were pregnant. Hayes Alan Taft, M.D., was convicted of performing illegal abortions by a Cuyahoga County jury on September 17, 1947.

He would go to jail for a year and a day. "I can stand that," Dr. Taft told his son, "but I'm not sure that I can stand the worry about what will happen to you and your mother."

"Can't you appeal?" asked Everett, who was sixteen.

"I haven't hurt anybody," Dr. Taft said. "I've taken women who were pregnant with babies they didn't want to have. I've anesthetized them and freed them of the pregnancy. Is there anything worse in the world than making someone mother a child she doesn't want?"

"I don't know," the boy said. "Can't you tell that to the lawyers?"

"The lawyers tell me," Dr. Taft said, "that there are no grounds for an appeal."

Hayes Alan Taft, M.D., died in the Mansfield State Penitentiary on May 15, 1948, at the age of fifty-one. It was said, but never proven, that he was strangled while resisting a homosexual rape.

The Taft house was sold and Everett's mother, a gourmet cook, purchased a small coffee shop in downtown Cleveland. She took an apartment over the store where, late at night, her son went to sleep, missing the half-timbered house in Shaker Heights, wondering about the roaches that invaded his new spare room, and smelling the greasy hamburgers that sizzled on skillets a floor below. Across hundreds of such nights, Ev Taft decided that he would not attend medical school, although his grandmother placed tuition money in a trust. His father had practiced medicine, helped people. For that he was disgraced, then murdered. At seventeen, Ev Taft decided that nothing in life was as important as making money. He knew then that he would become a lawyer.

He built his law practice without pretense, specializing in negligence cases and divorce. Within five years he had six attorneys working for him. Ev had a special way of coddling—some said bribing—insurance adjusters, and he was able to make more than a hundred thousand dollars a year, mostly from auto accidents. One associate called Ev Taft, "King of the Crack-ups." The title made Everett Taft uncomfortable, but his respect for money and his fear of losing it dominated him. Some nights in his own new colonial in Gates Mills, he awoke imagining that roaches crawled on the linen walls of the master bedroom and that the smell of sizzling hamburger grease again assaulted his nostrils.

A black outfielder for the Cleveland Indians changed

Taft's life. The ballplayer rammed a Buick Riviera into the trunk of a stalled police car directly in front of Taft's office near Public Square. A fifty-seven-year-old detective claimed back injuries and sued. Taft was pleased to meet and to represent a major-league outfielder. He settled the case quietly and reviewed routinely the ballplayer's income tax returns. He was surprised to see that the outfielder was grossing only thirty thousand dollars a year.

"The papers say sixty thousand dollars," he said.

"The papers is right, but the Indians has done me a favor. They spread my money. I get a little less each year, but I get it for more years. That way my taxes aren't so bad."

"Oh, no," Taft said in real excitement. "You've got it backwards. You're doing the Cleveland Indians a favor."

"I ain' with ya," the outfielder said.

"Money has value," Taft explained.

"I'm with ya there."

"So whoever holds the money has the value. He can use the money. He can buy things. He can make investments."

"So?"

"So the ball club is holding your money and maybe making investments with your money."

"Like what?"

"Like lending your money to some other company that needs money at, say, eight percent interest. We call that buying a bond."

After fifteen minutes, the outfielder said, "I ain' sure I got all you told me, but you helped me with the honky cop. I trusts you."

The outfielder's contract was due for renewal and Taft spoke with several officials of the Indians. To his surprise, they agreed to continue deferred payments in the future and to pay the ballplayer three percent annually on the money that was deferred. "What the hell?" an Indian executive said. "We can invest what we owe him at six percent. If we pay him the three, we're still ahead."

"You're being generous and we appreciate it," Everett Taft said.

"I'm a baseball man," said the executive. "Not a bandit."

The outfielder mentioned his modest change of fortune in clubhouses and soon Taft was negotiating deferred income contracts for a dozen major-league ballplayers at interest rates of two to four percent.

At first it seemed almost a dalliance. He could make more money out of one welder, whose hand had been crushed by a drunken driver, than he could with ten puny-interest baseball contracts. But after a while, the lawyer envisioned a larger field. He would not merely negotiate contracts for athletes. He would establish and run their bank accounts. He would make investments for them. He would have an assistant prepare their income tax returns. He would put them on weekly allowances. Thus, he, not the ball clubs, would have the use of their money. And as a lawyer, rather than a baseball man, he surely would not pay *his* baseball clients interest. Instead he would charge them fees. Thus, Taft Total Sports Representation, Inc., was born and chartered, for technical reasons, under the laws of the State of Delaware.

With his absolute command of flattery, Taft performed famously with the press. Each reporter who approached him about Taft Total Sports was rewarded with a compliment for writing style, journalistic integrity, or both. Taft then revealed insignificant bookkeeping records "not for publication but to show you how we operate." Important writers were rewarded further. Taft bought them dinners in the company of his English receptionist, Trish Wilford. It was said that no lawyer since Clarence Darrow enjoyed a more admiring press.

Using the ballplayers' money, Taft became more affluent than his late father. He acquired a Mercedes—a Rolls would have been overstating—and equipped it with a two-way telephone. He made it a point to meet visiting columnists at Hopkins Airport and let them use the car telephone to call their wives, or ballplayers, while he rolled along the expressway. The good publicity brought more business. What began as a small subsidiary of a drab, successful law practice, exploded when Peter Seitz liberated baseball players from the old system of reserve clauses. On December 24, Taft took thirty-one telephone calls from major-league baseball players, who wanted him to represent them. As Trish Wilford pointed out, all but three were placed collect. Johnny Longboat, of the New York Mohawks, paid for his call.

"Mr. Pitcher," Taft began.

"Beg pardon."

"You are *the* Mr. Pitcher to me."

"I've got some business to discuss," Johnny said.

When they met in a suite at the Plaza Hotel, Taft ordered two steaks, a bottle of Scotch for John, and two bottles of Perrier for himself. "I like to drink," he said, "but I've been going like a helicopter blade. New York today. Houston tomorrow. Atlanta after that. It looks like twenty-six separate stopovers just this month." The giant baby face grinned. "I might as well have skipped law school and been a ballplayer. How you doing?"

"That's what I'm here to find out."

"Good," Taft said. "Very good. Hey, look. Sit down. I want to ask you, do you have a hard time managing your money?"

"Not too hard a time, now," Johnny said. "I do wonder what will happen when I'm through."

"That's natural," Taft said. "Let me tell you something about this society. It's hard to make a buck but it's harder still to hold on to a buck once you've made it. That's because everybody in this society has a common enemy."

"I have a prominent enemy in baseball," Johnny said.

"We'll get to that," Taft said. He stood. He wore a fitted, three-piece suit, charcoal blue with a chalk stripe. "Baseball enemies are something I handle fine. The enemy that's tougher is ourselves."

"I don't follow," Johnny said.

"You're not supposed to follow me yet. We make money and we want to spend it; we're urged to spend it. You drive a sports car?"

"A station wagon."

"That's good. But the way things work, with television commercials and the rest, somebody's always after us to spend our money. And we do. We listen to what they tell us. We're only human. We buy the things the advertisers push, whether we need them or not. That's called extravagance and it's part of what I mean. But the biggest enemy, which truly is part of ourselves, is the U.S. government."

"Internal Revenue Service," Johnny said.

"You're following me now," Taft said.

Over lunch, the lawyer offered a seductive proposition. Through confidential sources, he had learned the salary of every pitcher in the major leagues. He had, therefore, an accurate idea of Johnny's relative worth in the new free-agent market.

"About how much?" Johnny said.

"As much as half a million for each of the next three years."

"Each?"

"I'm not promising," Taft said. "The Mohawks will yelp and argue about the side benefits you get from playing in New York. Commercials. Media exposure. That sort of thing. But I'll start with the half-million figure and we'll try to stay in that neighborhood." Taft sipped his

Perrier with lime. "What are you going to do with all that money?"

"Make love to it."

"That's a funny line," Taft announced. "Like the comedian who said, 'Happiness can't buy money.' But remember, Johnny, the only time you make jokes *about* money is when you *have* money." Taft explained that he could open certain high-interest-rate bank accounts on John's behalf and would mail regular, computer printouts showing how Johnny's money was being spent. Mortgage. Insurance. Whatever. He would put the Longboat family on a kind of computerized budget that would include a personal allowance for Johnny of two hundred fifty dollars a week.

"I don't much like computers," Johnny said.

"Neither do I. But they work."

"What will all this cost?" Johnny said.

"Nothing."

"Now *you're* being funny."

"Not at all. I charge twenty percent of your gross. You know the difference between gross and net."

"Net is what you have left."

"Right," Taft said. His answers were quick and the tone that came out of the enormous infant face sounded neither patronizing nor abrasive. Everett Taft had mastered a most lawyerly art. He could be adversarial—and certainly his demand for a twenty percent commission could have been a point of hot discussion—without appearing to be argumentative.

"After we get you straightened away, Johnny, you'll have more left than you'd have had without me. The benefits from tax shelters will amount, conservatively, to more than twice my fee." Taft sipped his soda. "Of course, you can do all this by yourself, if you want to study five thousand pages of tax codes, and take four years off from baseball to go to law school."

Johnny liked to believe that he moved with care on important matters. He had turned down several offers for his life story out of a prudent regard for his own privacy. (He was willing, he said, to collaborate on a pitching instruction book, but nobody seemed to want to publish that one.) He had been sensible when Brad Moresby tried to bribe him. John recognized baseball, or at least the locker room, as a world peopled with large child-men, like Raunchy Kauff. Against that background, he perceived himself as thoughtful, even calculating.

But, except when he pitched, Johnny was not a calculating man. He was an artist at the game of baseball; he brought control there, cold thought, intensity reined by discipline. Away from the pitcher's mound, he tended to relax and to allow his intensity to gallop. His marriage to Becky Rae was born of sorrow, hurt, and haste. His affair with Christina, now ten years old, screamed of recklessness. He could well lose almost everything Taft was promising if Becky Rae turned angry and hired a gelid-eyed divorce lawyer like Roy Cohn. When he considered such possibilities deeply, Johnny realized that he was less prudent than he elected to believe. But considering these depths burned him to agony. Life is not a contest to see how long one can hold one's hand in a fire without shrieking. Johnny pitched often and won. He handled the press. Why then probe places where agony lurked?

"You're hired," he told Everett McKinley Taft.

"I have a contract for us in my dispatch case. I was hoping to get you to come along with me."

John signed the document, three simply written paragraphs, mostly defining the twenty-percent fee for Taft Total Sports Representation, Inc.

Taft handed him another paper. "This is a power of attorney," he said. "It gives me the right to run your bank accounts, manage your investments, and find you tax shelters."

"Suppose something goes wrong?" Johnny said.

"Like what?"

"The government disallows a tax shelter."

"The worst that can happen," Taft said with a small, boyish smile, "is that we go to Leavenworth together. Things could be worse. At least you'll be going to prison with your lawyer."

John smiled in turn and handed Taft the rights to his financial future. "One point," he said.

"What's that?"

"My prominent enemy in baseball is the Commissioner."

"When you make an enemy," Taft said, "you don't play around at the service entrance."

On occasions when Taft grew tense, his face lost no placidity, but he did develop a peculiar mannerism. He would blink quickly and repeatedly for several seconds. Then his pale eyes vanished beneath fluttering lids.

"What does Commissioner Moresby have against you?"

John told the story of the bribe offer four years earlier and how Commissioner Moresby had responded and how, finally, the Commissioner acknowledged the report in writing.

"Where is that acknowledgment now?"

"The original is at home in Ridgefield. Xerox copies are in vaults at two different banks. It would take three simultaneous fires to wipe me out."

"Pretend you're on the witness stand. Do you swear that those copies exist?"

"I'd rather affirm."

"Accepted," Taft said, and stopped blinking. "You understand," he said, his voice rising slightly, "who's in trouble here?"

"Me," Johnny said. "The Commissioner will never get me one of those hundred-thousand-dollar broadcasting jobs when my arm gives out."

"Wrong. *You* behaved with honor. *Moresby* risked the integrity of baseball to protect a crooked brother. If this ever came out, I'd bet—I shouldn't say bet—that you'd be a bigger hero than ever and former Commissioner Amory Moresby would be looking for work." Taft sipped his soda. "A hundred-thousand-dollar-a-year broadcast job. I'll get you two hundred fifty thousand dollars."

"But what I have never will come out," Johnny said.

"Why not?"

"I won't tell you. Just take my word. My affirmation. It can never come out."

"But how can Total Sports give you total sports representation if you don't give me total information? You know I'm not only an agent but a lawyer. You know about confidentiality. If I ever broke a client's confidence, I would be disbarred."

The affair with Christina Moresby still held Johnny in an ecstasy that Germans call *liebestod*. Love-death. A few people knew about it, but only as gossip. He was not going to let Taft's sumptuous French provincial Plaza suite become a confession box.

"I'm not trying to be rude," Johnny said, "but we have a business relationship. I've signed your contract. I'll tell you anything you want to know about my finances. That's as far as I'll go."

"So where are we?" Taft said.

"Where we were. Facing the reality that there is zero chance of me broadcasting 'Games of the Week' even if I offered to do them free."

Taft blinked several times and sighed slightly. "Well," he said, "it probably won't matter anyway. With the investments I'm going to make, you won't need a broadcasting job. Besides, you're not as funny as Garagiola."

"What kind of investments do you have in mind?"

"Right," Taft said. "Good question. Never invest in

anything you don't understand. Have you ever heard of Freeport?"

"It's on Long Island."

"Not that one. It's a little plastic sort of place in the Bahamas. Slightly better winter weather than Florida. About three hours from New York by jet. Through certain confidential sources, I've learned about some land available down there."

"Valuable land?"

"Not yet. But in a few years that land is going to be in the middle of a maze of hotels and tourist shops and gambling casinos. *Then* it will be very valuable, indeed."

"I don't like it," Johnny said.

"Why not?"

"Casinos. Gambling. No."

"Johnny," Taft said, "I'm not a quick-buck into-the-market-Tuesday-pull-out-Thursday guy. This project will take years to develop. We buy land now, with Mohawk contract money and maybe some bank money as well. By the time we're ready to sell to the guys in the gray fedoras who own casinos, you'll be out of baseball."

"Maybe," Johnny said.

"Not maybe," Taft said. "The timing is going to be perfect. Do you have anything morally against gambling?"

"As long as the tables aren't rigged, people have the right to lose money any way they want."

"So?"

"Yes," Johnny said. "All right. Let's buy the land."

"Within ten years, less time than you think," Taft said, "you'll be an international capitalist."

"What's that land around Freeport look like?" Johnny said.

"Flat. Very, very flat."

"A little like Oklahoma land," Johnny said.

"No," the lawyer said. "It isn't like Oklahoma land at all."

* * *

In the corridor outside Gus Vermont's office at Mohawk Stadium, two weeks after the Peter Seitz decision and the Plaza meeting, Lawyer Everett Taft blinked rapidly.

"This is up to you, Johnny," he said. "If you think you can do better for yourself in Vermont's office without me, go ahead. I'll tear up the power of attorney. I won't charge you any fee. We haven't moved on the Bahamian land deal, because you have nothing to move with yet. So if you want me, I'm here, and if you want to bargain for yourself, just go ahead."

"I'm a professional pitcher," Johnny said. "Vermont is a professional bargainer."

"You're thinking well," the lawyer said, "but remember this—I want Total Sports always to be totally frank—we don't have all the weapons I'd like to have. You won't let me bargain with Kansas City, or the Red Sox, and some of Vermont's bluster may be real anger. If he stays as determined as he seems to be, he damn well will cut you off when you throw your last fastball." Taft blinked five times in quick succession.

"Isn't that a chance we have to take?" Johnny said.

"I was hoping you'd say that."

* * *

Back in the presidential office, Vermont was curiously mild. No, he would not pay Johnny $500,000 a year. He would not pay him $400,000 a year, either. "You're talking," he said to Taft, "about a three-year deal?"

"I'm willing to talk about a three-year deal."

"That's what I have in mind," Gus Vermont said. "Three years. Now I don't know what Walter O'Malley will do with the Dodgers and I don't know what George

Steinbrenner will do with the Yankees, but the Mohawks have a sort of top-line policy to contend with this free-agent madness."

"Namely?" Taft said.

"That there will be no million-dollar contracts. No ballplayer is worth a million-dollar contract."

"Then you are offering Johnny $333,333 a year," Taft said, "for each of the next three seasons, if he stays with your club."

"That might be arranged."

"Fine," Taft said. "I can certainly respect your million-dollar barrier, but I want to do it in a slightly different way. I'd like to see Johnny paid $250,000 a year for each of the next three seasons. I want him to get a $240,000 bonus for signing right now. This afternoon. If I can add, and I believe I can, that comes to a total of $990,000. We get the use of some money we need now and you get to save about $9,000 in the long run."

"Inflation will eat that up," Vermont said.

"Talent is expensive," said the lawyer.

Vermont and Taft stood and exchanged hard looks and shook hands. While a secretary named Mrs. Donadio typed pages of changes into the old-form baseball contract, Vermont opened his office bar and drank two Scotches with his finest pitcher. Everett Taft sipped Coke. "I don't mind telling you, Mr. Vermont," Taft said, "that when we were working out this deal, I had some butterflies. What a butterfly stomach does *not* need is hard liquor."

At 1:08, black-haired Lucille Donadio was finished typing. She went to another office and returned at 1:11. She bore a check payable to the order of John L. Longboat for $240,000.

"Don't lose it, John," Vermont said, in a voice without inflection.

Johnny grinned.

280

"I'm not making a joke," Vermont said. "I told you if you kept the lawyer here what the terms were. You chose to keep the lawyer here. That's *your* choice. *My* choice is that when you're through pitching, you leave the Mohawks' organization for good."

"We have to go now, Mr. Vermont," said the lawyer, taking John's arm.

Walking toward Everett Taft's rented limousine, John said, "Can you figure out what the hell was going on in there?"

"Oh, sure. It wasn't complicated. Not unusual."

"I mean the shouting and then the drink together and then the warning."

"He was blustering," Taft said, "to make you get rid of me. When he saw that you wouldn't, he stopped blustering. It didn't make sense to make more noise. He's a businessman. The warning was just the mark of a hard loser."

"He's still an unpleasant bastard," Johnny said.

"Just a businessman."

"But do you think he really meant that business about kicking me out of the organization?"

"Do you want to scout kid pitchers in Sioux Falls, South Dakota?"

"No, but I don't like that possibility being closed."

A uniformed driver opened the limousine door. "I almost want to laugh," said Everett Taft.

"Nothing's funny," Johnny said.

"You're looking at things upside down," Taft said. "Hey, driver, show us how you can make this baby move." He turned to Johnny. "I have just gotten you the biggest bonus in the history of baseball. Two hundred and forty thousand dollars. Not over three years. Not spread. Right now. And with the quarter million in your pocket, you're worrying that in three years you won't get a job that you don't want."

"I guess," Johnny said. The limousine started silently. John looked at the check. Two hundred and forty thousand dollars. Probably twice what his father had earned in an entire lifetime. He felt no elation, but rather a faint queasiness, as though somehow he had been given something he did not deserve.

The limousine proceeded across the Bronx, toward a highway that would lead Johnny home to Ridgefield. Door-to-door limousines was one of Total Sports' services for this day.

As they passed the skeletons of old middle-class apartment buildings, windowless now, inhabited by squatters and vermin, John heard over and over again the voice of Gus Vermont saying simply, "Don't lose it, John."

He endorsed the check to Everett McKinley Taft.

Chapter 12
2:41 P.M., October 14

JOHN OPENED the eighth inning with a fast curve, meant to snake downward near the knees of Rocco Lombardo. As he released the ball, John recognized that it would not bite across the black line that etches the inside corner of home plate. He had launched the pitch too far outside. The curve would be low, which is where he wanted it to be, but low over the center of the plate.

He had made a mistake. Good major-league batters make very high salaries by hitting mistakes, and Lombardo was a very good batter. For all his thickly muscled shoulders. Lombardo's chest was lean; he swung with a lethal, fluid quickness. He drove a line drive that carried a yard to Johnny's left, whining as bullets are said to whine in flight, and buzzing, with the sound of angry wasps, as the stitches bit against the air. The baseball spun onto the grass in short center field. A single. A routine major-league single. The crowd made a moaning sound. Johnny had lost his no-hitter and the subdued moan was the fans' eulogy.

Johnny kept all expression from his high-cheekboned

face. Look the same after a base hit or a strikeout. That was a code of his professionalism. You concealed agitation, pain, joy, from spectators and opposing ballplayers. In that regard at least, a pitcher was an actor. The no-hitter was gone and he heard Ken Osterhout, the kid at shortstop, chattering, "Good try, John. Helluva ball game, buddy." He turned his thoughts to Roosevelt Delano Dale.

Low-ball hitter. John threw a fastball he wanted to carry inside toward the black letters on Dale's uniform shirt that read "Mastodons." The ball moved down and Dale lined it over Anton Dubcek near first base. Johnny's right fielder, Dwayne Tucker, of McCook, Nebraska, fled toward the foul line, hoping to snare the baseball with a dive.

Abruptly Tucker slowed. No chance. He played the line drive as it caromed off the right-field fence. Johnny ran to back up third base. The no-hitter was gone. The Mastodons had runners at second and third. Nobody was out and his shoulder was again beginning to ache.

Cy Veitch folded his arms across his chest and the Mohawk infield moved in. Cut off the run. Don't let the bastards score. Now a ground ball at an infielder would freeze Lombardo at third. But playing closer to home plate, each infielder sacrificed range. Another theorem in the geometry of baseball. A hard grounder two strides from an infielder would mean two runs.

John threw a change of pace and got a strike on Jake Wakefield of Longview, Texas. A sinker missed the outside corner. Johnny whipped a curve through the pain in his shoulder and the pitch bounced two feet in front of Raunchy Kauff. The catcher boxed the ball and blocked it. Aesthetics were gone from Johnny's pitching. He was a struggling, forty-one-year-old man. Cy Veitch called time and walked toward the mound.

"I got Torchyzer ready in the pen."

"I want to finish," Johnny said.

"How much does he have left?" the manager said to Raunchy Kauff.

"He just missed a couple inches, till that last curve."

"Torchyzer's fresh," Veitch said.

"I want to finish."

"And I want to win," Cy Veitch said.

"I just have to reach back a little farther," Johnny said.

"Yeah, but is there anything left to reach for?"

John looked at the manager, pleading with his eyes. Veitch walked a tight circle, spat, and said, "Gimme the baseball."

"Goddamn," Johnny said.

"The baseball."

"If you pull me and they hit Torchyzer," Johnny said, "the newspapers and Mr. Cosell will have your ass. They'll second-guess you from here to the Super Bowl."

The manager put his hands on his broad hips and looked sidelong toward the press box. "All right," he said, "but we got to get out Wakefield. Then we walk Brown and make Jed Jackson our out man. He don't run good."

"I'll get Wakefield," Johnny said.

"Keep the baseball," Veitch said. Then, celebrating his indecision, the manager walked purposefully from the mound.

John threw a good tailing outside fastball for a strike, and followed with a high spinning change. Wakefield overswung and lifted a soft pop fly that Jap O'Hara caught alongside third.

There was one out, as Johnny walked "Hometown" Brown. Jed Jackson couldn't run much. The Mohawk infield moved into double-play position. John would have to throw down-breaking stuff to make him hit over the baseball, hit a grounder. Through pain, he broke off two sharp overhand curves. He had two strikes. Peripherally he noticed a scuffle in one of the boxes behind the Mohawk dugout.

* * *

Rob Brownell reached for his field glasses in the press box. "What's going on?" asked Townsend Wade.

"Kidnapping at the ballpark?" Prissy Coe asked.

But Brownell was gone, a good reporter hurrying to a scene. By the time he reached Box 101A, Johnny Long-boat had struck out Jackson with a third, snapping curve. Dammit, Brownell thought, if the curve had not been quite so good, Johnny would have gotten his ground-ball double play.

"Who were those people?" Brownell asked Trish Wilford, who had been sitting beside Everett Taft. The English woman looked pale. "I don't know," she said. "They practically dragged him. It was horrible."

"Admiral," Brownell called to Commissioner Amory Moresby in Box 100. "Do you know who those men were?"

"They identified themselves as federal marshals." Moresby's frosty face was frozen in a grin. "Apparently one of our leading advocates of ballplayers' rights has gotten himself in trouble with the law."

"How?" Brownell said.

"I don't have any idea." The Commissioner's gray eyebrows waggled. "But it does look as if the ballplayer's counsel may need counsel for himself. Can I put you off the record?"

"For one minute," Brownell said.

"Criminal counsel is my off-the-record guess," announced the Commissioner of Baseball.

* * *

Johnny was working on Hummin' Herman Calhoun. More breaking stuff. Just keep the pitches low and away.

He got two strikes on Calhoun, but the other pitcher

was a competitor. In a dogged way he beat the next three curves into foul territory.

John tried a fastball half a foot outside. Calhoun lurched and nicked the pitch so that it carried back to the screen.

"Stay careful, Johnny," Cy Veitch bellowed. That was a voice signal. It demanded more curveballs. John's shoulder throbbed. Still he would have to go back to the overhand curve. It would hurt, but damn, he wanted to strike out this glowering, insolent black kid, who was all guts.

* * *

Brownell called the New York *Standard* from the press box at Mohawk Stadium to report the apparent arrest of Everett Taft.

"We got it, Rob," said an assistant city editor named Mike Weiss.

"How can you have it when it just happened?"

"We got a tip from one of the federal D.A.'s for the Southern District of New York."

"They just came with four marshals and picked him up at the ballpark."

"They came with four marshals and one of our photographers. The chief D.A. says he loathes publicity. He means he loathes it when he isn't getting any. We promised him a little chunk of tomorrow's page one."

"What's the charge?"

"Charges," Mike Weiss said. "Plural. Rob, it comes down to something like this. Taft took money from a couple of dozen athletes and promised them a tax-free windfall in the Bahamas. A few ballplayers bragged and the Feds got wind of it. The government doesn't much care for tax-free windfalls. Some special officers began poking around."

"I need the phone," said a reporter from the *Des Moines Register*. "Soon as I'm through," Brownell said.

"The kicker," Mike Weiss said, "is that there wasn't any land. This lawyer, Taft, had some fake deeds drawn and the ballplayers were too damn dumb to check, much less fly down to Freeport to visit the investment they thought they had."

"But pay-outs," Brownell said. "Sooner or later, Taft would have to start making pay-outs."

"Sure," Weiss said, "but he's always signing new ballplayers, and there's fresh money coming in there. He intended to take a little of the new money and spread it around among his old clients. Ponzi. Insull. I forget who. The fake pyramid game."

"But why?" Brownell said. "Taft told me his practice was making him five hundred thousand dollars a year."

"The D.A. is still developing that part of it, so this is off-record, but apparently Taft was in a jet-set sports betting ring, with some pretty big names, like Bradford Moresby. They seem to have had a long run of terrible luck. You know, compulsive gamblers. They're all sick. Rich or poor, they're like newspapermen. They never have enough money."

"I'm trying to make some sense out of this," Brownell said.

"We've run a quick check on Taft," Mike Weiss said. "His father went to Mansfield Prison in Ohio. An illegal abortionist. About all that makes sense is that somewhere in Everett Taft's family tree there crawls a crooked gene. How's the game?"

"Read my piece," Brownell said. "Thanks, Mike."

The Des Moines reporter began to dial a downtown hotel. Brownell heard him say, "We might go into extra innings, honey, so stay in bed a little longer."

* * *

Johnny Longboat reached back, as he had promised his manager he would, and threw an overhand curve that broke to the knees along the black line on the outside corner of home plate. Pain stabbed Johnny's shoulder. Calhoun struck out.

"We need some runs," Simonius Veitch proclaimed in the dugout.

"You really pitched," Ken Osterhout said to Johnny.

"That's why they pay me."

"What happened in the box seats?" Harry Truman Abernathy asked Lefty Levin.

"It looked like an arrest," Levin said. "It looked like four big F.B.I. guys come into the ballpark to arrest Everett Taft."

Johnny strode to the intercom connecting the dugout and press box, and asked for Rob Brownell. "Just pitch," Brownell said. "I'll tell you in the clubhouse."

"Goddammit, tell me now."

Brownell recited what he knew. "So that's the bad news. I don't know what it means to you."

"Nothing," Johnny said. "It means nothing to me. It means I got to get ready to pitch the ninth."

But it did mean something. Most of the proceeds from the $990,000 contract would be gone, beyond hope of recovery. Johnny kept $5,000 in a small bank in Oklahoma, frail armor against the onslaught of disaster. His house in Ridgefield, more valuable with every wave of real-estate inflation, had been mortgaged, possibly beyond its worth, at Everett Taft's insistence. ("Remember, Johnny, every dollar you come up with is that much more casino land, and every dollar you pay in interest is a write-off.") Johnny wondered vaguely if his equity in the Ridgefield house would match his next quarterly bill for federal income taxes.

John watched Hummin' Herman Calhoun throw fastballs past three of his teammates. The kid seemed actually to be getting stronger. Johnny reached for his own glove. He was forty-one, famous beyond secret boyhood dreams of fame, loved by fans, admired by colleagues, and paid more to pitch a single game than his dead father had earned in any individual year.

He was also broke.

* * *

Aching shoulder or not, Johnny looked toward the mound as a place of safety. Broke. His life had turned into an attacking ocean, the way they said that waters got near the Bahamian village of Freeport when a hurricane approached. He'd be dammed if he would let himself be drowned.

Stay in the game. Give them a ninth inning to remember. Then the heat would be on the cold-eyed kid, Calhoun. Maybe the pressure would make him bend, if only a little, and maybe, then, the Mohawks could break through.

Johnny worked too carefully on Spider Webb and lost him when a 3-and-2 change of pace slipped high. The pain was worse. The hell with the pain. He wasn't going his father's way, with a pickled liver. The arm would have decades in which to rest.

Duke Marboro rapped a good curve toward Bad Czech Dubcek. The first baseman bent stiffly and the ball glanced against his shin. Dubcek winced. The Mastodons had runners on first and second. "Hey, Bad Czech," bellowed Frenchy Boucher. "You played every bounce right except the last one."

Now Whitey Wright would try to bunt. John beckoned Jap O'Hara in from third. "He's gonna bunt toward you. Throw to first base. Get the out. Then I'll walk Lombardo and come clear of this thing with Tucker and Dale."

O'Hara was chewing tobacco. "Urp," he said, meaning yes.

"Get the goddamned sure out," Johnny said.

"Urp," O'Hara repeated and moved back toward third in a swaggering trot.

John wanted Whitey Wright to bunt. Frenchy Boucher wanted Wright to bunt. This was one of the rarest of baseball moments. Offensive strategy and defensive strategy coincided, although for different reasons.

If Wright swung, he might bounce into a double play. A good bunt precluded that and would advance both base runners. That was Boucher's thinking, as simple as a Little League text.

But a successful bunt would mean runners at second and third. Then Johnny would deliberately walk Rocco Lombardo, the man who had broken his no-hitter and the most dangerous hitter on the Mastodons. He did not want to pitch to Lombardo with the game on the line, and an ache in his arm, in the ninth inning of the seventh game.

He threw a low fastball, an easy pitch to bunt, and Wright tapped it toward third. Jap O'Hara scooted in, made a deft bare-handed grab and turned and looked back toward third.

But Jap O'Hara was the third baseman.

He had fielded the bunt. That meant his base was left uncovered. There was nobody covering third. O'Hara looked toward second. Ken Osterhout stood at the ready, but it was too late to force out Duke Marboro. By the time O'Hara looked toward first base, Whitey Wright was two strides from the bag.

"Don't throw," Johnny roared. "Don't throw it away."

O'Hara held the ball and nodded. He moved to the mound. The swaggering trot had vanished. He held his head down.

"Sorry, John," he said.

Johnny glowered.

"I musta choked."

"That's right. You fucking choked. Now give me the fucking baseball."

Nobody out. Bases full. And the hitter was Rocco Lombardo, who impassively pumped The Godfather behind his neck, to loosen the thick muscles in his shoulders.

Chapter 13
Ridgefield, Connecticut, Christmas 1979

"YOU DON'T KNOW how to be a father." The cry rasped from the throat of the fourteen-year-old boy, who sat amid a chaos of Christmas gifts in front of a mountain of brightly colored packages in which the gifts had come. Mechanical hockey. Electronic football. Gallactico. A new baseball glove. A teal-blue fitted blazer.

"God, son," Johnny said. "Just enjoy your presents."

"You can't buy me." Jerry Lee Longboat stood up and slammed the new glove against a stone fireplace. "I don't want a fucking baseball glove."

"How dare you say 'fuck' to me and your mother on Christmas morning?" Johnny Longboat shouted at his son.

* * *

It was not simply that he didn't understand the boy; there were increasingly frequent periods when he didn't *like* him. Lately, Jerry Lee alternately confused and angered Johnny. He looked at Jerry, who was short, like Becky Rae, and high-cheekboned, like himself. Jerry Lee was nicely muscled and, for fourteen-year-old reasons, chose to wear jeans and cowboy boots in a colonial home on a historic ridge in Connecticut. From the hilltop, when the suburban haze lifted, a man could see both the Hudson River and Long Island Sound. Colonials and Redcoats had waged battles for the nameless ridge in 1789.

But here was the boy, dressed much as Jerry's father had dressed in the winddrift country of Oklahoma. Johnny looked at his son and saw his father, dead eleven years; in a sense a boy was his father and his son at the same time. Confusing.

"I can't stand it when the two of you scream at each other," Becky said. She was drinking a Christmas morning bloody mary.

"I'm sorry," Johnny said. "What I can't stand is dugout language in the house."

"What do you know about the fucking house?" Jerry shouted.

"The *fucking* house?" Johnny said, controlling his tone.

"Yeah, the fucking house. What do you know about it, Dad? You're never home."

"I have to travel," Johnny said. "My job makes me travel."

"I don't care about your job," Jerry shouted.

"My job keeps you in cowboy boots and jeans."

"I already told you, Dad. You can't fucking buy me."

Becky Rae rose to pour another bloody mary.

Merry Christmas to all, Johnny thought.

✳ ✳ ✳

Long ago, when Johnny imagined fathering, he thought of a smiling, merry son, to whom he would tell stories. First about the earth and sky, a limitless blue sky that suggested all at once innocence, promise, adventure, and infinity. He would tell the child about dry western land, and about places where the mountains preside and about the ancient, comforting New England hills. In the freedom of his own imagination, Johnny would explain to the smiling, merry, imaginary son how sky and earth, mountains and hills, had been created just for him. There would be times for playing catch, and times for talking books and studies. There would be money to buy things and go places. They would grow together and walk silently on silent paths, joined by their love and the beauty of being alive and the glories of an earth and sky made just for them.

But always for good and seemingly important reasons, he never told Jerry the stories he had imagined and even half completed in his mind. There was a hard game to pitch next day, or a Mohawk promotion he was ordered to attend, or a banquet where he could earn a thousand dollars by addressing other peoples' fathers and sons.

Or, quite simply, it was summer.

Jerry Lee shopped with his mother at Squashes' under the old maples on Main Street in Ridgefield and John sat in a hotel coffee shop in St. Louis, trying to calm himself after a ferocious game against Bob Gibson at Busch Stadium. He meant to offer Jerry Lee almost everything his father had not offered him. Comfort. Sobriety. Constancy. He had tried to be a good father, but the fourteen-year-old who shouted "fuck" this Christmas morning was a stranger. He looked at the boy and became his own father and wondered if his own father, too, had found a stranger in his home.

Jerry steadfastly refused to become an athlete. He liked to sketch what he called "pretend" places, but disdained Becky's suggestion that he draw things he actually saw: the Williamsburg blue colonial, the English yews along the driveway, the swimming pool with the diving boulder behind it.

He seemed to like rock music and delighted Johnny when he was eleven by asking for an electric guitar. But after Jerry realized that fingering and plucking demanded hard practice, he left the guitar under his small brass bed and made himself content by listening to tapes and records played so loudly that rock noises crashed through the house.

At the age of twelve, Jerry began to get poor marks and he and Johnny had their first hard arguments. John demanded an hour each evening without rock, during which Jerry was to do his homework. Jerry refused. Johnny confiscated his son's stereo. Jerry then all but spat. "You can't make me do this schoolwork. You can take away my stereo and you can beat me up, all right, but you can't make me do this schoolwork."

"I want to help you study," Johnny said. "You're learning things about Babylon and I want to learn with you."

"No."

"What do you mean 'no'?"

"You want to learn, Dad? The first thing to learn is what 'no' means."

Mrs. Grimaldi, the guidance counselor at Ridgefield Middle School, suggested a child psychiatrist in Stamford called Howard Frankel.

Dr. Frankel was what he called an anticompetitivist. Family therapy, he said, was an embryonic field, pardon the pun. It postdated Freud and Jung and even Karen Horney. His own belief, Dr. Frankel said, was that American competitiveness washed over from the business world and the academic world into the home. Competition made great corporations, such as Boeing, and competing for grades was an important early step in the creation of American physicians, who, Dr. Frankel said, were indisputably the finest in the world. But when carried into the home, through no one's fault, competitiveness created nonsupportive situations. Instead of everyone helping everybody else, someone was always trying to win.

The floor of one of Dr. Frankel's offices was covered with an intricate pattern of tracks for electric trains. Separate transformers controlled three small locomotives: a sleek imitation of an Amtrak diesel, a black model of a nineteenth-century steam-powered machine, and a drab replica of a freight engine. The tracks wove and interwove, from the starting place to parallel points marked "finish." Having his patients operate and sometimes race the trains was one of Dr. Frankel's unique diagnostic tools.

It was important to have control, he said. Too much speed would run any of the three little locomotives off its track.

You could use strategy. The intricate tracks crossed at many places and, with some planning, you could ram another locomotive and derail it.

"Is that allowed?" Johnny said.

"You make the rules," said Dr. Frankel.

"No ramming," Johnny said.

"Yes, ramming," Jerry said.

"That's quite interesting," said Dr. Frankel.

"What's the idea of the game?" Becky Rae said. "To reach the finish first?"

"You make the rules," said Dr. Frankel. "The Longboat family makes the rules."

"I want to win," Jerry said.

"You see," Dr. Frankel said, and his face brightened with self-pride, "you can all play with different sets of rules. You can try to win, Jerry, and you can try to produce a three-way tie, Mr. Longboat, and you, Mrs. Longboat, can do either, both, or neither."

"I'm not sure I understand the rules."

"Reluctance," Dr. Frankel murmured. "That may be the most significant symptom of all."

"Let's race," Jerry Lee said, suddenly dominant.

"First, you have to pick your locomotives," Dr. Frankel said.

"I'll take that plodding old freight job," Johnny said. "I saw a lot of them back in Oklahoma."

"I wanted that one," Jerry said.

"You've got it," said the father.

"No," Jerry said. "I'll take the diesel."

The Longboat family sat on the floor of a lime-green room, while Dr. Frankel, a portly, bearded, vested man, stationed himself in a rocking chair and rested both hands on his belly. Dr. Frankel's tracks had been laid in a maze of detail. Ovals and figure eights wove and interwove so that it was impossible to tell at first which course each locomotive was to run. The track crossings—collision points—were obscured by tiny stations, fashioned to look like brick, and white-steepled churches and clustered houses set amid small models of snowy fir and spruce.

"You're the diesel engineer, son," Johnny said. "Are we going to triple tie, or have a race?"

"Just do what you want to do, Dad, and let me do what I want to do."

"If that's what you *want* to want," Johnny said, and glanced at Dr. Frankel to see it his deliberate word repetition provoked a smile.

The psychiatrist appeared to ignore the father. "Humor," he said toward a lime-green wall, "is often merely a device for self-protection."

"I still don't understand the idea of this game," Becky Rae said.

"The idea is not to understand," Johnny said.

"Very insightful, Mr. Longboat," said Dr. Frankel.

The psychiatrist smiled a distant smile. He had been watching families play with his trains for eleven years. Some were competitive; others were competitively noncompetitive. He had never seen a major-league baseball player work the train game before; he had never before met a major-leaguer. As a boy, Howard Frankel was heavy and slow. He was "Porky" Frankel to his peers, who always made him play catcher in their pickup games. He played tennis now, three nights of cardiovascular exercise a week, with a competence developed across eight thousand dollars worth of lessons. But Porky Frankel was not an athlete and this great athlete in the lime-green office pierced his professionalism. How would the ballplayer work the train?

Jerry Lee commandeered the deisel. Johnny deferred to Becky Rae, who chose the nineteenth-century locomotive, a replica of the lonesome train that carried the corpse of Abraham Lincoln home to Springfield in April of 1865. That left the Amtrak for Johnny, who said, "I think I'd rather fly."

Dr. Frankel gazed just over Johnny's head at a print of Remington's "Rifleman," on the lime-green wall.

John considered the track his train would run. It began with a straightaway, moving to a rising curve. Then the track bridged a blue cellophane stream and faced an intersection—danger—at a tiny red brick station marked Putney, Vermont. Later there was danger in a forest of painted cardboard birch and at a station called White River Junction. Becky's track curved more often, but exposed her engine to collision only once, at Putney. Jerry Lee had the longest straightaway, but then would have to negotiate a severe turn.

"Ready at the transformers?" asked Dr. Howard. "At three now." He counted evenly, running the word "three" into a drill sergeant's "Go!"

Jerry Lee sent his locomotive hurtling. Becky started slowly, her face severe and suddenly old with concentration. John moved his Amtrak at a moderate speed.

At the first turn, Jerry Lee's diesel sprang from the track and clattered heavily into the base of Dr. Frankel's rocking chair. "Shit," the boy cried. "Oh, fuck."

"It's only a game," Johnny said.

"Who needs your fucking advice?" Jerry Lee said.

"Continue, please, Mr. and Mrs. Longboat," said the doctor.

What John wanted now was a two-way tie. He would like to traverse the curves and bridges, the tiny forests outside the make-believe towns, at modest speed under control. Then he would like to finish tied with Becky Rae. It startled him when she rammed her Lincoln locomotive at full speed into his engine, dashing the diesel from the tracks at the miniature railroad station labeled Putney. The Amtrak fell heavily to one side, wheels still spinning, and lay immobile, as though wounded.

Becky's suddenly old face showed a tightening at the jaw. She moved the lever on her transformer, but the Lincoln locomotive would not move.

"Something's broken," she said, angrily.

"No," Dr. Frankel said. "In derailing your husband's train, Mrs. Longboat, you've upset your own train just enough to break the electrical contact. He's on his side, knocked out, and you can't move."

"Meaning," Johnny said.

"Let's try another race," said Dr. Frankel.

✳ ✳ ✳

Excerpt from a letter from Howard Frankel, M.D., to Mr. and Mrs. Johnny Lee Longboat, Paynter's Mill Road, Ridgefield, Connecticut 06877.

> I have reviewed your family situation with care, placing special emphasis on your son, Jerry, as you requested. In addition to seven exercises in the train game, I have administered the Lumpe-Borquet test, a psychological probe, and certain standard examinations to measure intelligence.
>
> Jerry is extremely bright and in happier circumstances would probably test in the 93rd percentile. That is the kind of score which we associate with admission to an excellent preparatory school. However, he now tests in the 54th percentile. It is impossible to determine whether this is a function of his refusal to keep up with his schoolwork, or his resistance to being tested, or to his condition, which I diagnose as agitated depression.
>
> Be aware that I am making no criticism when I state that the circumstances of your home are far from

usual. As a baseball player, Mr. Longboat must travel a disproportionate amount of time. It is also my judgment that the intense emotional demands in his work—or what he perceives as intense emotional demands—detract from the psychic energy he can bring to his nonpitching duties of husbanding and fathering. Mr. Longboat's income is tied to his performance in a manner I can only describe as threatening.

The child, Jerry, however, is in a crisis situation. My suggestion is immediate removal from the home environment and enrollment in a special school such as Chestnut Hill Academy, near Willingboro, New Jersey. The emphasis at Chestnut Hill is on behavior modification, rather than on academics or athletics. Ongoing family therapy is a built-in requirement at Chestnut Hill and the distance from Ridgefield is not so great as to severely inconvenience the parents.

A period of two years there should help the boy significantly to approach his potential. The same period can be used by Mr. and Mrs. Longboat to rebuild—or build from scratch, should that be necessary—a more romantic relationship. I do not believe starting from scratch will be necessary. Deep residues of affection remain apparent.

I am available for further consultation.

A bill for my services is enclosed.

Howard Frankel, M.D., P.C.

Chapter 14
3:10 P.M., October 14

ALWAYS WHEN great pitcher faces great batter the game is cobra and mongoose. But no one knows, until the turn at bat is done, which one will play mongoose triumphant and which will play the corpse of the venomous snake.

Rocco Lombardo, The Muscular Medici of San Jose, pumped the black bat called The Godfather, behind his muscled sloping shoulders. Then he walked quickly into the batter's box, with strides that seemed to shake the earth.

He was thirty, a splendid age for a great hitter. At thirty, you still swing with a young man's quickness. You pound the fastball. And you also possess when you are thirty and a great hitter a veteran's sense of how to use that quickness. You've seen ten thousand major-league curveballs. You've faced the guiles and rhythms of a thousand pitchers. You have youth's quickness and you have also developed something the British once called gamesmanship. You know how to bully, when to lay back, what to anticipate. The great hitter at thirty is quick and strong, part Hercules, part hustler. It is an intimidating, dangerous age.

Ted Williams hit forty-four home runs when he was thirty. Stan Musial batted .346. Ty Cobb hit a rousing .371. Babe Ruth? At thirty, Ruth suffered through an abysmal season, but this, proclaim the honest historians of baseball, was occasioned by persistent gonorrhea, at a time when the uses of molds of the genus penicillium were not fully understood.

Black-haired, sharp-featured, confident, Rocco Lombardo allowed a smile to rush across his face. He knew, as hitters and hunters know, his adversary was wounded. Rocky would wait for his pitch. Then he would find it, said the rushing smile, drive it long and settle the seventh game.

Lombardo looked to the mound. The pitcher, Johnny Longboat, was tired and in pain. Lombardo stroked The Godfather back and forth across home plate. The smile reappeared and transformed into a grimace.

Staring toward the hitter, Johnny knew what he had to do. He had to strike out Lombardo. That was the very essence of the seventh game, and now the very essence of his career. He felt pain in his right shoulder, but no fear. He was submerged in a reasoning process. He would strike out Lombardo with no waste at all. He would strike him out with three pitches. He was determining the sequence of pitches that would fool, confuse, and disorient The Muscular Medici from San Jose. There was not room in Johnny's mind to think as hard as he had to think, and also to feel fear.

Kauff flashed two fingers and moved his glove behind the black line on the outside corner of home plate.

John's life, his thirty years of throwing baseballs, the agonized minutes of this October afternoon, came down to what his father had said in Oklahoma. "You snap 'em that good overhand curve on the first pitch, son, and you put a little terror in the best of 'em."

"You mean you scare them into backing away from the plate, Dad?"

"You can't get the good ones a-scared-a the ball. If they got a-scared, they wouldn't be the good ones in the first place. With a curve, the way you're gonna throw the curve when you get older, it's something else. It's the way the ball jumps down, falls off the table. You give 'em that amazing curveball and you get 'em thinking. 'Hey, how in hell am I gonna hit a pitch like that?' "

"I don't know how you mean that puts terror into hitters."

"The terror is that your snaking curveball is gonna make them look ridiculous. There's nothing worse than that, son, looking ridiculous in front of friends and strangers."

Johnny nodded at Raunchy Kauff. The curve leaped toward the plate, spinning and buzzing and buffeting the air. The ball might have been riding a wire. It approached just below Lombardo's belt and suddenly lashed downward toward his ankles. The baseball caught a shade of black and an inch of space parallel to Lombardo's front knee cap.

"Steey-up," bawled Umpire Danny Merullo.

"Hey-John. Hee-yup. 'Attababy. You can do it. You can get him for us, Johnny-boy." The major-league infield as chorus.

"Fucking low," bawled Frenchy Boucher from the Mastodon's dugout.

"Where was it, Dan?" said Rocco Lombardo.

"Close enough for you to swing at," Merullo said.

"Hey, Merullo," Boucher yelled. "You forgot your glasses and your white cane and your fucking one-eyed Seeing Eye dog."

Lombardo winced, and he had reason to wince. Antagonize Merullo now and the strike zone could grow to mammoth size.

303

"Damn good pitch John threw," Lombardo said, making peace. He stepped out of the box and pumped The Godfather behind his shoulders.

Change-up now, Johnny thought. The fine curve had surprised Lombardo. He would be eager now, less certain that John was wearing down. One good curve had altered the balance. After that perfect first strike, Johnny Longboat had become the aggressor.

"When you got the fuckers pull down the shade. Pull down that fucking shade and they is dead. Whoops." A whistle. "Goodbye Dolly Gray." Johnny heard not his father here, but his long-dead Pittsfield manager, Harry (The Whistler) Schulte. All the best advice he had been served across all the years was sounding in his head. That was another reason Johnny felt no fear.

Kauff showed three fingers. Incredible how pitcher and catcher think as one; incredible and inexplicable. John nodded.

He rocked until his toeplate touched the sky. The Oklahoma windmill. Magic. A steel whip for an arm. Then, as he released the ball, John pulled down Harry Schulte's window shade.

Fortran, the great computer system, had tapped the line: Do not throw Lombardo change-of-pace.

John's change spun and bit the air and hung. The Godfather flashed.

"Steey-up two," yelled Danny Merullo.

One more, John thought. One more.

"Hey-up-a-baby, 'atta-baby, way to fool 'em, Johnny-boy," chattered the chorus infield.

John blinked and saw Christina as she had been that morning, weepy and lubricous in the harsh dawn light.

Chapter 15
Moresby Point, 9:15 P.M., October 13

HE HAD CALLED to end the affair, or ask her to bed. He was not sure which. She had spoken in a murmur, come up, come up.

But what about the husband, Brad Moresby?

He would be spending the night in town at the New York Athletic Club, first a rub and then a sauna and then the bar. She was to meet Brad in the Wahoo Room of the stadium next day, the day of the seventh game. Christina's night was free; her sand-castle home was free, and she felt lonely.

In Ridgefield, John told Becky Rae that he needed a night of private contemplation.

"You can have that here," Becky Rae said. "There's extra bedrooms."

"I better go be a hermit," Johnny said. He said he would drive to a men's athletic club in New York City for a rubdown and a solitary night's sleep. It was odd, he told himself, how easy it was to mirror a lie off a truth.

* * *

He and Christina sat in the darkwood bar, where John drank Perrier, flavored with bitters and slices of lime.

Christina sipped slowly at an iced mixture of vodka and skimmed milk.

"I know you don't want to talk about tomorrow's game," she said.

"Today's game," Johnny said. "It's tomorrow now. According to my watch, 12:25."

"Scared?"

"Apprehensive. If this is the end, I want it to end properly."

"How many things actually do end properly?" Christina said. "Baseball careers. Lives. Love affairs." She wore a green sleeveless blouse and fitted white slacks. As she fetched drinks he noticed the downy arms and that the years had treated her body kindly. Sometimes, when Chris was tired, you could see faintly purple fatigue under her eyes, but her body—was it her body now or after so many seasons also partly his?—was lissome as a girl's. He thought of garlands and children dancing 'round a maypole.

"I'm shortly to become forty years old," Christina said.

"That happens to everybody," Johnny said, "after they've lived 39 years." What was it the psychiatrist with the locomotives had said? Humor was often a means of self defense.

"I have to think of the rest of my life," Christina said.

"You don't have to be afraid of it," Johnny said.

"Do you realize how long we've been together?"

"Sixteen years."

"And isn't that absurd?" Christina said. "A brief affair. A dalliance. I was a girl and I saw a handsome, black-haired high-cheekboned baseball player from Oklahoma, whose dark eyes twinkled with intelligence. You know that about yourself, Johnny. When you were young and fresh, you actually twinkled."

He looked at the bubbles in his soda water.

"And I thought, recklessly, I think I'll try him."

"And?"

"Johnny, you were a very easy lay."

He burst out laughing. "You weren't exactly Mother Teresa yourself."

She smiled with him, but when she spoke she was serious. "Where am I now?" she said.

"Oh, roughly where you were when we started."

"No. I have a master's degree in the history of architecture. I didn't have that then. I've painted enough watercolor landscapes to know that I'm no more than a dabbler. I've completed six short stories, which have drawn me forty-one rejection slips, all instructing me, in preprinted form letters, that I am not the female equivalent of Chekhov."

At her urging they had read Russian short stories together and Chekhov's story "Misery" brought tears to Johnny's eyes.

"I am, in short, an aging, still attractive, nowhere lady. I have a husband whom I don't love and a married lover I'm not strong enough to leave. I possess a modest variety of skills and talents, but to support myself I should probably have to become the receptionist in the offices of a perfume company. You know Gilbert and Sullivan?"

"Not very well."

"I am the very model of an unliberated liberated woman."

"You're too harsh toward yourself," Johnny said. "If the press gives me a damn dumb write-up, I say, 'The damn dumb press.' If you get a dumb rejection letter you blame yourself."

"I admire so much, I love so much, that single-minded confidence of yours."

"I can't do many things," Johnny said. "Dance the way you dance, or sing those show tunes. I came to you a hick. Do you think I'd seen Juan Gris paintings in Oklahoma? Or read Chekhov? Even now, I can't write anything more than a speech for father-son night at the Harvey School in Katonah, and all I can paint is my garage. But there's that one thing, pitching ball games. I am one hell of a pitcher. One hell of a confident pitcher of major-league baseball."

"You have that," Christina said, "and you'll always have that."

"Oh, no I won't," Johnny said. "I've seen the great ones coming back to old timers' games, drinking a little more each year, and going more to fat. Their features start to spread across their faces and they never say much about their lives. All they talk about is how things used to be. Stengel and Durocher and the cocktail waitress in Kansas City who could pick a quarter off a table with her . . . well, you don't want to hear."

"With her pussy," Christina said. "You've told me."

"The old timers' eyes get deader every year. There was that game in 1959, or '49, or was it '39, but fewer and fewer remember, and fewer care. What's the worth of yesterday's ball games, or last year's pennant race? You look at old newsreels and the film is grainy.

"You start out to be a ballplayer, which is a wild and adventurous dream. There're millions of you. Sometimes I think the lucky ones are the people who don't make it. They play some good minor-league ball when they're twenty, twenty-one, and then they're cut and have to go to work.

"It hurts at the time, but it's no tragedy. The ones who don't make it have to go to work, and that forces them to lead natural lives. The ones with intelligence become businessmen, or teachers, or even lawyers, and they build their lives the way lives are supposed to be built. Strive through your twenties. Strive through your thirties. Stay around your house. Raise the kids right. At forty, there's a bigger house. At fifty, you're a vice-president or a principal. I know some businessmen and lawyers at fifty, who're god-

308

damn young. But ballplayers at fifty are old men. It's all behind them. They crammed the whole damn thing into maybe ten years, ten years of playing major-league baseball. After that, there's nothing but a mess of memories.

"In ten years, Chrissie, you'll still be writing and painting. Maybe you'll even be published. If I'm not careful, ten years from now I'll be doing nothing more than telling Little Leaguers, who don't much care, how I pitched to Carl Yastrzemski and Rocco Lombardo."

"Your mind is made up."

He had been speaking so intensely he missed her meaning.

"You see us as separate, not together, ten years from now."

Johnny walked toward her and put both hands around her waist, surrounding her with his long fingers. "Still tiny."

"No babies to swell me." She looked sorrowful and severe at the same time. "I have a thing or two to tell you."

"Oh, sure."

"Don't kiss me, Johnny. Please don't kiss me right now."

He removed his hands from her waist and stepped backward. Nothing heavy, Chris, he thought. I have the seventh game tomorrow and that's weight enough for nine men. Please, Chris, he thought, nothing heavy.

"I want to know if you intend, finally, to marry me." She stood in front of the bar, poised and vulnerable. The mixture made his heart beat faster. He wanted to pierce the poise and then, when she cried out, to comfort her.

But he was pitching tomorrow. Or later today.

"You're not divorced."

"I know," Christina said. "This is weak of me and demanding and even corrupt." She shook her head, stirring her straight blonde hair. "I don't like the part of me that has put up with Bradford all these years, and I'm asking you to help me, Johnny. I'm admitting I need help."

Christ, how he wanted her at that moment.

"We'll get divorced together and we'll get married together and ten years from now you won't need your baseball pension, or any lawyers with land deals or things like that. I've saved some money. Enough so neither of us would ever have to worry."

"I need a day to think," Johnny said.

"After sixteen years," Chris said in a strained voice, "you still need one more day."

"You know about the emotional thing with me. I don't believe in divorce after a child is born."

"Jerry doesn't even live with you any more. He's off at Chestnut Hill. You don't see him that much anyway."

"And maybe that's wrong," Johnny said. "Maybe he should still be living with us. It's a gamble. A child is a gamble. They're all gambles, Chris. I guess I was my daddy's gamble and Jerry Lee is mine. But you know from your husband, when you gamble to take certain risks and hope to win." He sighed. "Would you put a little cream of barley into this French fizz?"

"You want a Scotch?"

"Yes."

"Then ask for a Scotch. Stop being cute."

"I'll get my own." He poured a strong jolt of Dewar's into his glass.

"I have another thing to tell you," Christina said. "If you don't decide tomorrow between Becky Rae and me, then I'll decide."

"Wait a minute."

"Don't wait-a-minute me. This double existence—or is it half existing?—is tearing me apart."

Johnny drank. "So if we don't get divorced together,"

he said, "you'll settle in for good with your decaying Ivy-Leaguer husband."

She looked at him without a sign of emotion. "I don't know what I'll do. I know this. I won't be seeing you any more. I mean that, Johnny. I love you and it would hurt badly to break us up. But it would hurt more badly not to. And the only way I can conceive of surviving our breakup is to make it clean and absolutely final." Her voice was a shard of glass; he had heard her talk that way to Moresby once. "You know the song. 'So Long, It's Been Good to Know You.' We've sung it together when we were drinking in that silly little room you got us in the Haystack Motel."

"You were the only one who stayed on key."

"I'll give you your extra day, but tomorrow after the game, when you're finished pitching, either you come get me, or I'll never again be there for the getting."

"Life is a bitch," Johnny said, putting off thought. He looked at his drink. He had so desperately wanted to avoid heavy conversation this evening; this night before the day of the seventh game. He drank his Scotch. *Look into the pewter pot/and see the world as the world's not.* A poem. One of her poems. Housman's, really, but she had taught it to him. The drink felt good. The poem was a world away from the Oklahoma Winddrift Blues. The music between John and Christina made a dissonance.

"You remember long ago between us?" Johnny said. "Do you remember the first time?"

"I try very hard *not* to remember." Chris sounded strong but when he embraced her, the tanned downy arms moved about his neck.

As he took Christina, blares of thought sounded.

Loveless marriages. Was that what joined them? That would not be sufficient to sustain them, once the loveless marriages were done.

311

Corruption. Her word not his. Brad Moresby was corrupt, like the Commissioner. But what about themselves, John and Christina, locked in a love without end, without commitment?

Five-cent philosophies. The nickel Socrates.

Harry Schulte, the ten-cent philosopher intoned from a cemetery John had never seen, "Never have sex with a woman before a game."

She made a loud cry as he entered her. Then, shrill as violins and pain: "I want to have a baby, John. Your baby."

"What Chris? What's that?"

"Don't worry, lover." Her voice receded and all at once became sad and dry and weary. "I've assumed the position. Go ahead. I'm still taking the fucking pills."

* * *

She wore a cornflower-blue apron, and only an apron, as she brought him breakfast on a flowered tray. "A small omelette with the finest herbs I have," she offered. She smiled without much cheer and he saw lines as delicate wedges around her mouth and fatigue's faint purple under her eyes.

He sat up and stretched carefully, alert to any discomfort in his pitching arm. "You have a lovely body, John," Christina said.

"For a forty-one-year-old man."

"You aren't old."

"Except as a pitcher." He reached for her carefully across the breakfast tray. "Blue becomes you," he said and spun her gently so he could see her buttocks. "The absence of blue becomes you more."

She smiled, still without cheer. "I slept well," Johnny said.

"I slept hardly at all," Chris said. "I drank too much vodka and milk. I'm not made up. I feel like the wrath of a hungover God."

"Why didn't you sleep?" Johnny said.

"Concern. Anxiety. And there was a physical reason. You made love to me so intensely and you came so quickly that when you went to sleep I was still excited."

"I owe you one loving, slow, seductive night," Johnny said. "Maybe, if I win, we can find a way to sneak somewhere. Maybe Bermuda."

"All the talk last night wasn't simply talk, Johnny. There can't be any more sneaking anywhere." She placed her hands to the face she had not yet made up and began quietly to cry.

He felt overwhelmed and picked at the omelette.

"May I have an answer now?" Christina said. "It's a new day, sort of."

"You deserve an answer," Johnny said, "but it's too much for me this morning. I have to get my head into the game."

"Could we at least do it now, even if you have to do it quickly, one more time, this time with love?"

"You deserve whatever I can give you, Chris, but I can't do it even quickly now. I have to pitch."

She wept more deeply. He rose and began dressing, walling himself off from her sobs, walling himself from his own confusion.

It was the morning of October 14 and he had to get down to the ballpark to pitch the seventh game.

"I need your love," she said. "I need your body. I need your cock. Don't you realize how difficult it is for me to say those things?"

"I have to pitch," Johnny said. He finished dressing in a glum and sour mood. He felt ashamed to be leaving her, all but naked, and sexually thirsty, but he felt a stronger drive to win the game. Already on this October morning, he and the seventh game were becoming one.

313

Chapter 16

3:12 P.M., October 14

ONE PITCH.

He knew if he could reach as deeply as a man can reach and find that one pitch, he could take the bat out of Rocco Lombardo's hands and things would be good. Things would be very good. He would get the next two hitters and the Mohawks finally would steal the run that won the game. If he could reach . . .

And then?

He was thinking too much. Johnny breathed deeply twice. He would go with his overhand curve.

The crowd was standing at Mohawk Stadium and the crowd sound was a rising rumble touched with apprehension, but meant to encourage him.

Patches of his life were scattered through the rumbling crowd. The Commissioner of Baseball, against whom John had tested his own integrity. That mettle had not bent, not even a millimeter. Gus Vermont, who had tried to sign him to a yellow-dog contract. Brad and Chris Moresby. They would look stylish and aristocratic in newspaper photographs the next day. Save for Brad's nose. It was now a bulb. Becky Rae sat amid younger, giggling, lip-gnawing, uncertain baseball wives. More ball-players were getting divorced than in the old days. Except for Ev Taft and Jerry Lee, who was leashed to that special school near Willingboro, all of his life but himself was in the rumbling crowd that meant to encourage him.

He was still thinking too much. Forget the fastball. The old speed had been lost on the long road from Oklahoma to New York. "You're a pitcher," his dad had said, "when you get the sense to know that if you get in trouble, go with your best pitch."

Don't try the change. Even off-stride, Lombardo was strong enough to stroke the ball between the outfielders and clear the bases.

Johnny's pride and his power were the overhand curve. His shoulder hurt. It hurt a ton. Another curve would hurt, push the pain one level higher. But for this pitch, Johnny believed that he could fight through any pain. The important thing was to go with his pride and his power.

Kauff flashed one finger, then two fingers, then three fingers. This was a code to confuse the runner at second base, who could see the signals the catcher pumped between his legs. Only the second sign had a meaning. Two fingers. Curveball. Kauff squatted behind the outside corner of home plate.

Johnny breathed again and nodded. His body strained into his graceful pitching motion. Rock back. Extend. Raise the left foot until the toeplate reaches toward the sky. Windmill and at the moment of release, snap that right wrist with all your strength.

Incredible, shocking heat tore Johnny's shoulder. His eyes closed and opened, opened and closed. He could not control his eyes or the sounds he was making. He saw the earth and sky. The soft grass of Mohawk Stadium bruised his face.

He did not know where he was. His stomach made him feel that he was falling. The white heat in the shoulder yielded to sharp, repeating electric shocks. He opened his eyes. Somewhere, far off, ballplayers were running toward him. The crowd was making a noise like lowing cattle or was it the bark of attacking Dobermans? He was not sure which. The white, electric pain stabbed again and again, making him twist and roll and groan.

"John. John. Stop cryin', Johnny. Please stop cryin'." Raunchy Kauff's face was over his.

"What happened? Jesus Christ, my shoulder. I broke my shoulder."

"You threw a helluva pitch. Take it easy, Johnny."

"It looks like a dislocation," Doc Youmans said. "It looks like he threw the curve so hard, he tore his shoulder apart."

"Forget the fucking shoulder," Johnny said. "The shoulder is dead."

"It'll pass, if you can relax," Doc Youmans said. "The quicker you relax, the sooner the pain will ease up. These things hurt like a living bastard quick, but they get better in a hurry. Don't get up. Don't try to get up. We'll get you strapped. Then pop a pain pill. You'll feel fine."

The stabbing shocks were tolerable now. "I said forget the fucking shoulder. What happened to the pitch? Did I strike Lombardo out?"

Kauff leaned over Johnny, his large, grapefruit face wincing and distorted. "John, you threw a perfect pitch. The ball come up there whistling and looking grand. Then it fell right off the corner of the table."

"Then I got him," Johnny said. "Okay. Okay. Now Torchyzer has to get the next two guys."

"Except one thing," Kauff said.

"What's that?"

"The Big Dago went down for that curve like a fucking moose going down for a salt lick in July. He hit the fucker into the center-field seats."

"A grand slam home run," Doc Youmans announced,

dully. "Take your time. Don't hurry getting up. You may feel a little dizzy."

"They got us, 4–0?" Johnny asked.

"They got us, 4–0," Kauff said.

"But you told me," Johnny said, "that I threw a perfect pitch."

"Yeah, dammit, Johnny, but this is some fucking league. This is the all-time league. This is the league where even perfect pitches get hit."

Where even perfect pitchers can be beaten.

* * *

The final score was 4–0, and Rob Brownell would write in *The New York Standard* that the Mastodons defeated the Mohawks with a mammoth home run.

* * *

The Commissioner of Baseball scurried—with as much dignity as one can affect while scurrying—to the winning clubhouse. He praised Frenchy Boucher and the Mastodons as "exemplars of all that is finest and most competitive in our national game."

"Thank you, Mr. Commissioner," said Frenchy Boucher. He was not quite certain what exemplars meant, but hell, it had to be praise. His guys had won. "That means a lot to me, coming from a great man like you, sir."

The Commissioner would grab ten minutes of network camera time before walking more slowly to the losing clubhouse.

* * *

The Mohawk physician, Larry Greenberg, a cousin of Gus Vermont's, explained that Johnny had badly stretched (but not torn) ligaments crucial to the implacement of the arm in the shoulder socket. "It isn't serious," Dr. Greenburg said, "although I imagine the pain must have been frightful."

"Bad, Larry," Johnny said, "but not as bad as losing."

317

"As far as normal function goes, your right shoulder will come around, with rest and certain exercises I'll prescribe."

"Pitching?" Johnny said.

"That's not a normal function."

"Be straight with me, Larry. Be clear, distinct, and straight."

"It isn't likely Johnny," Dr. Greenberg said, "that a man of your age suffering this kind of injury will ever be able to pitch again."

Were Greenberg's eyes wet, or did Johnny imagine they were wet? The doctor looked away, then offered John a bottle of codeine pills.

"I don't like pills. It's not that bad now."

"But it could flare up tonight. A sudden shift in bed while you're asleep. Here." Greenberg put the bottle into Johnny's left hand. "I'm sorry, John," he said. Yes, Dr. Greenberg's eyes were wet.

Being careful with the shoulder John took fifteen minutes to dress. Certain ballplayers, boyish Kenny Osterhout, sleek Harry Truman Abernathy and ancient Quincy John Coleman, stopped at his locker and gently shook his hand. "Final score don't mean nothing," Coleman said. "I'm here to shake hands with a winning pitcher."

The Commissioner entered among a scramble of reporters, including Prissy Coe and Rob Brownell. A television technician said it would take a minute to get the cameras set and Commissioner Moresby scowled. "But this will be aired?" he said. "You're not going to cut away from this to some silly Hollywood game show."

"You'll have five minutes of network time, sir," a white-haired producer said, "and that's a promise."

"Prissy," John said.

"Yes?"

"I'm delighted we recognize each other with our clothes on."

"Oh," she said, in sorrow, "how can you joke?"

"I thought you'd stay on the other side, run with the winners."

"I had to touch base there, but the story is here. I learned so much watching you today."

"Such as?" John said.

"Such as courage," Prissy Coe said.

He would miss this gritty young woman reporter, Johnny knew. It was a shame that she was coming into sportswriting just as he was leaving baseball. He could have enjoyed working with her as much as he enjoyed working with Rob Brownell.

Still wearing his black and gold uniform, Rocco Lombardo made his way through the scribbling, tape-recording reporters. "I just want you to know, John, you threw me a curve as good as anybody ever threw. I dunno how I hit it and if you threw that pitch again, I couldn't hit it in ten thousand years."

"You hit it when you had to," Johnny said. "Congratulations."

"Naw," Lombardo said. "I come over to congratulate you." He put an arm carefully over Johnny's shoulder. "You are guts, Mr. Longboat. You are Mister fucking guts."

"And you're a gentleman," Johnny said to his conqueror.

Someone turned on floodlights and Commissioner Amory Moresby mounted a footlocker. Eyeing a network camera, he began to speak. "No team that played as valiantly as the New York Mohawks did today can be said to be a loser. And to my right, where Johnny Longboat is congratulating Rocky Lombardo . . . well, had all the world been combed, we could not find a finer pair of princes."

Suddenly Rob Brownell leaped onto the footlocker and grabbed the microphone from Commissioner Moresby's hand. "My name is Rob Brownell," he said, "and I'm a reporter for *The New York Standard.* A good reporter. I want everyone to know that Commissioner Amory Moresby is a fraud. For ten years he's been covering up for a betting ring that involves his brother."

Hypersensitive to libel, ABC cut at once to a commercial for radial tires. But eighty million people had heard Brownell's charge. There would certainly have to be an investigation. Amory Moresby stood silent in shock.

"Now why did you have to go and do that for?" Johnny shouted from his locker. "Now you're gonna get in trouble at the paper."

"Doesn't matter," Brownell shouted back. "I can always find work in my father's bus company."

"As what?"

"A dispatcher. I don't drive buses very well."

* * *

Outside the dressing room, police held off a crowd of fans. Inside the barricade, Chris Moresby stood to the left and Becky Rae stood to the right. Chris looked slim and elegant in a pale-gray tailored coat. Becky Rae was shorter, rounder.

Johnny walked toward Chris. "Love," he said. "Have a good life."

She was a wounded fawn. "It's over then?" she said. John nodded and then, in one more enactment of mankind's long inability to make a suitable farewell, he touched her left elbow lightly and said, "See ya."

Becky hugged Johnny. She was too moved to speak. "Now cheer up, Beck," Johnny demanded. "We've got no money and no prospects but we have to drop our friend Kauff off at his house in Greenwich. At least we'll have good company riding home."

"Are you all right?"

"I will be shortly, but you'd better take the wheel."

* * *

From the back seat of the Longboat station wagon, Kauff said, "Watcha gonna do now, John?"

"Go back to Oklahoma, if it's okay with Becky."

"It's okay."

"I can teach some, if they'll have me. Gym. Maybe even Freshman English. Coach baseball to kids who want to learn. Indian children especially. Our family owes a debt to Indian children for something that happened long ago."

"I won't see you no more," Kauff said, and began crying.

"You'll make new friends," Johnny said. Then, to Becky Rae, "On the way to Oklahoma, maybe we can pick up Jerry Lee from Chestnut Hill School."

"If he's ready for us and we're ready for him," she said. "We've got a lot of work to do, Johnny. Family work."

The conversation was punctuated by Kauff's sniffling in the back seat.

John placed his left hand on the back of Becky's neck with infinite tenderness. The station wagon picked up speed on the Bruckner Expressway.

"Honey," he said, "it's a good thing they give you three score years and ten, because I sure as hell fucked up the first forty-one."